MW00612287

KEEPERS OF THE SWORD

OTHER BOOKS AND AUDIO BOOKS

BY GUY MORGAN GALLI

Lifted Up

Shadow Hunter

KEEPERS OF THE SWORD

A NOVEL

GUY MORGAN GALLI

Covenant Communications, Inc.

Cover image © Nejron.

Cover design copyright © 2014 by Covenant Communications, Inc.

Published by Covenant Communications, Inc.
American Fork, Utah

Copyright © 2014 by Guy Morgan Galli
Interior monastery image copyright © 2014 by Emilee Dummer
All rights reserved. No part of this book may be reproduced in any format or in any medium without the written permission of the publisher, Covenant Communications, Inc., P.O. Box 416, American Fork, UT 84003. The views expressed within this work are the sole responsibility of the author and do not necessarily reflect the position of Covenant Communications, Inc., or any other entity.

This is a work of fiction. The characters, names, incidents, places, and dialogue are either products of the author's imagination, and are not to be construed as real, or are used fictitiously.

Printed in the United States of America
First Printing: September 2014

20 19 18 17 16 15 14   10 9 8 7 6 5 4 3 2 1

ISBN 978-1-62108-190-6

For Zoram, who for so many years had to endure the animated scripture stories' weak portrayal of him. You and your descendants deserve to have your story told.

ACKNOWLEDGMENTS

To Paul Featherstone, whose profound love for the Book of Mormon inspired this story all those years ago,

To Clark Ward for his selfless gifts of knowledge,

To Hannah who is never afraid to say it how it is,

To all those friends who took the time to read a good story and offer suggestions to make it better,

. . . Thank you.

PROLOGUE

A SINGLE TRUMPET BLAST SOUNDED over the din of the angry crowd as the prophetess, shackled and bound hand and foot, was led to the front of the rostrum.

Hundreds of Israelites had turned out for her public trial, leaving the fields and marketplaces unattended to heap vile curses and condemnations upon her—not for any criminal act but for pricking the conscience of the people. The truth, like a sword, had cut them to the very center.

The High Priest, dressed in traditional and ornate priestly garments made of only the finest linens dyed in blues and purple and scarlet, stepped to the stone balustrade and raised his hands in a vain attempt to quiet the crowds.

"This woman who stands before you," he said once he could be heard above the frenzy, "is accused of being a false prophet and drawing the people of the Lord away from the faith!" More curses from the crowd. "She blasphemes the word and power of our God!"

The crowd's hate boiled over again.

"The law is clear," the High Priest continued, feeding into their fear and loathing, reciting to them the law. "Thou shalt not consent unto him—or her—nor hearken unto her; neither shall you pity her or spare her or hide her: but thou shalt surely kill her . . ." He couldn't finish reciting the punishment as prescribed by the law because of the clamor and outcries for her death. He raised his hands above his head again in an attempt to quiet the people. "Thine hand shall be first upon her to put her to death and afterward the hand of all the people!"

The murderous mass was whipped into a hysterical and bloodthirsty rage. But the High Priest was not the only one feeding off the crowd's energy. Seated next to him was the commander of Israel's military force, or at least what was left of it since the Babylonian invasion and conquest. He, perhaps even more than the High Priest, understood why this morning's trial was necessary. The once-proud people of Israel felt abandoned. The One True God had forsaken them, though none but a few—like this woman—dared speak it aloud. This trial, like the others over the years, was a distraction; a means to channel the people's fears away from taking real steps toward change. It was so much easier to blame their situation on someone else. Even if that someone was God. Where was He when the invading hordes rode through the city, leaving only devastation in their wake? Why did He not stay the invading armies with His almighty hand? Why did He turn a blind eye when they ransacked and defiled the Temple? Did he not hear the cries of the mothers who were forced to watch as their sons, young princes and heirs to nobility, were taken as slaves to the court of King Nebuchadnezzar? Had God lost His power to protect and save His people?

Maybe He had never had the power to begin with.

But lately these so-called prophets were becoming more persuasive in their declarations, conveying real purpose and concern. Words were the precursor to action, and action meant change, and change was the last thing he, the High Priest, or many of the others who had managed to maintain some level of power and control since the invasion wanted right now.

The military man allowed a sly grin to crease the corner of his mouth. At least for now.

The High Priest again raised his voice above the noise of the crowd.

"Elisheva!" he said, addressing the accused woman. "What say you?"

The masses quieted and hung on her response as the prophetess stepped forward.

"Repent," she started, speaking with a firm resolve laced with love and genuine concern. "Repent and again find favor in the sight of the Lord! Our fight is not with Babylon; it is with sin and disobedience. It is only by the will and hand of the Lord that Israel can once again be free."

The people cried out, as if one, for her silence. But she was not done. "You who profess to worship the God of Abraham, Isaac, and Jacob; you who practice the traditions of our fathers but whose hands are unclean— the time is coming that the first shall be last and the last shall be first!"

One of the Temple guards reached out to take hold of her and silence her, but she pushed him away with her shoulder and continued to speak, matching the intensity of the people below in one final exertion. "You accept the words of prophets long dead, as long as it suits your needs and practices, but you condemn and persecute those who speak to you now! I speak that your ears may hear, that you may not forget that God is the same yesterday, today, and forever."

She turned to a man dressed in full military raiment sitting to the side of the dais, and she leaned forward as if to touch him with her words. "Do not trust in the arm of the flesh, for wo unto that man who would lead an entire nation into destruction!"

Though he did not show it, he was alarmed by her accusation. Her death could not come quick enough.

The prophetess then turned and faced the High Priest. "And wo is the man, called of the Lord but afraid to stand for the right, who walks in darkness because he fears the light!"

"Enough!" the High Priest yelled over the outrage of the people. "We have heard enough! Need we hear more to find her in violation of the law? She has blasphemed God; she has blasphemed His people!"

The congregation was already chanting her sentence: death. But the High Priest would not be satisfied with her death alone. He and the others had discussed this before. They needed to end this madness once and for all. The High Priest leaned over the stone railing, sweeping one hand out over the people.

"Is there not one among us who would speak for her? If there is but one, I will spare her life! Is there no one who would plead for her life?"

While the High Priest worked the crowd into a frenzy, the military commander deftly scanned the crowds of hundreds, looking for the one or two who might betray their traitorous beliefs. At one point, he spotted a large young man who had paused at the periphery, and for a moment he thought the boy might speak up, but he just lowered his head and continued on.

Disappointing.

The verdict was unanimous. The old woman would be stoned.

No pleas for mercy crossed the prophetess's lips as she was dragged through the city to the pit dug and designed for one purpose. She was thrown into the center as men gathered around her, each carrying stones ranging from the size of a fist to the size of a man's head. She looked up, past her accusers, toward heaven and began uttering a psalm of David as the first stone was released.

CHAPTER ONE

ZORAM GATHERED HIS BELONGINGS IN short time under the direction and supervision of the caravan master. He didn't have much, just a strong leather satchel and a personal bag with food, water, and other provisions for the short journey home. With some effort, he looped the heavy satchel across his neck and over his shoulder for extra support. He was a healthy, muscular young man approaching his twentieth year, but his strong frame strained, and he groaned under the initial onset of weight.

"I had forgotten how heavy this was."

The caravan master did his best to smile, his skin dark and rutted from his years of traveling the desert routes. "I'm sure the camel will now walk with a lighter step." His eyes creased at the corners and showed surprise that Zoram took nothing else from the laden animals. "You travel light," he said. "I feel bad taking full fare for your travels."

"Bad enough to return a portion?" It was Zoram's turn to smile.

The caravan master climbed onto his horse, a beautiful desert stallion, and laughed deeply. "It would take more than feelings for me to part with money."

"That's why you stay in business."

The caravan master pointed down a wide and well-traveled road. "This will take you to Jerusalem." He checked the sun. It was midway across the sky. "But you will not make the city by nightfall on foot." He leaned in close, as if what he was going to say was a closely guarded secret. "You'll see a rocky trail off to one side where the road runs along the ravine. It cuts across the mountain and will save you an hour or two. It's not an easy road and not passable by caravan or even by horseback in places, but you're young and strong and should fare well."

Zoram reached out and took the old guide by the forearm. "You are a good friend." And friends they were. The desert—where the life of each caravan member depended upon the actions of others—had a way of making friends out of strangers.

"Your father will be proud of the man you have become."

Zoram's response was choked off by a sudden surge of emotion. He had been gone for such a long time.

"May the wind always be to your back," the caravan master offered.

"And in the face of your enemies." It was a peculiar farewell common among desert travelers, but now, after having crossed the vast deserts and wastelands, Zoram understood its significance.

"May whatever god you worship keep you well and safe, my friend."

"Thank you, Samir." Zoram watched as the caravan master pulled sharply on the reins and urged his horse to catch up with the caravan that would continue its passage to Tyre, Damascus, and farther north along the shores of the Great Sea.

As Zoram watched the caravan creep away, the reality of this day struck him with a weight rivaling that of his heavy cargo, and an anxious feeling knotted his stomach. He closed his eyes and turned his face to the sun, letting its warmth wash over his being and cleanse the ill feelings from his heart. He had been looking forward to this day for over ten years, and now that it was here he wasn't prepared for the emotions that assaulted his every sense.

He was home.

With new resolve and his feelings back under control, he set out toward the city he had precious few memories of. The road was, indeed, busy, and Zoram passed many groups of smaller inner-city and village commerce caravans. It was an odd feeling to hear the language of his childhood spoken so freely and in such abundance. It had been too long since he'd been able to use it. He stumbled through the first few greetings as he passed people on the road but was pleased to see how quickly the tongue of his youth returned to him.

As the sun started its long descent into the afternoon, he spotted the rock path the caravan master had told him about, and after a brief deliberation, he decided to take the less-traveled road. His shoulder was beginning to feel the strain of his satchel's weight, and he figured he had to do everything he could to reach the city before the sun set and the gates were shut and locked for the night.

The climb was arduous as it cut up and around a large mountain, though compared to where he had lived the past years, these "mountains" of Judea were little more than hills and mounds. After the initial climb, the path leveled out and traced the outline of the unspoiled countryside. It was breathtaking. He had traveled through a good part of the known world on his return home, and he was always struck by how varied and beautiful the different lands were. From the snow-capped mountains of the north to the lush jungles of the east, even the deserts, with nothing but jagged rocks and sand dunes as far as the eye could see, all possessed an exquisite and tangible beauty that Zoram could not ignore.

Truly great is our God, he thought as he viewed the land promised to Moses and his people: a land of milk and honey, a land choice above all others, a promised land. Soft green hills interspersed with tufts of uneven sheep grass and outcroppings of white stone gave a special quality and character to the landscape. It was unlike any other place he had seen.

Gnarled cedars and Joshua trees dotted the mountainside, and he decided that he needed to take a break in the shade under one of these small outgrowths. The muscles in his shoulders and neck nearly cramped as the heavy burden was removed, and he had to stretch to keep them loose. Zoram opened his other bag and removed a bota of fresh water, a hard biscuit, and strips of dried, salted meat. The day was at its hottest, and he knew he had to rest if he was going to push through and reach Jerusalem by nightfall. He ate hungrily, washed it down with a swallow of water, and then laid back and closed his eyes.

A thousand thoughts clamored through his mind as he relaxed his body. What would it be like, he wondered, to be home? Truly home. As he thought about it, he realized, perhaps for the first time, that he had never really had one. Sure, there had been places he had lived with friends and people he knew and loved, but even as a child he had known that when he was old enough he would leave to learn his trade. And as that time approached and he had overheard that he would go much farther away than his father or any of their fathers' fathers had gone, his home in Jerusalem took on the feel of only temporary lodging. And now, after what seemed like an entire lifetime, Zoram was finally coming home: a place to live his life, to accept and live out his duty to his people and to God.

As he lay there, beads of sweat cooling as they trailed down the side of his head, he heard a voice, a faint cry that pulled him from his thoughts. Zoram opened his eyes but didn't move, listening carefully for the sound again. Nothing. Just the wind through the branches as it wandered across the rocks and grass. He closed his eyes again, but as he did, the sound repeated, just as faint as before but longer and more desperate.

It was a cry for help.

Without thinking, Zoram leapt to his feet, turned his ear to the wind, and waited. He didn't have to wait long.

The plea for help was coming from over the far hills. Throwing his bags over his shoulder, he ran after the sounds of distress. As he topped the hill, a surge of energy flooded his muscles and focused his thoughts. In the small canyon below, two men dressed in what appeared to be military uniforms were having fun pushing a woman back and forth between each other. Her dress was ripped, and parts of her headscarf were torn and scattered. They were laughing and stepping from side to side to prevent her escape, like two cats playing with a mouse before the kill.

Zoram's instinct and training took over. He had a small knife at his belt, but he didn't suspect he would need it. Sprinting toward an old juniper, he shed his satchel and bag, broke off a dead branch about the size and length of his arm, and started down the hill.

The noise of the splintering wood startled the two men, who looked up almost long enough to let the woman escape. One of them caught hold of her arm though and threw her to the ground. She let out a painful cry as she tripped over a small outcrop of stones.

Zoram didn't bother ordering them to leave her alone. He knew men like these and knew that the time for words was long past. One of the men, the larger of the two, ran headlong toward Zoram, yelling something that might have resembled a war cry on a battlefield but, delivered as it was, was just a feeble attempt to frighten the newcomer.

It didn't work. It would take more than that to frighten Zoram.

Zoram slowed his advance, baiting the soldier to increase his. Just as the two of them were about to collide, the soldier pulled back his right fist, announcing his intention and target. Not only did Zoram easily avoid the strike, but he delivered his own to the man's solar plexus. He doubled over as Zoram continued on to the second tormenter. But the second would not be taken out so easily.

The other soldier stood his ground with sword drawn, the blade pulled back, expertly awaiting Zoram's attack. Zoram switched tactics, giving the soldier what he wanted by running toward him and raising the branch. As Zoram had planned, the soldier delivered a swift and decisive downward strike, splintering off part of the dead wood. But the man's sword also embedded itself into the heart of the tree limb. Quickly using the small advantage, Zoram twisted the branch, pulling the weapon from the soldier's jarred grip and tossing it aside. Unarmed and alarmed, the soldier scrambled backward and tripped on the uneven ground. Zoram took a step toward him and stood, towering over him.

The soldier forced his words over heavy and labored breathing. "You will be killed for this! We are . . . we . . ."

"Are lucky I don't finish you off where you lie," Zoram finished, only then realizing that he was speaking in a language they didn't understand. He tried again in Hebrew, fearing that it wouldn't carry the same threat or authority as he tried to recall the words.

The first soldier was regaining his wind and struggled to his feet. Zoram moved quickly and threw the off-balance giant toward his friend, who tripped. They tumbled over each other.

"You will pay for this!"

"You keep saying that," Zoram replied, "but you have yet to prove it."

"You will hang for your actions against members of the king's army."

For the first time since hearing the woman's cries for help, Zoram paused to consider something he hadn't before. He was returning home to take his place alongside his father as an advisor to the king. He was not simply some do-gooder who could right every wrong he came across, sweeping in to save every damsel in distress. There were laws that needed to be upheld and processes to be carried out. If these men were, indeed, on official state business, then he had just established himself a criminal.

But while part of him told him it might have been a mistake to charge in and intervene, the other part reminded him that they had been abusing the office of their uniform and needed to be stopped. Whatever this woman had done, she did not deserve the treatment he had witnessed.

The smaller of the two soldiers pushed the bigger one off and got to his feet to face Zoram. "By order of the king, I demand you step aside!"

Zoram sized the little man up. "The king? Since when did the king of Israel begin condoning the treatment of women in such a cruel manner?" It wasn't a question that required an answer.

The soldier held Zoram's hard stare for a brief moment and then made a sudden and frantic move for his sword, which lay just out of reach. Though Zoram was closer, the soldier was quicker and reached it a split second before Zoram, but it really didn't matter. Zoram wasn't going for the weapon. Before the man could grip the sword's hilt, Zoram struck his arm just above the elbow, using his fingertips to dig into and crush the nerves. This would temporarily paralyze the man's arm and send a shock of sharp pain that would fill the entire arm and spill over into the chest. The soldier immediately let go and pulled back. Zoram kicked him back to his accomplice and picked up the sword, a crude version of an elegant weapon.

"For an attack of this nature, I would be justified in killing you where you stand." Zoram's Hebrew was returning in a great flood. "The sanctity of womanhood is not to be dishonored and should be defended by all decent men. If she has committed a crime, then—"

"I-I . . ." The woman, still in shock from the terrifying ordeal, tried to speak but could only form a few sounds.

"She knows where he is," the little man said.

His companion finally had regained his breath. "She's hiding him."

"Who?" Zoram asked.

"A fugitive. A madman."

"A prophet." The bigger man froze, realizing his mistake; his words hung over them.

Had Zoram heard right? "A prophet?"

"A heretic," the smaller of the two said. "A traitor wanted for questioning before the High Priest, and if you have any sense at all or value your freedom and even your very life, you will stand aside and let us complete our charge."

Zoram looked at the woman, holding her ankle, her eyes wet and bloodshot, a fount for the tears that stained trails down her face. But as she sat there looking up at the three of them, there was no fear in her eyes. Anger, yes. And defiance. But not fear. He had to admit he hadn't known or even associated with many women in his lifetime. He had heard of the power some of them had over men, but until this moment he had never known what that had meant. She was fair to behold, perhaps his own age or a little older, with olive skin and eyes that affirmed intelligence and maturity. He could not imagine for a moment that she had done anything to warrant such treatment and abuse. And if she was harboring a fugitive, that was a matter for the authorities to sort out, not mercenaries who thrilled on inflicting pain and terror.

But with his attention momentarily on the woman, he was distracted long enough for his captives to flank him on either side. Zoram still had the sword and wasn't concerned with being overtaken, but gauging by their positions and distance, he knew they had a plan.

"I don't want to hurt you," Zoram offered. "But I cannot let you take this woman. If you would allow me to escort her to the city, perhaps we could all come to some sort of resolution."

"And split the bounty for what she knows?" the little man scoffed. "We tracked her all the way out here. He's here, hiding somewhere in these hills, and she knows where."

"Command of a garrison has been offered for his capture—"

"Or death, and we're not leaving without her."

"So step aside, and we just might forget we ever met."

Zoram considered his options. "And what happens to the girl?"

The two looked briefly at each other. The little man had a wicked grin. "You can have what's left."

The woman tried to look brave but stifled another cry.

Zoram had heard enough. Without allowing the fiends to pool their collective intelligence and form even a half-witted thought, he sprang toward the bigger of the two. Jumping high in the air and spinning to build momentum, Zoram brought the flat side of the sword down on the man's shoulder. The soldier was unprepared for the unorthodox move and wasn't sure how to block the attack. He raised his hands, but the wide metal blade connected where his neck met his shoulder. Zoram knew he had broken the soldier's collar bone. The man fell backward in excruciating pain, his right arm rendered useless.

Zoram then turned and ran toward the little man, sword raised high overhead. Thinking the strike was going to come from above, the soldier grabbed the discarded branch and positioned it over his head. Zoram jumped across the small distance between them. But instead of driving the sword down with the full force and momentum of his assault, Zoram brought his feet together and delivered a smashing blow to the man's exposed midsection, kicking him off his feet. The soldier landed on his back, confused and unable to breathe.

"You're a disgrace to the uniform and to all of Israel!" Zoram wasn't angry. He was . . . righteously indignant. "You claim to be officers of Israel, and for that reason, and that reason alone, I will let you live." He stepped menacingly toward the bigger man, who scrambled over next to his cohort. "Now get out of my sight!"

"You will regret this!"

"We shall see. Now, go! Before I change my mind. Or shall I let the woman decide your fate?"

As Zoram stepped closer, they twisted to their feet and crawled like frightened dogs up and over the hill. He followed them to where he'd left his belongings, then stood and watched them run away, making sure neither felt a sudden surge of courage and returned for more.

When he was convinced they weren't coming back, he picked up his things and turned his attention to the woman at the bottom of the hill, struggling to get to her feet. He hurried to her side to help, but as he neared she pulled away.

"J-just go!"

"You're hurt. Here, let me—"

"G-go away!"

Zoram noticed that her speech was forced and not natural. "Did you hit your head? Did they hurt you?"

"No. J-just go. I'm f-fine."

Zoram unconsciously took a step back, puzzled and not certain how to take this peculiar woman.

"D-don't look at m-me like that," she said with labored effort. "I'm f-fine."

Zoram was embarrassed that she had seen him staring at her. He tried to smile. "Please. Let me look at your foot. I have some training in these matters." A long pause later, she consented, and Zoram gently took her ankle and foot. It had swelled and was tender to the touch.

"Can you move your toes?"

She could, barely.

Zoram smiled again. "I don't think the bone is broken, and it will heal straight, but you must rest and stay off it. Do you live far from here?"

She looked away and didn't answer.

"Is there someone nearby I can take you to?"

Still nothing. Zoram was starting to become annoyed with her distrust. Didn't she know he was trying to help her? He had just risked his life to save hers. What additional proof did she need that he meant her no harm?

"You'll never make the climb without help. I know you've just been through a lot, but you need to accept my help." She was still looking away. "Before they come back."

Zoram waited a moment or two for her to change her mind but finally began to think there was nothing he could do for her. Maybe she wasn't right in the head. Maybe she was lost or confused. Maybe she really didn't understand what he was trying to say. But he knew better than that.

Zoram exhaled loudly and stood, draped his satchels over his shoulder, rested his hands on his hips, and said, "Well, I can't just leave you here."

Without asking permission, he took hold of her arm, swung her around, and slung her over his shoulder. She immediately started to kick and scream, demanding to be put down, but he just put one hand over her legs to prevent her flailing feet from causing any real damage and used the other to steady her over his shoulder.

"I guess I'll have to bring you along."

But he'd had second thoughts about his plan the moment she left the ground. Though not a large or heavy woman, she was no petite thing either, and the weight of his cargo hanging from one shoulder coupled with the resisting and writhing body over the other threatened to bring him down.

Now that he had her complete attention, and while he still had the strength to do so, he put her down gently, facing him. He opened his mouth to ask his questions again, but before a word could cross his lips she slapped him. Hard.

"No!"

Zoram rubbed the sting from his cheek. "I guess I deserved that."

"J-just leave m-me alone." She turned and walked away, trying to keep her weight off her injured foot, but she hadn't gotten far before she crumpled under the pain and went to her knees. Zoram moved in to help her.

"Please. I can help. I want to."

She looked up at him, and he realized that they hadn't even been properly introduced.

"My name is Zoram."

She continued to look at him, fixed on his big eyes. "My n-n-n—"

Zoram shook his head gently. "It's okay."

But instead of accepting the gesture of compassion, she looked upset. "D-don't do th-that."

Zoram was embarrassed again but didn't know why. "Don't do what?"

"M-my sp-sp-sp . . ." She stopped, unable to complete the word. "D-don't try to help m-me like that. It hurts."

"Sorry." And he was. He hadn't meant to offend her.

"R-Rebekah," she said suddenly and then smiled in relief. "M-my name is Rebekah."

"Rebekah," Zoram said, almost in a daze. There was that power again, this time the spell cast with the utterance of her name. This feeling of compassion, of . . . longing was unfamiliar to him. He hoped his words didn't betray his new feelings. "It's a pleasure to meet you."

Whether she finally accepted that she truly needed the help or saw that he meant her no harm—or perhaps a blend of both—Rebekah held her hand up, and Zoram took it. "I know of a p-place. It's not f-far from here."

He had never stood so close to a woman, and he clumsily tried to position his arm carefully under hers and around her to support her and keep weight off her foot. Rebekah blushed and smiled at his awkward attempts to get close enough to her to really help.

"Th-thank you," she said softly, and the two of them started farther down the hill.

CHAPTER TWO

LABAN WALKED SLOWLY, DELIBERATELY, AS he inspected the ranks of his elite guard: The Fifty. These men, fifty in number, made up his personal army, set apart from the hundreds, maybe thousands, of common soldiers who fell under his command. These men were hand selected and had proven their worth by their prowess and unusual proclivity to winning at any cost. This small band of privileged few were a feared faction of men, obedient killers and machines of war unlike any other army of the three kingdoms.

He could not have been more proud of their training, their performance, or their loyalty. These were the elements of an unstoppable force. All under his command.

His men had been eagerly awaiting this day, as they did every three months, looking forward to the testing. Later tonight any one of them might be forced to prove their worthiness and their right to remain numbered among the ranks of The Fifty; others would hope to join their ranks. For most of them, the limits of pain and endurance would be reached and put to the ultimate test. Some would succeed. Some would fail. This is what made them the most feared garrison of soldiers Israel had ever produced. These periodic competitions were an excellent way of ensuring that only the best numbered its ranks. Under Laban's special command, no one was promoted or given privilege due to mere longevity. Laban believed that was how armies became soft. To stay sharp, a blade must be constantly ground down and the rough edges smoothed off until only a fine, strong edge remained.

Laban nodded proudly then turned and faced the group of twelve young soldiers who would participate in and endure the testing for the first time. These were men identified by their commanders as having shown unusual skill in combat and had been invited to attend. These potential new recruits put on a brave face, but Laban could almost taste their fear. The testing was only spoken of in hushed voices and was shrouded in mystery and obscurity. Rumors had circulated of blood oaths and secret brotherhoods, and while there was no truth to them, Laban did nothing to dispel them. Power was best maintained by fear; and Laban's Fifty were definitely feared.

"Listen up!" Laban called out in his most stern and commanding voice. "Tonight you are given the chance to become one of us. Tonight you all stand on equal footing. Some will challenge." He waved his hand across the line of new recruits. Then he turned toward his elite guard and waved his other hand over them. "And some will *be* challenged. And in the end, only the best will be numbered with The Fifty."

A nervous and anxious energy passed through all in attendance. The training camp was in a natural amphitheater cut into the side of the hills just outside the city walls. Torches were lit and lined along the perimeter to compensate for the fading sunlight.

"The rules of the testing are simple. Those who are not yet part of us will compete with one another in each of the four branches of warfare and vie for the opportunity to challenge our ranks. Only the best will be allowed to approach us. There are no second chances; there is no room for error. Succeed and you will be honored. The rich will be begging you to wed their daughters; the finest wine will be yours for the drinking. There is great privilege in being one of us." Laban paused. "But you already know that." He chuckled.

Laban walked up the steps to the stone platform that overlooked the arena and took his seat. He was joined by Hanoch, his lieutenant and the closest thing Laban had to a friend. Hanoch had been with Laban nearly seven years and had helped in the creation and ongoing preservation of The Fifty. He was a skilled fighter and one of the best soldiers Laban had ever had the chance to battle. And Hanoch's large and imposing presence did much to instill both fear and confidence in the men at the same time. Laban nodded to Hanoch, who motioned for The Fifty to spread out and surround the field while the new recruits formed an inner circle.

The testing began with a competition of long-range skills: the sling and the bow. Targets were set up on the hillside, and potential recruits were given one chance to strike closest to the center mark and ranked accordingly. The lowest two were summarily dismissed.

Next, their medium-range skills were tested in the javelin and spear. Again, targets were mounted, and the two that hit farthest from the mark were sent away. Of the original twelve that began the testing, only eight remained.

These first two rounds, though necessary to weed out the weaker combatants, were a bit of a bore for Laban. It was the next stage that would prove to be entertaining and stimulating. Knowing what was next, members of The Fifty formed a circle around those who were left. With a nod, one of Laban's men stepped into the inner ring and tossed six swords into the center of the arena. Laban stood and raised his arms to quiet the raucous crowd.

"Two of you will be allowed to challenge The Fifty," Laban announced, pausing to give the candidates enough time to realize that there weren't enough swords for all of them. He smiled. "Try not to kill each other."

Where some hesitated, others seized the chance to narrow the odds and picked up more than one weapon. One soldier in particular stood out during this violent free-for-all. He was a short, stocky man who seemed to be able to anticipate the attacks of others, disarming and injuring them but always stopping short of killing them. He was clearly their superior. When there were only four left standing, Laban called for them to stop.

"Very good!" he said. Then, "Men, the swords." Three of his guards gathered up the weapons. The four remaining recruits were hurt and breathing heavily with exertion and near exhaustion, but they moved with confidence and pride, as they should have.

"You!" Laban called to the clear victor. "What's your name?"

The stocky man stepped forward while the others all gave him room. "Bani, my lord."

Laban leaned close to Hanoch. "I like this one already. Shall we see how good he really is?" Hanoch smiled. "Bani, you show great promise. You are decisive and quick to action. Do not disappoint me."

Hanoch stepped to the edge and called out a name.

"Gideon!"

Murmurs spread from members of The Fifty, and a section of the circle parted to let a giant through. Gideon made even big men look like children. He was almost a full head taller than most everyone there and was almost as thick as he was wide. The man resembled a tree trunk with legs. Bani had almost no warning as Gideon rushed him and grabbed hold of his tunic, delivering a crushing blow to his jaw. Bani hit the ground hard enough to bounce. He was stunned for a moment but quickly rolled to his side and then to his knees. He shook off the effects of the strike, though not in time to defend against the next round of attacks.

Bani raised his arms in a basic defense, but he was not strong enough to buffer the attacks and took a merciless beating. Right, left, right. Gideon's fists were unhindered by Bani's weak resistance as they bruised and bloodied Bani's face and midsection. It was a massacre, but the crowd cheered with every devastating hit. Finally, Bani could take no more punishment and stayed down as Gideon taunted him, motioning him to get up. Gideon circled him a couple of more times and then relaxed his stance. He turned and looked up at Laban.

"Finish him off," Laban said flatly.

But Bani had heard the command too and forced himself to his feet. Gideon reached out to take hold of the new recruit, but Bani wasn't ready to go that easily.

Digging deep down for every scrap of strength he had left, Bani drove his foot to the side of Gideon's knee, breaking it and bringing the giant down to his level. Clasping his hands together, Bani pulled back and delivered a sharp blow to the giant's left temple. When his opponent went limp and fell face-first to the ground, the recruit knew he had won.

Bani stumbled around the arena for a moment, trying to regain his balance and finally stopping to stand over the still body of his opponent. The arena was silent, the rest of The Fifty stunned and confused at what they had just witnessed.

Laban, however, was smiling. After a moment he said, "It seems that David has just beaten our Goliath," and started laughing. "Welcome to The Fifty, Bani!" The arena was filled with applause and cheering as the garrison circled around to welcome their newest member.

Laban had decided long ago that the risk of injury to his personal guard was not only worth it but, in fact, necessary. He had no use for weak men populating his ranks. Each member of The Fifty knew that he may need to prove his value and superiority at any given time. If beaten, especially by younger potential recruits, they would forever give up their place among The Fifty. Death had a certain finality to it.

But then, in contrast to the celebration all around them, a single soldier separated from the crowd and walked, with labored steps, to the vanquished member. Laban leaned in close to Hanoch. "Who is that?"

"Salah. Gideon's brother."

"The Fifty had two brothers?" Laban mused. "What a proud mother they must have had."

Salah stepped to the body of his brother, knelt, and touched Gideon's lifeless face gently, as if in disbelief. With his fingertips he brushed Gideon's hair from his eyes and then pressed his forehead to his brother's. He could not stem the flow of tears. As if he suddenly realized his show of weakness, he stood tall, defiant.

"He's dead!" Salah called out over the praise and approbation. He then looked up at Laban. "He's dead!"

The applause died as quickly as it had come to life. A heavy silence settled on the arena.

"I'll handle this," Hanoch offered, but Laban put a hand on his shoulder to restrain him.

"No, I want to hear what he has to say."

"As you wish." Then Hanoch called down to Salah. "You may speak, but mind your words carefully. It is Laban, leader of The Fifty and Keeper of the Records, who you address."

Salah spat in the dirt, turned, and searched the crowd until he spotted his brother's killer. Enraged, he lunged for him but stopped at Laban's command. "Stop this! You will not touch him!"

Members of The Fifty quickly formed a barrier to protect their newest member. Frustrated, Salah turned to Laban.

"He killed Gideon! You cannot let his death go unpunished!"

"He knew the risks, as everyone here does. Your brother was careless. That is what killed him, not this new recruit."

Unable to vent his anger in any other way, Salah raised his fists to the night sky and released a vicious scream. He took a threatening step toward Laban. "You sit there, untouchable with your position and calling, all the while making us fight for our membership, for our very lives! My brother should not have been challenged. Not in this manner. And so I invoke the right of challenge. I challenge *you*, Laban!"

The arena was silent, shock and astonishment captivating the audience.

Laban didn't move, keeping his gaze fixed on this brother of Gideon. Hanoch started to speak, to condemn the words and stop this madness from going any further, but Laban stayed him. "No," he said to his friend. Then he spoke louder, for all to hear. "Salah is right. A leader must be trusted by those who follow him. Without that trust I may have purchased your backs but not your hearts. I am reminded that I have not, indeed, faced the testing for a good number of years." Laban shed his coat and formal military armor and began down the steps to the arena floor. "So be it."

When he reached the ground, he rolled his shoulders and tilted his neck from side to side to loosen up. Looking to the soldier holding one of the swords, he held out his hand. He was given the weapon. Another was given to Salah.

"I assume you won't object to foregoing the other stages of the testing and getting right to the swordplay and hand-to-hand combat—that's what you meant by your challenge, is it not?" Laban's overconfidence and arrogance would have been sickening to other men, but to The Fifty it was a source of pleasure and sick delight. Laban was their leader, and though it was true that none present had ever seen Laban defend his position over them, none of them doubted for a moment that he was superior in every skill of battle and combat.

Laban took a casual defensive stance. "Don't let anything but fear stop you," he said with an inciting half smile.

Salah took the bait and unleashed his anger on his commander, using every attack, every angle, every offensive strategy and tactic he knew, but Laban deflected and parried them with confidence and ease, taunting him to try other moves and attacks.

"Is that all you have? I now see where the weak link in our collective armor is. It's clear to me which brother possessed the skills." Laban easily deflected Salah's blows. He enjoyed the display of degradation and humiliation of this traitor who would dare embarrass him in front of his men. He would show them all what a mistake it was to—

Sudden pressure and a sharp pain in his upper left arm extinguished his mirth. He parried the next strike and stepped back. Salah paused and remained fixed on Laban. Still unsure what had happened, Laban looked to his men, who all stood staring and in shock. A hush had fallen over The Fifty. Then he registered that the pain in his arm remained. He touched his arm and pulled back fingers smeared with blood.

His blood.

A dark rage overshadowed Laban. A tremor began in his chest and quickly spread through his arms and legs to his fingertips, engulfing his whole being. *No one strikes Laban! Laban is not cut. He is not defeated. And he is not humiliated in front of his own men!*

The time for games was over.

Laban re-gripped his sword hilt and growled, charging the wretched fool, unleashing a relentless attack on his challenger. Over and over he swung from above, from the side, spinning to build momentum, advancing with every strike. It was all the young man could do to defend against the full fury of Laban.

Fear having long since replaced his grief from losing his brother, Salah retreated until he stepped on a small stone and tripped, falling backward to the ground. But instead of letting up, Laban continued his rampage. Then, with one particularly vicious strike, Laban jarred the sword from Salah's weakened hand. Salah looked up, terrified, eyes searching for mercy.

But mercy was something Laban did not possess.

Spinning the sword, he gripped it tightly with both hands, raised it high over his head, and drove it deep into Salah's chest. Laban let out a feral cry that echoed through the arena and into the night.

Laban's chest heaved, and the sound of his heart threatening to burst from his chest soon subsided, but he still kept his grip on his weapon, buried almost to the hilt. Looking around, he was angered to see only stunned silence and was about to take out his wrath on the whole lot of them when the new recruit, Bani, clapped. He was followed by another and then another, and the next instant the outside amphitheater filled with thunderous cheering and applause.

Laban laughed and stood, withdrawing his sword and tossing it on the ground next to the body. He turned around, slowly basking in the approval and admiration of his men. He had proven, here and again, that he was deserving of his title and position. Each soldier showed his renewed support and loyalty, and with each nod of consent and word of praise, his confidence swelled. Until he met the gaze of Hanoch, who only gave him a disapproving shake of his head.

CHAPTER THREE

REBEKAH LED HIM THROUGH THE hills and along paths that, from afar, looked impassable. A few times, Zoram had voiced his concerns that she had made a mistake and taken a wrong turn. But always the pathway opened up, and they would continue through new almost-hidden canyons and trails. He finally decided to trust her and walked in silence.

"We're almost th-there," she said eventually.

As they passed through a small stone rift at the base of an odd-shaped mountain, he expected to find a cave and scattered rubbish and debris. Hermits and self-proclaimed holy men often suffered from delusions that made living in organized and established societies impossible.

"And this place we're going, you're certain he'll be able to help you?"

Rebekah smiled. "Th-they are good p-people."

Zoram smiled back and then noticed that the path through the natural rock walls was smooth and well maintained. It was absent of the neglect he had expected, and he was unprepared for the sight that greeted them as they passed through.

The sun had just set, washing the skies in purples and oranges and reds, which magnified the beauty that lay before him. The small ravine had opened up into a wide valley with steep mountain walls on all sides, perfectly secluded from the rest of the world. The ground was flat, and grasses grew from one end to the other. There were trees of several varieties spaced throughout, giving the enclosed landscape an open and wide feeling. Sheep and cattle were corralled, as were several horses, all content and preparing to bed for the night. A well was situated on the far side. And near the center but slightly to one side was quite possibly the largest and most ornate tent Zoram had ever seen. From where he stood, it appeared to be at least twenty paces across. Other smaller tents surrounded it.

An older boy spotted them, dropped a bag of feed, and started running for the tent.

"Papa! Papa!"

At the far end of the field, two men attending to a small group of flightless fowl stood up and watched Zoram and Rebekah hobble into the well-kept secret sanctuary. The men looked at each other but made no move to approach or intercept them. From around the back of the main tent stepped an elderly woman with wash draped over her shoulders and dripping down the front of her. Some young girls, most likely daughters, looked out from behind her, their dress sleeves dark from helping with the chore.

This was not just the hideout of a single man but the estate of an entire family—and a wealthy family at that. None of this made any sense. He wondered what manner of man this patriarch must be. It was peculiar.

A moment later the tent flaps opened and out walked an elderly man dressed in formal and expensive desert robes. He looked regal as he answered the call of his young son.

"His n-name is L-Lehi," Rebekah said softly. "He is a g-good man."

Lehi stepped forward and was joined by his wife and daughters, hiding behind their mother. As he neared, Zoram could see that the man's demeanor—strong, handsome—matched his vestments, and any fear or hesitation he'd had about bringing Rebekah here melted away.

Lehi called out as he walked toward her. "Rebekah? Is that you?" Even his voice spoke to his gentle authority and command. "Dear, are you all right?"

Lehi's wife gave the wet clothes to one of the girls and hurried ahead to meet them. She took Rebekah's other arm. "Child, what happened?"

"She ran into—" Zoram started but Rebekah cut him off.

"I t-tripped."

Zoram looked at her briefly, surprised she had just lied to the woman trying to help her, but suspected that now might not be the best time and place to talk about her harrowing ordeal.

The elderly matriarch smiled at Zoram. "Thank you . . ." she said, waiting to fill in his name.

"Zoram, ma'am."

"Thank you, Zoram. You are very kind."

"The ankle isn't broken," he explained, "but she needs to lie down."

"The Lord will bless you for your acts this day." Then to Rebekah she said, "Now come with me. Let's look at that foot."

As Rebekah hobbled toward the tent, Lehi stepped close and wrapped his big arms around Zoram, embracing him. Zoram didn't resist, not wanting to be impolite, but he was uncomfortable with this display of affection from a man he had only just met. Lehi must have sensed this and released him after only a moment, but he kept hold of Zoram's shoulders.

"Thank you. May the Lord bless you and return the kindness you have shown this day tenfold."

Zoram nodded his thanks for the formal blessing, unsure what the customary response might be. He was still uncertain his rusty Hebrew was understood, and he had almost no knowledge of Jewish customs and traditions. Lehi smiled and slapped his shoulder in another show of appreciation and fatherly affection. He moved to Zoram's side, and the two of them watched the women disappear into the tent.

"Rebekah is a very special woman. Her father, Ishmael, and I are the oldest of friends. She's very dear to us."

Zoram didn't know what to say, so he kept his tongue.

"She didn't trip, did she?"

Zoram looked at Lehi, surprised at the direct question. But he didn't have to answer. It wasn't really a question.

"She is fortunate you came along when you did. We all are." There was an edge of sadness to his voice.

After a moment of reflective silence, Zoram told him what had happened. "They followed her from the city. They were looking for you. But she would have rather died than tell them."

Lehi sighed and looked over his estate. "Soon none of us will be safe here either. Why is it that troubles seem to follow some? My family doesn't deserve to be uprooted again. We've made a good life here. They are happy here. It will be difficult to leave when the time comes."

"I don't understand," Zoram said. "The soldiers said you were wanted for questioning. That the High Priest wanted to talk with you."

Lehi chuckled but it was without mirth. "Oh, they're all too happy to talk. The problem is that no one wants to listen. But I trouble you with matters that are mine and my family's to bear. Come. You will share the evening meal with us and stay the night."

"No, thank you. I must get back on the road to—"

"Jerusalem? You'll never make it before all light is drained from the sky. Besides, you'll never find your way back to the main roads in the dark, and the countryside is full of many dangers."

Zoram still felt like he needed to try. He was already a day late from the caravan. "I appreciate the offer, but I must try. Please understand—"

"I insist. You will be at great risk if you venture out tonight, and I could not, in good conscience, let you venture out tonight. It is not often that we have guests to our table, and tonight my good wife is serving spiced lamb with *beid hamine* and *tzimmes* with honey. You won't want to miss it." Lehi jabbed Zoram's ribs good-naturedly. "Although it may forever ruin the meal for you because no one seasons it like my good wife." Lehi laughed deeply and slapped Zoram on the shoulder again. It was clear Zoram wasn't going anywhere, so he joined Lehi, walking toward the tents.

Lehi instructed his son Sam to show Zoram to his tent. Lighting several hanging lamps with his own, Sam followed his father's instructions, but there was something in his movements and his words that led Zoram to believe that he might be slower, mentally, than other young men his age. Not a disability but rather a simple, childlike mind—a mind that many young men would have grown out of.

The tent was immaculate and well furnished, with a divan, table, and wash basin filled with warm water and topped with a polished silver mirror that cast an almost flawless reflection. The blankets, coverings, and pillows were all of the finest tapestries and silk. Incense was lit and filled the spacious room with a sweet smell that soothed Zoram's body and mind. These comforts were unlike his past living arrangements—sparse rooms of stone floors and walls, a thin mattress of sheep's wool, and thick, uncomfortable blankets to keep out the cold mountain air.

In one corner stood a small stove. Sam set to work filling it, and the tent soon filled with radiant warmth that completed the air of the room. On the divan were folded white linen garments and costly robes and apparel. Sam pointed them out. "My mother thought you might be able to wear these. They belong to my younger brother. You and he are about the same size."

Zoram had never felt anything so smooth, so fine, as these garments.

"She also said for me to take the clothes you're wearing, and she and my sisters will wash them. She said they looked like they had crossed a desert." Sam smiled.

Zoram almost laughed. "Your mother is a very insightful woman."

Sam turned his back and let Zoram wash and change. In the corner, Sam spotted the heavy satchel Zoram had carried. He started to unlatch the leather strap holding it shut. "What's in here?"

Sudden and intense feelings of possession and protection overcame Zoram, and although he knew it was just simple curiosity and he had nothing to fear, he reached out to stop Sam from touching it.

"Don't!"

Sam was startled by the forceful rebuke and pulled away, hurt and confused. "I'm sorry. I didn't mean . . ."

As quickly as those feelings had arisen, they vanished, and Zoram knew he had overreacted. He tried to apologize. "No. I am the one who is sorry. It's just—" Zoram stopped, suddenly aware that they'd been joined by one of the older sons. He had a look of disapproval across his face.

"Sam!" he said sharply.

Sam cowered at his brother's voice before lowering his head, snatching Zoram's traveling clothes, and scurrying out of the tent. Only half dressed, Zoram met this brother's hard, coercive stare with one of his own. He had known men like this before, men who used their size or strength or influence to bully others into submission. Zoram wasn't afraid, but he also had no reason to challenge the brother or his authority.

"Sam was just—"

"Dinner is ready," he said simply then left, leaving Zoram alone to extinguish his heated feelings for the clear display of arrogance and intimidation.

Zoram finished dressing and entered the main tent to the most delicious aromas he had ever breathed in. The family was gathering around a large table set just off the ground and surrounded by an abundance of cushions.

"Ah, Zoram! We're so pleased you're joining us. Come, you will sit here," Lehi announced, moving to his left and motioning to the spot to his right. The eldest son, angered at this usurpation of his place at the table, stood and stormed out of the tent—but not before looking long and hard at his brother, who looked around sheepishly then got up and joined his brother's protest.

Lehi sighed. "Don't mind them. They're good boys. They will have forgotten the whole thing by morning."

Lehi's wife, Sariah, and his girls then brought in the plates of food and bowls of soups and broth. After Lehi invoked the blessing, he dished

Zoram's meal before the rest of the family partook. Zoram's reluctance to indulge as a guest dissolved with the first bite. The food was of the most exquisite flavor he could ever remember tasting. Of course, he had little to compare it to. Caravan food, though sustaining and somewhat nutritious, lacked appeal to the senses, and during his time away, he'd eaten little more than rice sometimes flavored with honey or a little goat meat. Zoram wasn't sure if they ate in heaven, but if they did he couldn't imagine anything better, and he let Lehi and his wife know this.

Sariah smiled and blushed. "You are too kind."

Lehi chuckled. "You see, Mother. It's not just me who thinks so."

Zoram ate largely in silence and listened as Lehi and the others discussed chores and other work that had ensued that day. They reported on the flocks and the gardens, on their health, and on general household management. Zoram raised a brow, though, when Lehi mentioned preparations for another trading expedition to Egypt.

Sam became very excited at this news. "Can I lead the team this time? I know the route."

Lehi smiled and clapped him on the back. "I suppose there are few who know the routes better, isn't that so?"

"Yes, Papa."

"Can you load the camels without help?"

An excited nod.

"And drive the teams across the Goshen deserts?"

More nods.

Lehi looked to his wife and met her smile. Then back to Sam. "You make a good argument. It would be an honor to have you by my side."

Sam smiled, looking thankfully between his parents, then returned to his meal. After another round of small talk died down, Zoram voiced a question he'd had since sitting for dinner.

"Is Rebekah all right?"

Sariah looked pleased with the inquiry. "She's fine. You were correct about her foot. It's not broken, but she needed the rest and I *urged* her to stay in bed. I will pass on your concern in the morning."

Zoram was suddenly embarrassed and stumbled through a thank-you before returning to his food.

Once they finished the meal, and after they all heaped praise and thanks on Sariah and the girls, Lehi insisted on walking Zoram to his tent via a circuitous route. The skies were clear, the weather was warm, and the stars were bright enough to cast a soft glow on the small valley.

"Thank you, again, for returning Rebekah safely to us. She has become like another daughter to me and a dear friend to my wife."

After a moment of silence, Zoram spoke his mind. "They wore military uniforms and commanded me to turn her over in the name of the king."

"Zedekiah has been . . . confused since being appointed, but I believe he wants to do the right thing. It isn't the king who concerns me; it's those advisors and counselors who surround him who pose the biggest threat to Israel." There was no fear or anger in the man's voice—just sadness and maybe a hint of regret.

There was another stretch of silence.

"You have invited me into your home, treated me with more hospitality than I deserve, and fed me like a king, all without knowing anything about me."

Lehi inhaled deeply the fresh night air. "Is there something else I should know? I know all I need to. You risked your life to save the life of a stranger and bring her to safety. You have a good soul. That is all I need to know. Your reasons for being there are your own, known not only to you but also to God, and I am content knowing that He knows."

Zoram considered his words and grinned at their heartfelt simplicity. "Well, thank you."

Lehi continued to lead Zoram through their property. "Will you need help finding your way in the morning? Sam has become quite fond of you. I'm sure he wouldn't mind showing you the way."

Zoram smiled. "Thank you, but no. I should have no trouble finding the trail again. Offer my sincere thanks to Sam though."

Lehi nodded. "I will see that your clothing and provisions are left at your tent. I do not rise as early as I used to, so let me say farewell to you now as I suspect you'll be gone before I'm up."

Lehi embraced Zoram again, but this time it wasn't the slightest bit uncomfortable and, in fact, caused Zoram's eyes to tear, thinking of the embrace he would soon be able to share with his own father.

Zoram expressed his thanks once again, retired to his tent, pulled back the silk sheets and thick blankets, and tried to fall asleep.

שומר החרב

Zoram had not been asleep long when he was awoken by the sounds of an emotional conversation coming from the main tent. He didn't mean to eavesdrop, but there was no way not to listen. And the more he did, the more intrigued he became.

Someone—a boy or man, he couldn't tell—was crying.

"There was nothing you could have done, son." It was Lehi.

"But there was. All I had to do was speak up, and she would have been spared."

"What?"

"That's what he said. He said that if anyone would speak on her behalf, he would free her."

"And you believed him?"

"I wanted to speak, but my tongue wouldn't form the words. I was a coward."

"You have never been a coward!" Lehi's tone was firm but filled with love.

"Then why couldn't I speak?"

"There is a time for everything under heaven: a time to speak and a time to be silent."

"But why didn't God save her? She had done nothing wrong. What if God was waiting for me to speak up? What if I was supposed to save her? And I didn't."

Lehi didn't respond right away. "And what if you had raised your voice in her defense?" he finally said. "What then? I can tell you that she wouldn't have been released and you would have been taken and stoned as well." Lehi's voice dropped. It was softer, more gentle. "And the Lord has more in store for you; I feel it."

There was another pause. "I promise you, Father, I will always speak up. I will always choose what is right, regardless of the consequences. They have gone too far. There must be something we can do."

The son's plea for action went unanswered, resonating against the silence of his father's weighty consideration. "I will take it up with the Lord. But for now, get something to eat, then retire to your tent. Rest if you can. Solutions usually present themselves after a good night's sleep."

"Thank you, Father."

There was the rustle of clothing and the firm resolve of father and son embracing.

"You're a good boy," Lehi said softly. "If all fathers could only have a son like you."

Zoram was touched by this simple exchange and fell back asleep with the warmth and love of a father's words resting on his ears.

CHAPTER FOUR

JHAROM SAT ATOP THE CITY wall scanning the countryside for any sign of his son, but as the last of the day's light faded into night, so did his hope that today was the day Zoram would return.

Not today, he thought. Perhaps tomorrow.

Zoram's last letter had arrived months earlier and had been sent just prior to his final preparations to return home. He had included the anticipated caravan route and the expected window of time they would pass by Jerusalem. Though caravans were often at the mercy of the weather, and sometimes governments and outposts, Jharom had hoped and prayed that his son's travels would be without incident.

A hundred thoughts crossed his mind—and only a few of them did not result in his son being stranded, robbed, hurt, or worse—and Jharom had to rein them in, reminding himself that his son was no longer a child. In his letters, Zoram sounded so strong and confident in his newly acquired skills and knowledge. His son had learned so much more than Jharom had anticipated. He could not wait to sit up all night, listening to his son's stories and benefiting from his teachings. Jharom had received a handful of letters over the years, and it had been a strange experience to watch his son—his only child—grow up on parchment. When his mother died, Zoram became everything he had left, his sole reason for hope and his only outlet for love.

And he was half a world away.

Jhoram was ashamed to admit it, but there had been many times since his wife's passing that he'd wished he could bring his son home, wanting to see him again, needing to hold him close. But he never voiced them to anyone. Not even to God. How could he? Zoram had gone away to learn the secrets that would allow him to return and take his place as Israel's new

Keeper. His responsibilities were to be great, especially in these dark days of Israel's occupation. Jhoram's feelings were selfish, and even during his most lonely hours, he knew deep down that Zoram was doing the right thing, serving God and His people.

Jharom had sat atop the northern wall every night for a week, hoping, waiting for the first glimpse of Zoram. He was sure it would be today.

He sighed, offered a short prayer for his son's safe arrival, scanned the dark countryside once more, and resigned himself to wait another day.

As he began to move from his precarious perch high atop the outer wall, he spied movement approaching the north gates. His first instinct, hoping against hope, was to call down and tell his son to be patient while he unlocked the gate, but something in the way the figure moved through the dark trees and up the small hillside unnerved him. Intrigued, he watched as the figure kept to the shadows and froze when a far-off shepherd called out for a lost sheep.

Thieves and other criminals preyed on those hapless or lost souls who found themselves outside the protection of the city walls, which were shut and locked after dark. But something about the way in which this man moved kept Jharom's attention. He moved with purpose, winding his way along the base of the wall, cloaked in almost total darkness. The moon would not rise for several more hours, and the light from the stars did little to illuminate him.

Jharom hurried along atop the wall, moving toward the Damascus Gate, and wondered if the sentries—

The sentries were gone! There was no one manning the flanking towers.

Jharom walked to the edge of the wall as far as he could and watched in horror as this stranger simply pushed on the heavy wooden door and entered, passing through unchecked and unnoticed.

Where were the guards?

Jharom thought it best not to yell out, warning the intruder to hide or run away. Instead, he hurried down the stairs in the middle of the wall and through the streets of the city, hurrying to the courtyard just inside the gate. As it was every night after dark, the city streets were deserted, and he was painfully aware of the noise his sandaled feet made on the cobbled streets. He stopped at a corner and carefully looked around. Everything was quiet and still.

He'd missed him!

Jharom held his breath. If he couldn't *see* the intruder, maybe he could *hear* him. Nothing. Then a shadow caught his eye down one of the intersecting streets leading toward the upper city. No longer a young man but still in fair shape, Jharom sprinted after the figure. He knew he was now making noise on the otherwise silent streets, but that didn't matter. Jerusalem was a maze of streets and alleyways, which were difficult enough to navigate during the day. He knew that if he let the man get away now, he may never find and apprehend him.

Fortunately, the figure was not in a hurry, concerned more with keeping out of sight than being chased. As Jharom approached, closing the distance between them, he had the thought that this was really a matter for the city guards or military. His calling was not to track down criminals or risk his life to stop a thief. *Where is everyone?* he wondered. Not only were the posts above the gate vacant, there was no military presence anywhere within the city either.

The sounds of his feet must have been louder in his own ears than what carried through the night air. His approach seemed to go unnoticed by the intruder. The moment Jhrom could discern the man's hooded cloak, the man became aware of his pursuer and turned around, his face masked in shade. Frantically the intruder darted down one of the side streets.

"Stop!" Jharom ordered, knowing it would do no good. But he had to try something as he chased.

The dark figure was quick and would have likely escaped, but he tripped over two stacks of bagged grain as he rounded a corner and fell to the ground briefly before scrambling to his feet and continuing in a full run. Jharom chased blindly, becoming turned around and lost, even in his own city. He was surprised when he ended up back in the abandoned courtyard where he had started. He paused, hoping he hadn't lost the other man, when he caught dark movement at the gate and then the figure was gone.

Not one to simply give up, especially as he was convinced that this was no ordinary thief, Jharom followed the man outside the city wall and into the valley beyond. The figure was light on his feet and seemed to fly along dirt trails, down the hills, and through the thick vegetation. Whoever he was chasing was skilled in deception and flight.

But what Jharom lacked in speed and stamina he made up for with intelligence and cunning.

Instead of following along the slope of the hill, Jharom cut across the valley and made his way to higher ground. Whoever he was chasing would either be forced to return for another attempt at entry or run away. Either way Jharom should be able to spot him from his new vantage point. He walked parallel to the valley for a minute or two before his hastily made plan paid off, and he spotted the dark, fluid figure crossing from the valley floor to one of the olive gardens planted along the natural ridge.

Jharom moved quickly to intercept him and reached the figure just as he entered the thick olive trees, catching him by surprise and tackling him to the ground. Under his robes the man was thin and lithe but very strong, and he leveraged his own weight, using Jharom's size against him and throwing him off balance. The thief, or spy, or whoever he was, expertly shoved his palm out, connecting with Jharom's chin and ear with such force that it stunned him momentarily. But he wasn't beaten that easily. Kicking the back of the man's legs paralyzed the would-be intruder and brought him back to the ground, giving Jharom time to stand and resume his tackle. But the little guy had one more trick up his sleeve.

Literally.

Jharom's years of combat instincts seemed to sense the small knife a split second before he saw it, giving him just enough time to create a small space between the thin, curved blade and his neck. As he lurched backward, though, he brought his foot up and connected with the man's hand, snapping it at the wrist.

The man screamed out in pain, alarming a horse tied up nearby.

Where did that come from?

The cloaked figure staggered and stumbled to his feet and almost fell on the horse, pulling himself up into the saddle. And with a sharp kick, he rode off into the night. Jharom slowly got to his feet and dusted himself off. The more he thought about what had just happened, the angrier he became. The tower posts were abandoned and the gate left unlocked. And as much as he hated to entertain the thought, there was a traitor in their midst—a wolf within the folds of the flock.

שומר החרב

Laban emerged from his scented bath water and paused, admiring the man he saw reflected back at him in the mirror. Most men his age had begun to lose their youthful, muscular form and shape by now, but the body that stood before him had never been in better health. His chest was still defined, and his stomach flat and hard. His legs were perfectly shaped and his arms strong. He had to admit he seemed to be the perfect specimen of a man.

Not taking his eyes from the polished brass mirror, he clapped his hands out in front of him quickly, and half a dozen nubile and scantily clad young women fell upon him with towels and robes. It was late, but he had needed to clean up after his own "testing" earlier that night. And one of his . . . *position* could not be expected to bathe alone.

Or without beverage.

Laban reached for the familiar carafe of wine, never far away, but instead of pouring a cupful, he decided to drink right from the wide opening. It had been a long day. And looking at his present company, it promised to be a long night too.

Some of the newer girls giggled as they dried him off while others whispered yearnings and desires into his ears as they dressed him. He almost spilled his wine. Laban loved the attention, their soft hands caressing him, their fingers running through his hair as they anointed and rubbed him head to toe in sweet oils and perfumes. He reached out playfully, encouraging their fervid attention and promised them all time with him later.

With two girls on each arm, Laban made his way through his lavish quarters to the banquet hall, where a meal fit for royalty and in quantities to feed a dozen men was laid out before him.

His position was not without benefits, he mused.

"Laban." A voice spoke from behind them. Several of the girls gasped and yelped at the sudden sound, but Laban had sensed him the moment they had entered the room.

Hanoch was leaning against the wall, digging at his fingernails with a small dagger.

Laban stiffened. "Ladies," he said with a dismissive tone. There were groans of displeasure from all of them. Two refused to leave and clung tighter to him, one on each arm.

"Oh, please," one said and then the other, tugging Laban teasingly between them and casting upon him their most seductive looks.

But Laban was no longer in the mood. He pulled away sharply from the one on his right and used his hand to slap the face of the other. He had raised his hand to lash out against them again when a woman's voice at the dining hall door stopped him.

"Girls!" An older, stout woman—not unattractive in Laban's eyes—stood at the door with a stern look about her. The young women scuttled out of the room past her, their heads bowed in shame. "Forgive them," the house matron said.

Unsure what to do with the built-up energy, Laban waved his hand several times in dismissal, and she left with a slight bow, closing the door behind her.

When they were alone, Laban stepped to the banquet table. He was very selective as he picked through the food, choosing only the best cuts of meat and the freshest, plumpest vegetables, and breaking off pieces of bread that were perfectly browned. When he was done with his careful selection, he took a seat along one of the walls next to a window. The cool night breeze felt good. He drank deeply, emptying his carafe.

"Ah!" he exclaimed when it was gone. "That's better."

"It's amazing you have any staff at all that will voluntarily serve you," Hanoch said, moving to the table to pick from the food Laban had left behind.

"What do you mean?" he said, sounding offended.

"The way you treated those girls."

Laban waved a leg of lamb in the air. "They're too much trouble. Do you want one? Have two if you'd like. Just tell the matron on your way out, and she'll arrange everything."

Hanoch dismissed the offer with an uninterested shake of his head. He sat with Laban in silence for a moment. "The woman who was stoned this morning—what was her name?"

Laban grunted his uncertainty and lack of interest as he ate.

"She spoke harsh words against you and the High Priest. You should have gagged her, like I suggested. You had best be careful about these public trials. It's dangerous. For a moment this morning, I thought there might be a voice brave enough to speak up. What would you have done then?"

Laban shrugged and took another bite. "Kill them both. You see, I don't care about any of them—I am Laban, commander of the armies of Israel, captain of The Fifty, and Keeper of the Records!" His voice became louder with each title.

"Well, you should care." Hanoch finished another bite then set his plate down. "That soldier you killed tonight . . ."

"What about him?"

"You shouldn't have."

Laban held Hanoch's dispassionate, matter-of-fact stare for a long pause then tossed his plate into the wall. It broke, shards and food making a mess on the floor.

"What else was I supposed to do? He challenged me! He challenged my rank and my authority. He questioned my abilities in front of the entire command!"

"Not to mention his lucky shot."

Laban stepped passed him to the window. "I have to maintain control over my men. Any doubt in their minds, the slightest sign of weakness, and my ability to lead them is compromised. There is no room for doubt among The Fifty."

"You do remember that they were brothers, don't you?"

"Who died in a military operation."

"Who died in a *training exercise*," Hanoch corrected. "It was an exhibition."

"Who cares?"

"Their mother. And father, who is a member of the royal house, an advisor on trade and financial affairs. He is demanding compensation for his loss and has lodged a complaint with the king."

"Already? They haven't been dead long enough to get cold and already he is seeking *compensation*. I'll tell you what he should do: maybe he should mourn his loss first, then open his eyes and realize they were soldiers, and soldiers risk their lives every day. If they wanted a life of ease, they should have been merchants or performers. If he's such a family man, maybe he should take the consolation his wife will offer and make another son." Laban grinned wickedly.

Laban stood and visited the table again, this time sampling one of each of the varieties of pastries flavored with honey, cinnamon, nuts, and berries.

"Nevertheless, your little outburst, your tirade, will not go unnoticed or be forgotten anytime soon."

Laban shrugged it off and returned to the window, looking out into the night.

"I think you should begin working on a story. The men will back you up. If I might suggest—"

A forceful knock interrupted them.

"What!" Laban yelled.

The door opened. Both men recognized the man who dared interrupt their meal. Laban quickly put on a cordial face.

"Jharom, my old friend. What's wrong? Why are you up—"

"Forgive me, Laban, but I have the most disturbing news. The Damascus Gate was left unlocked, and no guards were posted at the towers."

"What? Slow down." Laban and Hanoch shared a concerned look. Jerusalem was a walled city, accessed by several gates. These gates—some large enough to pass a caravan through, others not much wider than a large door—were locked and guarded each night as a protection from the dangers the desert presented. An unlocked and unwatched gate invited trouble. "Unlocked? What do you mean? Start from the beginning."

Jharom did. He told them about spotting the dark figure and then watching him move for the gate. "It was as if he knew it was unlocked," Jharom said. "And it was then I noticed that the sentries weren't there."

Hanoch spoke up. "And what were you doing atop the wall at this hour?"

Jharom knew it was prohibited to be up there after dark, but his position allowed him certain legal discretions. "Watching for my son."

"Ah, yes," Laban said. "Your boy, the next in line . . . What's his name, again?"

"Zoram."

"Zoram, that's right."

"And you followed this thief through the city streets?" Hanoch handed Jharom a small plate of food, and he accepted it with a nod of thanks but did not eat.

"Yes. He moved as if he had specific purpose and direction."

"Did anyone see you?" Hanoch asked. When Jharom looked confused at the question, he added, "Is there anyone that can corroborate your story?"

Jharom shook his head. "The streets were empty."

"And then what happened?" Laban asked.

Jharom finished his story, relating the events exactly the way they had happened, leaving nothing out. Laban paced the room.

"This is, indeed, disturbing. Who else did you tell this to?"

"No one. I came right here."

"Good."

"If the gate was left open for this foreigner—" Hanoch began.

"Then we cannot trust anyone," Laban finished. "Hanoch, I want post assignments for all of the gates, not just Damascus. And I want you to handle this personally."

"Yes, Laban." Hanoch bowed slightly, acknowledging his orders.

Turning to Jharom, Laban asked, "Do you think you could show my lieutenant exactly where you were when you first spotted this man and then trace his steps for us?"

"Of course." Jharom set the plate down and started for the door with Hanoch falling in behind him.

"Jharom?" Laban's words stopped Jharom, and he turned. "Did you see him?"

"Who?"

"Your son."

"No. His caravan must have been delayed."

Laban gave a consoling smile. "I'm sure you will see him soon. And, Jharom? Thank you for bringing this to my attention. We will not rest until those responsible are found."

Jharom led Hanoch down to the city and up the steps along the back side of the outer wall. Hanoch followed behind along the edge to the spot where Jharom had sat waiting for any sign of his son, where he had first noticed the stranger.

"There," Jharom said, pointing to a patch of dark trees. "He was moving along the shadow line, like he . . ."

Jharom stopped. Something about this didn't feel right. Something since reporting the intrusion to Laban, but he couldn't identify it. Then it hit him, and for a brief moment he was afraid. "How did you know he was a foreigner?" Jharom asked.

Hanoch quickly and with great force and aggression struck Jharom's chest, pushing him backward and off balance. He stepped to the edge of the wall, losing his footing. He reached out to grab a hold of Hanoch, anything, but he only felt the cool night air between his fingers. Falling was an odd sensation. There was a pull downward at first and then a calm, except for the rush of the wind past his ears. He didn't think to scream out.

In this sudden peace, he noticed that the stars were bright and beautiful, and he wondered if his son, wherever he might be at that time, was looking at these same stars. His last thoughts were of years ago when he last saw and held Zoram. The boy had been so young. So handsome. So trusting. A greater calm came over Jharom, and he forgot all but his love. He sent a prayer heavenward, not for his own life but for the life of his son. His last thought was that he loved Zoram very much.

CHAPTER FIVE

ZORAM WAS NINE YEARS OLD when he was sent to a distant land to begin his training and fulfill his calling as this next generation's Keeper of the Sword. Some of his friends had come to see him off. None of the children really knew what the word *apprentice* meant, but they did know that their friend was going to be gone for a long time. Most of them had never before dealt with separation, so their anxiety was released by chasing one another around a small field as the adults talked. But though his friends played and ran and laughed, Zoram couldn't help but feel an enormous weight in his chest that made him not feel like playing.

For him, the days and weeks leading up to the morning's ceremony and farewell were a scary and uncertain time. He had always been told that one day he would have to go away, to leave his home to fulfill something his parents and the others called his "destiny," but it was all so foreign. And until recently that day had seemed so far away.

"Zoram!" It was his father's voice. "It's time."

The rest of the children stopped playing as well, not knowing what to expect but knowing it was of grave importance. Zoram faced his peers and tried to smile, but he was too afraid. One of his friends, Daniel, held his right hand out to him, palm facing out, then closed it into a fist. It was the sign between them to be strong. Zoram returned the sign, feeling a little better.

His father was waiting for him with a group of other men and women. He recognized them as people of importance in the city. There was even a representative of the king. Standing next to Jharom was a man who worked closely with him, the Keeper of the Records, and his two sons, the eldest who, like Zoram, was being groomed to succeed his father and one day take his place.

As he hiked the small hill to the road, his mother broke free of the others and ran to meet him partway, throwing her arms around him.

"Mother," Zoram said, embarrassed with the display of affection, especially in front of all his friends. But as he tried to push her away, she just held him tighter. A sudden surge of emotion washed over him, filling his eyes with tears and making it hard for him to breathe or swallow, and he hugged her back.

His mother started to cry.

"Miriam," his father called to her gently.

But Zoram's mother didn't let go, and though she didn't make a sound, he could feel her choking back her cries. He had been told he would have to be strong, especially for his mother's sake, but now, at this moment, feeling the love of his mother's arms around him, he wasn't sure he could be.

But for whatever reason, either his strength or his fear, his tears soon passed, and he carefully took his mother's hand and led her back to his father, who embraced them both.

The next few minutes passed in a blur for young Zoram. There were words of encouragement and congratulations and more handshakes and hugs to his father and mother. Today was a great day, many of them declared, and through all this, Zoram's hand never let go of his mother's.

One of the advisors to the king, a spiritual and holy man—though not the High Priest, Zoram noted—offered the Lord's blessing to protect and strengthen Zoram and to purify him into an instrument of good. Then the man who Zoram had often heard speak with the ferocity of a lion knelt on one knee and looked at Zoram with the eyes of a lamb.

"Though you may be far from God's people," he said softly, "you will never be far from God. He is the One True God, and He will be near to you wherever you go. Remember this." He smiled and affectionately rubbed Zoram's shoulder then stood and led the people away.

There was another brief round of good-byes, and when they were finally alone, his mother let down her guard and started crying.

"Miriam," his father said firmly. "We have to be strong. For Zoram."

She turned away in an attempt to stem the flow of tears but was only partially successful. His father picked up a large shoulder bag and hefted it to his back. "Come," he said. "We'll walk the rest of the way. Together. As a family."

The three of them walked in silence for a while as Zoram tried to make sense of what was happening to him and why. His father, and his father's fathers before him, worked in metal. Zoram knew that the secrets of turning heavy, clumsy iron into fine steel were closely guarded. He was being sent away to learn these secrets.

"Where is the Indus Valley?" Zoram asked. "Is it far? Is it as far as the Great Sea?"

His father looked down at him as they walked. "Where did you hear that name?"

"I heard two of the men speaking about it on the way over. They said it was very far away."

His mother struggled to stifle another round of tears and sobs. Even his father got choked up. "You heard right. It *is* very far away, but it's where the Lord wishes you to travel."

Little was known of these people, said to live in the tops of mountains that reached beyond the clouds. Zoram could not imagine a place so distant. But that was not all he overheard. He also heard men speak of the Babylonian Empire and the fortune spent to send him beyond its reach. His training was to be very different from his father's.

"Why can't you just teach me?" Zoram asked. "You're the Keeper of the Sword. Why do I have to go somewhere else to learn?"

"Because . . ." his mother started but was unable to finish.

"Because you are going to bring hope back to God's people," his father explained. "You are a very special child, Zoram. You have been chosen by Him who created all to restore honor to His land and this people. You will learn things I do not know, skills in smithing metals and techniques heretofore unknown to us. If God's chosen people are to survive, it will be because of your efforts and your faith."

Zoram heard the words but didn't understand. "So do I *have* to go?"

His mother suddenly burst out with a half laugh, half cry.

"Yes," his father said, smiling. "It means you have to go."

They made their way to the main roads just north of the city where they would meet up with the caravan heading east along the spice trade routes. Zoram mostly listened as his parents talked to and about him, reminiscing about funny or important times in his life. Some were more common, like the time he was playing in the palace with one of the young princes who knocked over a vase that had been a gift to the king from a visiting Egyptian dignitary. The prince, not accustomed to being in trouble, tried to persuade Zoram to lie and cover it up.

"And do you remember what you said?" his mother asked as they walked together as a family. "You told him it was always better to tell the truth. You knew that lies spawn more lies as you try to cover up the one before. We knew you were a special boy, even back then . . ."

Zoram just kept walking with a pleasant grin. He'd heard that story before, and with each telling, his response to his friend became more profound and thoughtful. He did remember that day. The vase was old and not that valuable—it was in a room where children were allowed to play, after all. And to be honest, he was more afraid of being caught telling a lie than for breaking the decorated fired clay. But his mother loved telling that story, so he let her. It made him feel good.

His father had timed their arrival in such a way that they wouldn't have a lot of time to sit and wait and worry. The dust cloud of the caravan could be seen coming around the first hill.

Zoram clung tighter to his parents' hands. "I'm scared. I don't want to go."

"Now remember, Zoram, first and always, that you are a child of God. You are on His errand. He will watch over and protect you, but you have to do your part. Be safe. God's protection does not always extend to cover foolish acts. If you are wise and obedient, the Lord will do his part."

His mother dropped to one knee to meet her son face-to-face. She wiped the tears that were now spilling down his cheeks. "I need to see your brave face. You are a Keeper."

"I'm not one yet."

She smiled through her own tears. "You will be. And you'll be back before you know it. This isn't good-bye; it's just a farewell, and I will pray for you every night. If you are ever afraid or alone you have just to close your eyes and listen. I will be there in spirit."

They hugged once more, and it was as if time stood still as the sum of a mother's love was expressed in that single, tight embrace.

ख़ेपेर ओफ़ ष्वोर्द

Zoram was given preferential treatment during his journey and was kept as well as a nine-year-old boy could be by men hardened by the dangers and perils of driving across deserts and hostile lands.

The caravan master had first objected to delivering this human "good" to lands far beyond the Tigris and Euphrates, but when the request was made by the king of Israel and accompanied by a considerable fortune— almost double what the caravan master had made over the course of his entire lifetime—he had consented and given his word to watch over and care for the boy until he was delivered safely.

But the task had not been as bad as the caravan master had imagined. The special emissary wasn't the spoiled child he had expected, given all the fuss and expense. In fact, he was just the opposite. The caravan master spoke a little Hebrew and could communicate some with the boy, and many times he let the boy ride in front with him, making observations about the land, the political unrest that seemed to plague the world, and other topics he couldn't, or at least *wouldn't,* speak with his men about.

Zoram was pleasant and respectful, and he was a quick study, learning the positions of the stars, the phases of the moon, and how to find food and water in the desert. He even quickly grasped how to organize the men to make their travels more efficient. A couple of times the caravan master had suggested that the boy come and work for him, that there was much money to be made and many adventures to be had leading caravans, but Zoram remained true to his charge and politely declined.

After his first week, Zoram begged a simple log book from the supplies and began a journal of sorts to record his thoughts and experiences. It gave him comfort on nights that he painfully remembered what—and who—he had left behind. He also used it to describe the exotic and varied lands they traveled through, and when words could not describe it, he had drawn pictures. He'd lived his whole life in Judea and had only traveled as far as the Great Sea once with this father, so nothing could have prepared his young mind for the sights that passed before him during the nearly five months of his caravan travels. From the beautiful expanses of sand and dunes of the Arabian deserts to the fertile rivers and valleys of Mesopotamia, Zoram was held in awe at all of it.

They stopped in the city of Babylon for three days as supplies were loaded and unloaded before making the journey across Persia. The caravan master took it upon himself to show Zoram around the city and told him of the political and economic woes of this once-great center of civilization.

"Remember this," he had advised Zoram after walking past a section of the city that lay in rubble and ruin. "It is wise to keep one's finger on the pulse of every city and country you find yourself in. Armies conquer, kings are overthrown, empires rise and fall, and one day you may find that your friend has become your enemy."

He slapped Zoram on the back. "But do not worry of these things. A caravan represents trade, and that means money, and everyone loves money." He laughed, and they continued on.

For the next month, the days seemed to blend with one another. They passed through the kingdoms of Elam and Persia between the shores of a great southern sea and the mountains to the north, stopping only briefly to trade and refresh supplies. It was not until they crossed a river the caravan master called the Sindu that Zoram's journey took on a new look and meaning. It was beyond this river, he was told, that his new home awaited him.

They were strangers in this land, and being men from the West, they were not trusted and were kept under constant and strict escort. The caravan master had only traveled this far east twice before, so he knew very little of the language and customs. He was, however, able to surmise that there were great tensions between the two kingdoms of this land: the Kuru and the Panchala. Fortunately their escorts were of the Panchala and could deliver them safely to Zoram's final destination.

Zoram kept a log of their journeys, describing the strange deserts, lush forests, and odd animals, including a wild tiger. He also noted the strange and heathen practices. It was all so frightening and exciting at the same time.

The days were getting shorter, and he noticed the air and weather getting colder. He had never felt cold like this before. Winters in Israel were wet and the nights were cold, but this weather seemed to bite at any piece of uncovered skin. Even the fires did little to stave it off.

One night he was told that his journey with the caravan was quickly coming to an end and that he would be taken the rest of the way under special escort. Zoram was surprised to feel many of the same feelings he'd had when he left his mother and father. He'd never had an adult friend before, and those feelings of attachment and longing to remain with the caravan master confused him. He was ashamed that he started having thoughts of abandoning this journey and staying with the caravan. But even the caravan master seemed to know that this was the right thing to do.

Zoram's time to part with the caravan arrived a couple of days later. His new escort was comprised of two men, both strangely dressed in robes of a deep mix of orange and red and riding small, stocky horses with long manes and hair. Another small horse was tethered behind, presumably for him.

"Sh-or-hm," one of the men said, trying to pronounce his name in their strange tongue. Zoram was suddenly more afraid than he had been when he left his home. He looked up at the caravan master.

"Will anyone speak Hebrew?" His friend shook his head. "Then . . . then how will I understand them?"

The caravan master smiled and touched Zoram's ears. "Listen."

There were no hugs or long good-byes. Zoram suspected the caravan master would miss him, but he also knew that this was business.

The goods had been delivered as promised.

Unlike his trade route companions, these strange men traveled in silence with a serious, solemn feel about them. And although it frightened him at first, the longer they rode, the more he felt a real sense of purpose and quiet resolve. He had never seen men like this before, but something in their manner made young Zoram think of his own priests back home. But where the priests of Israel wore costly and colored apparel, being some of the wealthiest and most influential citizens, these men looked like they were among the poorest. Still, there was something about them that inspired confidence in the boy's heart.

But that confidence was quickly dashed as they passed through a small rocky canyon. Braving the stiff, biting wind, Zoram saw for the first time that their trail wound up the face of the largest mountain he had ever seen. Thick white snow covered the peaks, making them seem impossible to climb.

Zoram must have gasped out loud because the men turned and looked at him. "Are we going up there?" He pointed.

For the first time, the men smiled at each other and said something in their strange language. They nodded, pointing in the same direction Zoram had, and said something he knew meant yes. Then they laughed again, urging their strong horses up the path.

Zoram had never had to offer a *sincere* prayer before. His prayers, like so many of Israel's, were scripted and specific to the need. There was a prayer for the cattle, another for the crops, and still more for sickness, peace, and repentance. But there wasn't one he was aware of for climbing a narrow, rocky, and icy path up the sheer face of a mountain. So he just made one up. And despite the darkness and the cold wind that howled through the rocks, he felt a warmth stir within him. This peaceful feeling helped him better understand what the great prophet Elijah meant when he said that the Lord was not in the wind or the earthquake or the fire but in the still, small voice. And it was this quiet voice that whispered to his troubled heart that even out here, so far from home, he was not forgotten or alone.

They rode for hours in the ever-increasing dark. The moment they passed through a tall, narrow mountain pass, though, Zoram had the sudden fear of falling. Their trail now snaked along the edge of a canyon so deep he couldn't see the bottom. He was abruptly dizzy and felt sick. It was all too much for him. He was exhausted, cold, and hungry, and the sight of the abyss that stretched out below them scrambled his feelings to a point that he couldn't take anymore.

Where was he? What corner of the world had he been sent to? Was this all some kind of mistake? He was going to die here, plummet to his death, and never see his mother again. Would anyone send word? Would anyone even care?

But then he saw a light in the darkness ahead on the far side of the canyon. He had to squint against the whipping wind, and he carefully let go of the reins with one hand to wipe the snow and water from his eyes to get a better view. He wasn't imagining it. It was really there: a light perched on the top of the mountain—several lights, actually—illuminating what looked like a small city surrounded by a wall with several different shapes and rooflines beyond it.

His guides started speaking between themselves in quick, sharp sounds. They were animated about something. But they weren't happy. They both turned and looked at him, and one spoke to him, motioning him to move faster. They must be late.

With a lighted goal in sight, Zoram was able to turn his anxiety into an excitement and anticipation of reaching his goal, and that peaceful feeling crept back into his heart as he held on to his surefooted steed.

When they reached the monastery, the main gates were opened, and Zoram was quickly rushed inside. Disoriented from fatigue and the cold, he was pushed across a large, ice-covered courtyard into a large hall lit with dozens of fires and lamps. The instant warmth felt wonderful but was nothing compared to how good his heart felt to see the room filled with other children, boys, like him.

Yes, he thought. *We were late.*

He must have paused at the sight because the next thing he knew, he was being pushed again, guided forcefully to a place on the floor next to another boy. Were they all here to be apprentices too? Sitting cross-legged, he wiped away the water dripping from his hair into his eyes and looked around. The boy next to him looked like he was maybe a year or two older than Zoram, but it was hard to tell. The boy's facial features were smooth and rounder than Zoram's, and his eyes were different than any other eyes Zoram had ever seen. They were small and flat, but they were also kind and intelligent.

Behind this boy, on either side, stood men who had similar features and were dressed like he was, in silks and robes with intricate designs and shapes. The men looked very protective of the boy and reacted when Zoram was made to sit next to him. Feeling uncomfortable at being seated next to the boy in their charge, Zoram started to inch away from him.

The boy reached out, though, and put his hand on Zoram's knee. Surprised by the touch, Zoram looked at the boy, who held his look for a moment then smiled. Zoram physically and mentally relaxed and smiled back.

Zoram put his hand on his chest and whispered his name. "Zoram."

The other boy understood the gesture and put his hand on own chest. "Wu Yien."

Half a world away, small and insignificant compared to the mountains peaks and valleys that surrounded them, Zoram knew that he had not been forgotten by his God. The Lord had watched over him, delivered him safely, and given him a gift, a pearl of great price whose value far exceeded the riches of kingdoms, a source of strength and solace to men when all others abandoned him.

Zoram had made his first new and best friend.

खेपेर् ओफ़ ष्वोर्द

Nothing could have prepared young Zoram for the life that awaited him at the high mountain monastery.

He didn't sleep well the night he arrived. He was cold, he was scared, and he was feeling alone. Part of him wanted to run away, but where would he run to? It was terrifying for a young boy to be so far away and unable to even speak the language. Did his mother and father know it would be like this? Would they have sent him if they had? If he ever needed the comfort his mother had promised him, he needed it now.

After the strangely dressed men finished speaking to them, the boys were all paired up and escorted through the dark streets to their quarters. Fortunately, Zoram was paired with the boy he had sat next to during the orientation. While they couldn't speak to one another, they communicated their shared trepidation and supported one another with smiles and nods.

Zoram tried to force sleep to take him, but it wouldn't come. His friend had fallen asleep shortly after climbing into bed. The wind howled through the wooden slats covering the windows, adding to Zoram's unease. Eventually, though, exhaustion overtook him, and he did rest. But not for long.

The next morning Zoram was awakened by the ringing of a large brass bell. The sound filled every corner of every room at the monastery with a solemn, almost religious atmosphere. And while it was startling at first, the resonating tones served to calm Zoram's nerves and unwind his knotted stomach. After a small breakfast of cold rice and strips of salted meat, the boys were all taken outside and lined up. Here they were stripped of their individual clothing and given robes in what Zoram would later learn was a symbolic gesture that, despite the circumstances each boy had come from, they were now all equals in their apprenticeships. As soon as they were dressed, four of the masters, with razors and bowls of hot water, proceeded to shave each boy's head. Some of the boys began to cry as locks of their hair fell to the ground, but Zoram did his best to keep silent and still. Their hands worked swiftly and with great skill, and before he knew it, his dark curls were blowing away in the morning breeze. He reached up and felt his scalp, pulling his hand from his neck all the way forward over the length of his smooth, bald head. It was a singular sensation that allowed him to smile for the first time that day. He looked over and caught Wu Yien's eye. He was responding to his new look in a similar manner, with a similar smile.

Their first few weeks were spent following the masters around the monastery, performing work and receiving instruction by word, gesture, and example. None of the boys knew it at the time, but during these long and tedious days, they had learned more than how to sweep halls, gather firewood, mend walls and fire pits, and the host of other chores they had been required to complete. They had also learned enough of the language to begin communicating with their new instructors. Zoram found that he could understand what they were telling him even though he couldn't yet speak the language. But that ability, too, came shortly and with little effort.

Finally, however, their training began, but not in the manner Zoram had imagined. The sun was warm the morning the apprentices were all taken to the center courtyard and instructed to form a circle around its perimeter. One of the masters, the Sadhus, stepped into the center of the square. He held loosely in his hand a sword whose blade was made of a light, reflective metal Zoram had never seen before. This must be the steel he was sent to learn how to fashion and forge, he thought as his excitement began to rise.

Bending deeply at the waist, the Sadhus performed a sweeping bow to his spectators. Zoram noticed that Wu Yien was the only one of the boys who returned the bow, and he quickly followed suit. The Sadhus smiled briefly at Zoram before exploding in a stunning and astounding series of strikes and defensive moves, moving and using the sword in ways Zoram had never seen before or even thought possible. The Sadhus's movements were quick and fluid as he jumped and spun around, cutting and defending against what seemed like an army of imaginary assailants. Zoram was mesmerized by what he was seeing and could scarcely contain his rush of exhilaration. Would he be taught to wield a sword like this? He inhaled deeply at the prospect.

When the demonstration was over, the master bowed and left the courtyard but not before winking at Zoram, further fueling the boy's passion for the upcoming instruction and training. Another master stepped into the center of the square. Older and with a gentle presence, this was the head of the monastery, the High Sadhus. He waited for the boys to quiet down and turn their full attention on him. Speaking slowly and deliberately for their benefit, the High Sadhus explained the reason for the morning's exhibition.

"The sword is not the weapon; the Sadhus is the weapon," he was clear to point out. "The sword is merely an extension of his skill. Before you can create weapons such as this, you must learn to wield them with perfect knowledge and intuition. But to wield the blade as you have just seen, you must condition yourself, train yourself, temper yourself. You must *become* the blade."

He smiled and looked over the apprentices. "And if you're committed and devoted with your whole heart, you will become the weapon." His gaze rested on Zoram. "Then, perhaps, it will be the *sword* that will wield *you*."

खेपेर ओफ़ ष्वोर्द

The next months were filled with physical exercises and routines Zoram had never seen even soldiers undertake. They began every morning, one at a time, stretching their legs atop a stone wall that lined one of the courtyards. At first Zoram found that he couldn't even reach his toes but gradually became more limber, reaching past his heels and nearly folding his body in half. Their training consisted of push-ups and tossing rocks back and forth to each other, increasing the size of the rocks to what amounted to small boulders. In one corner of the monastery, there was a pit where they conditioned their fists and built muscle by repeatedly punching the fine sand. It was also at this station that they practiced gripping tightly woven bags filled with sand, one at a time, with their fingers in the shape of a claw, picking it up, flipping it over, and then repeating the exercise with the other hand. They also hit their hands and arms and legs with poles wrapped in blankets to toughen up their muscles.

And then there was the running—always running. Up steep hills and over rocks. At first Zoram couldn't go far or for very long. The air seemed thin, and he found it difficult to breathe; but over time his body adjusted, and he could sprint and almost keep up with his masters.

खेपेर ओफ़ ष्वोर्द

It was a full year before they were given wooden swords and taught the basic movements of this elegant weapon. Their year of training had made their reflexes quicker, and each boy had a greater awareness of his body. They were all stronger, leaner, but if Zoram thought his physical training to this point was intense, the weapons training made the past year look like playtime. Zoram practiced basic movements and routines until he thought he would collapse or the sword would fall from his hand out of sheer exhaustion. But always at the close of the day, his spirit was strengthened knowing that he was working toward a greater good, praying that his efforts had been acceptable before the Lord.

One morning, during their third year of training, instead of the regular unarmed combat exercises, they were led into one of inner halls and told to gather around a small fire pit. The pit had been cleaned out and emptied of all rocks and ash. Zoram thought that was unusual until the High Sadhus joined them, holding two thick, woven bags. He then dumped the contents into the wide pit. Two snakes spilled out, hissing and slithering as they staked out their new environment.

"Those are cobras," Wu Yien whispered to Zoram. "Most deadly."

Once the boys' initial shock of seeing the serpents passed, the High Sadhus shared the purpose of the morning's lesson. "Observe how they fight. Animals are uninhibited with form or technique. Their every movement is pure and natural. Watch, then we will discuss what you have learned."

Zoram was repulsed at first by the idea that one or both snakes would die today just to make some point, but he was quickly captivated by what he saw. The cobras circled the stone pit once or twice before approaching each other, rising off the ground almost a full arm's length. Their heads, flared and revealing the circles and loops on their necks, rose next to each other and slowly intertwined. They began pushing one another, each trying to keep balanced and remain upright. It was a tense but graceful performance as each snake twisted and turned, attempting not to kill the other but to slam its opponent to the ground. Once on the ground, each snake was quick to tower over the other in the fight for dominance and superiority. Finally, one cobra was clearly the victor, rising to its full height as the other stayed down, exhausted and defeated. The defeated snake was caught, quite easily, by the High Sadhus, who snatched it with the thick sack turned inside out.

After some discussion with the apprentices about what they observed, the High Sadhus explained, "Not all contests need result in death. There are rules to follow, patterns to accept, to be one with your opponent. But not all fights will be so graceful."

Another Sadhus entered the room with another bag. Whatever was inside was desperately trying to get out.

"Watch as mortal enemies engage one another."

The other bag was opened, and a small, furry animal was let loose in the fire pit with the cobra. It had a pointed head, a long body, and an even longer tail.

"Behold the mongoose," the High Sadhus said. "Watch as the rules of the fight change."

The victorious cobra from a few moments ago, dormant since his prior contest, jumped to life, using its raspy hiss and spreading its neck to ward off the animal. The apprentices stepped back to a safe distance. The mongoose, however, was not deterred. The two natural enemies circled one another. The cobra struck at his opponent with lightning fast movements, over and over, but each time missed. As fast as the snake was, the mongoose's reflexes were faster, dancing just out of reach of the fanged and deadly strike. Then, as the cobra struck again, the mongoose dodged the strike and bit the back of the snake's head. The cobra fell dead instantly. The mongoose cautiously backed away then approached and struck again, making sure the snake was, in fact, dead and no longer a threat.

There were many things the boys learned from this demonstration. From the cobra they learned grace and persistence, and from the mongoose they learned defense and patience in waiting for the opportune time to strike. Zoram wasn't sure how he felt about this new line of training.

Over the next few months, the boys observed many other animals fight. Some lessons were conducted in the monastery, like a snake and praying mantis, while others were conducted in the villages at the base of the mountains. Here they were fortunate to study the fighting styles and methods of the tiger, the monkey, the bear, the crane, and other birds. Each animal possessed its own unique style of fighting and protecting itself. And while it saddened Zoram to watch these beautiful creatures fight and kill each other for his instruction and benefit, he was grateful for the knowledge they imparted to him. He had a new respect for nature and each of God's creations and reverenced them for their sacrifices.

The primary purpose of these observations and exercises was to incorporate these animal movements into their own style of fighting and combat. It was a singular and unique experience for Zoram. During one of these practice sessions with the other apprentices, Zoram was called out by one of his instructors.

"What are you doing?" he demanded.

Zoram bowed. "The snake style."

"Does the snake think about how it should move?"

In that moment Zoram was painfully aware that his movements felt deliberate and unnatural and was embarrassed that his instructor could see it, too. He lowered his head. "No."

"But what if I still can't do it right?"

The instructor smiled. "Who is to say what is right or what is wrong? Do you or I judge the snake as it moves and strikes? Right and wrong vanish, leaving only the snake moving naturally and as it should."

Zoram nodded, glimpsing for a moment the wisdom his instructor was trying to bestow upon him. He would reflect on this moment of instruction for years to come as he learned to let go of how he *thought* he should strike or defend and trust his instincts and training to move appropriately in the moment. Keeping one's head clear and free from the clutter and concerns of analysis was the difference between the victor and the vanquished.

खेपेर ओफ़ ष्वोर्द

Finally the day came, and they were all ushered into a large structure in one corner of the monastery. A nervous excitement rippled through the young men as they stood outside the large wooden doors. The forges had been off limits to them during the years of their physical and mental conditioning. Zoram had to admit that there had been days and even weeks at a time that he had forgotten about the reason for his apprenticeship entirely. But today, as he stood shoulder to shoulder with the others, he offered silent thanks to the Lord for his training to this point. Not all of the apprentices had successfully survived the years of instruction. Some were injured and forced to return to their homelands; others simply gave up under the pressures and demands. But Zoram had stuck with it. Though he had to admit he owed much of his determination and strength to the young man at his side. Wu Yien had been a faithful companion and brother to him over the years, and it was this combined strength that served to reinforce and fortify each of them during the long and exhausting days of training.

"You have each proven your worth and dedication to what our order has to offer," the High Sadhus began. "It is our honor to instruct you further in the arts that, together, we will master and elevate to new heights."

With a ceremonial unlocking of the armory doors, they were all ushered inside. A blast of heated air struck them as the orange glows of the many fires, furnaces, and hearths assaulted their senses. Standing close to him, Wu Yien closed his eyes, breathed in, and smiled. For Zoram the smell of charcoal and acrid smoke reminded him of the days he'd spent with his father heating and shaping metal into weapons that the armies of Israel would use to defend their laws and their God.

This was his destiny. His calling.

The final stage of his apprenticeship had begun.

His life, he knew, would never be the same.

CHAPTER SIX

SEEING JERUSALEM FOR THE FIRST time after all these years was surreal. Zoram had almost forgotten what the city looked like. And although some of the surrounding landscape had changed, the Temple, shining prominently atop Mount Moriah for the whole world to see, was an almost forgotten symbol of God and His supremacy.

But a great deal had happened to the city and the land of Jerusalem since he had left. In the ten years he'd been gone, the Assyrians, who had conquered Israel nearly a hundred years earlier, had themselves been conquered by a new empire: the bloodthirsty Babylonians. His father's letters had only lightly touched on the conquest, careful not to say or imply anything that might be considered traitorous in the event their correspondence was intercepted somewhere along the way. But his father had said enough, and in his young mind Zoram had imagined the entire city destroyed, similar to the ruins and rubble he had seen parts of Babylon reduced to. He was proud and happy to see that, for the most part, the city itself remained intact, a further witness, he thought to himself, of God's favored blessings and protection.

But as excited as he was to see the city of his early childhood, the thought of seeing his father again, after nearly ten years, lifted and carried his tired feet. He had so much to tell his father, so much to share, so much to teach him.

As Zoram approached the north city gate and joined others pressing to enter the city, they were all stopped by Temple guards, flanked by menacing men in military uniform, and directed to the western gate. There seemed to be a matter of some concern farther down the wall. It took him nearly half an hour to enter through this smaller gate, to pass the tax collectors, and to declare his purpose for entry. It felt good to finally say the words.

"Returning home."

He received apprehensive looks from the gate sentry but was allowed to pass with only a small tribute, which Zoram was only all too happy to pay.

He was home.

The city streets had not changed much during his absence, although everything seemed smaller than he remembered. He suspected, though, that everything from one's childhood would seem smaller given the perspective. The streets were crowded with men and women and animals of every variety, almost beyond capacity. Everywhere he looked there were merchants and buyers bartering and swapping goods and money. Men yelled to the passing crowds to attract new customers and herald their products or services. It was organized chaos at its finest.

Zoram breathed in deeply. Ah! He had missed all this. On occasion he had visited the markets in the valleys and surrounding mountain villages where he'd lived, but there had only been scant goods to trade. It was a harsh land, and survival depended on being able to trade what excess you had for the excess of another. Their markets were nothing like this!

As remote and desolate as its geography made it, Jerusalem was nevertheless a crossroads, the hub of several great and competing kingdoms and empires, and its markets were favored and prized as a great oasis of the desert. There was gold from Nubia and Upper Egypt, cotton from the shores of the Nile, spices and incense from the East, lumber from the north, and more food than one would think possible in one location. It was truly a wonder to behold.

At the money changers, Zoram exchanged a single small gold ingot for pieces of silver and brass which he could use throughout the market. He bought a strip of tender salted meat and a small loaf of bread, still warm from the baker's oven. It was no spiced lamb, and truth be told he wasn't really that hungry, but there was something about eating food bought on the streets of Jerusalem that gave him great satisfaction.

A light tug on his shoulder satchel immediately caught his attention, and without thinking Zoram swept his hand under and around the pickpocket's arms, pinning them with his other hand and pulling him in close. The thief was no more than a child, and by the terrified look in the boy's eyes, Zoram knew he was relatively inexperienced in his career. Big cities bred crime the world over. In places where everyone knew everyone else, crime was low because no one wanted to harm or steal from a friend or neighbor. But in a place like this, with more than a hundred thousand people living and working on top of one another, it was easy to victimize a stranger.

Zoram wondered what quality of life this boy must have to persuade or compel him to risk imprisonment, or worse, for whatever valuables might or might not be inside a purse or satchel. Was he hungry and stealing to provide food for himself and his family? Or did he have other reasons for taking what wasn't his?

Zoram leaned in close to the boy's face and whispered a warning in his new tongue, scaring the boy further. Then Zoram smiled and pushed the boy away, letting him go. He ran off and disappeared almost instantly into the dense crowds. Whatever the reason for their chance meeting, Zoram knew he had to be more careful. He was not living a sheltered life anymore and would feel better the sooner he reached his home.

Home, he thought as he walked through the marketplace toward the upper city. He'd never really had one before. When he was living here as a child, he'd known he would leave. And then, of course, when he was away, he knew that was only a temporary residence. But today, unlike anytime before in his life, Zoram was finally someplace he would live out the rest of his days. His journey was over.

He was home.

The crowds thinned as Zoram followed the winding streets that traced across the natural slope of the hillside. Here, the city took on a new feel. The upper city was where the more influential of Israel's citizens lived and worked. Men sat on verandas, eating morning meals and discussing business, politics, and the future of the city. More than one looked down on Zoram dressed in his old—but clean—clothes. Zoram just smiled and nodded and continued on his way.

With every turn and climb, his feelings of excitement became more pronounced until he stepped at almost a run as he approached the finish line to what seemed like a lifelong race.

But then a sharp sound challenged his elation and pierced a hole in the pit of his stomach. From open windows he could hear the sounds of mourning and cries for the dead. He had some distant memories of funerals when he was a child, and he remembered the women, usually friends of the deceased family, who would noise the passing from this life into the next according to tradition. It had been a frightening occurrence then, and those same feelings of dread returned at their sounds this morning.

But the cries were not coming from a single residence. Zoram could identify at least four households from which the sounds of wailing could be heard. He didn't like the panic that was rising within him. He quickened his step, now driven with a fear he couldn't explain. He needed to get home.

Up the street. Around another corner. The sounds continued.

And then—

There it was—his childhood home, the residence that had housed his family for several generations. It was a beautiful sight, and as suddenly as his fear and worries had appeared and choked his happiness, they were left behind at the street as he climbed the steps to the doors. They were locked, however, and he had to knock.

A moment later he was met by a member of the house staff. "The house is not taking mourners," he said abruptly and started closing the door. But there must have been something in Zoram's shock that caused him to stop.

"Mourners?" Zoram's worst fears flooded back in a sickening wave. Strength began to leave his legs, and his heart started beating faster. His face felt hot. "What has happened here?"

Zoram then noticed the man's shirt had been torn, and he knew.

The servant's eyes were bloodshot and wet from tears. "Israel's Keeper of the Sword is dead. But how did you not . . . Who are you? Why are you here?"

"I am Zoram," he heard himself say. The house and sky began to spin. "I've come home."

שומר החרב

"Anat! Anat!" the kitchen servant called out, running to the guest wing of the house. "He's here! He's returned!"

Anat looked up from the divan but made no effort to rise. The man she had loved like a father was dead, and she was still in shock. "Keep your voice down."

"Of all days, he returns today. The poor man."

Anat's curiosity outweighed her displeasure with the staff. "Who? Who's here?"

"The young master. Zoram."

That got her attention. "What?"

"He only just arrived. He is resting in the reception hall.

Anat was on her feet. "Help me," she ordered, running a comb through her hair while the kitchen help dressed her and made her presentable.

"How do I look?"

"Beautiful. Now go to him. He is alone. He will need someone to comfort him."

Anat took a deep breath and tried to put on a smile but quickly changed her mind given the circumstances.

Zoram was lying down being attended to by the house staff. His coat had been stripped from him and replaced with a clean white linen robe; his shoes had been removed and his feet washed. A small plate of cheese and bread was being brought from the kitchen, which Anat took and brought to his side.

"Zoram?" Anat said softly. He was even more handsome than she had remembered. And as she looked down on him, she could still see that little boy she had played with and known as a child. "Are you all right?"

She regretted the words the moment she spoke them. Of course he wasn't all right. He'd just been told his father was dead—and on the day that was supposed to be a joyous reunion. But to be fair, she thought, she hadn't imagined in all these years that they would be reunited like this. It was supposed to be a happy meeting of childhood friends all grown up. They were supposed to rekindle their friendship—and possibly something more.

She took one of the clean towels, dripped it into a bowl of fresh water, and started rubbing his forehead and face with it. Zoram was in a stupor, a daze at the sudden news, but he started to come around at Anat's voice.

"I am so sorry. We all are." That was better.

Zoram finally focused on the voice above him. "Who are you?"

Anat was devastated, and her disappointment shone through briefly before she could compose herself and tried again to smile. "Anat. When we were young . . . Remember? It's me."

Zoram didn't appear to recognize her. "I'm sorry. I don't . . ."

Anat continued to smile, this time with compassion. "I understand. You've been through a great deal this morning. Don't worry, though, you will remember. But for now just know that you are loved and supported in this time of trials."

"Thank you."

Anat continued to caress his face with the cool cloth. "Leave everything to me."

שומר החרב

Anat expertly organized the house staff to see that Zoram's quarters were refreshed, that hot water and new clothes were delivered to his room, and that a light meal and wine was prepared. And though the staff worked and supplied him what they could, Anat took it upon herself to give him what he really needed.

Information.

"What happened?" he asked a short while later when they were alone.

"No one knows," she answered softly. "All we know is that he . . . he fell."

Zoram remembered the scene earlier at the north gate, and a forceful wave of nausea threatened to void his stomach. This was not supposed to be happening. "Is this how God rewards the faithful?" he said aloud but only partially aware.

"What, dear?"

"Who found him? When did it happen?" Zoram stood walked to the window. "I should have returned last night, like I'd wanted to. I shouldn't have listened to him."

Anat was confused. "Who?"

But Zoram had already moved on. "What if he was waiting for me and slipped?" He didn't want to think, even for a moment, that he was partially responsible for his father's death, but it *was* possible. He needed to know. "Who found him?" he asked again, not really expecting Anat to know, but she stumbled through an answer.

"One of the wall guards . . . before sunrise. Word spread quickly throughout the city. Everyone loved your father. Jharom was a good man, a faithful servant of the people. An emissary from the Temple and the High Priest visited as soon as they could. None of us could believe it." Anat was getting choked up. "I still can't."

Zoram kept closing his eyes, squeezing them tight, hoping to wake up, hoping this was all a dream. But each time he opened them to see Anat doting on him, he knew he wasn't going to wake up from this.

Simply wishing wasn't going to make the pain go away. In fact, for him it seemed that pain never really went anywhere. If he was going to distance himself from the pain, he would have to be the one to move. He had to move away from it. Not physically—although he had thought briefly about running away—but mentally and emotionally.

The city now seemed dead. The life and activity that he recalled from his childhood were gone. But Jerusalem hadn't changed. Zoram had. His life was now empty. Loss creates a void in one's heart, in one's life that, if left empty, begins to eat at the very essence of who you are, leaving only a husk of who you once were. He had known men to be consumed from the inside out with loss. The only way to avoid this fate was to fill that void, that hole within him with something—*anything*—to restore the body and mind and make him "whole" again.

Zoram still had his calling to accept and fulfill, and while he had always imagined that it would be under the careful and deliberate tutelage of his father passing the mantle, so to speak, the fact remained that he was now, officially, the Keeper of the Sword, chosen and called of God. And now that responsibility would be passed to him.

He only hoped he was strong enough to shoulder it.

Zoram looked at the lavish house around him. He had been born into a family with a destiny to fulfill and service to render. He had always expected to be schooled by his father in the practical and daily responsibilities before assuming the title, but that was just not to be.

There would be time to grieve later. Today there was much to do, and Zoram consciously put his doubts and blame aside.

"Anat?"

"Yes?" she said, obviously eager to do his bidding.

"I'll need someone to help me with the customs and traditions for . . . a situation like this. I've been away for so long I have forgotten them." He turned and looked right at her. "Will you help me?"

Anat's eyes teared up again, and she smiled. "You have but to ask, Keeper."

Zoram smiled back. "Thank you."

שומר החרב

Word of Zoram's untimely return spread throughout Jerusalem like a grass fire.

At Zoram's request, Anat sent for a priest to assist him through the bereavement and rituals prescribed by the prophets and the law. The mourning process, called the *avelut*, was a practice deeply steeped in ritual.

First, Zoram was instructed that he must recite a blessing and acknowledgment that God was above all: *Blessed art Thou, Lord, our God, King of the Universe, the True Judge.*

Next, he was told to rend his shirt, as this was a symbol of the suffering and anguish man feels when loved ones are separated from them by death. He couldn't explain why, but that simple act did seem to provide release for much of what he was feeling.

A group of men from all levels of government and society, including many of his father's household servants, formed the *chevra kadisha* to see that the body was properly handled, washed, and prepared for burial. Zoram was grateful for the outpouring of support and genuine love and insisted on staying close to these men throughout the day. He hoped that directly participating in the many ceremonies would bring closure and dispel the feelings of helplessness that plagued him.

As soon as he was able, he followed them to the place of Taharah, near the Temple, where bodies were washed and prepared for burial. The sight of his father's body lying on the large stone table, covered with a white sheet was almost too much for him to take. Before the men began the washing and ritualistic dressing of the body, Zoram asked for a minute alone.

As strong as he had pretended to be thus far this morning, the minute he was alone, he broke into tears. "Papa," he said softly, pulling the sheet back, remembering the last time he had seen his father, listening to his words of counsel that had given him insight and strength and peace during the ensuing years. The time he had spent away was made bearable by the assurance that he would see his father again.

Zoram had been close to his father, partly because of their common destiny but also because Jharom had always been an attentive father. He had always made time for Zoram, balancing his duties as Keeper of the Sword and his duties as husband and father. Despite his father's faithfulness, Zoram had always been convinced that Jharom had loved him and his mother more than his obligation to the kingdom. And though he had no immediate plans for marriage, he had always looked forward to making Jharom a grandfather. His father had earned that privilege.

Zoram ran his fingers lightly across his father's hand and down his arm.

He repeated the words of the blessing again, trying harder now to believe them.

As he reached deep down inside to remember everything he could about his father, he used his thumb to clean the dirt from Jharom's face and picked at the mud and grass caked to his pants and shoes. It was calming to him, and the tears dried up. After a few more minutes, he covered up the body again and called for the others.

The rest of the morning was spent washing and purifying Jharom's body. Anat explained that according to the law, the body must be cleansed completely, and any jewelry must be removed, symbolic of returning to God in the manner that one left Him. She helped remove Jharom's two rings and gently handed them to Zoram. He accepted them with a solemn nod then watched as his father's body was washed and dried from head to toe. Like the other rituals, this one too put Zoram's mind and soul at ease. It was as if the Lord knew how best to calm the troubled heart.

When they were finished, the temple priest joined them again, carrying a small pile of clean, white burial clothing, which the men dressed him in. The final article of clothing was a white sash that was to be tied in the form of the Hebrew letter *shin*, ש, standing for the word *Shaddai*, one of the names of God. With the priest's permission, Anat helped Zoram tie this.

The body was now prepared, but as the men moved to carry it outside, Anat stopped them. "Wait," she said, picking through the things she had brought from the house and finally producing a worn prayer shawl. Though he had long since forgotten it, Zoram immediately recognized his mother's *tallith*, and he reached out for it. Before he knew what he was doing, he brought the familiar shawl to his face and breathed in. His mother's scent still lingered on it. She had worn the shawl as a constant reminder of her faith in God and as a prayer to Him. How many times had he taken the knots between his own fingers and recited the prayers with her? He had reflected on her faith many times over the years and now to be presented with this.

"Where did you . . ." were all the words he could form.

"Your father kept it," she started, "after she died. He loved her very much and couldn't part with it."

But as much as Zoram wanted to keep it for himself, he knew he couldn't. He laid it carefully across his father's chest, close to his heart. Where Miriam had always been.

Zoram stepped back and nodded for the men to proceed. The body was carried out of the room adjacent to the Temple grounds and placed tenderly into the coffin that had been prepared by the men of the chevra kadisha. Before the lid was closed, Zoram was given a handful of dirt poured from a small urn. He was confused.

"It's dirt from the Temple Mount," Anat explained as the small crowd waited. "Sprinkle it over the body. This way, your father is never far from Israel."

He did, and the coffin lid was closed, never again to be opened. Zoram feared that there were parts of his heart that wouldn't open again, but he quickly dismissed those thoughts. He would just have to fill the void. It was the only way for him to heal.

For the first time in many hours, Zoram looked up and became aware of the men and women around him. He only recognized a few of the faces of those in attendance. He was a stranger in a strange land. Anat seemed to sense his loneliness and took his hand.

The coffin was carried from the small courtyard, down the streets, through the western gate, and out to the small spot of land that had been dedicated for the internment of his family's line. As they walked, they were joined by scores of others as they passed through the cries and sounds of those who mourned his father's passing. By the time they reached the burial ground, Zoram wondered if there was anyone left inside the city walls. It was an impressive tribute to the memory of his father. It seemed that all of Jerusalem had come to honor the life and passing of their Keeper. Zoram suddenly felt inadequate to follow his father in his duty.

The High Priest, a man named Pashur, called the people to order and offered the eulogy, called the *hesped*, touching on points of his father's life and accomplishments in his public service as well as on his love for his wife and son.

"He was an exemplary man," the High Priest concluded, and the crowds offered a reverent amen.

Zoram noticed the long shadows stretching across the hillside plot. The day was drawing to a close, and what a day it had been. Had it all really happened? But the freshly dug grave removed all doubt. He was exhausted. All had gone according to custom and tradition, and for that he was grateful. His father deserved a good memory, and Zoram had helped give him that.

Just then a voice startled Zoram and everyone present, calling out from behind them, "How merciful is our God!"

Standing atop a small outcrop of rock was an old man with his hands outstretched in front of him in both a pleading and welcoming manner. He had an imploring look. His words were not meant to incite retaliation or hatred but, instead, had a sincere plea to them. His beard was full and white, and it cast a shadow on his face that gave him a charismatic draw. And then it struck Zoram. He knew this man.

It was Lehi.

CHAPTER SEVEN

Zoram noticed right away that the man before them didn't look much like the man he had seen only the night before. Lehi's hair was now stark white, and he looked much older. What could have possibly happened to turn his hair from a rich, dark brown to white overnight? It just wasn't possible. But here he was.

And it wasn't just Lehi's hair that had changed. His jolly demeanor was replaced by a strong, firm, and commanding presence. He was still the same man, with a spark of happiness in his eye, he just looked more sure of himself as he spoke to them from his elevated hilltop.

"Thus saith the Lord: Repent!" Lehi continued. "And taste of His mercy."

The people were stunned at his strong words, but the High Priest was not so easily taken aback.

"Lehi?" Pashur said in disbelief.

Lehi smiled with an edge of defiance. "You wanted to question me. Here I am."

Pashur was angered and flustered at the public challenge. "You are not welcome here! This is not the time nor the place for your words of discord and dissent!"

"But they are not my words. They are the words of the Lord, and He—great is His mercy!—has commanded me to speak them."

"This is not the time for your foolishness! I command you to be silent or—"

"Or what? Will you silence me as you did Elisheva?"

"You have no right—"

"The blood of that righteous woman is on your hands. And though you may silence the messenger, you will never be able to silence the message"—Lehi looked from Pashur to the surrounding people—"or He who sends it."

Pashur stood taller and took the offensive against this interruption. "God is silent in His heaven."

"No," Lehi said confidently. "He speaks, but it is you—all of you—who do not listen." Voices rumbled through the crowds. "So he sends those unafraid to stand before you and who are more concerned with offending God than offending the hearts of men."

"Men like you?" Pashur accused. "Men who would spread discord and lies? Who doubt God and His goodness and His chosen people? This is heresy!"

The High Priest scoffed and seemed pleased with his accusatory response. "We grow tired of this madness. If God were to speak again, do you not think he would do so to men chosen and called up to the people? But does He make Himself known to me or to the other Temple officiators or the rabbis? No. You would have us believe that He speaks through men and women unlearned in the commandments and the law—opportunists who can only prophesy of doom and destruction and who prey upon the downtrodden and submissive."

Lehi knew better than to take the bait. "The Lord speaks of mercy and redemption. If all you hear are words of punishment, perhaps that is what you are meant to hear."

Pashur was visibly upset at being called a sinner in front of these influential and powerful citizens but restrained his tongue, likely for fear of losing his temper and tarnishing his image. Lehi must have sensed this and took advantage of the silence to share the impressions of his heart.

"I knew Jharom well," he said, holding Zoram's gaze for a brief moment, "and I can speak to the man's pure heart. His love for his king and this people was surpassed only by that of his love for his family and God. I would risk offending him and all he believed in if I were to remain silent when I was commanded to open my mouth."

"Commanded?" Pashur asked, sounding incredulous. "Does the Lord now speak to you?" He laughed.

Lehi became very serious. "In a dream."

"A dream, you say? Well, then, it must be from God. That, or a piece of spoiled meat." He laughed again, and the crowd joined in, taunting and tempting him to tell them his dream.

So he did.

"Last night, whether I was awake or asleep I cannot tell, I was carried away in a vision in which I saw the heavens opened and saw God sitting on His throne, surrounded by concourses of angels who were all singing and praising His name."

Cries of blasphemy echoed among the people, but Lehi continued undaunted. "And then one, like God, descended and stood before me and gave me a book and bade me read it."

There were more cries and taunting. "What did it say? Tell us!"

Lehi then took a more serious and aggressive tone. "The Lord has seen your abominations and your wickedness! You claim to honor and revere the prophets long dead, yet you stone those sent before you. Oh, ye hypocrites! Wo be unto you who deny God's power and might and unto those who rely on their own arm instead of the arm of the Lord; you who would rather perish by the sword than look to God and live!"

Zoram found it interesting that, despite their obvious and vocal anger, the people all stepped aside as this "prophet" walked among them, giving him room to move untouched. It was then that Zoram noticed the military presence on the outskirts of the funeral gathering. Had they always been there? Had he just not seen them before now?

"But great and marvelous are the works of the Lord," he said, sweeping his arms to encompass the mountains, the trees, and even the great city behind them. "The Lord is all powerful, and His goodness and His mercy are without bounds." His words were strong but loving, like a father addressing a wayward child. "Come unto Him, please, and repent and look unto Him for deliverance."

What he said next struck Zoram as no other words had before. "If you do not," he said, "Jerusalem will perish."

A hush fell over the crowd, and in that moment no one dared speak. Zoram was moved. He had never heard words like these spoken with such clarity and filled with such conviction. It was inspiring. It was what he imagined his father would have wanted.

Then he saw her. Rebekah. She must have come with Lehi. He smiled to see her leaning on a crutch and suddenly yearned to go to her, to speak with her. She saw him and returned the smile. But at that instant a chorus of ugly words and shouts erupted, shattering the peace that had reigned for a few blessed moments. Someone picked up a stone and threw it at Lehi, but it went wide. There was movement behind Zoram as several soldiers pushed through what had quickly turned into an angry mob.

Zoram knew what they were going to do, and he was not about to let it happen. Not here. Not now.

Zoram sprang into action, rushing to intercept the two closest soldiers before they reached Lehi, knocking the one into the other, toppling them both to the ground. He then took a defensive position between Lehi and the other two guards.

"No!" Zoram commanded. "You cannot do this!"

But the soldiers paid him no attention, one of them drawing a small blade to emphasize their intent to lay their hands on Lehi and arrest him. Words at his father's funeral were one thing—weapons, however, were quite another. Zoram calmed, centered his feelings, and waited for the predictable slice through the air between them. The move was meant to scare off any resistance, but when it came, Zoram moved with the downward strike and instantly took control of the dagger. It was a common intimidation attempt used by inexperienced fighters and easily defended against. One experienced in the art of war, as his good friend had once called it, knew that it was more important, not to mention safer, to control the *man* rather than the weapon. And with the soldier's hand firmly within his control, Zoram disarmed him quickly and without effort. He pushed the man away and picked up the knife, facing the last soldier.

"Stop!" Zoram tried again. "You will not—"

The other soldier lunged at him, a similar blade at the end of his fully extended arm. It was a foolish attack and one that left him open to any number of counterattacks. But Zoram only needed to use one to neutralize the action without harming the attacker. Deflecting the arm and blade with his left hand, he stepped in close to the soldier instead of away from him, extending his own arm and running it up the man's neck and throat. The soldier fell to his back, stunned and momentarily unable to breathe.

Zoram then spun around to face any other attackers, his training and instincts in command of his actions. There was only one more—a tall, muscular man—and Zoram could tell by the way he stood and carried himself he was not going to be easily overpowered like the others.

Zoram heard whispering words from the crowds, picking out the word *fifty* from several of them. One of the first soldiers he had pushed to the ground looked up at the man facing Zoram and scuttled backward to his feet, mumbling a name in fear: Hanoch.

Hanoch stepped closer but made no move for the sword at his side. "You will step aside. This man is a fugitive, and you are interfering with the king's official business. Is this man's life worth your own?"

Zoram was not intimidated by the threats but knew he would have to be careful with this one. He sensed that he possessed the skills to support his confidence.

"He has done nothing wrong," Zoram asserted. "You and your men are—"

Hanoch scoffed. "My men? *My men* would not have been so easily defeated. Now move aside."

Knowing what fate had awaited Rebekah as a means to find Lehi, Zoram could not let them take him. He picked up one of the short swords littered at his feet. "He is under my protection."

Hanoch glared at Zoram with hard eyes. "That's too bad."

In one quick, fluid move, Hanoch drew his weapon and closed the distance between them. It was a bold and fierce attack, difficult to defend against with his small blade. Zoram pivoted to his right and narrowly missed being sliced up the middle, deflecting the larger blade weakly with his own. But the attack did not stop there. Hanoch continued to move, spinning and building momentum as he brought his sword over his head and straight down. But where the lethal strike would have connected with lesser trained men, Zoram instinctively finished his pivot, tumbling in a forward roll to get clear of the sharpened metal. Then, taking advantage of his low stance, Zoram swiftly swept the back leg of his attacker hard enough to knock it out from under him. Not wasting a moment, Zoram pinned Hanoch's weapon hand with his knee and brought his knife to the man's throat. He stopped the instant he heard a loud voice behind them.

"Enough!"

Hanoch relaxed under him, and Zoram turned his head slightly to acknowledge the voice, but he never took his eyes off his attacker.

"Hanoch!"

At the sound of his name, he released his weapon and surrendered.

"You disgrace us! Get up!"

Zoram eased his knife from the man's throat and carefully moved off him. He then tossed the small blade away. Hanoch got to his feet, livid, and glared at Zoram with a look that clearly conveyed his intent to kill him.

Zoram turned and faced the man who had power and authority to stop their mortal combat. He was tall and charismatic, older than Zoram but no more than ten years his senior. He wore a brightly colored military uniform with gold-decorated chest plates and arm and leg shields. Around his neck was a scarlet cape that complemented his full, formal military regalia.

The military commander dismissed Hanoch with a curt look then turned toward Zoram and bowed. "Forgive us. Rest assured this insolence and show of disrespect will not go unpunished. Please accept my deepest apologies"—he bowed again, deeper—"Keeper of the Sword."

As soon as he spoke those words, Zoram remembered where he had seen the man before. Years ago; when he was a boy.

"Let me introduce myself. I am Laban, Keeper of the Records, and I offer you my deepest and most sincere condolences. Your father was a great man, an example to all of us, and a good friend. It feels as if a part of me has died with him."

Out of habit, Zoram returned the bow. "Thank you."

Laban looked around for Lehi, who had disappeared in all the commotion. A brief look of aggravation flashed across his face before he regained his regal manner and control. "Let there be no further interruptions! Let the memory of Jharom, our great Keeper, be preserved this day, and may his son," he declared, pointing to Zoram, "find peace and solace in our prayers."

The words soothed the crowd and brought feelings and emotions back to levels more conducive to a funeral. After a long pause, the High Priest continued the ceremony and burial as prescribed. Blessings were pronounced and praises uttered to God as the body was lightly lowered and laid to rest in the freshly dug earth.

Following the High Priest's lead, Zoram took three handfuls of dirt and tossed them, one at a time, over his father's coffin; then he stepped back and watched as many of those present filed by the grave and did the same. He was certain this practice carried with it deep symbolism, but he didn't know exactly of what. Some uttered quiet prayers on his father's behalf, while others just moved past in silence. When they had all gone, Anat wanted to stay, but Zoram politely told her that he really needed to be alone. She looked disappointed but tried to smile and told him she would wait up for him, regardless of the hour.

But if he was honest with himself, there was only one person he would have wanted by his side right now, and she had disappeared with Lehi.

The sun was nearing the horizon and those members of the chevra kadishas who had remained behind to bury the body looked to Zoram for permission to begin so that the task might be completed in time.

Is the day spent already? he thought to himself. On one hand, the day had passed so quickly he could scarcely believe the position of the sun and the length of the shadows, and yet emotionally it was as if his entire life had been compressed into this single, exhausting day.

"Sir?" One of his father's staff spoke.

Zoram snapped out of his stupor and looked around, aware that there was not much light left to the day. He got to his feet. Dusting himself off, he reached out and took one of the shovels. The others gave him a quizzical look.

"What are you . . . ?"

"I'd like to help."

Several of them exchanged worried expressions. "It's generally not allowed—"

"But I need to. For me. To put this day behind me."

They all looked to the Temple priest, left behind to oversee the ceremony. He was a young man, and by his confused look, it was clear he had never been presented with this request. After a moment of nervous deliberation, he smiled and nodded. There are times to do things right, and then there are times to do the right thing. He even picked up a shovel himself and helped.

And there, under the calm skies and mild Judean evening, Zoram buried forever what might have been, and he firmly resolved to accept whatever the Lord had in store for him.

שומר החרב

Laban joined Hanoch on the tower balcony overlooking the western hills. He handed Hanoch a cup full of wine.

"Here," he said, thrusting it at him. "You need to calm down and relax."

Hanoch knocked the cup to the floor in a fit. "It's okay for you to kill the one responsible for your public shame and humiliation, but you order me to stand down and *relax*."

Laban joined him at the railing and looked down at Zoram and the others filling the grave. "If I hadn't stopped him, he would have taken your head off." Laban took a deep drink from his own goblet. "Or at least cut you from ear to ear. Either way."

"The fight wasn't over! If I'd only had—"

"Did you see him fight, though?" Laban said, interrupting his lieutenant, not really listening to him and still watching the scene below them. He started to laugh. "I mean, the way he dropped low and used his momentum to avoid your attack and then spin and sweep your leg. It was brilliant. It would seem that our new Keeper has learned more than simply working with metals."

"I *will* kill him. Make no mistake about it."

"Yes, yes, of course you will . . ." He trailed off in thought.

After a contemplative stretch of silence, Laban's view shifted out into the darkening hills. "It looks like we've found our elusive voice in the wilderness. Did you at least have the presence of mind to send your spies after him?"

"They lost him. But two of our men followed the girl deep into the mountains yesterday. We'll find him."

"But now that we know his name, surely there's someone who knows where he lives." Laban took another drink. "I had always suspected Lehi had fled during the invasion. He has only showed his face a few times over the years. It's interesting, isn't it? A man of his wealth and position does not just disappear."

More silence. More wine. "How many men will you need?"

"None," Hanoch said proudly.

A smile crept across Laban's lips. "Take a dozen. From The Fifty. Make no mistakes this time."

Hanoch didn't like the insinuation and stormed past Laban.

Laban continued to look out over the countryside. "You can't hide forever. I'll find you, and when I do, there will be none left to rally the people or oppose me."

He tilted his glass back and drained his cup. The sound of giggling girls entering his room filled him with a shiver of anticipated pleasures.

CHAPTER EIGHT

THE HEAT FROM THE MASSIVE furnace blasted Zoram as he pulled from its flames the blade he had been forging and shaping for the better part of two days. After smelting the iron from freshly mined ore then transforming it from simple iron into the stronger and lighter metal known as steel, he had spent the last few hours hammering and shaping the superheated metal.

What he had learned over the years of his apprenticeship could not be calculated or recorded. He knew now why it was necessary for him to leave his home and travel so far away to learn this skill. Forging steel was not something one just learned how to *do*—it was a process of conditioning and *becoming* a master of the art. This is what the Lord and His people required of him. There was great wisdom and inspiration in their decision to send him here. He only hoped he could work his art to make his father proud.

Hammering flat the steel blade on the heavy anvil, Zoram took pride in his latest creation. He held it up to the light filtering through the wooden slats over the windows. He ran his fingers over the steel blade. It was still rough and far from its sharpened and polished state, but it was straight and—

"Beautiful," a voice declared behind him.

Zoram smiled at the sound of Wu Yien's voice. "How long have you been standing there?"

"Long enough to watch you caress and fall in love with a piece of metal." Wu Yien chuckled. "We need to find you a woman. There was this peasant girl in the market last month who—"

Zoram picked up a soiled rag from the table next to him, spun around, and threw it at his friend. Wu Yien swatted it away, and the two of them laughed lightly.

Wu Yien stepped closer, his hand outstretched. "May I?" Zoram handed him his most recent attempt. Wu Yien held it up to the light. The length of metal was flawless. "You have a gift. Truly." He continued to feel his way along the hammered and heat-treated metal. "Does the High Sadhus know of your skills?"

Zoram was flattered with the observations and praise, especially coming from his friend. Wu Yien had been given special treatment and instruction since their arrival. His apprenticeship was supported by a much larger endowment than Zoram's, which had afforded him additional attention. But where other boys might let this prestige and standing go to their heads—resulting in spoiled and self-indulgent behavior and attitude— Wu Yien had never once given off an air of superiority. He was a humble, grounded, and dedicated student—Zoram's best friend and brother.

Wu Yien ran the blade along his two fingertips until it balanced perfectly on them. A look of concern wrinkled his brow. "It's off by a span."

Zoram knew that a perfectly balanced sword pivoted at the base of the blade where it met—

"The hilt," Wu Yien said, realizing his oversight. "Of course. You may be a finer sword smith than the instructors. Perhaps my gold should be deposited with you instead."

Zoram looked away, embarrassed. "If I have any talent, it's because God grants it to me."

In a sudden and unexpected movement, Wu Yien spun around and struck another student's sword hanging on a rack. After a sharp *clang,* Zoram's blade continued to ring and sing throughout the empty rooms.

"Beautiful," he said reverently. "If your God could bestow upon me skills like yours, I may be tempted to add Him to my worship." Zoram tilted his head and gave him a mildly disappointed look. Wu Yien cracked a sheepish smile. "I know, I know. He's your One True God. You know I respect your belief, as peculiar as it might be."

Wu Yien tossed the blade back to Zoram. "You are clearly able in making them, but shall we see if you are equally talented in wielding them?"

Zoram had been itching for another chance to best his brother and removed his heavy leather apron with an eager smile. Hastily he attached two small metal rods to the base of the blade by wrapping a strand of leather to fashion a makeshift hilt and handle. Wu Yien picked through the other swords in the room, deciding on one that their masters regularly used in examples and lessons. He led Zoram outside to the central square.

The sun was bright, and both young men squinted and shielded their eyes from the intense light. The late summer air was warm, touched by the occasional cool breeze from the surrounding mountaintops perpetually covered in heavy snow. They had scarcely reached the center of the square before word spread of their contest.

Both Wu Yien and Zoram were known for their intuitive use and mastery of the sword. All the apprentices spent a great deal of time training with swords to give them insight and intimate knowledge of the weapons they were creating. It was one thing to understand the concept of a blade's balance, for example, yet quite another to feel that a sword was clumsy or weighty in hand. Where was the joy in forging a blade if you were unable to use it, to experience it, and communicate with it? But of all the students, two stood out—Wu Yien and Zoram, one from the east and the other from the west, brought together, their friendship forged not unlike the steel each now held at the ready.

Of the two, however, Wu Yien was clearly the master. His use of the sword in combat had risen to a level of deadly artistic expression. When he was young, he'd received private training and tutelage from his royal attendants. These men were more than mere stewards, they were all trained experts. They'd given Wu Yien additional instruction and training in the use of the sword. Fortunately for Zoram, the young prodigy needed someone to practice with. But Zoram had proved to be more than just a sparring partner, displaying an uncanny predisposition in his martial training. Though he never vocalized it, Zoram attributed this natural aptitude to the special calling God had given him and that he was preparing to fulfill. It was quite evident that he was not forgotten and that God was still very much interested in his training and development. Zoram couldn't quite explain it, but he never felt complete or at peace unless he had a sword in his hand.

Zoram blocked out the faces of the onlookers and took a relaxed and open defensive stance, starting with the sword in his left hand and "hidden" behind his left arm. Moving his arms in wide, rotating circles, he dropped to a strong low stance and brought the sword across his body. Reaching under his left hand, he gripped the hilt with his right hand. It was a flashy and impractical move, but the crowd that had gathered around them seemed to enjoy the theatrics.

Wu Yien could not have been more proud of his protégé. Then, as if a heavy curtain fell over his countenance, all traces of pleasure disappeared from his face, replaced with a cold seriousness. "Defend!"

Wu Yien then executed a flawless series of strikes and thrusts that challenged every skill and defensive technique Zoram had ever learned. Wu Yien struck at his head, his chest, his legs and arms, spinning and surprising Zoram with diversions and deceptions, but Zoram was equal to the trial, sweeping and blocking and feeling with the sword in his hand. He had learned not to think about the attacks and how to defend against them. Thinking took too much time. Each attack could be defended against in any number of ways. To be conscious of these choices took time—time one did not have when the stakes were high and life was at risk.

The well-trained body will feel when and how to move, they had been told when they were young, but it wasn't until years later that Zoram finally understood and experienced what the instructor meant. Zoram recalled one evening when he'd been tired from being pushed without mercy by his instructors, further than he thought possible. Finally, and without realizing what was happening, he surrendered and stopped telling his body *what* to do and just let it *go*. He moved in ways he couldn't remember being trained in, much to the astonishment of everyone else in the combat room—with the exception of his friend. Wu Yien just nodded as Zoram tapped into a strength that so few men and women ever realized. Zoram was still bested, but the more he practiced, the more he conditioned his body to perform and the more trust he had to just relax and let his body do what he had trained it to do.

Today was no exception as he seemed to sense where the attack was coming from and where it was intended to strike, only partially aware of his own defensive actions.

Wu Yien finally stopped and smiled, not even winded by the relentless exercise. The crowd held their collective breath and remained silent, sensing the exhibition was not yet over.

Wu Yien settled into his own strong, defensive stance. "Attack!"

And Zoram did, again letting his body dictate and control his every move. His strikes were lightning fast and fierce, uninhibited by the clutter of where or how he *should* strike. Zoram just let his hands and feet, his body and mind, command his blitz of strength and steel, pushing Wu Yien back toward the steps of one of the annex storage houses. But his old friend displayed no concern or worry. In fact, a glint in his eye revealed just the opposite.

With Zoram's next move—a long, leaning thrust standing on one foot with his other arm outstretched behind him to balance the attack—Wu Yien decided to end the contest. Moving almost too quickly to be seen, he deflected the blade and spun around, striking Zoram with a fist. Zoram, however, pulled back to avoid most of the force and continued in that backward direction, jumping and completing a back flip to put space between the two of them.

Both Wu Yien and Zoram paused and reset their combat stances. Wu Yien was the first to stand tall, relax, and lower his sword; a wide smile accompanied small, proud nods. It took Zoram another second to transition from instinct to awareness that the fight was over, and then he lowered his weapon as well.

After a short pause, the spectators erupted in applause and cheers. Zoram looked around, somewhat surprised. He had forgotten that he and Wu Yien had drawn a crowd with their little contest of blades and skill. Their peers then flocked to them, praising them with words and pats on the back. Zoram was smiling now, feeling the energy and adrenaline drain from his shaking limbs, pleased with his performance. But then many of the young men abruptly stopped talking and stepped back, parting to let the High Sadhus approach. Zoram turned around and saw him. He was startled and bowed.

"Is this your blade?" the old master asked.

Zoram immediately offered up the sword, still in his deep bow. The High Sadhus took it from extended hands, turning it over as he examined it in the bright sun.

"Who helped you with this?"

Zoram kept his head down. "No one, Master."

"You fashioned this by yourself?"

"Yes, Master. Sorry, Master."

The High Sadhus chuckled. "Sorry? You have nothing to be sorry for. Your skills are extraordinary and have far exceeded our teaching."

Zoram stole a quick glance at Wu Yien, who just smiled. "Thank you, Master," he said, standing tall again.

The High Sadhus handed the newly forged blade back to Zoram and bowed himself. "No. Thank you. You bring us honor."

Zoram and the others were stunned. Thus far, and over the past eight or nine years, respect had been demanded and shown in only one direction. It was not to say that their teachers and instructors and the others were not patient and polite, but this was a unique gesture and one that astounded everyone present, both master and apprentice alike.

Zoram's chest felt as if it might burst with pride, but in his heart he gave all the glory and honor to his God.

खेपेर ओफ़ ष्वोर्द

Dinner regularly consisted of steamed rice, vegetables, and the occasional piece of meat, though Zoram had learned early on not to ask what it was. After they were done and had cleaned up, the remainder of the night was, as a rule, theirs to do with as they saw fit. Many would play games of chance or sit around fires and talk of the places they each called home, but usually the day's grueling work of smelting ore and pounding and shaping the blades left the boys exhausted and crawling into bed. But occasionally, on clear nights like tonight, a couple of them would sit out on one of the many stone terraces interspersed around the perimeter overlooking the deep valleys below and speak of whatever was on their minds. Sometimes they didn't speak at all.

That night Wu Yien brought a small carafe of rice wine. Zoram was not fond of the taste nor did he like the headache the next morning, but he let his friend pour him a small cup anyway.

"You should be proud of yourself," Wu Yien said, referring to the demonstration earlier that day.

"One of these days, I might just defeat you."

Wu Yien smiled. "I believe you just might . . . if you only had more time."

"What do you mean?"

"They say our apprenticeship is nearly complete. I've heard we go home in the spring." He poured himself another small cup. "When you return home, what role will you play?"

"Role?" Zoram looked out past him. "I will be the Keeper of the Sword."

"I know what your title will be, but what will you do? Will you lead your armies? Train the generals?"

Zoram considered the question but kept his eyes on the colors of the setting sun playing on the mountain peaks towering all around them. "I'm not certain. It's hard to explain. As the Keeper, I guess I'll represent the strength of my people. I remember my father being an advisor to the king. I guess that will be my responsibility as well."

"But what will you advise him *on*?"

Zoram didn't answer. He didn't really know. He had been a child. He knew that his father had been a trusted advisor to the king, but he really didn't know on what matters. But he took some comfort knowing he would have time to learn under his father's guidance.

"Your talents are without equal at fashioning blades from this new metal, this steel, and with the exception of me, you could defeat anyone here with its use, but these skills do not a great leader of men make." Wu Yien sat up straight with new excitement, pouring himself yet another cupful of wine.

"You see, the strength of an army does not lie in its number of soldiers or the weapons they use or even how well they use them."

Zoram was only half listening. His friend was very educated and was prone to giving him these "lessons" from time to time. "Then what does win the battle?"

Wu Yien touched the side of his head. "Strategy. How and when an army moves is key to its success or defeat. Answer me this: if your army outnumbered your enemy's twenty to one would you attack?"

"Twenty to one? Of course."

"No. No, you wouldn't. You should surround them but not attack. It is better to keep an army intact, preserve them, convince them to join with yours, and you have increased your strengths by their numbers. So what about five to one? Would you attack then?"

Zoram looked at him sideways. "No?"

"Yes! Yes, you would. Five to one and the spoils outweigh the risks and would justify an attack. But now, what if you only outnumbered them two to one? Should the wise general order the attack?"

Zoram shook his head. "I give up. Tell me."

"The wise general now divides his enemy's army and conquers it in pieces. You see, strategy must be applied to each battle, each engagement, but so often men of action—kings and generals—believe that what works once and for one circumstance will work again and again. Eventually they are kings and generals no more."

Wu Yien poured another cup of the bitter drink. "I've been study-ing the recorded battles of my people for as long as we have been keep-ing records. It is the wise man that learns from his mistakes as well as his accomplishments." He took a sip. "But more from his mistakes."

Zoram had to admit this was a new concept to him—planning a battle not just by strength in numbers or geography but planning the actual fight itself. As simple as it was, he had never thought of it before. It made sense.

"Victory in battle is achieved even before the first arrow is strung or the first sword drawn. Deception is essential to success on the battlefront."

"Deception? You mean lies?"

"I mean strategy. If you are a large army but appear to be small, what is your enemy likely to do?"

Zoram shrugged. "Send a smaller army to meet you?"

"Or become careless and give away not only their numbers but their plan of attack—all information you can use, if you're looking for it."

"And end the fighting quicker."

Something in Zoram's comment aroused another wave of excitement in Wu Yien's demeanor, and he produced the dagger he always carried with him. It was small and ornate, a favorite of his. He pulled it from the scabbard. Even in the fading twilight, Zoram noted that it was a masterful blade.

"A blade can be strong and tempered and made by the greatest masters using the greatest skill, but what happens the more and longer it's used?"

Zoram didn't know where his friend was going with this, and his words were starting to become muddled. "You're drunk."

"Perhaps." Wu Yien smiled. "But I'm also right. Answer me. You know. What happens to the blade that is in continuous use?"

"I don't know."

Wu Yien's anger flashed for the briefest moment as he slapped his hand down on the stone bench they shared. "Yes, you do!" He immediately regained his composure. "The edge begins to dull. It is the same with men and with armies. Strike quickly and strong. The longer an army is engaged, the more its resources, morale, and commitment dull." He sat back, leaning heavily on the rail. "Remember that when you advise your king."

Wu Yien *was* drunk, struggling to pour another cupful. Zoram looked around and waved over a passing monk. His friend offered no resistance as he was helped to his feet and escorted to his room. "Remember what I have said. There is more to war than men and weapons. There is a skill, an *art*, to war that separates the victors from . . . those who are dead."

Zoram tossed his cup of rice wine over the side of the railing and let those last words resonate for a time. Wu Yien was right. He was always right when it came to matters of warfare. He was a brilliant strategist, Zoram thought, but an even better friend. If what he said was true and their time left together was short, he would miss Wu Yien most. These were formative years, when lifelong friendships were forged. It didn't seem right to sever them like this. He always knew it would happen someday, but he was unprepared for the deep emotions and feelings of loss he was now experiencing as the reality of this impending separation settled in.

It was true that Zoram would remember this night for years to come, but not for his friend's lessons in military tactics.

Tonight, Zoram's life would change forever.

खेपेर् ओफ़् ष्वोर्द

Clouds had rolled in, first distorting the quarter moon and then blocking it altogether. A cold wind had picked up and now blew in from the higher mountains, carrying with it the promise of the approaching snow. The seasons were peculiar at this altitude. Spring and summer struggled to break free of winter's dominance and supremacy, able only to give a month or two of warmer mild weather. The nights were still cool, but the sun felt good during the day. When winter had relented long enough, though, it returned suddenly and without mercy. Zoram suspected the number of nights to sit outside without being bundled up were limited. And that, too, compounded his heavy heart.

As a thousand thoughts flooded through his mind, some of them leaving pools in his eyes, he was interrupted by one of the monks serving in the monastery.

"Young master Zoram," he said, bowing and holding a folded leather parcel tied with frayed straps. "For you. From home." Zoram accepted the small, weathered package. "It was waiting for you in the village. It was misplaced earlier. Our apologies."

Zoram bowed his head in return. "Thank you."

Correspondence was a rarity at the monastery. He had only received two other letters from home over the years, though he suspected that more had been sent. The means to deliver written correspondence across such great distances and through so many kingdoms made communication nearly impossible. He treasured each roll of parchment more than if it had been carved in gold. These words and letters were his only tie to his home. Though written by the hand of his mother, Zoram believed he could actually feel the love of his father radiating from her script as well.

But in addition to words of love and encouragement, these letters also bore the news of his homeland, news that was less than uplifting or promising. His first letter, received many years after his arrival, told of Israel's conquered fate and the devastating accounts of young men, the elite and privileged of their nation, being taken captive into the heart of Babylon by their new masters. Though his mother had never said it, Zoram knew that if he had stayed behind, he most likely would have shared that fate. His thoughts had reached out to his childhood friends, to Daniel and the others, and he had sent many silent prayers heavenward over the years for their safety and well-being.

The following letters had been blissfully free of news of politics and the dire straits Israel must have been experiencing. His mother had chosen, instead, to write of faith and hope and of the mercy of their One True God. He had read and reread her letters daily, cherishing her warm and gentle words for months.

But not this letter.

Not these words.

The letter was written in his father's hand. The greeting, though proper and caring, lacked the warmth of his mother's words. Though he was now a grown man, there was something about a mother's love that he didn't think he'd ever outgrow.

As he sat in his room, reading by the warm glow of lamplight, he read as his father began to describe his mother's illnesses, her exhaustion and fainting spells. He forced his eyes to read on, fearful of what end they might reach, what news his father was trying to prepare him for. And then he saw the words.

His mother was dead.

How long ago had these words been written? There was no reference to the time or the season or even the year. Was this all new? Should he still mourn? He wanted to cry, but he couldn't. He was numb. It was like a void had opened up inside him and drained his every feeling. He let the letter fall from his fingers to the floor and cast himself upon his bed.

But sleep would not come. He lay there well into the night, but the feelings of regret, grief, and even doubt filled his heart and mind, and his eyes would not shut. He watched as his lamp ran dry, the flame growing smaller and smaller until, without ceremony, it just ceased to be.

Much like life, he thought. So fragile, so illusory.

His wandering thoughts eventually turned to his own faith contrasted with the faith of his instructors and the people of this land. Their religion was filled with many gods, each having power over a different natural element or aspect of their lives. Emphasis, however, was not placed in appeasing or petitioning these deities. Instead, the people focused on achieving a new consciousness that placed every man—all mankind, in fact—on a journey to reach a state of what they called "enlightenment." This goal, this state, was not commanded by their gods but was sought out voluntarily to become at peace, or at one, with all of creation. It had continued to be a foreign concept to Zoram because the God of his ancestors, though He loved His people, demanded sacrifice and obedience to the many commandments and laws.

As he lay there, he recalled one particular man who had visited the monastery a few years earlier. Zoram and the other apprentices were not permitted to meet or see the man and were confined to their quarters for the three days he stayed with them, but Zoram and Wu Yien had sneaked into the reception hall and caught a glimpse of the stranger. They had gathered from what little they overheard that he was a young man of some eminence and esteem, a prince of a neighboring kingdom who had forsaken all in his search of this enlightenment. He didn't appear to be much older than them. The night they had stolen in, he was speaking of the origin of suffering, that it was inherent in life and that it was caused by attachment and longing for what one didn't have. The man's words rang especially true tonight as Zoram lay there suffering the death of his mother. This young prince had gone on to assure them that it was possible to overcome longing and attachment, and hence, the suffering associated with loss. He had explained that this could be accomplished by following a prescribed regimen of wisdom, ethical conduct, and meditation.

A large part of his instructions that night was that our individuality, our separateness, our "self," was merely an illusion; that we were all, in reality, connected to all things and people around us. Once this was understood and believed, then there was nothing to want, nothing to be deprived of, and nothing to cause us to suffer. The stranger had left the monastery that night after leading them in a session of deep meditation, focusing on strengthening them from within, and pronouncing his blessing on all of them. The young man's words had resonated with Zoram for many nights to come, always when he felt the longings to return home, to work next to his father, to embrace his mother.

But Zoram could not be comforted, not by his faith or the faith of his masters. He supposed, with a sense of cynicism, that he still had a long way to go toward his own personal enlightenment.

When he could take being confined in his room with his thoughts no more, Zoram got up, threw a blanket over his shoulders, and ventured outside. The cloud cover was thick, and the courtyards and houses were all dark. Everyone was asleep. He walked quietly along the stone paths and made his way to a small garden terrace set back from the rest of the monastery. This had always been Zoram's place of refuge when the stresses of his studies became too great. Carved into the rocky hillside, it offered a view not only of the curved and steeply pitched rooftops but also a breathtaking panoramic outlook of the mountains and valleys that surrounded them. They called the mountains the Himavant, or "abode of snow" in the native language, and they had always served to inspire him and lend him strength. Even at night, under the dimmest of stars, it was a sight to behold.

But tonight there was only darkness.

He was trying to make sense of the news. Not of his mother's death specifically—intellectually, he knew all men and women died, that death was the natural balance of life. He remembered the words of the holy books read to him as a child, that to every thing there was a season and a purpose under heaven, that there was a time to plant and a time to sow, a time to laugh and a time to mourn, a time to be born and a time to die. It was God's plan. But Zoram found himself snared in the trap of questioning his mother's death and the timing and fairness of it. If he was going to return in the spring, why could God have not waited to take her? Could He not have given them a little time together? A small moment to embrace? It seemed cruel to take something so precious and on the brink of his return. Would it have been so difficult to extend her life just one more year? Hadn't he served faithfully, sacrificing his time, talents, and very life to serve God, and this was how he was repaid?

But through his guilt and pain, a small but strong voice warned him against doubting and finding fault with the Lord. Was it not written that His ways are not our ways? And standing there in the darkness, insignificant and small in comparison to the grandeur of creation all around him, who was he to counsel the Lord? If his mother had ever shared similar feelings, he could not remember it. She must have possessed great strength and faith to prepare and send her only child to the far ends of the earth, trusting in the Lord, that He would care for Zoram where she could not. He remembered her kind and encouraging words and recalled her expressions of love in the months and weeks before his departure, and he knew that, as difficult as his leaving was for her, his mother had never questioned God's will or doubted Him.

And neither should he.

Zoram closed his eyes, lifted his face to heaven, and visualized his sadness and doubts and guilt being carried off on the currents of the cold wind. His heart felt a little lighter, the tears were released and began rolling down his cheeks, and just as she had promised him, he could feel her arms tight around him.

He didn't want to open his eyes. He didn't want to let go. But then a curious light began to dance on the back of his eyelids, and he wondered if the clouds had parted to reveal the moon.

He opened his eyes to the most peculiar and perplexing sight he'd ever seen.

The clouds were still thick, but a light gradually grew brighter from behind them, revealing their many layers and dimensions as if it were daytime. In the distance he heard a faint peal of thunder, but this was unlike any lightning he had ever witnessed. It didn't flash; it remained constant, the light growing in intensity, brighter and brighter until—

A ball of fire as bright as the sun burst from the clouds at an incredible speed and shot through the air, leaving a trail of flames and smoke. The ball crossed the vast expanse of the valley in the blink of an eye before impacting the face of the mountain on the opposite side of the valley from where Zoram was standing. A few moments later there was a thunderous noise that shook the ground.

Zoram just stood there, shocked and in awe, as he watched the fire quickly cool and disappear into the dark, rocky mountainside. He could do nothing but stand there, unable to even breathe.

What marvel was this?

Noise started to build from the sleeping quarters below as lamps were lit and students and teachers alike emerged from their beds, frightened and wondering what commotion had awakened them all. Zoram watched them gather in small groups, speaking in excited tones and voices, and he knew it was only a matter of time before he was noticed. Then all eyes and ears would be turned to him for an explanation.

But what would he tell them? He didn't know what he'd seen. But a confirmation calmed his heart. When asked, he would tell the truth: he didn't know.

But as he fielded and failed to answer their many questions, the High Sadhus gave him a look that told Zoram the old man knew that Zorma's answer was not quite the truth. Instead of pushing, the venerable master respected his answers with a nod and a smile.

Returning to his room later that night, Zoram now found that sleep was eager to claim him. He was exhausted, and as he lay there, drifting into the soft embraces of sleep, he was struck forcefully with one thought, a single and consuming purpose.

He needed to see for himself what miracle had fallen from heaven for him.

CHAPTER NINE

ZORAM BLINKED HIS EYES A couple of times. He was disoriented for a moment or two. The shades were drawn, but the faint slivers of light let in the early traces of the approaching dawn. For a brief but hopeful moment, he wondered if the events of the day before had actually happened. But the soft bed, warm blankets, and empty feeling in his heart confirmed that he was, in fact, without family, without friends—alone.

Without allowing his mind to dwell on these thoughts, he rose and quickly pulled on clothes from an adjacent closet, recognizing many of his father's things. It was a surreal feeling to be surrounded by the effects of the single most influential man in his life but whom he could only recall from a handful of exchanges. But there was more to this oddity. Standing there, he also felt as if he were that man. His father. He was now the Keeper of the Sword, but he didn't know exactly what that meant, and all the clothes in the world couldn't hide the feelings of inadequacy he now felt.

He rummaged through the loose shirts, formal coats, ceremonial cloaks, and many pairs of shoes and boots. He had all he needed to put on the façade of his father, but without—

His thoughts halted at the first sight of it. It appeared to be discarded and forgotten amid the mass of clothing, uniforms, and other formal attire. One of his father's blades—a single hilt long sword. Zoram remembered this one. His father had let him play with it when he was a boy. At the time he'd to struggled to lift it with both hands, clumsily swinging and chopping at the air or trees; now it felt light in his rough, calloused hand. It was heavier than the swords he was used to handling, made of heavy iron, with spots of rust along the edge, but it was well balanced and a fine weapon.

His father had been an exceptional craftsman.

Zoram felt better immediately and found his way outside and onto the roof. There he focused on centering his mind and body, only marginally aware of the approaching dawn as he practiced the combinations of attacks and defense tactics, gliding as it were on the rooftop. He moved with a slow, relaxed grace that should have seemed to be out of place considering the sword in his hand. His every move was slow and deliberate—from his firm and rooted stances, which provided his sure foundation, to the wide and sweeping cuts and blocks. He focused on his breathing. Deep, in through the nose, imagining that each breath carried with it peace and a calm energy that circulated through and filled his body. And then out, expelling the poisons and negativity from his system. This moving meditation had been his routine for the past years, and it had served his heart, mind, and body well. He needed this time to get centered and refocus. He was one with his surroundings, feeling and experiencing the sky's transformation from a dull gray into a heavenly sea of blue, the few wisps of clouds igniting with a fiery blast of color heralding the sun's approach.

Below and all around him, the city of Jerusalem was beginning to awaken. Sounds of merchants setting up their shops and of corralled animals floated up from the city streets below. Occasionally the aroma of fresh baked bread or roasted meat was carried on the morning breeze, and his morning meditation was made that much sweeter.

But it was movement just beyond the city wall that caught Zoram's attention, causing him to pause and watch with some interest. A dozen soldiers, armed and suited for light battle, gathered on horseback. Then another soldier, suited like the others but with more gold and a bright red cloak, approached at a full gallop. He proceeded to circle the men as he bellowed out words Zoram imagined to be motivation. They were too far away for Zoram to hear, but he could tell by the loud inflections and resulting rousing accord that orders were being given and a plan of attack explained.

Their commander then brought his horse around in a full circle. Zoram recognized him as the man he had fought the night before. Hanoch.

Hanoch continued around one more time before he stopped, facing another man, who Zoram hadn't noticed before. He was standing atop the city wall, supervising their send off. With a wave of this man's hand, the small army had their permission to ride off toward the north. As Zoram turned and watched them ride away, he caught a glimpse of their commander's face. It was Laban, the Keeper of the Records. Laban must have sensed he was being watched and turned around quickly, locking far off stares with him. After a long beat, Laban turned around sharply, his cape whipping around him, and stalked inside the wall tower out of sight.

Zoram considered what he had just witnessed and turned his attention back to the men on horseback, just now cresting the hill and disappearing over the rise. Where were they going? They were too big to be a scouting party and too well armed to be a diplomatic delegation. And something about the hour in which they left didn't feel right. But what did he know about Israel's current military affairs? He had only been back a day. Already it was clear that "coming home" was definitely not what he'd imagined and romanticized it to be.

Zoram took another moment to stretch before returning from the roof and back inside his family estate. The calm he had just created was quickly torn apart by the loud voices he overheard.

"What do you mean he isn't there?" It was Anat's voice, shrill and in a panic. "Where could he be? You don't think he . . ."

"No, no," another voice, an older, maternal voice assured her. "I am sure he's just—"

"Just what?"

"Maybe the young master went for a walk?"

"And somehow locked the doors and gate behind him? Maybe he didn't come home last night. Maybe he met with thieves and—"

"No, no. He returned home safely."

"I didn't see him."

"Perhaps he was careful not to wake you. But his bed was slept in."

"Then where *is* he?"

Zoram stepped into the room. "Is there a problem?"

Anat and the house matron looked over, startled. Anat rushed to him, threw her arms around him, and squeezed tight.

"You're all right! God be praised! You had me so worried."

"Yes, I heard. But I'm not a child."

Anat pulled back, visibly hurt by the implication. "I didn't mean to . . . I'm sorry."

Zoram flashed a smile and touched her shoulder. "I know you didn't."

Anat noticed the sword in his hand. "Where were you?"

"Clearing my mind."

The matron stepped forward. "Did you sleep well?"

"Yes, very. Thank you. Forgive me, but much of yesterday is still lost in a fog to me."

She offered a motherly smile and put her hand on her chest. "My name is Naomi. I'm the head matron over the—over *your* household."

"Thank you, Naomi."

"Are you hungry?"

Zoram returned her warm smile. "It won't be cold, leftover rice, will it?"

Naomi looked confused. "Sir?"

"Nevermind. I'm sorry. Yes, breakfast would be wonderful. Thank you."

"But he can't," Anat blurted out. "He's in mourning. He must eat the meal of consolation."

Naomi shot her a disapproving look. "It is his *avelut*. It is his decision." She then returned her attention to Zoram. "Would you like boiled eggs and stewed lentils?"

Zoram tried to keep a straight face as to not offend Anat's concern for him and the adherence to tradition, but he couldn't quite do it. "No. Thank you. A more . . . traditional meal would be great."

Anat would not leave his side, following him through the house and talking incessantly about how worried she was and how she'd feared the worst when his bed was found empty. Zoram finally had to excuse himself, telling her that he planned to bathe and that he would meet her in the dining hall later. She again stumbled through an awkward apology and backed out of his quarters.

He didn't give her much thought as he washed from the morning's exercises. He couldn't remember ever having bathed in so much warm water. He must have as a child because it all felt somehow familiar, but for the past five months, his bathing had consisted of dipping a towel into a pot of water—only occasionally warm. And while some of the men of the caravan paid a few coins for a night in a bathhouse in the cities as they crossed the deserts, Zoram had refrained, hearing that more than simply bathing transpired there. So now to fully immerse himself in a tub of warm and scented water was a wonderful and distinctive sensation. He was pleased to find that clothes had been chosen and laid out for him, and he dressed slowly, deliberately.

Naomi gasped as he entered the dining room. "My, if you're not the very image of your father." Zoram didn't know what to say, and he felt sadness return for a moment before it was replaced with the warmth of the comment and the love the entire house had for his father.

Breakfast consisted of several plates of breads and cheeses and fruits—dates and figs sugared and soaked in a bowl—and a tart drink that he couldn't place. "This is delicious. What is it?"

"Pomegranate juice. It was your father's favorite."

He took another sip. "It's very good," he said, instinctively bowing his head in gratitude.

Naomi was flattered. "There is no need to bow here. This is your home. We're here to serve *you*. But I've seen you do it many times since you arrived."

"Habit, I guess. It was common and expected where I was living. I didn't mean to make you uncomfortable. I'll stop if you—"

"No, Master Zoram. If you wish to bow, you go right on ahead and bow whenever and to whomever you want to."

Zoram smiled and nodded his appreciation. She smiled and nodded back.

"Tell us of this place you went to," Anat said. "I heard it was farther away than any Israelite has ever traveled. That it was to the edge of the world."

He paused, reminiscing. "More like the top."

"What?"

"The mountains. Where I stayed," he said between bites. "They were nothing like you—I mean, *we* have here."

"We?" Anat's eyes lit up, and she sat a little taller.

"Israel. Judea. What we have here are mere mounds of dirt and rock compared to these mountains."

"Oh," she said, trying to hide her disappointment.

"It was unlike anything I had ever seen, like something out of a story adults might tell children when they're young to inspire their imaginations—"

A loud knock at the front door interrupted them. Naomi rested her hand on Zoram's shoulder. "Please. I'll see who it is."

Zoram could hear the door open and a loud, firm voice instruct her to give something to the Keeper. After the door closed, she returned with a roll of parchment and gave it to him. "This is for you."

"Who was it?" Anat asked.

"He was sent from Laban."

"The Keeper?"

Zoram untied the parchment.

Anat's curiosity was tinged with concern. "What does it say?"

"It's a summons. From Laban. He wants to meet with me."

"When?"

"Now."

Anat moved to get up, but Zoram put his hand on hers to stop her.

"We can't keep him waiting," she protested.

"*We* won't. But I might. This is my house, after all. And I've just sat down for the morning meal. I think whatever it is he wants can wait a little longer."

Anat nervously settled back down.

"Tell me about him," Zoram asked.

"Who?"

"Laban. I vaguely remember the boy who was being groomed to become the next Keeper of the Records, but I didn't think it was him."

Anat glanced quickly to Naomi and then back to Zoram. "He was the younger son. His older brother . . . when the Babylonians came . . ." She shook her head.

"And his father? The Keeper?"

Again, Anat looked at Naomi. This time the house matron answered. "It's unclear. Some say he gave up on life after the death of his son."

"But others say he was poisoned." Anat dropped her voice to just above a whisper. "The Babylonians have spies everywhere."

Zoram just nodded, placating her suspicions but not believing them himself. "And Laban found himself bearing the mantle of Keeper."

"He's a good Keeper," Naomi added, "and a cunning general. He's a very powerful man. There are many who speak ill of him, but Israel needs men who are unafraid to do the right things."

It was clear to Zoram that these last words were also meant as a plea to cast aside any fears he may still have. "Men like my father?"

The matron's eyes watered suddenly. "Men like your father."

The rest of the meal passed in relative silence. Naomi had found a way to say what was on her mind and in her heart while Anat ate quickly, clearly preoccupied and concerned with the delay in responding to Laban's command. But after insisting that he help clean up, Zoram finally answered the call from the Keeper of the Records.

שומר החרב

For four or five generations, Laban's family had lived in a detached house and estate that was officially part of the royal palace. Zoram recalled once, when he was a child, asking his mother why, if they were Keepers too, they didn't live like Laban's family. It was all so enticing to a child—having servants to wait on your every wish and whim, clothes and exotic foods from the world over, being recognized and envied by everyone else. And while Zoram's family had a staff and never went without anything, it was somehow different. His mother had explained that their family had been offered similar palacial quarters but had opted to remain at their humble family estate. "We are servants of the people," she had explained with a comforting smile. "It just doesn't seem right."

He was met at the steps of Laban's house and escorted through the lavish estate. Every hallway had alcoves and niches filled with vases, mirrors, and silks, the tile polished to a reflective shine. Maybe it was because he had lived a modest and stark lifestyle for the past ten years, but the blatant and obvious display of wealth and privilege sickened Zoram. He had passed men, women, and children along his journey—many in this very city—who teetered on the verge of starvation every day. It didn't seem right that so much wealth was accumulated by so few.

His escort halted in true, rigid military form just inside a room lit brightly by the morning sun streaming in through an intricate lattice work that lined a full-length veranda spaced with wide marble columns.

Laban stood with his back to Zoram, facing the window. He was dressed in bright colors of fine silk and tightly woven cotton. He wore light military armor trimmed with gold that was clearly more for show than function.

The room had the look and feel of a library. There were several tables set up in the center of the rectangular room, each with parchments, quills, and inkwells opposite empty chairs. Along the walls were shelves full of scrolls and books bound in leather and other animal skins, filling the air with that musty smell that lingered from old texts the world over. Zoram had spent countless hours in ancient libraries during his training, studying the tests and trials, successes and failures of those metallurgical masters who had gone before him in the pursuit of perfecting their art. Whether the library was hidden away in granite mountains half a world away or here in the deserts of Judea, there was little difference.

At first, this intellectual display surprised Zoram, and then he remembered that Laban, in addition to his military responsibilities, was the Keeper of the Records. It was his sacred charge to record and protect the law and the words of the prophets. The fact that he was also a military leader, though unique in the history of the Keepers, was not prohibited as far as Zoram knew. Their callings were not exclusive, but as Jharom had always taken his role with such complete devotion and without distraction, it felt almost wrong to see Laban dressed as opulently as he was.

Laban kept his back to Zoram for another moment before turning around. He wore a serious and somber expression. He then bowed. "I have said it already, but it bears repeating: we are all grieving the loss of your father. He was a good man and a faithful Keeper."

Zoram held his stare for an uncomfortable pause then stepped closer. "I'm sorry. We haven't properly met. I knew your brother, and I remember your father . . ."

Laban's compassionate demeanor was replaced briefly with a look of contempt but then returned almost as fast as it had left. "Of course, but I remember you. This must be confusing to you, especially in the wake of your father's untimely accident." He strolled over to the wall covered with scrolls. "No, it was never supposed to be. The calling, the title, the responsibilities were never meant to be mine. They belonged to my father, my brother, but the Babylonian invasion took them both from me." He extended his arms at his side, palms facing front. "And here we are. You and I are the same."

Zoram didn't respond as Laban stepped toward one of the tables and examined the writings, only partially completed. "Your return has been eagerly anticipated. A small fortune was expended on your training. They say you know how to fashion a new, stronger kind of metal, something not even the Babylonians or the Egyptians possess. Is this true?"

Zoram didn't take his eyes off Laban's. There was something about him that Zoram didn't like. It may just be his smug personality, or perhaps it was simply the man's air of arrogance that repulsed him. But whatever it was, he knew he had to shake it off and cast it aside. Like him or not, Zoram needed him. They were two halves of a whole. Israel needed them both if they hoped to survive this latest occupation and the darkness that accompanied it.

Zoram lightened his appearance with a smile. "Of course. I live to serve Israel and the One True God."

Laban quickly crossed the distance between them and put his hand on Zoram's shoulders. "I know you do. We both do." Then Laban quickly moved his hands to Zoram's shirt collar and, before the young Keeper could react, forcefully pulled in opposite directions, tearing it, ripping the fine outer garment.

Zoram recoiled and became defensive but stopped short of action when he realized he was unharmed. With a firm look he demanded an explanation.

Laban smoothed the shirt over Zoram's shoulders as if had done nothing wrong or warranting an explanation. "You are in mourning," he simply said. "It is tradition."

But Zoram knew there was more to it. It was not merely to help him comply with the law. Laban's actions were debasing and clearly meant to establish his position and prominence in their shared responsibilities. Zoram had never forgotten his place in this charged and holy partnership. While theirs was nearly a partnership of equals, they were not designated as such. God was a God of order. The Keeper of the Sword was technically the servant of the Keeper of the Record, a nuance Laban sought to emphasize. But now was not the time or the place to push back. As it is in war, so it is in relationships: observe your surroundings and plan your strategy before committing to the first action. Zoram didn't understand Laban's need to establish himself as the superior, but he would simply accept the behavior and actions for what they were and take them into consideration as he charted out his course as the new Keeper.

Besides, he thought, he needed to strike a balance with Laban. They were, after all, inseparably connected for the rest of their lives. Zoram touched the torn spot. "I suspect there has been a great deal of mourning these past few years."

"That there has been, my friend," Laban said, moving to a pair of divans along the wall. "More than any nation should have to bear. War is truly hell on earth."

Zoram followed. "It must have been painful—losing your father and your brother so close to each other. And if I remember correctly, your mother passed away when you were young."

"It's true," he said, looking away and out through the lattice. "I never knew my mother, so it was very difficult when my only family died and in such short time of each other. I guess in that regard you and I are alike— both alone, trying to do the best we can without the benefit of mentoring or example."

Zoram reflected on this for a moment. What Laban said was true, and Zoram began to see him in a new, more compassionate light. At least he'd had the memories and words of a mother to cherish despite his absence and separation. This last year had taken a toll on all of Israel.

"Tell me how it happened."

"He was traveling with a small company of settlers to Damascus to deliver copies of the law when they were ambushed by a horde of Babylonian mercenaries and bandits who prey on the fear and utter defeat of the people. He died defending the very records he was charged to protect."

Zoram was confused. "What? Who are you talking about?"

"My brother, the Keeper. I thought you asked how he died."

"No. I was asking about the conquest. My father's letter only mentioned it in passing, and I have heard very little since my arrival."

Laban took a moment to gather his thoughts before answering Zoram's inquiry. Finally, he took a seat just inside the balcony. "When you left, if I remember correctly, Israel had just shed its allegiance to the Assyrians and was now under the 'protection' of Egypt. But the Egyptians could not hold on to their power for long. The recently defeated Babylonian Empire, under the leadership of a new king, Nebuchadnezzar, rallied their military forces anew. With an insatiable thirst for power and dominance, they defeated the best armies Egypt could offer, and Israel found itself serving a new master. There was a tense, uneasy peace, but it was peace, nonetheless."

"And this is when Jerusalem was conquered and the city laid to waste?" Zoram was a little confused. Much of the damage he had seen throughout the city looked relatively new. "Did the Babylonians invade then?"

Laban shook his head. "After Egypt's defeat, Nebuchadnezzar sent a delegation of politicians and military advisors to ensure Israel's new allegiance. It was a peaceful transition, for the most part."

"Then what happened to the city?"

Laban leaned his head back and closed his eyes for a moment. "Jehoiakim was rash and a fool. After three years he stopped paying tribute to Babylon and aligned our forces with Egypt. Before our full strength could be realized, it was too late. We didn't stand a chance."

"You were serving in the military at the time?"

"Yes and no. I had already assumed the mantle of Keeper, but I still retained my position as captain of the armies. While it wasn't fully my decision to make, even I recognized that there was a time to fight and a time to pull back and regroup."

Laban's fist balled up and then released. "And then they took appalling actions to ensure our compliance and subservience. It's one thing to steal from our treasuries, to take our gold and silver, or even desecrate our Temple and steal our holy vessels, but to break our spirits forever . . . They took the one treasure we valued more than all others."

Zoram recalled the words of his father. "The children."

Laban nodded. "Our future. They took the best and the brightest, the sons and daughters of the spiritual, influential, and powerful, leaving only the poorest behind to pick up the pieces of the broken city."

"And our king?"

"Thrown from the city wall. His son Jehoiachin assumed the throne, but he only served three months before being deposed by Nebuchadnezzar, who personally chose the next king from the royal lineage—replacing Jehoiachin with an instrument, a figurehead, a young uncle to the king who would be easily controlled, one who knew where his power had come from, one who knew who his master truly was."

"And the records?"

"Safe. Your father was a cunning man."

Zoram appreciated the compliment. "And the Sword?"

Laban didn't answer right away. "It was destroyed."

"How?"

"No one is certain. It was in your father's possession almost continually during the siege. But it was discovered in the armory, the blade cracked and snapped at the hilt. I saw it with my own eyes. It was beyond repair. No one blamed your father. You can see, though, why the news of your return has become a matter of such importance."

"Because of the law," Zoram mused to himself. He may have forgotten much while he was away, but he could never forget the law of the Keeper of the Sword.

One Generation. One Sword.

"Because of the law," Laban confirmed.

"May I see it?"

Laban shook his head. "Your father melted down the blade, as is the custom."

"And what of the hilt?"

Laban thought for a moment. "I believe it's in the armory." He got up and pulled open a drawer from a bank of them along one wall. He reached in and produced a large brass key. "This is yours now." He tossed it to Zoram. "It fits both the treasury and the armory. As Keeper, they are both your responsibility, just as they are mine."

Zoram experienced a sense of reverence holding the key that had once been his father's. This key represented the legacy left to him by his father, a legacy that secured him in the long line of Keepers. The key felt heavy in his hand.

Laban remained silent for a stretch of time. A heaviness descended and settled on the room. Zoram sensed the change and looked up. "What is it?"

"There is one more thing," Laban started, a timid tone to his voice. "I am loathe to even bring it up, but I feel you need to know. It's about your father."

Zoram looked up as Laban turned, facing the open patios. He didn't speak for several beats. "Well?" Zoram finally asked.

Laban took a deep breath, his back still to him. "Your father had . . . an addiction. To games of chance."

These words could not have struck Zoram with more force if they had been physical blows. "That's impossible. He was a faithful man. It is forbidden."

"As are all vices. The Babylonian influence has corrupted even the very elect."

"I don't believe you. I have never known him to gamble."

"I know this must come as a surprise to you, but how well did you really know him? Childhood memories? A letter or two? Time can change a man."

Zoram still didn't believe it, but he was beginning to question the image of his father he'd had all these years. "And how do you know this?"

Laban turned around, a regretful expression darkening his face. "He was heavily indebted to me."

Zoram felt sick to his stomach, and his hands and jaw began to tingle and go numb. Was it true? Could it be possible? But as hard as Laban's words were, his next ones caught Zoram completely by surprise. "I fear I may have played a part in his . . . accident."

"What are you saying?"

"All I know is that unholy appetites, transgressions, and the shame of being found out can weigh heavy on a good man's heart." Laban sighed. "I only found out what the loans were for a short time ago. I was concerned. When I approached him, he denied it at first but then became angry, breathing out all manner of threats against me if I reported this to anyone. But then his anger turned to regret and remorse. I offered to help but told him I could no longer finance his habits. He thanked me, and we embraced. I truly loved your father. He was a mentor and like a second father to me."

Zoram just sat there, unable to stand. All strength had left him. It was as if everything he thought he was, everything he hoped he would be, was now fatally flawed. Could his father have been so weak as to find satisfaction in this wrong? Zoram didn't want to believe any of it, but Laban was right—he didn't really know his father for who he was, only for who he remembered and imagined the man to be. Had his death not been an accident or mere coincidence?

"When did you confront him?"

"About a week ago. I don't remember the day."

A disturbing and selfish story began forming in his mind. Could his father's guilt have been so great that he couldn't bear to face him? Zoram's heart had never felt so heavy. "Who else knows?"

Laban put his hand to his heart. "True to my word, I have not told a soul. I made a promise to your father. But—"

"But what?"

Laban hesitated. "But now his debt falls to you. I'm sorry. It is the law."

Zoram's feelings toward his father turned from disbelief and pity to anger for the selfishness of what Jharom had done. Deep down Zoram still harbored compassion and love for his father, but with this new revelation, he worried that his image of the man he idolized and who served as the very model for his calling was forever tarnished.

When he finally found the words, he asked, "How much?"

"How much? Oh, the debt? It was significant, but don't worry yourself with that now. You have weightier matters on your mind. I do not envy the circumstances of your return, and again, you have my deepest and most sincere sympathies."

"You are kind, Laban, and I thank you. But I will not let my father's debts go unpaid."

Laban held up his hand. "No, listen, the money is not important, and though I applaud your sense of nobility and integrity, I would as soon forgive the debt and relieve you of this stress right now."

"That's not necessary."

"I know, but you're the Keeper. You and I are a team. I don't want this to come between us."

Zoram felt the key still in his hand and rubbed his thumb over the smooth curves as Laban's news more fully registered with him and became clearer. Everything now rested on his shoulders. There was nothing he could do about the deeds and misdeeds of his father—those were his alone. The consequences of his actions, though, had spilled over into Zoram's cup, and he would drink those bitter dregs if he had to. He didn't think it possible, but his spirit, already drained by the death and burial of his father, had now been brought to a new low.

"You say this fits the armory as well?"

Laban nodded. "But no one expects you to begin work right away. You're just beginning the time of mourning. You need to grieve, to rest, and to heal. Do you need anything? Is your house staffed and able?"

"Yes, Naomi has been very attentive and kind."

"She's a good woman," Laban said, reaching down and taking Zoram's hand to help him up. "I have heard your father speak well of her over the years."

"You have shown me much kindness. I want to apologize for engaging your men last night. I understand that man was wanted for questioning but . . ."

"No apology is necessary. As I said before, it was I who have need to beg your forgiveness. They had no right to interrupt your father's service."

"I just didn't want people's last memories of him—"

"Stop. Please. Don't give it another thought. I have already dealt with those responsible."

Zoram smiled his appreciation.

"Now," Laban said, leading him out of the room, "return home. Rest. Eat. Get accustomed to your new life. There is time to do all you need to do, but for now, do those things that help you relax and clear your mind. You will be of no use to us with your heart this troubled. The hills are beautiful and fragrant during this time of year. If you require . . . company . . ."

Zoram shook his head. "No. Anat is company enough."

"Anat?" Laban looked surprised for a moment then smiled. "Did you know her before you left?"

"I don't remember her, but she remembers me."

"I'm sure she does."

"What is that supposed to mean?"

"Nothing. Only that she has spoken of you and your return for years. You must have made quite the impression on her."

"She was at the house when I arrived."

"She's a sweet girl. Take time to get to know her. Let her refresh your memory of the sights of the city and the countryside. This land is, after all, yours to help protect and defend. She would be all too happy to spend this time with you."

"Thank you," Zoram said as they reached the door. "I just may."

"If you need anything—answers, directions, or just to talk—you have but to ask. All I have is at your disposal."

Zoram bowed and left, more confused and conflicted than he had ever been in his life.

CHAPTER TEN

ZORAM DIDN'T KNOW HOW LONG he aimlessly wandered through the streets of the upper city. After Laban's news about his father, he didn't feel like going home; he particularly didn't want to speak with those who apparently knew nothing about his father's secrets. He needed some time to comprehend what all this meant. He needed time alone. To walk. To think.

Jerusalem was both foreign and familiar to him. Though his childhood memories gave him a sense of geographical orientation—he knew where the market was in comparison to the palace, for example—the "feel" of the ancient fortress-city was alien to him. He could attribute much of this to his own growing up and leaving childish notions behind. He was plagued, though, by the men and women on the streets who exhibited broken hearts and spirits. No one looked up as they passed one another; every man was an island, isolated and separate from each other. And it wasn't just directed toward him. He was still mostly unknown to the people. Once his name and face became more widely known, as his father's had once been, people would likely look up and acknowledge him out of respect for the title and calling. But for now his anonymity offered the solitude he so desperately needed right now.

It was all so hard to believe and accept. It sickened him to think that his homecoming had in any way provoked his father to take his own life. Did he have no faith that Zoram would understand and love his father, faults and all? The news of his father's death and the funeral had only produced a sadness for the years of association that they would miss out on, a longing to finally belong to a family. Laban was right; he didn't really know his father. And while Jharom had been buried just the day before, it was as if that day, so long ago, waiting for the caravan to pick him up, was actually the day his father died to him.

Though his mother continued to live in her letters.

His eyes began to suddenly tear as he thought of her. Not because of her death, or even the illness that consumed her life, but for other reasons that he couldn't quite clearly identify. He had never experienced grief like this before. Perhaps this was why the law, the commandments and religious traditions collected and passed down for generations, prescribed a time of mourning—not just to pay homage to the memory of loved ones passed on but to give those who remained behind time to clear their thoughts and quiet the questions that arose in their hearts. Perhaps Laban's counsel was sound. Perhaps he needed some time to sort out his own purpose and chart out a course for his return and eventual work on his calling. He wasn't thinking clearly. He would need time to become centered and strike balance in his new life here.

Zoram continued to wander. For how long, he wasn't sure, but the sun still hadn't reached its zenith, which only added to his discouragement and depression. The coolness of the morning air had not entirely fled in the day's heat. Oh, how he wished he could leave this place, leave everything behind and start over somewhere. He had skills and knowledge that were in great demand the world over. Maybe he could make a new life in Egypt or strike out to the northern lands and the sea-going Phoenicians or farther around the Great Sea to the new cities of Carthage or Rome that the caravan master had told him about. All he knew was that he didn't want to stay here. There was nothing left for him here. Despite his father's death, he had at least believed he had a legacy to uphold and fulfill, but now he wasn't even sure he had that to rely on. Jerusalem was a dead city. To be fair, all he had to compare it to was his childhood memories.

To children the world was alive and new and full of adventure; the grasses were always green, the skies always blue, and the waters always clear. But he didn't think his jaded view of the city was simply a distorted and skewed memory. If Jerusalem was base enough to corrupt a man like his father, Israel's respected and esteemed Keeper of the Sword, then what hope did Zoram have against its influence? Wasn't it better to leave with his life and what little hope he still had intact?

But through all the nagging and stinging questions, had he not given his young life in service to God? Why would God reward him with such pain and abandonment? But as soon as that thought crossed his mind, it was immediately driven out by the image and memories of his mother. She had given up all to send him away to serve a higher and greater purpose. He felt ashamed for blaming God for the actions of others as well as for his own inadequacies in dealing with them. And, still, despite the news concerning his father, deep down he refused to believe it.

As he approached a corner somewhere in the market quarter, a familiar sound reached his ears. It dispelled the self-centered and disheartened mood he had nursed since leaving Laban. Though it was not her *voice* that he recognized, Zoram knew Rebekah's unmistakable speech patterns. And she wasn't alone. There were other voices with hers, loud and mean. He picked up his step but stopped just short of rounding the corner, taking an inventory of the situation before jumping in.

He also needed a second to force himself to calm down.

Rebekah was surrounded by five or six young men, ten to twelve years in age, if he had to guess, each taunting and teasing her, mocking her stutter and throwing pebbles and small stones in her direction. Across her shoulders was a thin yoke with two large containers of oil, one hanging from each end. She was pushing through them, turning her head and trying to ignore them.

Then one of the boys found a rock about the size of a date and hurled it at her. Rebekah must have seen or at least sensed the rock and turned her back quickly. The stone missed her but hit one of the earthen containers, chipping it but otherwise not doing any damage. However, the momentum of her spin smashed the other container into the stone retaining wall lining the street, shattering the pot and spilling its contents onto the dry and dusty road.

More laughter erupted from the boys as they stuttered their jeers and insults. Rebekah fell to her knees in a frantic attempt to scoop up and save the valuable liquid. Another boy found a rock, this one larger, but Zoram had seen enough.

"Hey!" he hollered, running toward them with all the menace he could muster. As tough as they were ganging up on a lone woman, their cowardice overtook them in the presence of a real threat and sent them scattering. Rebekah looked around, surprised and confused at her sudden deliverance. Then she saw Zoram.

"Here," he said, stepping closer and getting to one knee. "Are you hurt?"

She turned quickly away and started picking up the pieces of the shattered urn but not before Zoram noticed the tears and the embarrassment in her eyes. He started to help her gather and pick up the pieces. "Let me help you."

He had no sooner picked up a large shard when she reached out and tried to knock it out of his hand. She missed his arm, however, and cut her palm on the sharp slice. She instinctively pulled back and squeezed her hand shut, trying to stem the blood and the pain.

"What? Why did you do that? Let me see your hand!" She continued to work in silence with her back to him. "Rebekah!" he said, this time with more force. Her hand likely needed attention, especially with all the mud and dirt.

"G-go away," she stammered. "You d-don't have to d-do this."

"Do what?"

"You saved m-my life, and I'm grateful, b-but you d-don't need to continue to feel his re-resp-ponsibility for me. I'm not helpless. I d-don't need your p-p-pity."

Zoram was shocked and even a little hurt, but her words forced him to evaluate his feelings. Were they just a result of his actions along that mountain trail? Was she right? Did he just feel sorry for her because of her speech impediment? It was possible, yes; and if he were honest with himself, these all did play into his feelings for her, but there was also much more to it. She was unlike any other woman he had ever known. Granted, he hadn't known many over the years, but she possessed a certain mystery. She was strong, intelligent, and attractive, with a softness that she guarded and kept safe. He wasn't sure exactly where his feelings toward her arose from; all he knew was that she was simply exhilarating to him.

Zoram removed the sash from his shirt and ripped it lengthwise down the middle. "I'm all out of pity. How about a little help instead?"

Rebekah's body language relaxed, and she turned about to face him, trying to return his warm smile. She held out her hand and unclenched her fist. Zoram took a moment to wipe away the blood around the cut. It wasn't as bad as it looked.

"It's just a scratch, really," he said, wrapping her hand with his sash. "But you should still have a physician look at it. Not that you pay much attention to my instructions, anyway."

"What d-do you m-mean?"

"Your ankle. You were on a crutch last night, and while that would *help* ease the pressure and strain to your foot, you really needed to be in bed, resting."

She looked away with a shy smile.

"And now not only do I see you out without your crutch but laboring under the weight of this yoke and heavy jars."

Rebekah didn't respond. She didn't have to.

"How's it feeling?"

"Still hurts, b-but it's b-better."

"You shouldn't be on it. The bones in your ankle need time to build up their strength again. If you fall again, you might actually break something."

Rebekah took her newly wrapped hand and held it with her other. "I never really t-told you."

"Told me what?"

"Th-th-th—" But Rebekah stopped, unable to finish, the sound getting stuck in the back of her throat. She looked helpless for a brief second before looking down so he wouldn't see her frustration.

Zoram noticed this, felt her sense of embarrassment, and finished her words for her. "Thank you?" he said, thinking that she would appreciate the help.

She didn't. In fact, the look she gave him was quite the opposite. "D-don't. I told you not to d-do th-that."

"Sorry." And he was. Again.

She then closed her eyes and seemed to gather and calm her thoughts. "Th-thank you." She smiled warmly.

Zoram nodded and, not knowing what to say next, worked in silence gathering the last of the pieces of broken pottery. He noticed again that she was comfortable with silence. So often people felt the need to fill a lapse in conversation with what usually ended up being a meaningless exchange. But he suspected that a woman like Rebekah, with her particular impediment, would have learned to embrace and enjoy silence at an early age.

"Is this olive oil?"

"Yes. M-my father owns m-many groves here and in th-the surrounding m-mountains."

A thought suddenly lit lightly on Zoram's mind, but he pushed it away for later. "Many groves, you say? He must be a wealthy man."

Rebekah looked embarrassed. "We d-don't want for m-much."

"Do you have a large family?"

"Wh-why?"

"Why what?"

"Wh-why d-do you want to know?"

Zoram suddenly felt as if he had done something wrong and had to explain himself. "Just trying to get to know you better."

"Oh," she said, blushing, and then turned to pick up the yoke and the other jar.

"No, let me get that," he offered.

"I can d-do it."

Zoram started to reach out to stop her but thought better of it. They both knew she shouldn't be putting that extra weight on her foot, but he knew better than to mention what she *shouldn't* do and expect her to go along with it.

"I know you can."

"I'm not helpless j-just because—"

"I wouldn't think of it. In fact, I think you just might be the strongest-willed person, woman *or* man, I've ever met."

"Th-then wh-why?"

"Why what?"

"Wh-why get to know m-me?"

Zoram considered the question carefully. He hadn't really given it much thought and hadn't expected to be pressed for an answer. He wasn't really sure why he was making the effort to get to know her. He just knew he wanted to. And that it felt right. So not entirely certain—or comfortable—about where this was going to lead, he made the quick decision to venture into unknown territory and just tell her the truth. "Because I have no friends, and I don't really want to be alone right now."

Rebekah was wholly unprepared for his answer and began nodding, a small smile cracking her tough façade. "Oh."

Rebekah had a mostly empty shoulder bag that they filled with the larger pieces of smashed urn before Zoram shouldered the yoke and carried the remaining container of oil. He walked with her through the streets of the poorer section of the city, dispensing oil to customers and clients. She continued visiting each one on the route even after the oil had run out, apologizing for having run out and promising to return later in the day to fill their orders at a discount for the inconvenience and hassle. Throughout all her interactions she never once mentioned the attack or blamed the lack of oil on anyone else. She simply apologized with a promise to make it right.

Zoram was impressed with her character and sense of integrity and responsibility. It would have been so easy to fault those insensitive and mean-spirited boys, and no one would blame her if she had—it would have been true, after all—but she didn't. There was no mention of the assault or the reason for the deficiency, and new thoughts and feelings began to replace the ones he had picked up earlier with Laban.

Though the vessel and yoke were both light now, he continued to walk with her, asking questions about her family. She was the oldest daughter of a large family. Her father, Ishmael, came from a long line of Bedouin traders, but his grandfather began buying fertile lands in and around Jerusalem and the Judean countryside, planting and growing olive trees. Since then, they had supplied the finest grade and most exquisite tasting oil found anywhere in the world. This focus on quality had built a financial empire and legacy unsurpassed by other businesses or merchants. It was an inspiring story of faith, vision, and hard work.

After a break in the conversation, Zoram spoke up. "Lehi speaks very highly of you."

"He is k-kind."

He held up the empty container of oil. "Is this how he knows you?"

She nodded and explained that Lehi was a wealthy merchant and caravan master with routes extending south through Egypt and past the Nubian deserts, north to Macedon, and east into Persia. He was a very shrewd businessman, well known and respected.

"And he carries your father's oil to the far corners of the world."

Rebekah smiled. "Th-they are good friends."

"By his words last night, I would have guessed he was a priest."

"He is a good m-man, a faithful m-man. He is also st-st-stubborn." She stopped and corrected herself. He wasn't *stubborn*. He was firm in his faith and the faith of his fathers. "Th-this has m-made him u-unp-popular with th-the High Priest . . . and others."

"Like Laban?"

At the mention of his name, Rebekah looked down and away, clearly uncomfortable. Zoram thought this curious. "Can I ask you something? About Laban?"

She answered with silence but looked at him, ready to receive the question.

"I've just come from his house and library. Tell me, do you trust him?"

"I d-don't really know him."

"But you know him—or at least *of him*—better than I do, and I trust your judgment."

She considered her answer. "He is v-very powerful. He is th-the K-Keeper, c-captain of th-the armies, c-commander of The Fifty. He is wealthy and has th-the king's ear. He m-may wield more power th-than anyone else in Israel."

Zoram understood completely. "And those with even a little power are tempted to abuse it?"

"We hear st-stories—"

"Yes, I've heard them too. I didn't mean to make you uncomfortable with my question. I'm sorry." Zoram flashed another smile and tried to make her feel better.

When he looked away from her, he noticed they had stopped in front of a large estate with merchants and businessmen coming and going through a side gate.

"Rebekah!" a woman called down from a second-story balcony. "You're late!"

Rebekah took a deep breath, clearly embarrassed. "M-my sister. Sorry—I m-mean th-thank you," and she took the yoke and empty jar from Zoram.

"No, thank *you*." Zoram's next words almost caught in his throat, and he worried that he might also start stuttering. "I . . . I would like to see you again."

She blushed again at his advance but didn't fully turn away, one eyebrow raised in hopeful anticipation.

"Is this where you live?"

"D-during th-the summer."

"May I call on you again?"

She scarcely contained her excitement. "I'd l-like that."

They parted, and he watched her turn at the door, look back at him one more time, and then go inside. He waited for another moment, feeling as if he might call out her name at the top of his lungs, but he restrained his tongue and just imagined it instead.

As he stood there, he became acutely aware that the weight he had picked up at Laban's house was lifted, and he felt new and hopeful for the future. Laban had all but commanded that Zoram not begin his work until his time of mourning had passed. He didn't know if it was part of the law or merely tradition, but it didn't matter. There would be time to sort out his feelings about his father later. He was inspired by Rebekah's example of taking responsibility for her duty despite events that transpired to prevent her. Was he any different? There were no degrees of responsibility, he concluded. Rebekah fulfilled hers. He would do the same.

He checked the sun. It was not yet midday. Ideally he should have begun his preparations at sunrise, but he was determined not to wait. In his coat pocket, he felt the key to the armory and treasury. Where it had been heavy at Laban's home, the brass was now cool and felt almost alive. It infused him with energy.

He was the new Keeper of the Sword.

He had a duty to perform.

A divine calling to fulfill.

שומר החרב

Though he had not visited the treasury for over ten years, Zoram remembered the way as if it had been yesterday. As he approached the upper city, he passed more men and women who recognized the young Keeper and tried to offer their condolences. Zoram thanked them but would not be detained or delayed, politely excusing himself, in some instances not even stopping. At the treasury he had to pass three separate guard stations to enter. Word of his return had spread sufficiently that merely a declaration of who he was, along with the showing of his key, was all it took to gain entrance.

Inside, the chamber was lit by several oil lamps atop wall sconces. Zoram's eyes took another moment to adjust from the bright afternoon sunlight as the soft, almost mystical glow of lamplight washed over what Israel had been able to save from the centuries of conquest and occupation. Scrolls containing the words of Israel's many teachers and prophets as well as genealogies of kings and influential families filled the room on shelves and in boxes. Pieces of gold and silver, used in kingdoms past as coin currency, were scarcely scattered in small coffers around the room. But for all of the obvious treasures, what caught Zoram's eye was an unassuming strip of cracked and dried leather hanging on one wall. He heart nearly leapt for joy.

It was still there!

To the uninformed observer, it would have looked out of place and wholly unimpressive; a forgotten piece of trash. But Zoram knew otherwise. He reached out and touched it gently, reverently. This humble strip of leather had saved a nation and united a people. If the stories were true—and Zoram wholeheartedly believed they were—this was the very sling that David had used to fell Goliath. It was an account told and retold for more than four hundred years and one that continued to serve as an inspiration to descendants of Israel. It had been a favorite of Zoram's as a boy. He and his childhood friends would take turns pretending to be both the giant Philistine and the faithful shepherd boy. It was humbling and exciting to think that here he was now, fulfilling his own destiny, his small role in the grand plans of God for His people.

But as inspiring as David's sling was, it paled in comparison with what Zoram had come to see. There, to one side, under a gold-trimmed purple covering, was Israel's most valued and treasured possession. Engraved upon the thin metal plates made of brass were the accounts of the creation and the lives of great patriarchs, the laws and commandments, and the history of Israel's kings. Of particular interest and reverence to Zoram were the psalms of David and the words of the great prophet, Isaiah, who never lost sight of hope in the promised Messiah, Israel's Great Deliverer.

Zoram reached out and removed the royal coverings. Despite the dim lamplight, the plates seemed to shine with a luster all their own, as if the light and truth contained therein would not merely depend on external sources. A feeling overwhelmed him, threatening to choke his breath and fill his eyes with tears. In that instant his whole heart was committed to the protection and preservation of these plates. He there confirmed before God that he was and would forever be their protector. As Keeper of the Sword, he would defend them with all of his might, mind, and strength. If there had ever been a doubt in his conviction or his ability to perform in this capacity, it was forever dismissed in that instant. He felt reborn.

He ran his fingers gently over the deep letters and impressions in the smooth metal, knowing that great care and effort had been put into each word, each letter. It was a labor of love and faith to engrave the words of peace and salvation.

Zoram reverently replaced the wrapping and began looking for what he had come for. Positioned over the table were two wooden pegs, conspicuously devoid of what they should be holding. He recalled seeing his father's sword hanging there when he was a boy, and the vacant space tugged at his heart. The records had been unprotected for too long.

He looked around the room until a glimmer of gold in the far corner caught his eye, as if desperately and silently calling out for him. Laban had said it might still be in the armory, but it wasn't. It was here. He pushed aside the other relics and artifacts and held the centuries-old sword hilt up to the light. Though it had taken many shapes and designs over the years, the material had remained the same, melted down and recast each generation to more perfectly form the symbol that would represent the nation's faith and commitment. The gold and precious stones making up the guard, grip, and pommel had been blessed during Israel's then-darkest hour with the promise that it would forever join man with what the blade represented, that only through the hilt could man be joined with and wield the Sword to offer protection.

It was made of gold, the most malleable of metals, to be reshaped to complement the ever-changing sword and style. It was all Zoram had left of his father's sword, and he accepted the challenge and responsibility that seemed to emanate from the sole remnant of the previous generation's Sword.

Zoram rubbed his fingers over the broken metal still housed inside the hilt. It was smooth, a clean break unlike anything he had ever seen before. There was no part of the blade protruding above the hilt's small, flat guard. It was a strange place for the metal to sheer off at and an even stranger direction. The natural direction for the metal to break was along the length of the blade, due to the forward direction at which the super-heated iron was hammered and shaped. But as he examined it more closely, Zoram could see that this fracture was completely horizontal and without even a jagged edge to reveal the metal's grain. It was very peculiar. Very peculiar, indeed.

On his way out, he informed the pair of guards standing as sentinels that he had taken the hilt and that he was heading to the armory to begin work on the new Sword. They both came to attention to pay Zoram the respect and honor that his title and calling both demanded and deserved. He was tempted to send one of the guards to fetch his satchel from his family's estate, but the contents were too precious to risk it to anyone else's care. The temptation to open it would simply be too great.

With an urging borne of righteous anticipation, he left the treasury and made his way to his estate with haste. Entering without announcement and with full purpose of heart, he retrieved the heavy leather satchel without being seen—the household was still in mourning and adjusting to its new master. Hefting the bag over his shoulder, the heavy steel inside felt remarkably light, as if the metal itself knew the time had finally come. He would now fulfill his destiny, and where fear and hesitation might have weighed upon other men's hearts, Zoram thought his would burst with exhilaration. Nothing else mattered to him right now.

Zoram reached the armory as the late afternoon sun cast long shadows across the palace. The armory was located near the treasury, and in no time, it seemed, he was standing in the antechamber facing the large wooden door. Behind it, he knew, held the means and tools to work his craft and fulfill his destiny. He was suddenly immersed in memories of accompanying his father inside, listening as his father told of his love of metals and fires. His father had shown him the purpose of the many tools a sword smith relied on. Zoram had an odd impression of being eight years old again, letting go of his father's hand so he could use the key and open the door to the room that had played such an important role in his family. That same key now rested in his pocket.

He announced his intention to the guard, who watched him in awe as he produced the key Laban had given him—his father's key, *his* key—and pushed open the heavy, wooden doors. A warm breeze flooded over him, bringing with it, over the musty smell of disuse, the scents of the trade. He breathed it in, savoring every trace. Today he was finally embarking on his own life's work, realizing the very reason for his existence, the test of his insight and passions, breathing life into his creation, and thereby into a city and a people who so desperately needed it.

The Keeper's armory and forge, like the treasury, were set apart and consecrated for a special and vital purpose and used only by the Keeper of the Sword—the military had its own forges and armories to meet its warfare needs. It was here that fire and metal and prayer merged to create something greater than simply a combination of the three. Here, the fires burned hotter than most men could imagine, hot enough to burn the flesh off a man's hand before the pain even registered. The forge would stoke a fire that burned without flame to molten even the strongest metals.

It was here, in the bowels of the hearth and forge, that a mixture of metals, the finest and purest, were cast and shaped by the muscle and will of the smith, heated and hammered in seemingly endless repetition until the sword began to take shape; it was where the master's skills were put to the test with each blade. But to the Keeper of the Sword, this process was partial and incomplete. Sword smiths were common enough in any kingdom. Even those who believed they were doing the work of their king, or even their gods, lacked the generations of sacrifice, commitment, and dedication that the Keepers perpetuated in faith and devotion.

The Keeper of the Sword was a simple title for a complex man and position. He was required to strike the balance between being warrior and priest where other men had failed. His was more than just a custodial role. Yes, he had responsibilities and answered to the king and to the people, but more importantly, he ultimately answered to God. The reality of the words dispensed by prophets and holy men and women of God had sunk deep into Zoram's mind and heart, and he did not just simply *believe* them; he *knew* them to be true and had lived his life by them.

But until this moment, his life's preparation had always been idealistic and somewhere in the future, something a young boy dreamed about and found comfort in during long and lonely nights. The armory was exactly as he remembered it. It was here, from his earliest recollections, that he had spent time with his father, identifying the tools he would someday wield, learning their names and how to properly use them, being groomed for the life he was destined to live.

He paused again and breathed in deeply, taking in every scent and essence. From the ash and residue from the hearth to the impurities burned out of the iron, leaving the pure metal to be shaped—it was all flooding back to him. Zoram stepped farther inside, brushing his fingers over the stone fireplaces and the iron anvil marked with nearly a century of scoring from the Keepers of past generations, giving it almost a personality of its own. On the tables were the hammers and tongs and chisels that, he suddenly realized, were probably last touched by his father. It was a connection across time and even life and death. He reached out, took one of the heavy leather gloves, and tried it on. His father's hands had been bigger and thicker than Zoram's, the result of a lifetime of exacting and rigorous work. The gloves extended up the arm to nearly the elbow to protect it from the white-hot flame and blasting heat. He could still feel the first time hot sparks had landed on his forearm and the panic he'd experienced until his father's blackened hands brushed them off his young skin and with them any pain or fear. His father could always make whatever troubled him better. He had that way about him.

Zoram closed his eyes. He could still feel the heat from the fires and hear his father's voice calling to him and lovingly enlisting his help. They were fond memories that now served to relax the last of fears that always preceded undertaking any forging. But especially this one.

Zoram missed him intensely.

He removed and replaced the gloves where he had found them on the table and then walked to the central hearth and oven. The stones and bricks were quiet and cool to the touch.

That was all about to change.

He could feel the muscles in his arms beginning to tighten, and his lower back seemed to ache in anticipatory protest for what he was going to force them to do.

Zoram stepped from the armory into the anteroom. The posted sentries snapped to attention. "If you will," he asked one of them, "I have a task I would ask of you."

The guard was honored. "You have but to ask, Keeper."

Zoram explained what he needed and when it was to be delivered. He had the guard repeat it back to him to ensure the man understood exactly what was required. The timing was critical.

"Sir, it will be done," he said and then was off.

Zoram watched him go for a moment then returned his attention to his surroundings and the place he would call home for the next . . . He couldn't finish his thought. There was no way to tell how long it would take. It would take as long as it took. It appeared that he had every tool and supply he would need. His father had kept the forge well stocked and prepped for Zoram's return.

"I'm not to be disturbed," he instructed the remaining palace guard, "for any reason. Do I make myself clear?"

"But what about food and water?"

"I said any reason. I'll be fine. Can you handle that and see to it that the next watch is also informed and clear on this request? I must not be disturbed."

The guard looked puzzled. "But what of the—"

"Have it left outside the doors. I'll come for it when I'm ready."

"Of course, Keeper."

And with that final instruction, the heavy doors were closed.

Rectangular windows had been cut into the top of one of the walls to let in natural light as well as to provide ventilation and fresh air. They were also angled in such a way as to remove a direct line of sight from the outside world and prevent anyone from spying. The work that was done in this forge was sacred and not for the merely curious or the insistent.

Zoram waited until he heard the door latch lock before opening the satchel. He reached inside and pulled out its heavy contents: a singular brick of metal roughly a span long and half a span wide and thick. Holding it up in the light, Zoram could see the several layers of different metals fused together one on top of the other. The brick, or billet, was smooth and perfectly shaped in preparation for its singular and unique purpose. Like all sacrifices worthy of the Lord, it was the finest, the firstlings of the flock, without blemish. The metal was perfect. No step was skipped or process rushed. Every detail of its creation was attended to with meticulous attention. For all intents and purposes, it was perfect.

Zoram took one last moment to simply behold the metal billet of his creation. He marveled that this was, perhaps, the most unusual and extraordinary alloy in all the world. His had been an unsurpassed spiritual journey just to fashion the metals and bring them home to Jerusalem, and he was eager to complete his life's design.

Zoram reached for his father's fire plow. He had used one similar during his time away, but there was something familiar, something inviting about using the instrument his father and his father's father had used to create the elemental force that made their work possible—fire.

The long, grooved length of wood was charred and worn nearly through; it would have to be replaced soon. A fire plow produced hot coal by pushing a stick of hard wood along a groove cut into a plank of soft wood. Zoram could only hope it had one last fire left in it. Taking the stick made from the branch of an almond tree and cut and shaped to a dull end, he began running it along the groove in the cedar plank in a plowing motion, over and over and faster and faster until black dust—coal dust—began to form and smoke at the base of the groove. Zoram quickly reached for a small bundle of tinder, about the size and look of a bird's nest, and tapped the smoldering coal dust into the center of the dry twigs and needles. He gently blew across the tinder, feeding the emerging flame with the fresh air it needed to grow. His father used to whisper to it, speaking a psalm or two until the fire ignited, and while that had seemed silly to Zoram as a boy, he now understood his father's peculiar practice.

Was he any better? Could he do no less than call down the powers of heaven to commence his undertaking?

"God is our refuge and strength," he began, reciting a favorite psalm of his mother's, one she used to sing to him, "a very present help in trouble. He maketh wars to cease until the ends of the earth; he breaketh the bow, and cutteth the spear in sunder; he burneth the chariot in the fire. Be still, and know that I am God."

The thin wisp of smoke gradually grew in size until, with a crackle, a small flame erupted and the tinder was quickly consumed. He tossed the ball of young flame into the hearth and carefully tended to the growing fire. This is how it always started. From small and simple things truly are great things brought to pass.

He watched the fire for a minute or two, mesmerized by the exchange and dance of heat and flame. It was marvelous. It was miraculous.

He could feel the call of the flame.

And the answer of the metals.

It was time.

The Sword would wait no longer.

CHAPTER ELEVEN

Zoram couldn't feel his fingers. The strips of cloth tied around them did little to protect them from the biting wind and numbing cold. But still he willed them to open and take hold of the next rock ledge or handhold. The storm from the night before had left a thin covering of snow on the rock face, which made climbing it that much more difficult. But he was determined to find it. He knew it had been a sign, a gift from God, to comfort and compensate him on the night he learned of his mother's passing. He had to reach it; if it killed him, he would reach and see this fallen star.

He'd had to wait a few days for the right time to take his treacherous journey, and during that time he could think of nothing else. Even Wu Yien had noticed his preoccupation, and while Zoram did not like keeping the secret, he had decided not to tell anyone what he had seen nor of his plans to retrieve it. Finally the time came, and Zoram's resolve was as strong as it had ever been. There was no hesitation or doubt. How could there be?

He had volunteered to join a small band of priests headed to the village for supplies. They had left before the first signs of dawn. The early morning air was so cold that ice had formed between the stones in the courtyard. Zoram wasn't sure if his shaking was caused by the sudden drop in the temperature with the approaching winter or his nerves and anxious anticipation that today was the day. Either way, they had scarcely left for the village when he had excused himself, explaining he had forgotten a task that needed to be done that day and parted with his company, returning toward the monastery. As soon as he was out of sight, however, he took another route, veering from the worn pathway and making his way around the wide valley and up the side of the facing mountain. He had regretted the deception, but he knew it was necessary. Though leaving the monastery was not strictly forbidden—they were permitted to spend some time outside its walls—he knew that permission to scale the sheer cliff would never be granted. If he was discovered, he figured it was better in this instance to beg forgiveness. Furthermore, he had rationalized, whatever had hit that mountain was meant for him and him alone. No one else must know.

Besides, he thought as he made his way in the predawn darkness, what he had said wasn't entirely a lie—he did have *personal* work to complete that day—it just wasn't completely the truth either.

Despite the clear skies, the temperature hovered just below freezing, and the fierce wind seemed to pierce right through his wool coat and hat, chilling him to his very center. There were no trails to where he needed to go. He was forced to make his own pathways, but he was fortunate as he pressed on through the early morning hours to discover a natural cut in the rock that led him around the bowl-shaped curve in the mountain terrain. While he had made good time on the linear stretch of his quest, every seed of doubt he'd had since leaving the warmth and safety of his bed that morning began to take firm root, blooming into full-blown despair by early afternoon as he faced the almost vertical climb now before him.

The next few hours were perilous as he took hand- and footholds wherever they led him, trying to fight his physical exhaustion and stay aware of where he was on the mountain as he scaled and shifted on the cold, frozen rock.

Taking a short break on an outcrop of rock wide enough to allow him to rest, he massaged his arms and legs, which ached from the ceaseless climbing, to prevent them from cramping. Zoram checked the position of the sun. Judging by its angle in the sky and the shadows it cast, he estimated that nearly ten hours had passed since he had left. He had fallen behind schedule. He wasn't going to make it in time. He hadn't come prepared to spend the night on the cliff face. If he didn't find whatever it was soon, he may have just traded his life, as well as the hope of an entire generation, to chase a piece of fire that he now feared disintegrated when it hit the mountain. He wasn't even sure what he was looking for, but still there was this drive from deep within him to hunt for it, to find it, and know once and for all why he had been shown such a vision that night.

There were worse deaths than the one traded for pursuing your dream.

A faint tapping sound accompanied by a few scattered pebbles falling with intermittent irregularity caught his attention over the soft howl of the wind. In a horrifying instant, he knew what this was. Falling rocks and gravel—rock slides were common during the change of seasons and a real threat to life in the mountains. He scrambled to press himself against the mountain wall as close as he could. At that very instant, larger rocks and dirt cascaded down, pelting the spot he had only just been resting on. But his fate did not include a reprieve from peril. His hand, numb from the cold and exposure, lost its grip on the ledge above him. His feet scrambled to compensate for the lost hold, but they too lost traction with the sudden weight shift. He was falling!

Zoram panicked as the sensation of free falling sent a chill through his bowels and chest colder than anything the wind could produce. He spread his arms and legs out wide, instinctively trying to find a rock, a ledge, a cavity, anything to grab ahold of. Everything was happening so fast. His fingers dragged down the sharp, icy granite. Then he felt a sharp pain in his left hand. Immediately afterward, his right foot jarred to a sudden stop as the most excruciating pain spiked up his leg and into his hip. Zoram cried out, but it wasn't until a full beat later that his brain registered that he'd stopped his fall. He fought the sudden and instinctive urge to push away from the mountain and instead searched frantically for a hold to give him time to regroup. His fingers closed around a deep cut in the rock.

Immobile and safe for the time being, Zoram closed his eyes and focused on his breathing. Slow. Deep. In. Out. When his panic finally subsided, he opened his eyes and looked around. He had slid down the mountain eight or nine times his own height, almost twenty-five cubits, a distance that had taken him the last hour or more to traverse. His heart sank when he considered the time it would take to make up the progress the last few seconds had cost him. But it was what it was, and it did no good to wish it were otherwise. He looked down. His foot had found a crack in the rock not much wider than his sandal. Beyond that the face disappeared, curving underneath him. If he hadn't stopped here, he would have lost touch with the mountain and fallen to his death. He chanced another look above him. He had made his way up the rock face at an angle. From where he was, there was no obvious way up the mountain. To his left the small jut of rock quickly merged again with the smooth and impassable granite. Fortunately the ledge continued to his right, but it curved around the cliff face and out of sight. He had no idea how long it ran or where it led to, but he didn't really have a better option.

He inched along the rock fissure, ignoring the pain in his foot and his hand, willing himself to move. The rock was slick from the dusting of snow left over from the series of storms over the past couple of nights. He noticed that his left hand was leaving red streaks on the white speckled rock as he shuffled along. But, he thought with some humor, bleeding to death was the least of his problems.

The wind continued to scream down the valley, trying, it seemed, to pry Zoram from the mountain. He refused to let his guard down for even a moment, knowing that doing so was all it would take to send him falling the rest of the way to his death. Then, as he reached and rounded the bend in the rock, the wind suddenly died for all its fury, and the world around him was peaceful. In the absence of the bitter, whipping wind, he could now feel the warmth of the sun on his back, instantly thawing him and returning feeling to his frozen frame. Zoram closed his eyes and focused again on his breathing, letting himself relax while he stood there. When his thanks for this short respite had been silently expressed, he looked beyond the rock before his face, only to have his continued gratitude escape his lips.

Before him stretched out a natural shelf that looked like it had been hewn out of the face of the cliff. While it was small when compared to the vast mountains around it, the landing that was no more than five or six paces across might as well have been the Persian expanse. He stumbled toward the center and collapsed, total and complete exhaustion overtaking him. It was then that his muscles chose to complain and knotted up in pockets of pain along every stretch of his body. It was so sudden and so intense that Zoram, a strong grown man, began to cry. But his tears eventually blended with tears of joy and thanksgiving. .

He lay there, forcing his body to relax, stretching his back and other muscles. He envisioned each of them being infused with warmth and sunlight, pushing from the tendons and sinews the pent-up tension from the climb and the fall. When he was certain he wouldn't hurt himself, he sat up and looked out over the wide valley spread out before him. It was breathtaking. But before he could fully savor and take pleasure in the magnificent sight, he felt a sharp, stinging pain pierce the strips of cloth shredded but still wrapped around his hands. Instinctively he moved to relieve the pain and pulled out a jagged shard of rock. But as he was about to angrily toss it away he stopped, noticing that it was unlike any rock he had ever seen before. It was thin and rounded and concave on one side, like it had been chipped off some larger piece. The tip, however, thin and sharp, was not brittle in the least. He then noticed its weight. He had never known rock to be this heavy, this dense. In fact, if he didn't know better, he'd think that it was—

Zoram looked around. The ground was littered with pieces of this dark rock. He stood slowly and with great effort to get a better view. There were hundreds of them scattered everywhere. Then he saw it embedded in the granite wall about eye level. It was the source of these strange slivers—a blackened mass three times the size of his fist. Surrounding this strange rock were scorch marks consistent with the fire and impact he had seen a few nights back.

This was it. He had found it!

Zoram picked up one of the larger pieces from the ground and struck it against the larger rock still embedded in the mountain granite. He hit them together, and the sound it made confirmed what he was beginning to suspect but couldn't bring himself to believe. These were not rocks at all. These were pieces of metal.

But how does metal fall from the sky?

Zoram was puzzled. He had never heard of such a thing. It was impossible, and if he hadn't seen it with his own eyes, he never would have believed it. Unwrapping his hand, he reached out and touched the mass. The surface was smooth and ice-cold. The rock—if that's even what it was—had streaks or veins of a lighter material crisscrossing and running through it. It was extraordinary!

Removing a small hammer and pick from his shoulder bag, he began chipping at the rock around it. The granite was brittle and crumbled with little effort, allowing him to easily free whatever it was from the mountainside. It was heavy, like a brick of iron, and clearly metallic. It must have been molten or at least extremely malleable as it fell from the sky and smashed into the rock cliff. Which would also explain the scattered pieces, he thought.

Cradling the metallic mass in his hands, he looked across the valley, spotting the monastery looking small against the backdrop of the

Himavant Mountains. Then, in a single moment of clarity unlike anything he had ever experienced before, the purpose and timing of all of these events combined into one purpose. This place, so far away; the news of his mother, delayed to that night; unable to sleep and alone to witness the falling fire; even his slip and fall down the mountain—everything in his life had led him to this moment. He was sent not only to learn the skills to serve Israel and God but also to be given the material to fulfill this calling.

Truly, he thought with profound reverence and faith, great were the ways of our God.

Gathering up all of the pieces of metal his shoulder bag could hold, Zoram secured the leather strap over his neck and shoulder and began the treacherous journey home, confident that if God had led him to this place, He would see that he returned home safely, the bearer of this wonder and this mighty miracle.

खेपेर ओफ़ ष्वोर्द

Two weeks later, the heavy, thunderous sounds of horse hooves filled the central square, driving away the morning's peace like a vicious storm. The High Sadhus had only a minute's warning of the soldiers' arrival and quickly moved to protect the apprentices from any harm, secreting them away in an upper room behind one of the larger temples, instructing them to remain there and keep absolutely still. Zoram's curiosity and concern, however, were not so easily contained.

"Who are they?" he whispered.

Wu Yien shook his head. Then, with a devious smile to convey his intent, he said, "There's only one way to find out."

The others voiced strained and whispered objections, but Zoram and Wu Yien paid them no heed and carefully made their way back down to the temple. Donning oversized and hooded robes, the two friends joined the other monks in the main square.

The leader of the five-man envoy wore the colors and insignia of the Magadha Empire. Politics was not a subject spoken of in any great depth by the mountain priests. Theirs was a world of inner peace and solitude. The skills they taught and the religion they professed transcended the politics of men and empires. But the fact that their many questions weren't openly discussed hadn't stopped Zoram and Wu Yien from learning a great deal about the world in which they lived.

The Magadha Empire was one of sixteen kingdoms that made up the Mahājanapadas, or Great Countries. Their borders reached from the land of great rivers to the east to the foot of the Himavant Mountains, where their monastery was hidden. And while each kingdom was largely sovereign and independent, the Magadha assumed control over the lesser, weaker governments. The Magadha Empire had been ruled by many dynasties over the years. Neither Zoram nor Wu Yien knew much about the current dynasty, but what they had heard did not paint the rulers in a favorable or beneficial light. They were ruthless and not to be underestimated.

The leader of this unexpected and unwanted party expertly reined his horse around in a circle before easing his steed to stop and dismounting. He was a short man of a slight build, accentuated by his sharp, trimmed beard.

"Where is your master?" he demanded, casting his voice with all the authority his position offered him.

The crowd parted and let the High Sadhus pass. He walked with confidence and purpose. If he was frightened or concerned, he did not let it show. He stopped, towering a full head and shoulders above the little man, but instead of using his size to his advantage, the High Sadhus bowed instead.

"How might we be of service to the emperor?"

"A lunar phase has passed since a manifestation of the gods lit up the night sky and was seen throughout all of the empire. The emperor's shaman has declared it a sign from the Indra, the Sky Father."

"We have seen no lights or signs in the heavens."

"We have traced its path to these mountains."

The High Sadhus appeared genuinely concerned. "We often retire early. Events in the night sky are so often lost to us."

The delegate was becoming frustrated. "Perhaps someone else then? A night sentry?"

"With the protection of the mountains all around us, and living so far from others, we have no need for guards or watches."

"Indeed," the little man said, casting his eyes over the crowd gathered around him. "Then you won't mind if I inquire of the others. The noise it made could be heard for many miles and in far-off villages. Surely someone heard this thunder . . ."

Zoram's stomach turned over and over and knotted up in fear. They had all heard it that night. If it was learned that the High Sadhus was lying, he would be punished and the monastery torn apart looking for what Zoram had seen and found. He held his breath, waiting for the High Sadhus to give his reply.

"Of course," he said gently, gesturing his hand over the others. "We will be happy to oblige the emperor and his delegate. But I assure you, no one saw this sign you speak of."

Zoram breathed easier, for veiled in his words was the command that no one was to reveal the sounds and events of that night. But why? It didn't seem right for the High Sadhus to risk everything, even their very lives, to hide his suspicion that Zoram had seen more than he was willing to admit that night. And then another thought struck him. Did the High Sadhus know he'd found something? Could he have found out that he had not traveled with the others to the village and had instead gone off in search of the very object that the Magadha emperor now sought? These new thoughts troubled Zoram.

If the Magadha emissary suspected the High Sadhus was lying or withholding information, he made no sign of it. His parting words, however, weighed heavily on Zoram's mind.

"Your continued loyalty to the Vedas is felt to the highest levels of government," he said as he mounted his horse. "But the emperor is fully aware that loyalty can be expressed in *other* ways. This sign from Indra is of great interest to him, to all of us, and any news of its sighting or whereabouts would be handsomely rewarded."

The delegate paused to let his words settle on the ears of those present. "But, of course, what is a small fortune to men of faith and devotion such as yourselves?"

With a call to the men, they left the monastery as loudly and as disrespectfully as they had arrived. No one spoke or even moved until the last sounds of their horses had faded and blended with the silence of the mountains. Wu Yien nudged Zoram. "Why do you think he lied like that? I mean, I didn't hear anything, but it was all everyone talked about for days. You said you heard it, right? What do you think it was?"

Zoram didn't trust his tongue to keep his secrets, so he kept silent. Had he done the right thing by not sharing what he had seen that night or, more importantly, what he had found? He had been so sure before, but now he doubted his deceptions and clandestine activities. If it was discovered that the High Sadhus had deceived the Magadha emissary, Zoram feared the worst—not just for the monastery and Sadhus, but for all of them.

Wu Yien, apparently not satisfied with Zoram's uncharacteristic silence, took him by the arm and led him to a back alcove where they could be alone.

"Hey!" Wu Yien whispered. "You saw something, didn't you?"

Zoram couldn't hide his shock. "No, why would you say that?"

"Do you take me for a fool? Just look at you. You may be able to deceive everyone else, but not me. I know you too well. Besides," he said with a mischievous grin, "you've never been a good liar. The truth comes too easily to you."

Zoram didn't know what to say, so he did the wise thing, remembering one of the proverbs of David—he that keepeth his tongue keepeth his life—and turned away.

"Look, if you don't want to tell me, I'll respect that—I'm your friend first and foremost. But as your friend, I stand ready to share any burden that might be yours. I can only hope you would be as persistent with me if the roles were reversed."

Wu Yien held Zoram's gaze with a serious and solemn look, communicating his sincerity and resolve to stand by his friend; then he broke into another grin.

"What?" Zoram asked, his own seriousness and burden suddenly interrupted.

"Nothing," Wu Yien replied. "I'm just dying to know, that's all. You know me well enough to know I don't handle curiosity well. I've got to know. What did you see?"

Zoram smiled. "And all that about respecting my decision not to tell you . . . ?"

"It sounded good, didn't it? You know, for a moment even I believed what I was saying." Wu Yien laughed.

Though Zoram joined his friend in a jovial chuckle, he still wasn't ready to confess and voiced the question pressing heavily on his mind instead. "Do you think anyone will speak up?"

Wu Yien considered the question for a moment. "Our masters are nothing if not loyal, but only a fool would underestimate the power greed has over the hearts of otherwise good and honest men. Kingdoms have been traded for a mere handful of riches."

"And birthrights sold for pottage," Zoram said thoughtfully, recalling the story of Esau and Jacob. Wu Yien was right. Human nature, the natural man, was a difficult force to contend with and overcome, and in a moment of weakness, even the most faithful and steadfast can fall. It was foolish to hope or think otherwise. And if—no, he thought—*when* news of the fallen star surfaced and made its way to the Magadha emperor, Zoram would need all the help and support a trusted friend could offer.

"Come with me," Zoram said, grateful for his friend's excitement and insistence. "There's something I need to show you."

Zoram quickly ushered his friend inside his quarters and placed a heavy stone at the foot of the door. Though all of the apprentices were given their own quarters, none of the doors was fashioned with locks or bolts. The feeling among their masters was that, while they acknowledged the need for privacy and solitude, locks on doors only invited secrets and division.

Zoram then moved to the window and secured the vertical wooden shutters. Confident they were alone, Zoram knelt at the wall at the foot of his bed and began carefully prying one of the stones free.

"It was already loose when I took the room," Zoram explained. "It would seem that all men have a need to keep secrets. Even here."

Wu Yien watched intently. "I may have to check my walls more closely."

Zoram pulled the large piece of the wall free; retrieved his shoulder bag, weighted heavily by its contents; and set it on his bed.

"What's this?"

Zoram took a deep breath to gather his courage. "Do you remember the night we were talking? I had just received a letter from home."

"With news of your mother's passing. You shared that with me. I'm so sorry."

"I couldn't sleep, so I spent a good part of the night reflecting on the toll this apprenticeship and these years away from home have had on me . . . and my family. I didn't know what to do. I felt that I was at a crossroads. Should I stay and continue my training or return home to what was left of my family? My heart was full of questions and doubts. The moment I had exhausted my reasoning and had almost given up all hope, something suddenly lit up the entire night sky, breaking through the clouds, as bright as the sun." Zoram was animated as he shared the story for the first time. "It had a trail of fire, and then, as quickly as it had appeared, it smashed into the side of the mountain across the valley. Moments later the noise from the crash filled the air and shook the ground.

That's when everyone awoke and ventured outside to see what it was, but by then the night was again dark and the clouds and snow had covered up any sign of the impact."

Wu Yien stepped closer to the bag on the bed. "And this?"

"I sneaked away one morning last week and nearly died making my way up the face of the mountain in search of . . . whatever it was I saw. In the end, I found this."

Zoram opened the flap and turned the bag upside down, spilling the charred metal and shards into the light for his friend to see.

Wu Yien cautiously reached out and picked up one of the smaller pieces. "What is it?"

"I don't know," Zoram admitted. "Best I can tell, though, it has the feel and weight of iron. At least one of the other, bigger pieces has traces of some other metals running through it."

"Incredible," Wu Yien whispered. "And you say this fell from the sky?"

"The granite was scorched around where it was embedded in the rock. And look at these pieces. This metal was superheated, like what we do in a forge, then cooled. See? It has the shape and feel of molten metal."

Zoram held one of the medium-sized pieces up to the light filtering through the wooden window slats. "I believe it came from God."

"For you, in your role as Keeper of the Sword," his friend acknowledged.

"And so you see why I must protect it at all costs." Zoram handed him the piece of metal. "You asked to know what secret I held. Now I have a request of you. Will you help me keep it safe?"

Wu Yien accepted the metallic rock with reverence. "Great must be your God to cause it to rain iron and other metals from the heavens. And you say that no one else knows of this?"

"I believe the High Sadhus suspects I did not share everything I had seen that night, but he has not approached me or asked about it."

"Then you have nothing to fear," Wu Yien said, offering the lump of metal back, "because I will go to the grave with this secret . . . on one condition."

"Condition?"

"When do we start?"

"Start what?"

"The process of turning what you have into something your God can use. We will turn this into the finest steel the world has or will ever see."

While the thought of his help appealed to him, Zoram was also concerned by his friend's enthusiasm. "I can't ask you to risk your placement or possibly your life with this."

"You can't *not* ask me at this point. Besides, we're friends, and what good is a friendship without the sense of shared danger? Admit it, you need me. You may be unparalleled at forging and fashioning the actual blade, but you'll need my help smelting, extracting, and purifying the metal." Wu Yien leaned in closer and lowered his voice. "What's more, I've learned of a new carbon compound to fuse with the iron ore in the production of the steel. I've experimented with it already, and I promise that you've never seen such a result as I have created."

Wu Yien leaned back. "Think about it; your God sends you to this place, a world away from the deserts your people call home, to learn steel and sword making. He also blesses you with talents unsurpassed by any other apprentice before and quite possibly after." Zoram started to protest, but Wu Yien held up his hand. "No, hear me out. And then he sends a letter to you the very night he causes this . . . wonder to fall from the sky. And then above all, if he hasn't done enough to prove that he truly is a great god, he sends me to be your best friend." Wu Yien flashed another one of his charming and somewhat mischievous smiles. "The way I see it, to refuse my help is to refuse your God's carefully scripted plan for you."

Zoram expected a hint of sarcasm in the words, but there was none. He was serious.

"And it would be my honor to help you and offer what skills I possess to accomplish this great task set before you by your God."

Zoram felt a burning within his heart. He couldn't refuse the offer, and the two of them started right away.

ख़ेपेर ओफ़ ष्वोर्द

Wu Yien was correct. Zoram did need his help and expertise in taking what the Lord had given him and turning it into something he could actually use. The process and practice of extracting the ore and separating it from the rock was well known to them. However, the material that Zoram had recovered was unlike any other source of ore he had ever encountered before. Once the material was superheated in the forge, Zoram and Wu Yien realized that some of what they'd both thought was iron was, in fact, another mineral altogether. And while it separated from the iron ore under intense heat, this other material—whether rock or metal, they couldn't tell—refused to completely detach from the iron. It was as if the elements that made up this strange metal refused to be divided asunder. The rock's strange behavior only served to encourage their finest efforts to smelt this unusual iron.

Iron, they knew from their years of training and instruction, was best produced at high altitudes where the air was thin. Zoram had always suspected that it was no coincidence that their mountain monastery was built where it was. And while their elevation aided in the production of the finest and purest iron, and consequently the strongest steel, it also proved difficult to keep the fires burning hot enough to sustain the incredible heat needed to smelt the ore. But their masters had overcome this potential problem with the design of their forge.

The central forge was a marvel of ingenuity and skill. Most forges were of similar design and construction the world over, but the one at the monastery was, as far as Zoram and Wu Yien could determine, unique. Like the hearths the young men had both seen in their homelands, this one was shaped in a semicircle to better keep and intensify the heat from the fire. But where this forge differed from others was the hole in the center of the hearth beneath the coal, where air was blown into the heart of the fire. Produced by a fan that was cranked by hand, the air passed up through this passageway, superheating the coal beyond its burning point, transforming it into the hard, porous rock called coke. It was this fuel that burned hot enough to melt metal. It was a blistering, unpleasant process, but the two friends took to the task under the cover of night with a greater purpose in their hearts that seemed to cool their minds and their bodies.

By sunrise the next day they had created a brick, or billet, of this strange mixture of metals that had fallen from the sky. But this accomplishment, as great as it was, was only part of the process of turning the iron into what they had been sent to learn, what the monastery was famous for from one end of the world to the other—steel.

The creation of steel, or what the Sadhus called *urukku* in their native language, was the deliberate and careful process of introducing other elements into the pure and smelted iron. This was the secret of transforming common iron, used the world over, into steel—unknown to all except the rare few willing to pay to learn its secrets. Zoram's masters mixed the iron with purified charcoal to make the hardened steel, but Wu Yien proposed they add something else. He held out a small leather pouch.

"What is it?" Zoram asked.

Wu Yien opened the small leather pouch and removed a pinch of a fine black powder. "The locals that mine it call it *mashim-kri*, meaning *black rock*."

"Is it coal dust?" Coal was sometimes ground up and used in the creation of lower quality steel.

Wu Yien shook his head. "They mine it like coal, and in fact, they once thought that's what it was, except it doesn't burn. Here, feel it." He poured a small amount into Zoram's hand. "It's smooth. There's almost no grit to it. The locals were using it to make black dyes, and it was only by coincidence that I observed the black rock powder and inquired as to its origin. Which got me thinking . . ."

Zoram was intrigued by the feel and composition of this black powder. It felt slippery, like oil, as he rubbed his finger across it, but it was clearly dry. "What possessed you to mix this with iron?"

Wu Yien cracked a smile. "I'll try anything once. Besides, when have I ever settled for being like everyone else or content with just doing what I'm told?"

"And you say you've already attempted it?"

Wu Yien reached to the small of his back and produced a small dagger. "It's not as well made as something you could do, but feel that edge. Look at the grain. And you should see it in the sunlight—it flashes between a reflection of silver and jet black, like it can't make up its mind what color it is."

Even in the lamp and fire light of the forge, Zoram could see that the steel was exquisite.

"Go ahead," Wu Yien urged. "Try to dull the edge or break off the tip. Whatever this black rock is, it makes the hardest steel I've ever seen."

Zoram didn't hesitate and jabbed the knife into the stone kiln as hard as he could. When he pulled it back and examined it, there wasn't even the smallest dent or indentation on the tip. There wasn't even a scratch on it.

"Truly," was all Zoram could say.

खेपेर् ओफ़ ष्वोर्द

They labored in secret over the next few nights, working through meals or staying late to finish their secret, and to Zoram *sacred*, work. They took their time, adding the black rock powder in precise measurements to their molten iron and other metals, eventually casting it into a billet of most unique steel.

But as amazing as their finished product was, Zoram was not yet satisfied with their work. There was one more level of steel-making that he felt compelled to achieve in the pursuit of a product worthy of his God and His people—a level that involved wresting from their masters' secrets that were forbidden to foreign students and apprentices. He would have to convince the High Sadhus to break the oath and make an exception. And he would not—could not—take no for an answer.

The High Sadhus was a man of great mystery and respect among all the masters and instructors at the monastery. He was regarded as a learned master in the arts of metallurgy and sword making as well as an artist and accomplished master of the blade and its uses. He was also looked to as the spiritual leader and guide. With his simple robes and quiet demeanor, he was both the letter *and* the spirit of their law.

In all his years since arriving as a child, Zoram had never had the opportunity to speak with him privately. Their relationship was one from afar, and until recently, when his blade-making skills caught the High Sadhus's attention, the day he had received the letter from his father, he had never spoken a direct word to him. Thus he was surprised when the great master agreed to see him.

Zoram was ushered into the High Sadhus's quarters. Where most leaders of men lived "above" those they lead or command, with displays of wealth and privilege others can't afford, Zoram was surprised to find that the High Sadhus lived and slept in a room identical to his and the other apprentices'. But where Zoram's walls were in large part bare, the High Sadhus's walls were decorated with charcoal drawings on parchments of the mountains and monastery from afar. And these were not simple sketches. The master's attention to detail and lifelike renditions gave Zoram pause. He noticed there were more in a small pile on the foot of the bed. The one on top immediately and forcefully caught his attention. It showed the mountain across the valley, the very spot where the falling star had hit. It was incomplete, and Zoram suspected that it was the most current work.

He must know!

Zoram hoped that his reaction to the sketch had gone unnoticed, but he knew, now more than ever, that the High Sadhus missed nothing.

The High Sadhus rose to meet him. "Ah, young master Zoram, it is good to see you."

Zoram bowed deeply and remained bent until he noticed the gesture was returned.

"To what do I attribute this honor that one of our finest young students has need to call on an old man?"

Zoram was more than a little intimidated by the close, one-on-one presence of his master. "With age comes knowledge," he started. "With knowledge comes wisdom; and with wisdom comes enlightenment."

The High Sadhus just smiled, pleased with his answer. "You are a good boy, Zoram of Je-ru-saa-lum. Did I pronounce it correctly?"

"You do me great honor in even remembering the name of my home."

"We occasionally hear stories, carried on the trade routes, of the lands of the West."

"Are they much different from the lands of the East?"

The High Sadhus pondered the question longer than Zoram expected, which only added to his nervousness.

"We hear of wars and rumors of wars, of empires coming to power and crumbling under the weight of their own pride and greed. But we also hear of good men striving to live their faith, men who sacrifice much to bring about change." The High Sadhus held Zoram's gaze for a beat. "No. There is no difference. Men are the same in any corner of the world."

Zoram bowed slightly. "I am honored and blessed by your wisdom."

The High Sadhus held up his hand. "Please, I am not one to be honored or praised. I am but a servant, an old man who finds great joy in the simple beauty all around him."

Zoram looked around his sparse quarters, acknowledging the many drawings and artistic impressions captured on scraps of parchment. "They are beautiful."

The High Sadhus smiled pleasantly. "Do you like them? The time I spend with them fills my life with an added measure of peace. Sometimes they express what is . . ." He reached for the unfinished one and looked at it longingly. "Other times they reveal what only the mind's eye can see."

Zoram hesitantly accepted the sketch from the High Sadhus. Unsure what to do next, he looked more closely at the charcoal images and shapes. Lightly drawn on the parchment, almost too light to be seen in the dim light, was the unmistakable streak crossing the skies and an impact site on the face of the mountain Zoram knew all too well.

"But I hide my works away," the High Sadhus continued, gently taking back the sketch, "and seldom show them to others. These are very personal. To me, they are sacred."

Zoram didn't know what to say, and the two of them stood in silence for a long moment. If he'd had any doubts as to what the High Sadhus knew, they were gone in that instant. Whether the High Sadhus had seen with his own eyes, intuitively knew, or had pieced it together from the events and accounts of that night, there was no doubt that he was aware that something had, indeed, fallen from the sky. But Zoram also knew that this knowledge would be forever safe and secure from anyone else who might seek it. But— "Why? Why would you risk so much to keep this secret with me?"

The old man smiled warmly, kindly, and with a sincere heart. "Because whatever fell from the sky was not meant for me or anyone else here. It was meant for you, and the universe conspired to ensure its delivery to you and no one else. You see, a gift taken that was not meant for you quickly becomes a curse. And when the gods bestow a gift of this magnitude, of this infinite value, it becomes the honor of honest men to see that both gift and receiver are cared for so that their entwined destinies can be written and fulfilled."

The High Sadhus lit the corner of the unfinished sketch with the small table lamp, placing it into a bowl as it quickly caught fire and turned to ash. "This is your *dharma*."

"My *what*, great sir?"

"Your dharma, your purpose, your destiny. It falls upon every man, wherever he may live, to seek out and fulfill his dharma. A man's dharma is comprised of three journeys."

Zoram listened intently.

"The first journey is to discover one's relationship to deity; to become aware that we are all spiritual beings, inseparably connected to a god and to one another. The second journey we must each undertake follows the truth that each of us possesses unique talents and skills, unlike anyone else in the entire world. Firm in knowing who you really are, it becomes the obligation of every man to then seek out and develop these talents."

"And the third?"

The High Sadhus smiled. "The third journey is to find and express ways in which you may use your talents in the service of others. It does no good to develop talents to hide them away for your own selfish pleasure. We must each ask how we can help, and in what ways we may serve the gods who give us and all mankind life. This is the law of dharma."

The High Sadhus peered deep into the Zoram's soul. "So I ask you, young Zoram from Je-ru-saa-lum, how might I be of service?" There was a glint of excitement and anticipation in his eyes, not unlike Wu Yien's eyes, as he looked up, awaiting an answer.

Zoram's fears dissipated, a feeling of relief and anxious exhilaration flooding his heart and mind. God had spoken to the heart of this great man, and Zoram immediately did what he had come here to do. He swiftly dropped to one knee before his master. "Teach me the way of folding Wootz steel."

"Wootz?" The High Sadhus cocked one eyebrow. "And where have you heard this word before?"

"Forgive me, Great Master, but my ears have heard of this, the greatest of steel, from the whispers of others."

"Indeed." The venerable teacher couldn't help but crack a smile.

"Teach me that I might fashion a sword to serve and honor the very God who sent this miracle to me. Help me to reach the full measure of my creation."

The High Sadhus thought for a moment then reached out his old hand and placed it on Zoram's shoulder. It was calloused and strong. "Great must be your God. It will be my honor to help you serve Him along your journeys." He took a deep breath to make the commitment. "So let it be done."

CHAPTER TWELVE

"YOU WANTED TO SEE ME, my lord?"

Laban looked up from his table littered with the picked-over remains of the midday's meal. He had eaten his fill but had only put a small dent in the elaborate and gluttonous spread prepared by his kitchen staff.

"Ah, Anat! Please come in!" He dismissed his servants and motioned for her to join him. "Please. Have you eaten?"

Anat was nervous responding to the summons. She had not spoken to Laban for a number of years, and memories of that time of her life were not pleasant ones. He had made it clear that he never wanted to see her again, so when she received word that he wanted to meet, her thoughts raced as she tried to conceive of any possible reason he would want to see her. So much so that she had made herself sick. "No, thank you."

"Then some wine, perhaps?"

She shook her head.

"Please?" Laban gave her an imploring smile. "This will all go to waste if someone won't share it. No?"

Struggling to contain her thoughts, she blurted out a single word before she could stop herself. "What—?"

Laban continued to smile at her. "Do I want? You always were one to speak your mind and get right to the point, weren't you?"

"I'm sorry, my lord. Sometimes I don't—"

"Think before you speak?" Laban took another bit of the roasted fowl. "That never was one of your strengths, was it?"

"Laban, I'm sorry. I didn't mean—"

Laban held up his hand to stop her. "No, Anat. I'm the one who should be sorry. I didn't ask to see you so we could dig up the past. What happened, happened, and there are certainly no regrets on my end as I hope there are none on yours. Will you forgive me?"

Anat could not hide her shock at the apologetic words that had just spilled out of Laban's mouth. Was it possible that he had changed during these past few years? Had the mantle of Keeper of the Records brought with it a maturity and perspective that now allowed him a measure of understanding and compassion? Maybe she had been wrong to judge him as harshly as she had. They had both been much younger then. Perhaps time did heal all wounds.

She was speechless but returned his smile with a timid one of her own and nodded.

"Good. Now, if you're sure you will not eat, will you at least sit while we talk?" He motioned to the oversized and lavish divan against the wall.

"Of course. And if the offer still stands, I think I will have some wine."

Laban poured her a glass and joined her on the couch. "So, how are your parents?"

Anat was taken aback by the question. What did he care about her parents? What did anyone care about them? "Mother is slowing with age," she said, feigning concern, "but her health is still good."

"I have always believed that your father bakes the finest breads in all of Jerusalem. He is a skilled artisan."

"Artisan?" She couldn't help but scoff at the compliment. "Thank you. I will tell him you said so." She had no intention of doing so.

An uncomfortable silence followed, and Anat was worried that he knew she was estranged from both of her parents and would likely never see them again. She feared that this had been some kind of test of integrity and that she might have failed. His next words, however, put this fear to rest and raised even more alarming ones.

"I saw you last night at the Keeper's funeral. You were standing with the family. I wasn't aware you were close to them."

Anat looked down and started to unconsciously fidget with the hem of the pillow on her lap. Did Laban know of her plans? Were they that transparent? She reined in her fears and cleared her throat. "Miriam and I met years ago. She was always kind to me, and we grew close to one another. She was a good woman."

"And when she died," Laban said, "her husband was left alone . . ."

Anat shot Laban a sudden look of contempt and disgust. "It was nothing like that!"

"No, of course not."

"Jharom was honorable and caring and held up remarkably well during her long illness. He was a *source* of strength and comfort to those around him, not a recipient."

"Yes, yes, I knew him well. He was like a father to me as well. Such a tragedy that he died on the night before his son's return. A pity, really. And how is Zoram . . . *holding up?*"

Anat wasn't sure where this question was leading and just looked at him suspiciously.

"I mean, first he receives news of his mother's passing—I assume Jharom sent word to . . . *wherever* he was. And then to know that he was one day late in reuniting with his father. He must be devastated."

Anat wasn't sure she liked where Laban was going with this. "I suppose."

"You are living in his estate, are you not?"

"He didn't return home yesterday," she said, almost apologetically. Laban betrayed a brief look of concern, mixed with . . . fear? "We learned that he locked himself inside the armory yesterday afternoon and hasn't yet emerged."

"Has he, now?" Laban looked as if in deep thought. "Is he not aware that his time of mourning prohibits work such as this?"

"Why does it matter if he—"

"Why?" Laban interrupted. "He's the next Keeper of the Sword and my counterpart in this most holy calling. I need to know that he is grieving and accepting the loss of his parents. I need to know that he's going to pull through, that he's strong and able to perform his duty when the time comes. If there has ever been a time that Israel needed a symbol of strength and resolve, it is now."

"But why do you ask me? You will see him and associate with him more than I will."

Laban got up and went to the table to pick at his meal. "A man puts on a strong face when in the presence of other men. To be honest, I'm worried about him. These next few days are critical to his emotional recovery. He needs to rest. He needs time to cope with his tragic loss. He needs someone he can turn to, someone who will care for and look out for him. He needs someone to spend time with him, to listen to him, to comfort him— someone who will let those who care about him know if he is showing any signs of overwhelming stress or behavior not considered appropriate during his *shinvet.*"

Anat may have been young, but she was not stupid. "You want me to *spy* on him?"

"No, no, no. Not spy on him. If that's how I communicated it, I'm sorry. No, I simply meant to make certain he takes the time he needs to grieve properly, that he doesn't attempt to return to his duties prematurely. We need to know we can count on him. And I'm not speaking just for myself. The body of the Sarim met this morning, and they share these concerns."

Anat almost choked on her drink at the mention of the ruling body of Elders. The Sarim was the real power at Jerusalem, made up of the wealthy, the aristocracy, the priest class, and the most influential families in all of Israel. Their official appointment was to sit in council with the king and his advisors, but for generations now, their words and wishes overruled even the king. What they decided was final; they *were* the law. Both Zoram's and Laban's families had served in the Sarim since even before accepting their callings as Keepers. If the Elders of the city were worried about Zoram, then maybe there was truth to Laban's concern.

"So," Laban continued after giving her a moment to consider the assignment, "will you help us?"

"Of course," she said, realizing how perfectly this task would fit within her own plans. "You have but to ask."

"Good," he said, refilling his goblet with wine and topping hers off. "You will report to me the doings of our young friend. I need to know that he is recovering. Go to him, comfort him, and know that you do all of Israel proud this day."

Anat raised her glass to meet Laban's when a sudden loud knock on the doorpost behind her startled her, causing the drink to slip from her hand.

"Excuse me," he said gently, picking up Anat's spilled cup. He then turned and stood at this full height, almost switching personalities as he called out in an authoritative voice, "Yes?"

A young man dressed in the uniform of the king's guard moved into the frame and stood at attention. "Laban, Keeper of the Records, the king requests an audience with you."

Anat watched as Laban eyed the palace guard closely. She sensed that it must have been unusual to be summoned in this fashion to the palace. Laban was not impressed or intimidated and quickly replaced his contempt with a pleasant look.

"Of course. Return and tell the king that I will attend to him as soon as I conclude my business here." He looked down and smiled at Anat, who weakly smiled back.

"With all respect, my instructions were for you to accompany me."

Laban walked to the table, replaced both cups, and picked at some of the food left from his meal. "Then you will wait."

The king's guard took a small step, venturing into Laban's quarters. "No, sir, I will not." He was then joined by two more guards similarly dressed, flanking him.

Anat could feel the tension that suddenly filled the room and glimpsed, again, the temper she remembered Laban possessing. The muscles in his jaw tightened, and his hand gripped his heavy brass cup. She held her breath, thinking he was about to throw it at the guard in protest, but Laban did no such thing. Instead he closed his eyes momentarily, inhaling deeply, and then set the cup of wine on the table.

He turned to Anat. "I do apologize for this interruption, but as the king beckons, I must obey. Thank you for taking the time to meet with me this afternoon. I will instruct my staff to come escort you out." He helped her to her feet. "Believe me when I say it was good to see you again after all these years. I hope that, between the two of us, we can help our young friend find the peace and happiness that awaits him."

שומר החרב

"Rebekah!" Hannah called out for the second time. "Are you even listening to me?"

Rebekah abruptly snapped out of her thoughts and returned to her work. Her sister rose from the table and looked over Rebekah's shoulder at her partially completed ledger. Though nearly two years younger, Hannah had long ago assumed a controlling role over Rebekah. In fact, all three of Rebekah's younger sisters treated her with disdain and disrespect. They all worked for their father, a man of impressive power and wealth who had caused no small stir and broken many traditional and social barriers by having his daughters do the work typically assigned to men. But as he was fond of telling them, and anyone else who asked, he was not one to raise a child—son *or* daughter—who didn't possess the skills necessary to contribute to their family and their society.

"Honestly," Hannah said. "You've been flighty, and your thoughts have been scattered all morning. You're behind on your reports, and you haven't even begun to fill your afternoon orders. I don't know what's wrong with you today."

"I do," Emalia said from the other side of the room. "She's in looooooove," stretching out the word in an obviously mocking tone.

"Ooh!" Eshel, the third sister, cried, laughing and giggling and adding her own insult.

"What is this?" Hannah said, feigning shock and surprise.

"I saw her with someone yesterday when she returned from the morning's lower-city run," Emalia reported.

"And was he there again, this morning?"

Emalia shook her head.

"Maybe it was just a coincidence, someone not walking *with* her, just *next* to her."

"Not the way he lingered."

"He lingered?" Eshel asked, astounded. "You mean, he actually *wanted* to talk to her?"

They all laughed.

"And he was carrying her cistern of oil," Emalia said.

"Well, there you have it," Hannah said, feigning disappointment. "It's not what you think at all. Rebekah simply hired a boy to help, who then waited around to get paid. Isn't that it?"

Rebekah lowered her eyes and refused to look at them. She knew enough not to be baited into an argument with them. She didn't want them to see how their teasing, even after all these years, still hurt and cut her to the very quick.

"No?" Hannah prodded. "That's not it? Then tell us. Who is this man you can't seem to take your thoughts off."

"Yes, yes. Tell us," Emalia said with a marked lack of sincerity.

Rebekah's sisters all paused to let her answer. The silence was heavy and made her sick to her stomach. Why was it that the ones she loved had the power to hurt her the most? She didn't speak. It really was none of their business. All three of them were of age and busy entertaining potential suitors. Was it so wrong that she wanted the same?

"So," Hannah started. "Tell us who has found interest in our Re-Re-Re—"

"Beh-Beh-Beh—"

"Kah-Kah-Kah," Eshel stuttered, finishing the taunt they had used more times than any of them cared to count since they were all little girls, from the time it became evident that their older sister wasn't going to simply outgrow her speech impediment. It had made her cry when she was young, but years of taunting had made her calloused to the insult. Today, however, the pain returned, this time running deeper.

"Come on," Emalia pleaded. "Who is he?"

"Did you say anything to him?"

"If you were smart, you just smiled and kept your mouth shut."

"Really, Rebekah," Emalia persisted. "I saw him from the upper window. Do we know him?" All three sisters looked at each other wondering for the first time if any of them might actually know this mysterious man in their sister's life.

"Well?" Hannah was done being polite, demanding an answer.

Rebekah looked up at each of them, searching for some remnant of kindness in their eyes, but there was none. There was only jealously and envy and disregard. She knew it was none of their business, and she wanted desperately to keep this small glimmer of happiness to herself, but she also knew she had to give them something. Their torment would be merciless. "I m-met—"

"In the market?"

"Is he wealthy?"

"Hush!" Hannah said sharply. "Let her finish."

Rebekah was grateful for the interruption. She had almost mentioned meeting him the other day in the hills outside of Lehi's estate but now thought it better to go with the story her sisters wanted to hear. She might be forced to share their encounter yesterday morning, but she would keep their first meeting forever in the secret recesses of her heart. She gathered up her resolve once again and tried to calm herself before speaking again.

She nodded. "Th-the m-market."

Emalia clapped her hands. "I knew it!"

"Whoever he is probably recognized you and saw a chance to marry into wealth and get out of the streets." Hannah rolled her eyes.

"And he helped you when you spilled half of the morning's revenue out of the kindness of his heart? Do you really think he loves you? Love requires friendship; friendship needs communication; and communicating, my dear sister, is not one of your strong points," Emalia said.

They all laughed, but Hannah eyed Rebekah carefully. "Why don't you spare yourself yet another heartbreak and just tell us the truth. He wasn't just some boy you met in the market, was he?"

Rebekah held her sister's harsh and condescending look as she decided what to say next. They wanted so desperately to keep her down. Maybe that was the only way they could feel good about themselves. It was sad and pathetic, and Rebekah felt sorry for them, just as she had their entire lives. Deep down she wished they would someday find peace in their lives. If they wanted to believe he was just a boy from the market, who was she to try to convince them otherwise? She didn't think Hannah would believe it if she admitted to it anyway. "Y-y-yes he w-w-w—"

"Save it. You and I both know your stutter gets worse when you lie. You'll never be good liar. So out with it. Who is he really?"

"Yeah," Emalia persisted. "What's his name?"

"Come on, tell us!"

They went the rounds over and over, teasing and prodding with intensity fueled by increasing frustration. As unpleasant as it was, Rebekah was not surprised at her sisters' behavior. It wasn't rare for her to be a source of jealousy. For reasons she couldn't understand, her sisters felt some compulsion to control her. When she was younger, she tried to tell herself that they were just being overprotective, that despite all the jabs and name-calling, they somehow, somewhere deep down, actually cared for her. And so she took the pain at their words, never totally abandoning her love for them. She owed the memory of their mother at least that much.

"I told you it was all in her head," Hannah scoffed.

"Give her more time," Emalia said. "Maybe her thoughts stutter worse than her tongue."

Eshel just laughed.

Other days and under different circumstances, Rebekah would be content letting them simply tire of their inquisitions and eventually leave her alone. But she had never felt this way before about anyone, not after what she had experienced that afternoon in the hills. Had it only been three days ago? She barely knew him, but she believed that what they had between them could be seeds of something much greater, and she was not going to stand by and let her sisters trample something so precious to her.

"Look, we can find out if we really want to," Hannah said, refusing to give up. "Surely there was someone in the courtyard or in the streets who saw you with him and knows his name." She leaned in and lowered her voice to just above a whisper. "And you also know that you don't want Emalia speaking to her friends about this. Just think what rumors they would spread. So just tell us. Tell me the name of this boy who occupies your mind and your heart so."

Rebekah's anger began to build. Hannah was right. They had all worked hard over the years to sabotage her happiness, and today was no exception. But if they were going to discover his name in any event, maybe it was better to control the situation the best she was able.

"Z-Z-Z—" Rebekah paused, took a deep breath to settle her conflicted feelings and calm her thoughts. "Z-Zoram."

Hannah and Emalia both were suddenly rendered speechless. Their mouths gaped open. Their younger sister, however, didn't recognize the name, and started on another round of teasing. "Z-Z-Zoram? Who's that?" Eshel quickly stopped when she saw the stunned looks on her sister's faces. "What? Do you know who she's talking about?"

"You're a liar," Hannah said to Rebekah.

"What are you talking about?" Eshel said. "Who is he?"

"Zoram, the son of Jharom," Hannah clarified, more as an accusation than any real clarification.

Emalia struggled with the words. "He's the new Keeper of the Sword."

"What?" Eshel exclaimed, looking sharply between Rebekah and her other sisters. "The Keeper . . . ? That's not possible . . . is it?"

All four of them remained silent for several long moments. Rebekah felt somewhat empowered and even a little proud of her announcement. She knew the rumors would start immediately and only hoped Zoram would understand. And though she tried to keep her feelings in check, she quite enjoyed the fact that, after all these years, it was her sisters who were now unable to speak.

Finally, Eshel couldn't take it anymore. "That's not fair!"

"It must be a mistake," Emalia agreed. "How would she have even met him? Her route doesn't even go near the upper city."

Hannah suspected there was more to the story. "How *did* you meet him?"

"She was planning this!"

"That sneak!"

"She was probably waiting for him to come home so she could—"

"So she could *what?*" Hannah interrupted. "Open her mouth and scare him off like all the others?"

"Maybe he just felt sorry for her."

"Yeah," Hannah agreed. "A gentleman showing pity on the p-p-poor stuttering girl."

Emalia and Eshel laughed, but Hannah kept her eyes firmly on their older sister. "Well, I never thought . . ." she said, just loud enough for Rebekah to hear.

"That's enough!"

The loud, commanding voice of their father put an abrupt end to the childish display. None of them had noticed him enter the back of the room.

"Hannah, what's going on here?"

"Nothing, Father."

"Nothing productive, I see that much. Is the morning's accounting complete?"

"No," Emalia started to explain. "Well, we were almost done, but then Rebekah—"

"Yeah," Eshel hastily added. "She interrupted and started ta—"

"Talking?" their father finished. "No doubt distracting you and taking you away from your work. Is that it?"

Eshel turned away, embarrassed.

"Hannah, see that your accounting is completed and turned into Joseph before the hour's end. Is there any reason this cannot be done?"

"No, Father."

"You are all smart and capable of this work," he said to all of them. "That's why you work for me. Or am I mistaken in this?"

They all hung their heads in shame.

"I said, *or am I mistaken?*" their father asked again. He was an imposing man with his large frame and full graying beard. He was kind, but he did command and demand respect.

"No, Father," they each said.

"Good. Rebekah? I will have a word with you. Hannah, see that her work is finished first."

"But—" Hannah started to protest but thought better of it. "Yes, Father."

"Thank you. Rebekah?" he said again, leading them through the house and out onto a small, private balcony. It had always been one of Rebekah's favorite places in the house. From here they could see the city spread out before them. Much of Jerusalem still lay in ruin from the Babylonian invasion nearly a year ago, and she wondered how it could ever be rebuilt.

But the sight before her had never stopped her from dreaming what it must have looked like when Israel was a free nation, when the world's emperors paid tribute to them and sought the wisdom of their One True God.

Across the valley, rising out of the filth and poverty of the lower city, stood the Temple. Built atop the mountain where Abraham was commanded to sacrifice Isaac, the House of the Lord was a constant reminder to both Jew and Gentile of His power and glory. A glory that she and others, including her father, prayed to live long enough to see again.

Her father's hand on her shoulder startled her and brought her back to the present. "Are you all right?"

"How m-much d-did you see?"

"Enough. You know they love you, don't you?"

She kept her eyes fixed on the city below. "Th-they have a funny way of sh-showing it."

Her father sighed. "I blame myself. I should have never given you so much responsibility over them when your mother died." He reached up and brushed her hair back out of her eyes. "You look so much like her. It's hard for me to see you and not feel that loss all over again. I still miss her."

Rebekah listened but didn't acknowledge her father's touch. "Y-you have D-Daniah."

"Yes, and I love her very much. She's been a great comfort to me these last few years. And though she has given me a daughter and another child on the way and has tried to make me happy, there remains a place in my heart for your mother. It's just . . ." He paused and looked out over the city. "I don't expect you to understand."

"B-because I'm not m-married? I haven't b-been in love? Is th-that it? B-because you're wrong. I have."

"Then why do you turn away every young man that shows interest in you? And don't say it is because of your speech."

"P-p-pity is not love."

"That's not true. There have been many men willing to look beyond your tongue."

"And into your t-treasury. M-men will d-do anything for m-money."

Her father took a deep breath and let it out slowly. "You are an intelligent, insightful, caring, and beautiful woman. If any man can't hear *what* you have to say because of how you say it, then he is not deserving of you and is not welcome in this family."

Rebekah was stunned, and in the few moments of silence that punctuated her father's words, tears began to well up in her eyes. She so seldom felt comfortable enough to let down her guard and relax when speaking about her handicap. To protect her feelings, she had constructed a wall to keep out the insults and injury that assaulted her because of the way she talked. Built brick by brick from her earliest memories filled with cruelty and mocking and cemented together with the many tears that soaked her pillow, she wondered at times if she would ever find love. Was it even possible to be loved by someone else when she didn't truly love herself? Frustration had been her lifelong companion. She had so much to say and contribute but couldn't. As hard as she tried, she couldn't force her tongue to work right, and so to protect her heart, she built this wall so high and thick that no one could breach it.

Until now. Until Zoram.

Her father was not often open with his feelings, and she had never heard words like these escape his lips. She imagined that they must have been hard for him to articulate. Growing up she had told herself that either he hadn't noticed her sisters' teasing or hadn't cared. Either story threatened the already fragile relationship they shared. How could he let them sling their insults without so much as a reprimand? Where was the punishment for what they did? Where was the justice?

Rebekah was sixteen when her mother passed away, leaving her oldest daughter with the responsibility to raise three younger sisters. She had two older brothers, but they were busy with the family business and starting families of their own. When her father remarried years later, their already strained relationship only got worse. And while she hated to admit it, she even questioned his love for her. Their worlds became farther and farther apart as he left her to assume the role of mother to her sisters. His new wife, Daniah, tried to love them as much as she did her own children, but the reality was that they were on their own.

Of late, her father's interest in seeing his eldest daughter married dominated every conversation, but while she had seen him change and soften over the years, the pain and resentment remained. And always the question remained. *How can you love someone else when you despise so much of who you are?*

But with these few words, she saw another side to her father, one not so much concerned with business profits, product quality, and trade routes but with genuine love, guarded and buried as it was, for his eldest child. She didn't think she could take it all in. It had been an emotional couple of days for her.

She reached out and placed her hand atop her father's, resting her head on his shoulder and smiling up at him. "Thanks," she whispered. His eyes were full, and suddenly she couldn't hold back the tears anymore. She wrapped her arms around his thick frame. It felt good to cry—not from pain but from understanding and peace.

After several long moments of just hugging one another, her father spoke. "Did I hear correctly back there? Is there someone who has caught your eye?"

Rebekah pulled back and nodded, wiping her tears with her sleeve.

"And does he hold you in regard too?"

"I th-think so."

"Do I know this man?"

"No. Well, m-maybe."

"Tell me his name. What does his family do? Where did you meet him?"

His genuine interest put her at ease. She took a deep breath. "Z-Zoram."

Rebekah watched as her father suddenly recognized the name. His brow wrinkled and his eyes widened. "The new Keeper of the Sword?"

She nodded and looked away, almost ashamed.

"Well," he said after letting the news settle in his mind. "It all makes sense now."

Makes sense? "Wh-what d-does?" This was not the response she had expected. What was he talking about?

Her father reached into his coat pocket and removed a leather parchment with the royal seal stamped into it. "I received this not an hour ago. In fact, it's the reason I wanted to speak with you. I needed to talk to you about it."

"Wh-what is it?"

"An order for oil."

Rebekah was still confused.

"With instructions to have you deliver it. You're even mentioned by name."

"A d-delivery?"

"To the palace. To the armory of the Keeper to be precise. Before sundown you are to deliver two hundred measures of our finest and most pure oil."

"Why?"

"I can't imagine, but who are we to question such a request? And for our best oil." Her father leaned on the stone rail. Pointing to a lush, green spot on the far side of the hill just beyond the city's eastern wall, he said, "Do you see this place? It is a new garden of olive trees. They're just now beginning to bear fruit. The oil they produce is unlike anything I have tasted anywhere. It is a special place. The soil is rich and the ground fertile. If the Keeper desires my best, then it will be from this garden.

"In fact," he continued, "the fruit has been so abundant and so plump that despite our best efforts we have been unable to prevent baskets' worth of olives from falling to the ground. When the harvesters enter the gate, they cannot help but trod on them, saturating the ground with oil." Her father chuckled softly. "The workers even have a name for this new garden."

"Wh-what is it?"

"They call it Gethsemane, the oil press."

CHAPTER THIRTEEN

"You go too far, Laban! Your actions, however justified they might have been in your own eyes, are unacceptable and bring shame upon my leadership!"

Laban stood before Zedekiah, Israel's king, a mere child in his twenty-second year. Laban was literally biting the inside of his cheek to keep from retaliating and responding in kind. Though the king was a fool, Laban needed to keep up the appearance of respect, or at least subservience. He couldn't risk alienating the royal house and jeoparding his appointment. And while he didn't think the king could undo his appointment as Keeper, he wasn't entirely sure that he *couldn't*, so he used the sharp pain in his mouth to focus his attention. He still needed the king to play a part in his ultimate plans.

"They were brothers. *Brothers!* And the only children in their family line." The king paced back and forth in front of him. "Their father has filed a grievance demanding compensation. Do you know how much the law provides for a loss of this magnitude? And they have every right to have it paid in full."

The king paused at a table, picked up some papers, glanced at them briefly, and then threw them down again. "I have read Hanoch's report, and it is sorely lacking. What do you have to say for yourself?"

Laban held the intense and furious stare of the young king long enough to diffuse his own anger. "Zedekiah, my king," he said finally. "They were soldiers. There are certain hazards that come with the profession."

"In times of war, yes; during battle, most certainly, but this was a training exhibition! A test to initiate new recruits into the ranks."

"There are always risks," Laban said unapologetically.

"But unnecessary ones like these that result in the deaths of our own men weaken my ability to maintain control. News of their deaths has reached too many ears. I cannot simply deal with this in private."

This determination was uncharacteristic for Nebuchadnezzar's lapdog, and Laban didn't care for it. "And what do you propose to do?"

The king looked to his advisors on either side of him. "*We* are going to make a public apology, and *you* are going to personally express your deepest regrets to the soldiers' mother and father and beg their forgiveness." He paused to let the seriousness of his words sink in. "And then I am going to pay their claim with funds from your personal treasury."

Laban could take this insult no longer. "You cannot do this! It's outrageous! They died in a training exercise—"

"At your hand!"

"They were insolent and offensive! They had no right being under my command!"

"So you killed them?"

Laban stopped his tongue this side of confessing. He knew the explanation offered in Hanoch's report. "No. Their deaths were unfortunate accidents." The words were bitter as he spoke them, but he took some comfort that he would not be forced to pretend his allegiance much longer. The time was soon approaching that he would be forever free of the king, but for now he still needed to play the subservient and loyal subject.

Laban bowed to the king.

"Then you will comply with my orders?"

"Of course, my king. You have but to command, and I will obey."

Laban could tell the young king was expecting more of a fight. He was clearly surprised, if not completely distrustful, of Laban's quick acquiescence. But what could he do? He hadn't been bred to lead, and he completely lacked the finer skills of controlling men. The king was chosen from those in the royal line who were left after the invasion. Laban had often thought Nebuchadnezzar was nothing if not a brilliant emperor who knew how to control and subdue nations. By personally appointing Israel's new monarch from the formal royal line—however obscure or far down that line it might be—he established direct control over the man while at the same time ensuring at least some level of support from the people, primarily the aristocracy and upper classes. History was replete with conquerors who were quick to replace the defeated regime or empire with men from their own political and military ranks, enforcing their rule by the sword. This was costly in terms of armies and supplies. In appointing a new king from the recognized royal lineage and giving him control of a small and insignificant army to serve the subdued nation, Nebuchadnezzar had only to focus his efforts on controlling one man instead of an entire nation. For all of his acts of barbarism and terror, Laban respected the man's genius.

"Is that all, my king?"

The king shifted in his seat and looked to the soldier who had escorted Laban to the palace. "My men saw part of your Fifty riding out at dawn. Was this another *training exercise?*"

"The king need not concern himself with trivial and routine matters of security."

"You and your personal garrison are never involved in anything trivial."

"I assure you it was nothing."

"Nothing?" The king looked at him inquisitively. "Are you certain it has nothing to do with the man who showed up at Jharom's funeral last night? Oh, don't look surprised. I need not attend these things personally to know all that goes on in this city. Do you think me a fool?"

Yes. "Of course not."

"I know well what you and the High Priest—what's his name? Pashur?—are doing. And while I can see and understand what drives the High Priest to seek out and silence these voices, your reasons are not so clear."

Laban had to admit he was surprised at the turn the topic of the conversation had taken. He only hoped his face did not betray his eagerness to speak to it. "I do not believe they are so different from yours."

"Mine?"

"Come now, my king. The time for false pretense is long past. I do not think my reasons for quieting these *voices in the wilderness* are unlike your own."

"And what would my reasons be?"

Laban looked to the king's advisors with some level of concern.

"You need not worry about them," the king assured him. "I keep no secrets from them."

"Very wise and very good, my king." Ever the naïve fool. "You know, then, that these men and women, these self-proclaimed prophets, call out for the people to simply accept Israel's fate and give up their will to fight for their freedom, all the while claiming it is God's will. You and I have spoken many times before about how to regain Israel's freedom and independence, but men like this criminal would have the people accept the rule of these foreign masters. And as you know, it's difficult to command a man's hands when his heart resists. If we are ever to be free of Babylon's chains, it will because we love freedom more than bondage."

"Yes, yes," the king said, not convinced. "We have been over this many times, and while my brother may have been persuaded otherwise, Egypt is no match for Babylon. This is clear from the invasion a year ago. Even with ten times our armies, we could never hope to defeat them and maintain that fragile freedom."

He was right, of course, but Laban had abandoned the truth years earlier to serve his own needs. "Forgive me, but on what advice do you base these conclusions? How well do you trust your sources? I don't mean to imply that any Israelite would mislead or lie to his king, but I have sources, reliable ones, that would challenge this. Egypt is much stronger than you may have heard, and they are eager to ally themselves with us."

"Impossible. My advisors are loyal, and our spies have never been wrong."

"Never? Did our spies give us adequate warning when Babylon swept across Judea as their armies killed without discretion or mercy? Did they warn us in time to secret away and save our children and heirs to the royal house? And do these advisors now counsel you to fight back? Or do they encourage submission and obedience?"

The king couldn't help but look briefly to his advisors with a hint of suspicion and doubt. "They advise, but the decisions are mine."

"Of course they are, good king, and no one can fault you for acting on intelligence that may be inaccurate."

"And what would *you* have me do, Laban?"

Laban was amazed how easily this boy-king could be swayed and manipulated, but the idea still must be his. "As the Keeper of the Records, I am not in a place to advise such a one as yourself, but as commander of the armies of Israel, I would suggest that you not decide anything in haste. Question what you are told; question even what I tell you. But know that once your decision is made, you have but to ask, and I and my Fifty and the whole of Israel's army stands ready to obey your command."

Laban bowed in respect and honor.

"You're a good man, Laban. Israel is fortunate to have a man of your caliber and integrity serving her."

"I live to serve," he responded, continuing to bow.

The king nodded his head in return. "I may have been too harsh earlier. The soldiers' deaths were accidental, after all. Perhaps the nation that they served that should repay their loss."

"No, I insist. You are correct—accident or not, they were in my care when it happened. Their lives were lost on my watch. It is only right that I assume this responsibility."

"Thank you, Laban. I will send someone by later today to handle the details."

"It will be my pleasure. Is that all, my king?"

The king dismissed him with a wave and a grateful look, and Laban turned and left, careful that no one saw the smile that couldn't be kept from creeping onto his lips.

שומר החרב

The king cleared the reception hall. "Except you, Ammon," he called to his chief palace guard, the one who had been sent to summon Laban. "The rest of you, leave us."

Ammon stood at attention, looking very uncomfortable as the learned men and lawyers gave him cross and suspicious looks as they filed out of the room. The king thought to defend his friend but decided it would only make the tense situation worse. Zedekiah didn't have many men he would consider friends, but Ammon was not like other men. Born into the priestly class, Ammon was a man of great faith and conviction who had given up the life destined for him in order to serve and protect Israel's new king and kingdom.

"Zedekiah?"

They had first met years earlier, before his unexpected and unwanted appointment to the throne, and Zedikiah had never had reason to doubt Ammon. They had grown especially close over the past year, almost like brothers.

"My king?"

"What? Sorry. I still haven't become completely accustomed to my new, *royal* name."

"Do you wish me to call you by another? Your given name, perhaps?"

"No, thank you. I must get used to it." Zedekiah continued to stare at the doorway. "I don't trust him."

"Who, my king?"

"Laban."

"What has he done to lose your trust?"

"That's just it. Nothing. But he has also done nothing to build it. He was not meant for his position and calling."

"Israel suffered a great loss when his father passed away."

"And so soon after his brother's death."

Ammon didn't respond right way. "I've heard the rumors, as well. You don't believe them, do you?"

"It doesn't really matter what I believe. What concerns me is what I see now. He is reckless and self-centered, with wealth and position to have much influence among the aristocracy and the Sarim. His thoughts and actions are indifferent to others, and all of that in one man makes him dangerous and worthy of our watchful eye." He looked back to Ammon. "From afar and hidden from his view, of course."

"Of course, my king, but he has spies of his own. Some, I suspect, among the ranks of your own household."

The king was not surprised to hear the concern expressed so directly. He knew this as well and had begun to conduct the affairs of state with this knowledge in the forefront of his mind. It was difficult enough to maintain power and control under the critical and watchful eye of his Babylonian masters without also having to worry about deceit and conspiracies from among the ranks of his supposed friends. "But we still need to keep apprised of his actions. He's up to something."

"Do you think the death of the soldiers had anything to do with it?"

Zedekiah shook his head slowly. "No. Perhaps. I don't know. I don't know what it is. You saw the way his position and demeanor changed so quickly? Behavior like that is the mark of a calculated plan. He's hiding something."

"Perhaps," Ammon reflected. "Or perhaps he realized the error of his ways and knew he was wrong to oppose you."

The king looked at his friend sideways. "Do you really believe that?"

Ammon shook his head and cracked a nervous smile. "No."

The king's mood lightened, and he chuckled softly. "No. I suspected as much."

The two were comfortable with silence and let a few moments of it pass between them.

"Let me ask you," the king finally said. "Am I making a mistake by even considering aligning with Egypt as Laban suggests?"

"I'm no politician and don't know enough to—"

"No, no, I'm not looking for a well-educated and carefully thought out analysis of the political and military risks. I have an entire court of such men. But I trust your instincts. I always have. What does your heart tell you?"

Ammon considered the question and his answer very carefully. "We all know what happened to both your brother and your nephew. Babylon is not an empire to underestimate in any way. Their armies are skilled and unsurpassed. They defeated the Assyrians and are unmatched in all the world."

"They didn't defeat Egypt."

"I don't think they *wanted* Egypt," Ammon said. "I am no military historian or strategist, but if Egypt had had the might to overcome a weakened and tired army, they would have had no better opportunity. I suspect that Egypt, with all her forces, knew they couldn't even defeat a weakened Babylon."

These last words upset the king's heart and stomach. Why had his own advisors never spoken this simple truth with such clarity? Perhaps they did have their own agendas. Perhaps they really didn't know. Either way he didn't need these men surrounding him and influencing his thoughts and decisions. But Laban claimed that Israel could, in fact, fight for its freedom, and he was, after all, commander of the armies.

"And one more thing," Ammon said with a serious and somber tone. "Nebuchadnezzar is not known for his forgiving nature. If even mere rumors of such treason and betrayal reach his courts, I dare not imagine what the consequences would be."

The king closed his eyes and pressed his palms to his temples. He was so confused.

"Are you all right?"

"Yes, I'm fine."

"Are you in pain? Shall I send for a physician?"

"No, it will pass. Thank you, Ammon. You continue to be one of the few men in all of Jerusalem who I can trust without reservation. You're a good friend."

Ammon bowed at the most high compliment. "My king."

"What I am about to ask of you is dangerous," the king continued. "It might even be viewed as deceitful and even traitorous. Laban is, after all, one of the most respected and powerful men in Israel. He will not take inquiry and spying in good form. If you refuse this assignment, I will understand and not hold it against you in any way. In fact, the mark of a good friend is to speak the truth, no matter how hard it might be taken."

"While I appreciate the offer to refuse your command, your will be done. I agree with and share your impressions. Laban's behavior is odd, at the very least, and deserving of further investigation."

The king was relieved. "Come to me personally with any news. After today I'm not sure who I can trust anymore."

Ammon bowed again and turned to leave.

"Oh, one more favor," the king called. "The new Keeper of the Sword . . ."

"Zoram?"

"Yes, Zoram. Would you send for him?"

"It shall be done."

"It's not urgent. I have been informed that he has begun work on the new Sword. Send for him, but unlike Laban, he may come at his convenience."

"As you wish, my king," Ammon said as he walked out the door.

Zedekiah was left alone with his thoughts. His life had been much simpler before having this crown thrust upon him. He was fortunate, though, to have Ammon serving in such close proximity to him. He was a good man and a friend to his family. But while Ammon had maintained his faith in the power and deliverance of God over the years, Zedekiah had not. His anger and disappointment in God were still fresh, as they were with so many others. Where was He when his friends were killed during the invasion taken to serve their new master in Babylon? Was His ear deaf to their cries? Was He numb to their pain? Where was His deliverance then?

The king slumped into the oversized stone throne and again pressed the palms of his hands over his eyes.

But, he reasoned, if one cannot turn to God during times of death and destruction, where else can he?

CHAPTER FOURTEEN

HANOCH WAS SHOWN INTO LABAN'S personal quarters without delay. He had been riding for the better part of the day. He was dirty, he was tired, and the news he bore was not going to please his captain. But there was also no reason to put his report off. The sooner he could deliver it, the sooner he could return home and get a well-deserved night's sleep.

The servant announced his presence with a knock on the open doorway. The room was dimly lit and the air warm and heavy. Laban was lying on a table, facedown, with only a towel to cover his nakedness while three young women massaged his oiled back and legs. At the sound, Laban turned his neck—a struggle in his relaxed state—and motioned for Hanoch to come in.

"You're filthy," Laban slurred, his face pressed against the table. "Take off your shoes." They were caked in dried mud. "In fact," Laban swung his hand and tried to snap. While he couldn't produce the sound, another young girl waiting in the shadows obediently stepped to his side. "You will join me. Draw a bath for my friend here."

"No," Hanoch simply said, standing at attention. "No, thank you."

"I insist. Look at you. I can scarcely bear the sight of you, not to mention your smell. Do you *have* to smell like horse sweat?"

"Forgive me, but a full day atop the animal under the hot sun has a tendency to bond the beast with its rider in foul and unpleasant ways. The day has been long, and I am wont to return home for the evening. With your permission I will make my report and be off."

Laban propped himself up on his elbows and stared at Hanoch. He was clearly upset at the refusal but shook off his ill feelings and forced a smile to his face. "Of course, my old friend. What news do you have?"

"I would prefer to discuss my report in private." He did not share Laban's trust in his young and eager staff. "What I have is for your ears alone."

There was a tense moment as Laban challenged his firm request. Hanoch wondered if he had gone too far in making such a demand. Who was he to question what company the Keeper kept and who he trusted with sensitive and confidential information? But the truth was that Hanoch had as much on the line with their plans as Laban did. To his way of thinking, that gave him the right to insist on a private audience.

"Fine," Laban said, clapping his hands and dismissing his beautiful attendants. Laban sat up and wrapped the towel around him as they scurried out of the room and closed the door behind them.

"Drink?" Laban asked, stepping to the small table under the window and pouring two glasses of wine. He handed Hanoch a full cup. Then Laban drank deeply. "So, tell me, what is this secret report?"

Was it possible that Laban had forgotten their mission? "Lehi was gone."

"What do you mean *gone*? Are you certain you were looking in the right place?"

"Without a doubt. We found a small ancestral estate. The gardens were tended, the well was full, and we could see where the tents had been set up. It was him, all right. It would seem that someone warned him."

"Impossible. There were only two men who knew we were mounting this operation, and they are both standing in this room right now."

Hanoch stiffened at the accusation. "If you think I—"

"Relax," Laban said, turning his back to pour himself another drink. "I know you did nothing of the sort."

"You should have let me kill him last night when he all but offered himself up to us. The audacity the old man had to show his face like that. He knew we were looking for him and used the funeral to hide from us and to spread more of his lies and propaganda to a captive audience."

"But he's gone, you say? Just as well. In fact, this might actually work more in our favor."

"I don't understand."

Laban took another deep drink. "You see, whether he's dead or simply run away, either way his words and influence cease. By killing him, we risk making him a martyr. But if he just left in the night—"

"Like a coward."

"Like a coward, then what weight do his words carry? I think Pashur should be informed of Lehi's sudden departure. He's the master manipulator when it comes to the matters of faith. Let him put a spin on this to erase forever the very name of Lehi."

"Unlike that other so-called prophet—what was his name? The one who continues to prophesy from deep within the prisons?"

"Jeremiah? Exactly. And he is a perfect example of what I am talking about. They made a mistake not just killing him outright when he first started to become a thorn in all of our sides. The longer he speaks, the louder his cries become—even in prison. To kill him now would only rally his followers to action."

"So we keep him alive . . ."

"Only because we cannot kill him. Well, not yet, anyway. You see, Hanoch, my friend," Laban said, starting to display the languid effects of the massage coupled with a full day of wine, "the one thing you need to know is that there is no right or wrong, or even action or inaction. If you would learn one thing about leadership, it's that in the end, there is only politics." He finished off his glass. "And damage control."

"So we just let Lehi get away?"

"Let him hide. But if he returns . . ."

"We kill him?"

"We kill him."

"And if he doesn't come back?"

"Then we go hunting." The thought of this brought a twisted smile to Laban's face, and he poured himself another glass of wine. "Quietly. We cannot let an enemy live to return and fight another day, now can we?"

"And what do we do with the new Keeper? The people don't need any more encouragement to renew their faith. They are an impulsive group."

"True, they are a capricious people, like children, but I have taken care of Zoram."

Hanoch couldn't hide his surprise. "*Taken care of?*"

Laban exploded in a sudden outburst of laughter. "No, no! That would be too much of a coincidence, don't you think? No, I have recruited someone in his camp to keep tabs on our young, enthusiastic friend and report his . . . doings." And though his laughter had come quickly, this last word was hissed through clenched teeth.

Hanoch had seen this sudden transformation before and took a step back. But instead of lashing out, Laban held his seething anger inside with only a faint strain in his voice to betray it.

"He has locked himself in the armory," Laban said. "As we speak he is working his trade and fashioning a new Sword."

Of all of Laban's undesirable traits, this one frightened Hanoch the most. The ability to turn emotions on and off suddenly and completely wasn't the behavior of a man in his right mind.

"Let him work his craft," Laban continued softly and with a menacing tone edging his words. "In the end it will make no difference. Let him try to save us. Sword or not, Israel's fate is already sealed."

Hanoch unconsciously held Laban's stare longer than he had intended. The next and final news of his report was no better than the others, and given Laban's mood swings, Hanoch wondered if it might be best to wait until morning to share this last news.

"What is it?" Laban asked bluntly. "There's something you're keeping from me. Tell me."

Hanoch didn't answer right away, debating still whether to reveal what he had obtained upon returning to the city. He had inadvertently glanced at words not meant for him and feared that the rest of the letter might contain ill news. But, he rationalized with himself, bad news delivered tomorrow morning would only be compounded by wrath at being made to wait.

Hanoch opened the bag at his side and produced a leather correspondence tied and bearing the imprint of the Babylonian Empire. "The messenger returned pursuant to the agreed-upon instructions. His instructions were to deliver it personally to you, but I couldn't risk him being seen anywhere near the city. He eventually relented and gave me this."

Laban took the leather package. "Jharom and his late-night vigil almost ruined everything."

Hanoch's stomach was turning in heaving swells. "If there's nothing else, I'll see myself out."

"And miss the latest news?" Laban started untying the leather cords.

"Those words are for your eyes only."

"Nonsense. You've been with me almost from the beginning and have read every word she's penned." Laban had a far-off look in his eyes and smiled. "Well, almost every word."

"What you share with me is your decision."

Despite his intoxication, Laban surely suspected something was amiss. "Of course it is." He tossed the parchment back to Hanoch, who struggled to react quick enough to catch it and not drop it. "Here. You read it first. This time *you* tell *me* what it says."

"Sir, no. It's not my place."

"Your place is what I tell you it is! Now read it."

The request had turned into a command. Hanoch resented the order but knew he had no choice in the matter. His hands trembling, he opened the small scroll and held it up to the light from the wall sconce.

"*My dearest . . .*" he started but stopped, looking to Laban for a reprieve. When there was none, he continued. "My dearest, my eyes and heart ache for word from you, but they find no solace in your silence."

Laban got comfortable on the divan and smiled. "I like the direction this is going."

"But it is with a heavy heart that I pen these words, for it was my desire to be with you and forge a union to bring peace to your devastated land." Hanoch stopped. He had seen this much of the letter earlier by accident and feared what the next words might convey. Reading this to Laban was a mistake. He was not one to take ill news well, and tonight's reports had done nothing to put his master's temper at ease. Hanoch needed to return the letter and leave him to read the rest of the words alone, but before he could hand it back, Laban was on his feet. He snatched the letter from Hanoch's trembling hands and, without a word, began reading intently. Laban's face flushed red as his anger intensified. Hanoch took another small step backward, but he dared not leave.

Laban finished reading the letter but remained fixed on the written words, unable to move and only scarcely able to comprehend their meaning. After a few stunned moments, he looked up at his lieutenant, those glowing embers fueled and barely contained beneath the surface.

"Laban?" Hanoch asked meekly. "What does she say?"

Laban looked up, his stare unfocused and wild. "She wants them. Now."

Hanoch knew exactly what he meant. This was not good news. "But that's not possible. We're not ready."

"She is to be given to another. The only way to stop it is to act now."

"This is a delicate plan," Hanoch protested. "It has taken the better part of the year just to—"

"I will not lose her!" Laban yelled and lunged at Hanoch. As fast and skilled as Hanoch was, he was clearly and admittedly Laban's inferior. Before he knew what had happened, Laban had pushed him against the wall and wrested the sword free from his belt. The blade was pressed to his neck.

"I have worked too hard these past four years to lose her now. There is no other option. If things are not ready, then you will *make* them ready. Am I clear?"

Hanoch had been on the receiving end of Laban's tirades many times over the years, and while he had never actually believed the threats would be carried out, tonight he was concerned otherwise. He struggled to keep his composure. To display even the smallest weakness or sign of fear would likely mean a sudden and certain death in Laban's fit of rage.

Laban pressed the sword harder against his neck. "I said, am I clear?"

"Yes, Laban," Hanoch managed to say against the pressure. "Perfectly."

Laban released him, turned, and threw the sword, which made a deep cut in the wall before falling to the floor, cracking the tile.

With the sounds of violence still ringing loudly throughout the room, Laban backed up against the wall and sunk to the floor. The letter was still clutched tightly in his hand. "I will not lose her . . . I just can't . . ."

שומר החרב

Her name was Amytis, the name given to her mother, and she was the most stunningly beautiful woman Laban had ever seen. Her skin was the color of honey and cinnamon, and her short, radiant black hair framed her delicate feminine features in a way he could only describe as angelic. Her figure was shapely yet firm, and it seemed as if his entire heart, mind, and body cried out in a sudden uncontrollable urge to be with her. He had never experienced anything quite like this before. He was no stranger to women, but what he felt when he first laid eyes on her went much deeper, was more intense, and he knew he would do anything to possess her.

She had but one flaw: she was the daughter of King Nebuchadnezzar, the tyrant and warrior-king who had just defeated the mighty Assyrians and now stood poised to invade and lay waste to all of Israel if he so desired. But none of that mattered to Laban.

He had first spied her during the victory procession through the city. He was serving in Israel's army at the time. They had been defeated without raising a single sword, and he found himself, along with every other soldier, compelled to bow before and offer his allegiance to their new masters. Laban's only thoughts had been of despair and anguish until he saw her. She was riding atop a muscular stallion, surrounded by a personal guard of men who more closely resembled giants. He couldn't take his eyes off her. She must have felt his wanton stare, for she turned and met his eyes for the briefest of moments. Laban flashed her a quick smile, and then she was gone.

The next few weeks were frenzied and chaotic. Laban learned, to his alarm, that with the deaths and executions of Israel's military commanders he was now the ranking officer of the decimated army. As such, he was summoned to the palace to answer many questions about Israel, its history, and its people. He might have resisted sharing intelligence about his home and heritage but for the presence of the princess. Upon learning that it was he who was to be questioned, she had insisted on being present. Through the use of an interpreter, he had answered all of her inquiries truthfully—how could he lie or deceive in the presence of such utter and complete beauty? His fervor loosened his tongue and cleared his conscience. He must have charmed and impressed her as well because the following night he received a summons to join Amytis in secret. The possibility that it might be a trap did briefly cross his mind, but he didn't care. He was wholly smitten with her and longed to be close to her at all costs.

They met several times over the next few weeks. The young princess had many questions about his homeland that he did his best to answer. The two of them talked well into the night, and the topics turned from official fact-finding questions to more personal ones.

She was thrilling and purely intoxicating! They met a dozen times more over the next month. He found himself acting as her private language tutor, talking and laughing with her. Her accent was strong but her voice sweet, which simply added to her exotic and forbidden charm.

Finally, he dared express the way he felt for her and how he had been smitten with her. It was a risky act. If his love was not reciprocated, it could mean his death. In fact, he was pretty sure that even if she did share similar feelings, he might still be killed for speaking his mind to a member of the Babylonian royal house. But he didn't care. What was death compared to a love like his? And if he didn't share his heart with her, he would regret it and curse his cowardice the rest of his days. But as he held her hands in his and confessed his love for her, she smiled and looked away coyly, and he knew that she felt the same way about him. What he'd asked next was even more precarious.

"Take me with you," he'd said. "I hear your father is preparing to return to Babylon. I cannot bear to be without you."

She considered the request but then took back her hands, explaining that while she would like nothing more, her father would never permit it. "As a member of the royal house, I am not free to marry for love. It must be arranged. There must be political value to the union." She looked at him with imploring eyes.

Laban was crushed more now than he had been witnessing the slaughter of his friends and fellow soldiers on the battlefield. The temper he'd had since a child threatened to surface, but he kept it well hidden and under control. "But I have little to offer your father."

"But you are of the royal lineage, are you not?"

"Yes, but I'm not in line for any inheritance or wealth." Laban's mind was furiously considering any means to keep from losing her. His family had some privilege and status, and yes, she was right about his lineage being of the house of Joseph, but he was second born and not even considered for the small honor his family was entrusted to bear. There was nothing keeping him in Jerusalem.

His heart and mind began to give way to panic and despair when he willed them to stop and continue to conspire and fight for her. He would not lose the princess now. "You said our union must bring value to the empire. What might satisfy this decree?"

Amytis thought for a moment, searching his eyes before turning away and walking to the window. "My father is consumed in his pursuit of the treasures of conquered lands and people."

"Even if I sold everything I own, I couldn't raise enough for your dowry."

"No, not treasures of gold and silver—he has more precious metals than he can use in a hundred lifetimes. What he desires are national treasures, treasures of *symbolic* value."

"I . . . I don't understand."

"For such a small kingdom, tales of the God of the Hebrews reach the farthest corners of the world. I am certain that a relic or symbol of His power might persuade my father to allow our union."

Laban shook his head. "The Assyrians took what they wanted when they swept through our city, and now you take what is left. The Temple is bare, the altar defiled—Israel has nothing left."

"But I—" She stopped and stepped closer, lowering her voice. "But I've heard stories of a magic chest, which holds untold power."

Laban was confused for only a moment then laughed out loud before he could stop himself. "The ark? You mean the ark of the covenant? You're only a couple of hundred years late. Most of us doubt it even existed. But if it did actually exist, it disappeared a long time ago."

Amytis looked down and away. "I just thought that if it still existed and was, say, hidden away from the rest of the world . . ."

"I'm sorry, Princess, but like I said, you would be hard pressed to find anyone who still believes that it was real. The ark is a story, a tale to inspire a fallen and beaten people. Think about it. If my ancestors did have some small measure of God's power, enough to lay waste to foreign armies, don't you think that Israel would have conquered the world instead of being subject to every army and empire that passes by?"

Laban put his hand on her shoulder, but she shrugged it off. He had offended her with his sarcastic answer. "Forgive me, Amytis. I did not mean to show you any disrespect. You were only trying to find some way for us to be together. I am truly sorry."

She looked up and offered him a weak smile. "Surely Israel must have some treasures left, something we could offer him?"

Laban turned and began to pace the room, racking his brain to think of something, anything, that he could produce or even *steal* to offer Nebuchadnezzar for her hand—and the rest of her. But Israel had nothing left. What he had told the princess was the truth. Everything Israel had of any value—their treasures, their gold, their artifacts—had all been stolen or lost over the years. Everything that had once made them a proud and prosperous people had been ripped from them. In fact, the invading armies had taken everything Israel held dear except their God, and even then most of the people had even abandoned Him during the almost continuous occupations. All they had were accounts, legends, and stories passed down—

Then the answer became so clear, so obvious. Why hadn't he thought of it earlier? It would be so simple. Excited, he took her hands again in his.

"I know what I can offer your father. I can give him something—the one thing—no other king, empire, or invading army has ever been able to possess."

The princess's eyes lit up with anticipation. "What is it?"

"It will take some time to obtain though. Will you wait for me?"

"Yes, yes."

"What I must do will not be easy, and there will be no going back once I accomplish this thing. I must know that what I do will not be in vain."

"Of course, yes. Yes, I will do anything you ask. Just tell me, what is this thing you can offer that no other has attained?"

Laban looked at her in all seriousness, pieces of a plan already coming together. "What can I deliver? Why, the only treasure my people have left. Tell your father, Nebuchadnezzar, that I will deliver to him the very heart and faith of the people."

CHAPTER FIFTEEN

"Z-Zoram?"

The soft voice was accompanied by an equally gentle touch to his shoulder, drawing him slowly out of a deep and restful sleep. Images of fires, hammers, and steel were blanketed in a residual heat of the work he had just accomplished, a heat that beckoned him to remain asleep for a little while longer.

"Z-Zoram?"

He slowly opened his eyes and smiled at the face that greeted him. "Rebekah."

Zoram looked around, confused for a moment as to why he was sitting on the floor. He straightened up. He started to get to his feet but was hit by a wave of dizziness that almost tipped him over. His legs felt numb, and the muscles in his neck and back were knotted up from slouching against the table as he slept. How long had he been sleeping?

He looked past Rebekah's warm smile and noticed bright sunlight filtering through the narrow windows that lined the upper walls. It was well past dawn. Was it midday? Was it the next day? Was it the day after? How long had he been working? His mouth was dry and his tongue bitter and swollen, but he didn't feel any other effects of dehydration. It must only be the next day. He had completed his work in only a day and a half. While not the fastest time he had forged and fashioned a weapon in, it was a miracle given the complexity and attention to detail he had demanded of himself.

"B-be careful. Here." She put a small cup of water to his cracked lips. "Easy. J-just a little bit. There."

"Thank—" He gulped the cool refreshment, his mind and body coming alive after the fast and deprivation. "Thank you."

He was taking deeper drinks now. He looked past her to the door, suddenly puzzled at her presence in the armory. "How did you get in?"

Rebekah's smile grew bigger. "It w-wasn't easy, b-but I'm a p-persistent woman."

"I'll bet you are."

"Here," she said, offering him a small basket filled with breads, fruit, and cheeses. "Th-this is for you. You m-must be hungry."

Zoram reached for the one of the rolls—still warm—and ate a bite of mild cheese with it. "I'm so glad to see you. I was also pleased to see that you got my message," he said, nodding toward the empty vat of oil in the corner. "I'm sorry I couldn't greet you in person when you dropped it off. I have found it necessary to remain focused and sequestered during the whole procedure."

Rebekah explained that her father had been confused when he received the request with specific instruction for her to deliver it, but he had dutifully responded. "He g-gave you sp-special oil."

"Special? How so?"

"F-from an ext-ext-ext—" Rebekah stopped when she couldn't finish the word and chose another. "An amazing new g-garden."

"It was remarkable. I have never used oil to cool metal down before, but after speaking with you in the city, I was struck with the idea to try it. Besides, oil is used to anoint and bless, and I figured the Sword, which is to represent the faith and resolve of Israel, deserved no less."

Rebekah looked around the room. "I've never b-been here b-before."

Zoram stuffed the rest of the bread and cheese in his mouth and planted his hands behind him to try to stand up again. Rebekah reached out and gave him her hand.

"This is the Keeper's armory. Not many are allowed in. This place is reserved for the making of the Sword to protect the records, the place where the Keeper can hone his skills. I only have a handful of memories of this place as a child. My father only allowed me entrance a few times. It's a sacred place and mostly off-limits, even to the heir to the title."

Rebekah appeared suddenly nervous and almost embarrassed. "M-maybe I should go."

"Please." He reached out and took her hand. "Don't." She looked at their hands and then into his eyes. She looked away but not before he saw her begin to blush. She gently tried to pull away, but he refused to let go. "I'd like you to stay."

Rebekah just smiled and left her hands right where they were.

"Tell me," Zoram said after a poignant silence between them, "do you know much about the Keepers?" She shook her head. "I often used to beg my father to tell me about them. I can still remember him sharing the stories in this very room when I was seven or eight." He was stricken with a flood of memories and sadness at his loss. "What I would do to hear him tell those stories once more. He was a much better storyteller than I am."

Rebekah gripped his hands in a show of comfort and then took a seat on one of the small benches that lined the room. "I'm sure you'll d-do fine."

Zoram took a deep breath to clear his thoughts and began telling her the history and purpose of the Keepers. Instituted under the inspiration and direction of the great prophet Isaiah, it was declared that there should be established two families, two men, whose only concern, whose very calling in life and existence, was to protect all that Israel was and would ever be. To one, called the Keeper of the Records, was given the charge to protect the history, accounts, miracles, and words of the great One True God. These records, once written on the skins of animals and then later on scrolls of vellum or parchment, were commanded to be recorded on metal plates to withstand the ravages of the elements, fire, and of time itself. Thin sheets of brass were fashioned to engrave the words and teachings upon, and it fell upon the Keeper of the Records to preserve the words of God. This was a holy and most sacred obligation.

But written records were not enough to save Israel. Possessing the words of God was useless without the courage and strength to believe and act upon them. Faith was necessary to salvation. Knowledge alone wasn't enough. God required of His people not only a willing heart but the strength and commitment to make a stand against the world and to protect the words of God. In a vision, Isaiah also saw a Sword, fashioned unlike any other anyone had ever seen before, to accompany and protect the words of God. It was to be a symbol of the people's action and conviction. Just as God continued to speak and the records grew, so too would the Sword be replaced and recreated for each generation. This was to be the practice so as to, at least symbolically, prevent the new generations from relying wholly upon the testimonies and faith of the generation before them.

So Zoram's family was bestowed the title of Keepers of the Sword—to serve and work in unison with the Keeper of the Records to ensure the cultural, historical, and spiritual survival of Israel. It was not a calling his family had ever taken lightly, always searching out the finest instruction and most advanced techniques on metalworking and forging. The Sword that would represent the faith of the people could not be of common construction.

"That's why I was sent away," Zoram concluded. "The advancements in sword and steelmaking far exceed anything this part of the world has ever seen."

Rebekah was captivated by his words, listening intently to the stories. "And th-that's what you were d-doing all d-day and all night?"

He nodded. "It takes time to forge and shape the steel. I guess I could have broken the process down and spread my work over the space of a few days, but I've found that steel is stronger when heated and shaped without letting it sit idle for too long."

Zoram could feel the utter joy and excitement he had for his art building within his breast. "You see, a sword is not just a thing. It is so much more than mere metal, or even a blade and hilt. If done with care, and in the hands of a master smith, each sword becomes a unique creation. If you listen closely to the whisperings of the metal, the sword will speak to you and guide you in its very creation."

She looked at him sideways. "Really?"

"It's true . . . but I guess it helps to be a little crazy."

Rebekah laughed lightly. It was the first time he had heard her laugh, and he couldn't remember hearing anything so sweet, so melodic, and so soothing in his life. What were these feelings he was experiencing? It was like a warm wind blew over him whenever she was around, comforting him and lending peace to offset whatever might be troubling his heart. He had looked forward to his return with a good deal of fear and trepidation, especially in the wake of learning about his mother's death. Then, when the news of his father assaulted him immediately upon returning home, he had considered fleeing the city and abandoning his duty. If it hadn't been for Rebekah's example the other morning, he just might have. He was amazed that the very thought of her kept him here, inspiring him to do what was right.

But why? He hardly knew her. Was it the fact that he had saved her life and now felt a sense of responsibility for her, that he was somehow her protector? He didn't think so. Maybe it was—

"Wh-what's wrong?" Rebekah asked, her laugh long since faded.

Zoram was jerked away from his thoughts, embarrassed now as he realized he had been staring at her without saying a word. "What? Oh, you . . . No, not you; there's nothing wrong with—I . . . I mean, you . . . I-I—"

She reached out and hushed him with a touch and a smile. "Hey," she said gently. "I'll d-do the st-st-stuttering for both of us. Okay?"

If he had any doubt left, it was removed with her warmth, sincerity, and strength of character to make light of her impediment. He was smitten by her—completely and unequivocally—and those feelings he'd had since first laying eyes on her grew and deepened.

"Deal."

Rebekah held his gaze for a moment longer and then looked around the armory. He knew what she was searching for. She was looking for the Sword, and while he had already decided to show her his night's work, he felt that she might actually appreciate the process of its creation. "Follow me. I'd like to show you something."

His excitement returned as he shared with her the process of forging the Sword that Israel, and especially Jerusalem, so desperately needed in the wake of their latest defeat. He explained that the metal a sword was fashioned from had already been smelted, purified, and formed into what was called a billet.

"Is th-that what was in your b-bag wh-when we first m-met?"

"That's right. For such a small package, its value was immeasurable."

She then went on to ask him questions, not satisfied to simply wait for Zoram to offer additional information. She was fascinated with the process and, as far as he could discern, genuinely interested. She wanted to know what the difference was between the iron they had and this steel. Zoram produced from his belt a small dagger, fashioned many years ago when he was just learning his craft.

"Iron is found in certain rocks and is mined from the ground. Extreme heat is needed to draw and separate it from the minerals and other impurities. Iron is strong and malleable and is the base metal in creating steel."

He could see he needed to explain it a little more. "It's like bronze. Bronze is the product of copper and tin. By itself, copper is very soft and used primarily as a decorative metal, like jewelry. But mixed with tin—another soft metal, by the way—the two are transformed into bronze, which is many times stronger and more useful. It is the same with brass.

Brass, the material our records are made of, is the combination of copper and zinc."

Zoram searched for a piece of iron amid the many tables until he found some. "You see, iron has been used for centuries to make swords, armor, spear and arrow points, and a host of other weapons and implements of war. But where iron possesses great strength, it is very heavy. It's also brittle. I know that sounds strange, but compared to other metals, iron must be thick to derive any level of tensile strength."

"T-tensile strength?"

"Sorry. What I'm trying to say is that iron, for all its uses, can be improved upon. When mixed with other elements, like charcoal, iron is made into steel." He handed her both the piece of iron and the small dagger. "Do you feel how light the knife blade is? Do you see how smooth it is? Now, it might surprise you to know that the blade is stronger than an iron blade two or three times thicker and longer. Steel is an amazing metal."

"So, th-the sword you m-made is like th-this?"

Zoram's smile widened. "Not exactly."

He took the small steel dagger from Rebekah and began to run his fingers along the sharpened blade. "As impressive as this metal is, our Sword could not be like other blades. Near the place where I lived during my apprenticeship, they mine a mineral that the locals call *black rock* in their native tongue. A dear friend introduced me to it and forever altered the work I would complete as Keeper of the Sword. This black rock, ground down to a fine powder, transformed iron into steel unlike any other found anyplace else in the world."

Rebekah continued to drink in Zoram's words and share in his enthusiasm. He thought about the metal itself and the incredible, miraculous story of its origins, but he resisted the urge to tell her everything all at once. It might be too much to take in one sitting. But he would tell her, and he knew it would serve to strengthen their collective faith in the One True God.

He then proceeded to tell her about a secret method of vastly improving on even the finest steel by layering it and then folding the steel upon itself over and over until it resulted in a thinly striped brick of dense steel.

"The masters I studied under called it Wootz steel—a strictly guarded secret. It had never before been shared with foreign apprentices, like myself. But the Lord desired us to have this knowledge and softened the heart of one man, in particular, who broke with tradition and shared it with me."

Zoram then led her around the armory, explaining the purposes of the forge, of heating the iron to a red glow, then flattening it out on an anvil by a constant and steady striking, then reheating it and flattening it out, repeating the process until the blade began to take shape. The metal was heated, formed, and shaped, and then cooled several times as the steel was tempered. Tempering the steel, he explained, made it more flexible while at the same time making the edge stronger and harder.

"This is why I sought out your father's oil. Usually the superheated steel is liquid-cooled in water." He shrugged his shoulders. "I decided to use the oil and noticed the steel seemed less stressed from the process and easier to form. The final steps of using smaller and more refined tools to create the straight edge are usually difficult, but last night they were almost . . . easy. It was as if the steel knew of its special destiny and was helping me to finish its creation."

Zoram let those last words resonate before asking the question he knew she was dying to hear. "Do you want to see it?"

She nodded enthusiastically. "Very m-much so."

Zoram had led them to a workbench in the back. Hammers, metal files, vises, awls, and a host of other metal-finishing tools were littered across the workspace. Off to one side was a long strip of green cloth. It covered something equally as long beneath it. "Go ahead."

Rebekah looked at him with a mix of surprise and disbelief on her face. "N-no, I can't."

"Please. There is no one I'd rather see it first. Go on. And to be honest, I'm curious to see how it all turned out myself. Much of those final steps is a blur to me. I was so tired there at the end I really can't remember what it looked like finished."

Rebekah reached out and gingerly—almost reverently—pulled back the fabric revealing the most beautiful and ornate sword either one of them had ever seen. The sheath was decorated with strips of gold and silver twisted and shaped into long loops and designs, while the hilt was made of the finest gold and precious stones.

"When the first Sword was forged and presented to the prophet," Zoram explained, "it is said that he held it heavenward by the hilt as he pronounced a blessing upon it and all other future Swords. While the blades are fashioned in each generation, the hilt has remained largely intact. The belief is that the blessings are channeled through the gold hilt."

She reached out and ran her fingers over the ornate metal, ever so lightly.

"Draw it out," he urged.

Using both hands, she picked it up. "It's lighter than I expected." She firmly took hold of the handgrip and carefully wrapped her fingers around the gold hilt. She smiled and nervously chuckled softly.

"What's that?"

"It feels funny."

"It what?"

"It's not bad. It just . . . tingles a little."

"Pull it out. Look at the blade."

With one hand around the handle and the other gripping the sheath, she gently pulled the two apart. The blade glided effortlessly with a whispered hum of metal on metal resonating in the air. Zoram and Rebekah were both held in awe at the sight before them. When the sound finally became too faint to be heard, Rebekah found the words to speak.

"It's so beautiful."

Any words Zoram might have added were caught in his throat. It was as if he were seeing the blade for the first time. The blade was more amazing than anything he had ever seen. He doubted even the High Sadhus had ever seen a blade such as this one, and in a wistful moment, he wished that his teacher and Wu Yien could see the great work he had accomplished. But the blade was not fashioned from his skill alone. This was the work of God. There could be no other explanation.

The blade, roughly the length of his arm, was covered with intricate waves and patterns of alternating light- and dark-shaded steel stretching from hilt to tip. The lines were fluid, like water, with images that resembled droplets, like the cross-sections of a hundred miniature trees. The loops and contours were soothing to the eye and almost demanded to be gazed at and pondered. Zoram had never expected or even dreamed of steel with these visual properties.

And then there was the blade's construction. The lines were as perfect as he or any other master could have formed them. The thickness was uniform on the blunt end, tapering down to a razor-like edge. He ran his fingers along the length of it as Rebekah held it. It was without flaw. There was no evidence of his hammering. Any imperfections he would expect from the rough surface of the anvil or the dents and pocks of the hammers were noticeably absent to his touch. A blade this polished and smooth was just not possible, even after hours and days of buffing with the finest stones in existence.

"It's magnificent," Rebekah said.

Zoram was so overcome with emotion and awe he found it difficult to speak. "I have never beheld such beauty, such perfection."

"God gives you this gift. You are His chosen Keeper."

"To bless His people."

Zoram cleared his throat and tried to rein in his full heart. "Here," he lifted the blade from her hands. "Lay it across your two fingers at the base of the blade, just above the hilt. Good. Now . . ." He let go.

The sword teetered slowly back and forth, perfectly balanced. "There has never been its equal, just as there is no equal to our God."

"Amen."

Zoram lifted the sword into the air, admiring it in the bright light, the peculiar properties of the black rock giving the blade an ethereal, otherworldly sheen to it. "Behold my first and most perfect creation. Behold the Sword of Laban."

Rebekah was shocked and clearly troubled at the declaration. "L-Laban? Wh-why th-that name? Why not Z-Zoram? You m-made it, after all."

Zoram started cutting slowly through the air, twisting and turning the sword in his hand in a rhythmic and fluid motion. His eyes never left the blade. "Laban is the Keeper of the Record. The Sword is created to serve and protect the records and their Keeper. That is the order of things. I and the Sword live to serve the word and will of God, embodied in the Keeper."

"B-but Laban?"

Zoram could hear the disgust in her voice. She, too, apparently harbored ill feelings for the Keeper of the Records. "I know, I know, but whatever your feelings are for the man, this is the way it was set up, inspired by the prophet. Besides, I'd never consent to it being named after me. It's not my sword. It belongs to all of Israel; it belongs to God, and the prophets have declared it the servant of the word. Like it or not, Laban is the Keeper of the Record, called and anointed as such. We honor God and His people by adhering to tradition and following the inspired commands."

"Forgive m-me if I d-don't."

Zoram found even her defiance attractive. She was a strong and beautiful woman. "Call it what you will then—the Sword of Faith, the Sword of Action, the Sword to divide asunder the things of God from the things of the world, the Sword of Israel, the Sword of God." He held it again into the light. "I will call it by the name prescribed under the law, whether or not I find the man deserving of the title or not."

Rebekah suddenly pointed. "Wait. S-stop!"

"What? What's wrong?"

"There. D-do you see it?"

"What?"

"There. On th-the b-blade."

Zoram stopped and held it out. Rebekah touched the elaborate designs that ran the length of the blade. "Here. Don't you see it?"

"Is that . . . ?"

Characters. Words, written in an ancient form of Hebrew calligraphy, were visible between the winding and twists of the blade's light and dark patterns. He shut his eyes tight. Was it a play of the light? Was it the result of a lack of sleep? But Rebekah had been first to spot them, and he could not deny that they appeared to spell out words. "I see it, but I can't quite . . ."

She ran her fingers over it again but more slowly this time and leaned in to see it more closely. "I think it says . . . *Protector*."

"But look! It keeps going. *Protector*," he read, "*of the Word*."

"No," Rebekah corrected him. "Not *the* Word. This word here means *my*—'*Protector of My Word*.' This was written . . ."

Zoram felt his strength leave him at the realization of what Rebekah's interpretation meant. "By the hand of God."

They didn't speak for a long moment, content staring at the words written on the blade of the Sword. There was no denying it. The words were as clear as if Zoram had inscribed them along the length of the blade—which he hadn't. "How is this possible?" he finally said.

Rebekah continued to run her fingers gently over the smooth steel surface, scarcely able to believe it. "It's a miracle," she whispered as a calm settled over the room, tangible and real.

Neither had words to adequately describe how they were feeling at that moment. Fortunately neither tried, both being comfortable with each other and with silence. Zoram's mind was called back to his mother's favorite passage of holy writ, the experience of the prophet Elijah, when God spoke not in the wind or in the earthquake or in the fire but in a still, small voice. He had the feeling that God was speaking to them now. He felt an outpouring of love and approval for his sacrifice and dedicated work and knew that his offering had been accepted of the Lord.

In the stillness of his mind a thought—an observation, really—lit lightly on his mind and in his heart. During the time Rebekah had touched and handled the Sword, her stutter and all signs of her speech impediment had simply disappeared. Vanished. Her words had been expressed as easily and effortlessly as his or anyone else's. What manner of small miracle had he been allowed to witness? The depth of love the Lord had for this special woman humbled him to even be in her presence. Part of him wanted to speak, to acknowledge this personal and divine manifestation, but the larger part willed him to be silent. Now was not the time.

He could see that Rebekah was having her own spiritual experience as well. Her eyes were filled with tears, but her face had a glow about it. They were tears and cries of joy.

Her eyes eventually drifted up to meet his, and in that moment, time stood still. To Zoram, the armory and the rest of the world melted away, leaving only her. He still didn't understand what he was experiencing, but he realized he didn't have to. What was there to understand about love? Pure and deep. She was perfect, and God had taken care to place her in his way. And while his understanding failed him, he trusted in the arm of the Lord.

She held his eyes, captivated and sharing like feelings. With his other hand, he reached out and gently touched the side of her face. A ripple and spark of energy passed between them. They both shuddered at the touch and moved closer to one another—

Zoram sensed the moment pass and the serenity flee an instant before he heard the metal tray clang to the stone floor. Startled, they both looked over to see Anat, shock and betrayal strewn across her features. She just stood there, unable to speak or move, fruits and other breakfast foods littered at her feet. She finally tried to form words but couldn't. She turned and fled instead.

"Who was th-that?"

But before Zoram could answer, the doorway was filled by one of the king's personal guards. "Zoram, son of Jharom and new Keeper of the Sword?"

"I am," he said, unconsciously taking a position between the armed soldier and Rebekah.

"Zedekiah, our great king, requests your presence and audience."

Zoram turned and looked to Rebekah. "Go," she said. "I'll c-clean up here." Her tone was as warm as her smile.

Zoram returned her affection and replaced the blade securely and effortlessly into place within the scabbard. He couldn't bear to leave her now and turned to glance one more time, only to see her smile lightly.

There was no doubt in his excited mind. He was in love, he thought as he followed the king's guard out of the armory. Absurd as it sounded, he was sure of it.

CHAPTER SIXTEEN

ZORAM WAS NOT PREPARED FOR the influx of memories and emotions as he approached and entered the palace. He had nearly forgotten the time he had spent here as a child, playing with the other children of important or wealthy families. As the only child of the Keeper, he was raised to stand apart from the other children. His playmates had been young princes or heirs to land and fortunes.

The palace, built on the upper slopes of the hills and separated from the Temple Mount by a wide valley, had been the ancestral home of Israel's kings since the days of David. Built and added to over the centuries by each succeeding king, the palace was now a conglomerate of centuries of architectural styles and influences. And yet, for all its displaced configurations, the palace maintained a quiet dignity of a noble house and birthright.

The farther they ventured inside the palace, however, the more Zoram was struck by contrasting feelings of despondency. Where gold and silver and silks once adorned the hallways, now there were only bare walls. Like Israel and its people, the royal palace was a mere husk of what it once had been.

As they walked in silence, Zoram couldn't help but notice his guide stealing frequent glimpses at the Sword Zoram carried. Finally, when the guard's curiosity was too obvious to pretend it didn't exist, the young man broke the silence with an eager question. "Is that . . . the new Sword?"

Zoram reflexively readjusted it in his hands and gripped it tighter.

"Forgive me, I meant no harm or disrespect, Keeper," the young guard apologized. "When I heard you'd locked yourself inside the Keeper's armory with strict instructions not to be disturbed, I hoped you had begun work on the new symbol of our generation's faith and hope." He paused as if embarrassed by his bold words and then continued leading the way in silence. Finally, he spoke again. "You cannot begin to know how badly we need you right now. For many of us, the hope of your return and what you would create was all we had left to look forward to. Thank you."

Zoram was taken aback with the sincerity of the young man's words. With the exception of Rebekah, he had yet to hear others express their faith so openly. It gave him a ray of hope in an otherwise dark time.

"If I may," Zoram said, "what is your name?"

"Ammon, great Keeper."

"Please, my name is Zoram."

Ammon bowed his head sharply. "Zoram."

"Ammon, you can let it be known that God still lives and has not abandoned or forgotten His people."

"Many have lost their faith," the guard replied.

"I know, or so I have been told. But I *know* God has not abandoned us."

"I do not doubt your conviction, but how can you be certain?"

Zoram held up the sword in his hand. "The story of its miraculous creation will soon be known to all."

Ammon took a confident breath and appeared to walk a little taller as they made their way to the king's personal reception hall. "Thank you for your faithfulness," he said softly.

The guard paused at the entryway and motioned for Zoram to wait. Then he took another step forward and announced, "King Zedekiah, high leader and protector of Jerusalem and all of Israel, I present to you Zoram, Keeper of the Sword."

On cue, Zoram stepped through the large doorway as Ammon excused himself and left them alone. The reception hall was only marginally more furnished than the rest of the palace. Lit by natural light streaming in through large balconies and windows, the spacious room was still devoid of the life it once possessed. It took a moment for Zoram to find the king sitting atop the raised throne chiseled out of stone but robbed of the gold and other ornaments one would expect to find on the symbol of a king's power. Zoram suspected that the sparse furnishing was by design, meant to remind the king and the people both of their conquered state and that the king was, in fact, powerless under Babylonian control. It served to dissuade any visiting foreign dignitaries or ambassadors from having even the slightest faith in the power and might of Israel. The sight was truly pathetic.

Zoram's attention turned from the room and the kingdom to the king. Laban was right—he was young. He couldn't have been much older than Zoram, maybe in his late teenage years or early twenties. But where the king's body still retained some of its youth, his face bore the weight and stress of the position. He looked tired despite the morning hour, dark rings already around his sunken eyes.

Zoram had the sudden feeling that he recognized him, but he couldn't quite place the face. The king stood and stepped down from the raised dais, and in the new light he looked even more familiar. Years ago? From his childhood? Yes. Then a name burst into his mind. "Matteniah?"

The king smiled wide, dispelling most of his distress. "Zoram!"

The two walked quickly to each other and embraced as brothers.

"It is so good to see you," the king said.

Zoram could barely contain his excitement. "Is it really you? Of course it is. But how . . ." he trailed off, unable to think clearly.

"You cannot begin to imagine the thrill in my heart when I learned of your arrival, though I am truly sorry to hear about your father. I don't remember meeting him but a few times. What I do remember and know from his reputation is that he was an admirable and faithful man."

Zoram welcomed the praise of the man he scarcely knew and further disregarded the unsettling words about his father that Laban had shared. He thanked the king and bowed slightly at the waist. They had known each other as children. Matteniah was of the royal lineage, but he had not lived at the palace. If Zoram remembered correctly, Matteniah had visited often and made many friends with his outgoing personality and hunger for fun and games. He had been so vibrant and alive back then, which explained why Zoram had such a difficult time connecting the boy from his youth to the gaunt man occupying the throne.

"But there is much I am eager to hear that you must tell me," the king said.

"Tell you? Of what?"

"Why, your time away. It must have been such a grand adventure going to lands so far away. Do you know that when you left we all used to play and pretend we were you?"

Zoram was a little embarrassed. "No, you didn't."

"It's true. We would all take turns being you, fighting strange armies in far-off lands—Oh! And the dangers!"

"The what?"

The king smiled and led them to a table and bench set up outside on one of the balconies. "Oh, we knew they weren't real, but we'd heard so many exotic and fantastical stories about where you had gone off to. Our young imaginations devised many daring adventures to fill up our days. So tell me, what was it like?"

Zoram chuckled softly. "I'm afraid your stories were more exciting than mine."

"A lack of dragons then?"

"Dragons? What do you know of dragons?"

"You know, those winged serpents of great power that are said to inhabit the tops of mountains in those Oriental lands."

"Oh, those. No, no, there were dragons all right," Zoram said in all seriousness. "They just kept to themselves for the most part. That is, except when they came to the markets for rice."

There was a pause, a moment when the king was unsure how to take Zoram's account, before they both broke into laughter.

"But seriously, Zoram, I know of no one who has ever traveled that far east. Tell me, does it differ much from Judea?"

Zoram relaxed and leaned back against the bench, a pleasant feeling washing over him. "It was the most incredible place on earth. It is a land of deserts and jungles, plains and mountains. And when I say mountains, I don't mean the hills that dot Judea. These mountains reach right into the heavens, where the tops are shrouded in the clouds and covered in snow all year long, mountains so tall that not even weeds and grass and trees will grow. But while they're rocky and barren, they possess a majestic beauty that defies words. There's not a more peaceful place in all the earth."

"And the people? Are they heathens? Are they as savage and godless as we've heard?"

Zoram drank from the cup before him. The wine was as sweet and delicious as his memories. "I consider it a privilege to have lived with them all these years. Heathen? Yes, in that they didn't worship the One True God; but they're a very spiritual and peaceful people. To be sure, there will always be individuals who act contrary to the teachings and practices of the majority, but as a whole, they are a people very much at peace with everyone and respectful of any gods their many apprentices worship."

He could tell that his old friend was a little disappointed that he didn't share any adventurous stories, and while Zoram had many tales to tell, now was not the right time to share them.

"But my stories must pale in comparison to yours. Little Matteniah, carefree Matteniah, troublemaker Matteniah—now the king of Israel."

His friend's smile melted away and was replaced by a far-off look of pain and sadness. "I always secretly wished I could have been you. At first because life at Jerusalem in the royal house and in the hills was all so boring. I wanted to live out the adventures we all dreamed you were having." The king paused. "But then I wanted to be you because you were far away and safe from the death and destruction that accompanied Nebuchadnezzar and his armies."

The king stood and stepped to the railing. "I was never meant to be considered for the throne. But life," he added with contempt and almost under his breath, "never unfolds the way one plans."

Zoram thought back to his youth, trying to recall anything about Israel's leadership and line of ascension to Israel's throne. But he had been so young and these matters meant nothing to him at the time. "Josiah was king when I left . . . I think."

"Yes," he said, lost in thought. "Josiah, my father, was a good king—or so I was told. I don't remember him much. He restored the Temple and fought bravely against the Assyrians. His successor was less . . . inspiring. Jehoahaz was king for a not quite a year before my oldest brother, Eliakim, was put on the throne. He took the name Jehoaikim when he became king; it means *the Lord raiseth up*. But he did nothing to raise anyone up except himself and his own ego."

The king slouched at the banister as if he had suddenly lost all strength. "We rejoiced when we first heard that the Assyrians had been defeated. It never occurred to us that this new conqueror might be even more ruthless and inhuman. Until it was too late. My brother was king when they moved through our lands. He was allowed to remain in Jerusalem until last year, when he was taken captive into Babylon. His son was taken shortly after. Which left me." The king looked out past Zoram at nothing in particular. "Most days I wish I'd had the courage to fall on my sword."

"Don't say those things. Life is the greatest gift of God and not ours to discard."

"I know," he said softly. "I know."

"But why did they choose you? As you've said, there were others in the royal line that they could have chosen." Zoram remembered what Laban had told him about their new king, but he wanted to hear how his friend saw his ascension and appointment.

The king didn't answer right away, but when he did, he made no pretense about it. "Because I was young and naïve and had no skills to lead a nation. This seems to be Babylon's way. They destroy all semblance of a conquered government and put in children who can be easily controlled. I'm a king with no real power."

He removed the thin crown from atop his head, held it lightly in his fingers, and stared at it. "This crown is heavier than it appears. I'm not the right one to lead Israel. I haven't been schooled in politics or negotiation. I don't even possess the skills to manage my office, let alone inspire men."

Zoram didn't like the defeated tone in his friend's words. "But that's why you have advisors and a court filled with men who are schooled and skilled in these things. No king leads by himself. It's impossible and foolish to think otherwise."

"I wish it were that simple. What you say is true, but what can a king do when he can't even trust his closest circle of friends and counselors? When those whose words you've believed and acted upon may have been lies and half-truths to further their own personal and selfish aims? Where is a young king to turn then?"

Zoram didn't think the king was in search of an answer, but one came to the Keeper's mind and he felt compelled to share it. "Have you inquired of the high priests and those who have no interest in political power? Surely their words would be of value and offer impartial direction."

The king couldn't help but scoff at this. "It's the priests and religious leaders I trust the least. You're naïve to think they're without personal ambition. There is great power in controlling access to God and His will and approval."

These last words struck Zoram's heart like a heavy weight. Had all hope and faith in Israel and its heritage been exhausted and replaced with loss and despair? It was one thing for the masses to be easily defeated—those who had lost quite literally everything they once had—but Matteniah had come from a faithful family, strong willed and influential for generations. Maybe he just needed to be reminded of that. "Then you do what all of Israel's great kings have done and turn to the one source, the one advisor, who will never deceive and whose word is sure."

"Who?" the king asked. "God? Do you really think He cares for us anymore? For years there was talk of miracles and of God's mercy, but where was God when the Babylonian hosts swept through our land, riding through the streets, desecrating our Temple, robbing us of all we hold dear? They killed all those who posed a threat to their occupation. Did you know they even took our young princes? You asked why they selected me to be king? It's because there was no one left. Do you remember Daniel? Or Hananiah or Mishael or Azariah? They were all taken captive and enslaved."

Zoram had played with every one of them as a child, and suddenly the reality of Babylon's conquest became much more real and personal to him. He still remembered Daniel holding his hands high in the air as a final wish of good luck the day Zoram left for his apprenticeship. He had drawn strength from that image so many times over the years. And now Daniel was gone, and possibly—

"Are they still alive?" Zoram asked suddenly.

"We hear stories from time to time, but they lead lives of servitude and constraint."

"At least they live."

"But what is life without freedom? Not to be permitted to pursue and reach your dreams, but forced to work and slave under the yoke of an oppressive master."

Zoram joined his friend at the balcony rail and gazed down at the lower city and market quarters of Jerusalem. "Most men live their entire lives a slave to many things—poverty, status, theft, circumstance, poor crops, even the weather," Zoram said. "The world is full of men who work their entire lives, living day to day, without any thought of dreams or loftier goals. Survival is their master. And though men and nature can take away everything they have worked for and achieved, there is one thing that remains theirs so long as they don't *give* it away—their faith and trust in God. Whether we are bond or free, slave to another or master of our own lives," he tapped his chest, "we control who we are in here. We are of the house of Abraham, Isaac, and Jacob; we are heirs to a noble birthright. We are the chosen people of the One True God, and no invading army or foreign tyrant can change that."

The king shook his head slowly. "Maybe we once were, but not anymore. He no longer hears our cries. He had abandoned us."

"No," Zoram said with the full conviction of his soul. "God is immovable. If we find ourselves distant and removed from Him, it's not because *He* has moved."

The king thought about this for a moment and then shook his head. "You're starting to sound like *them* now."

"Like who?"

"Madmen, these self-proclaimed 'prophets,' always claiming to speak for God but always quick to judge and call us to repentance."

"Is what they say all bad?"

"That's not the point. They have no right to pretend to know what is best for the people and the nation."

"Then who does?"

The king shrugged his shoulders. "The high priests, perhaps."

"And what do they say?"

"Nothing. The heavens are silent. They have been so for many years."

"Are they? Or perhaps the priests have just become deaf to heaven's voice."

The king turned away sharply. "See, there you go again, speaking like you're one of *them*." He then waved his hand in front of his face as if swatting at a fly. He was clearly frustrated. "But enough of this talk. I did not mean for our time this morning to be spent on these depressing matters." His eyes fell on the Sword at Zoram's side.

"I hear you locked yourself in the armory. My men could hear the sounds of fires and pounding hammers all day and into the night." The king's eyes flitted to the Sword. "Is that it? I didn't think it would take so short a time."

"That's why it was necessary to isolate myself," he said, switching roles from childhood friend to new Keeper. "Would you like to see it?" He unhooked the sheath from his belt and offered it to the king.

The king was silent for a moment while he examined the hilt and sheath. "The metalwork is exquisite. The designs are flawless and is this . . . ?"

"The hilt? Yes, forged and fashioned from the original gold and precious stones of the first Sword as the great Isaiah once held and blessed it."

Those familiar with the Keeper's Sword knew the tale of the hilt. In a time where the nation's gold and other precious metals and gems were seized and carried off by the invading Assyrians, the call went out for personal sacrifice in the name of the Lord. Enough gold was presented and melted down to forge the hilt of the Sword that would represent their faith. Enough jewels were donated to add the ornate decoration. The king loosely gripped the handle, feeling the power of this symbol of the people.

"Did you ever see my father's Sword?" Zoram asked.

"No. It was destroyed before I ascended the throne. I've heard tales of its magnificence, but as beautiful as it might have been, I cannot believe it comes close to what you have created. You have exceeded all expectation in your skill and craft."

"You do me great honor, Matteniah . . . I mean . . ." Zoram couldn't recall the king's new name.

"Zedekiah, but Matteniah will do between us."

"Of course, my king. But you have only just seen the scabbard and hilt. Please, behold the blade."

With one hand wrapped around the Sword's golden handle, Zedikiah gripped the gold-and-silver inlaid sheath with his other and pulled the two apart.

But it wouldn't budge.

The king tried again, pulling harder, but the blade was stuck. The two would not come apart.

Zoram was surprised and even a little embarrassed with the Sword's grand and royal debut. He remembered how easily it had slid from the scabbard no more than an hour ago. "There must be a stray lip of metal not folded properly," he offered. "Or a nick in the blade that's catching. Here," he reached out, "allow me to look at it and help you."

The king tried to free the blade one more time, tugging on it with increasing frustration, before giving it to Zoram. "Looks like you might need to return to your workshop and—" He stopped midsentence as Zoram removed the blade without any effort. In fact, it was as if the Sword leapt out of the scabbard at its creator's touch. Zoram, too, was taken aback by the sudden ease and handed the Sword back to the king half drawn. Neither said more as the king drew the blade out the rest of the way. But where the king's silence had previously been the result of frustration and embarrassment, he was now speechless at the sight of the blade before him. He held it aloft, stunned at its unsurpassed craftsmanship and beauty.

First the king's eyes, then the tips of his fingers, traced the alternating light and dark patterns that were engrained through and along the blade. "What manner of metal is this? This is unlike any steel I've ever seen before."

Steel, Zoram knew, was rare throughout this and every other region of the world. But his masters possessed the most unique techniques for forging the hardened metal. "This is no ordinary steel, my king. The construction of this metal is a special process, secret and closely guarded by those masters who instructed me. It's called Wootz steel. These lines and patterns are made by folding the finest steel and other metals over and over during the forging process. This gives the blade greater strength and allows for a sharper edge."

The king ran his thumb over the sharpened edge of the blade. "I see what you mean." He proceeded to turn the blade over and over in his hands, the sun catching and reflecting against the Sword's many lines and contours. "It's beautiful, but is it battle worthy or simply ornamental?"

Zoram smiled. He was hoping for just such an invitation. "Your highness, would you allow a small demonstration?"

"Here? Now?"

"Who's your most skilled swordsman?"

The king did not hesitate. "Ammon."

"The guard who escorted me to the palace?"

"Yes."

"Good. Call for him and have him bring his sword."

Ten minutes later, Zoram was facing off against Ammon in the center of the reception hall, surrounded by a dozen or so others who had heard of the exhibition of the new Sword. Out of habit he bowed and then took a loose, defensive stance, his left hand extended toward Ammon with his first two fingers extended skyward and the others touching at the tips. The Sword was at his side and a little behind him, the blade pointed down.

Ammon looked at his fellow guards and then to the king as if asking how he should respond.

"Don't worry," Zoram reassured him with a smile. "You won't get hurt."

"Ammon is a skilled swordsman," the king chimed in good-naturedly. "He was once considered for Laban's Fifty, but he refused. Maybe it is you who should be concerned." There was a round of chuckling from the king's men.

Zoram continued to wear his confident smile. "Then this should be a good show." He resettled into his defensive and receiving stance. "Attack me."

Ammon grinned at the challenge. He spun his own sword in his hand and flexed his shoulders and neck before launching a series of overhead strikes. Zoram easily parried the heavy blows. Traditionally forged iron blades connected with a thick, heavy sound, but the new Sword rang with a light, crisp noise and echoed throughout the stark room.

But the attacks were only halfhearted in intensity and speed, as was common in practice and exhibitions. Zoram needed real attacks to push the new Sword to its limits. "What are you waiting for? This is not a dance for little girls. I said *attack* me!"

Ammon looked to the king as if for permission before unleashing a fury of faster and more fierce strikes.

"This is more like it," Zoram said, still defending each blow with ease. The training he had undergone was so superior to anything Israel's military had that he struggled not to flaunt his skills and school the king's guard. But this was not a demonstration of his skills—there would be time for that later. Today's show was all about the capabilities and power of the Sword. But Ammon was still holding back. Zoram needed a way to increase the ferocity of the attacks to truly test the Sword's potential.

"Harder!" he urged. "Faster! Don't hold back! Strike me down! Good!" But it still wasn't enough. He needed Ammon to fight as if his life depended on it.

Or at least his honor.

"Is that all you've got?" he taunted between defending strikes and lunges. "If you're one of the best, I can see how Babylon so easily defeated you!"

This infuriated Ammon, as he had hoped it would. The young guard screamed in anger and unleashed a renewed, relentless offensive. Zoram now had to watch his form and position as sharpened iron flew at him from every direction without restraint or regard for safety. Ammon was, in fact, quite skilled, and Zoram blocked and parried the unyielding attack until he spotted the precise moment he could test his new blade.

Ammon raised his sword overhead and brought it down with enough force to literally cleave a man's skull in two. Zoram deftly pivoted to one side and sharply drove his blade upward with all his strength to meet the thick iron. But he did not mean to simply block or deflect the blade. Instead, Zoram's steel blade actually cut into Ammon's sword, slicing clean through the iron blade at a sharp angle.

The detached piece of iron fell to the tile floor, the loud clang bringing Ammon's attacks to a halt. For a stunned moment, the room was devoid of all sound except for the ringing and hum of the new Sword. Ammon, the king, and all of the onlookers stared at the disfigured blade and the piece lying on the ground. Finally the king stepped between the two combatants, both breathing heavily with the exercise, and picked up the piece of Ammon's sword. It was a clean slice, like an ax through a sapling branch. In time, the king turned his attention to Zoram and touched the steel blade. There were a few small nicks and dents in it, but it had remained in one piece, and even more remarkably had retained its sharpened edge.

"Incredible," the king whispered to himself.

Zoram lowered his weapon and extended his hand to Ammon. "I am sorry for my words. I didn't mean them in the least. Please forgive me. I needed to elicit an attack strong enough to demonstrate the Sword's full measure. You are a worthy opponent and skilled swordsman. If Israel had an army of men like you, there's not a nation in this world that could stand against us."

Still laboring to catch his breath and comprehend what he had just experienced, Ammon reached out and took Zoram's forearm. "Great is our God for returning you to us. I have much to learn under your instruction."

Zoram smiled and bowed deeply, giving the king's guard all the respect he had to offer. The king thanked Ammon and his men and dismissed them with their words of praise and wonder still caught in their throats.

Zoram and Zedekiah were left alone. "I have never seen a sword like the one you have created."

"It may have been worked by my hands, but I did not create it." His words were soft and reverent.

"I don't understand. Who made it then?"

"Let me show you something. Look closely at the blade. The patterns there. Do you see it? It's a miracle."

"Where?"

Zoram began to point to the spot where he and Rebekah had seen the characters but stopped, confused. "Right . . . here."

"What am I supposed to see?"

"Writing . . ." But now he wasn't so sure. Had he really seen it? He was certain of it. It had been so clear when Rebekah had pointed it out.

"Writing? You inscribed something on the blade?"

"Not me."

"What do you mean, not you? If you didn't, then who?"

The word caught in his throat. "God."

The king looked up with a mix of doubt and confusion. "Is this another one of your jokes?"

"I know it must sound crazy . . ."

"Maybe you spent too much time over the fire," the king said lightly. "Such exposure can surely cause your eyes to play tricks on you."

Zoram continued to run his fingers over the intricate designs. "We didn't see them until afterward."

"We?"

"It was as clear as . . . there!" he said, pointing to a length of the light and dark patterns.

"I see it, but what is it supposed to say?"

"Here." But Zoram paused, unsure now of their earlier find. The letters were not as clear. "*Protector of My Word.*"

The king studied the spot Zoram was pointing to but shook his head. "I don't see it. Are you sure?"

Zoram suddenly rubbed his eyes as the patterns appeared to shift and change. When he looked again, nearly all traces of the letters were gone.

"Maybe it was a trick of the light," the king offered his old friend.

"Maybe," Zoram reluctantly agreed, but while he was sure he had seen them before, the illusion of the patterns changing troubled him. The steel was hardened and tempered. It was physically impossible for the folded steel that made up the patterns to change. Wasn't it? He couldn't explain it.

"Well," the king said, "if you saw symbols and words in these patterns, then maybe they were meant for your eyes only. May I?" he asked, reaching for the Sword.

The king was still in awe of not only the blade but also the display of martial training and military application. "The army that possesses swords such as this will be unbeatable."

"No, my king," Zoram said, being brought back from his thoughts into the conversation. "A weapon, as strong and as sharp as it might be, is merely a tool—an extension of its user, nothing more. Given to a fool or a coward, a sword like this one would be useless, even dangerous. No, Matteniah, victory is not achieved by the weapons an army possesses but by the hearts and faith of the men wielding them. Men like Ammon. Focus your efforts on forging men like him, men who still love and have faith in Israel, not on the swords or spears or arrows they will use. I was once told that it is the faith and the moral cause that inspire and drive an army to victory. When they fight on the side of right—and truly believe in their cause—then regardless of the danger, they will be invincible."

The king didn't reply, his eyes still fixed on the Sword. Zoram wondered if he had even heard the words of advice and counsel. Finally, he reached over, took the sheath, and slid the Sword inside. "Maybe you're right." He then tried to draw the Sword out again but couldn't. As before, it was stuck. The king suddenly released a short burst of mirthless laughter. "It looks like your Sword doesn't like me very much."

Zoram offered an apologetic smile to try and ease the thinly veiled tension in the king's voice. "I'll look at it and repair the defect immediately."

The king set the Sword down and stepped to the balcony. "Is there hope in Israel? We used to be a strong people and a powerful nation. Kings would visit not to conquer but to offer tribute, seek advice, and form alliances with *us*. Where did we go wrong? When did the world change?"

"Maybe it wasn't the world."

The king acknowledged this truth with a sheepish grin. "You're starting to repeat yourself . . . and I think I'm finally starting to listen."

Sudden movement from the other side of the hall startled Zoram. He sprang to his feet but then stumbled backward, embarrassed to see that his reaction was caused by a young boy running barefoot across the floor.

"Daddy!"

The king set the Sword aside and bent over, scooping the little boy up in his arms. They embraced in a tight hug. "When did you get so big? I don't even know who you are anymore," he teased. "Who . . . who are you?"

"Daaaaad!" the boy said, drawing the word out as if to say, *You know it's me.*

"When did you arrive?" He looked around. "Where's your mother?"

"She said you were busy," the child answered. "But I sneaked away."

"Don't you think she'll be worried when she realizes you're gone?"

The boy shrugged his little shoulders. "I don't know. Maybe. But I wanted to see you. You never come visit anymore. Mother says it's because you have important work to do. Is that why?"

The king looked over the boy's shoulder and smiled at Zoram. His son squirmed and turned around, startled at seeing someone else in the room. "Sorry," the boy said.

"It's okay," the king said, putting the child down. "I want you to meet someone. Someone special. We were friends back when I was your age. I'd like you to meet my oldest friend, Zoram." Zoram straightened at the introduction and bowed to the lad. "Zoram, I'd like you to meet my son, Mulek."

The boy returned the bow. "It's a pleasure to meet you," he said in a tone much too formal and mature for his age.

Zoram was amused. "The pleasure is all mine."

Mulek walked over to Zoram with a confident and mature air about him. "Is it true you knew my dad when he was a boy like me?"

Zoram nodded and smiled.

"And did you and he play?"

Zoram looked to Matteniah. "We used to run and play ball, and lots of times we used to hide in the palace. The grownups didn't like that, and they'd try to catch us, but your father and I were just too quick."

Mulek smiled at the thought of his father, the king, getting into trouble when he was a kid. "Did you live in the palace too?"

"No, my family lived across the valley."

"Mulek," his father said, "Zoram is the Keeper of the Sword."

Mulek's eyes darted immediately to the sword on the table. "Is that real? Did you make it?"

The boy's excitement was refreshing. "Yes and yes."

"Can I see it?"

Zoram looked to his father for permission, which was given. "Of course. Here, let me—"

"I can do it," Mulek said, picking up the Sword.

"Now, the blade gets stuck—" Zoram started to explain but stopped, stunned, as the blade slid out of its sheath without any effort.

"Wow!" The child's enthusiasm was childlike and sincere.

The king was also shocked with the ease at which his son drew the blade. "Be careful with that. Please, put it down."

Mulek obediently laid it on the table. "Wow . . ." he repeated, his young vocabulary not yet large enough to express his awe and wonder as he beheld the Sword's unique designs running the length of the blade. Then he stopped and pointed. "Cool! How did you do that?"

"Do what?" his father asked.

"Don't you see it? These lines are words."

Zoram felt a chill run through him from head to toe. He exchanged a quick look with the king, unsure what to do or say next. The king stepped closer and looked over his son's shoulder.

"Can you read what it says?"

"Can't you see them? They're right there."

"Just answer my question, son. What does it say?"

Mulek's face wrinkled in concentration. "I don't know. It's so fancy."

"Try, Mulek. What do the words say?"

Mulek stared at the Sword, sounding out the letters to himself. Finally he spoke. "*Protector of My Word*, I think. Is that right?"

The chills returned, amplified, and a lump formed in Zoram's throat. He, too, stepped closer and looked at the blade. There they were! The words had returned, as clear as when he and Rebekah had first seen them.

"What's wrong?" Mulek asked, sensing that his father was troubled. "Did I read it wrong?"

"No," his father said with a quake to his voice. "You read it right." He cleared his throat. "Why don't you run along? I have a few more matters to discuss with Zoram, but I won't be long. I promise. Why don't you have Ammon ask the kitchen staff if they have any sugared fruit for you."

"Yes, Father," he said obediently. "It was nice to meet you, Zoram. Your sword is . . . pretty. Thanks for letting me see it."

"Yes, it is," Zoram said, his own voice faltering. "Thank you." And then Mulek was off.

Zoram replaced the blade, and the two friends took a seat at the table.

"His mother and I were young," the king started. "Little more than children ourselves, really. We thought we were in love, and I guess we were. We still are. To the shock and embarrassment of our parents, Mulek was born the next summer. The families arranged to marry us off privately and set us up in a small estate on the Sea of Chinnereth."

"What happened?"

"Babylon happened. When Nebuchadnezzar made it clear he was appointing me king, part of me wanted to run and hide. I couldn't risk my wife and child's lives or force them into a life of perpetual fear. If we had fled, we would be continually looking over our shoulders, wondering when the Babylonian bounty hunters would finally catch up with us. I made the decision then and there that I would leave willingly and quickly. Fortunately, our marriage and Mulek's birth were not known outside of a trusted few. I've been able to hide their existence since assuming the throne, but as you just saw, my son is less cautious than he should be."

"Your wife isn't the queen?"

The king laughed curtly. "No, of course not. My public marriage was all arranged. What could I do? I couldn't refuse her. What excuse could I offer and still protect Jerusha and Mulek? My marriage with Israel's queen is for show only. There is no love. And while the queen does not pretend to understand my emotional and physical distance, she agrees to produce heirs and live her life in what little luxury Israel can provide her."

"But isn't Mulek the rightful heir? Isn't he the next king?"

"I pray not. I've heard the accounts of what they did to the other kings who came before me. No one must ever know about him. Besides you, Ammon is the only one I have trusted with this secret. I love Mulek more than I thought I could love anyone or anything in this world."

"You have my word."

"I know . . . I know." The king looked down the hall where Mulek had run off to. "He's a very special boy. Sometimes I wonder if I have anything to teach him. He's always been a bright and sober child—so quick to do the right thing. I sometimes question my worthiness to be his father."

"It's clear that he loves you very much," Zoram said. "There's nothing a child needs or craves more than that."

The king sat in silence for a long time, apparently assessing Zoram's words. He then took a deep breath and forced it all out. "You'll take the Sword with you?"

"I'll keep it locked in the treasury."

"For what it is worth, the Sword has my blessing and endorsement. You've done a fine job with its creation. I'll see that the High Priest is notified of its completion. He'll want to arrange the public blessing ceremony, though after today I don't believe it's lacking in divine approval."

Zoram stood. "It is good to see you again after all these years, Matteniah."

"You're a good man. Perhaps we can do this again. Not the cutting of iron swords but this—talking. It's refreshing speaking with someone who . . ." the king searched for the right words, "who hasn't abandoned all hope, who hasn't lost his faith. Your absence may have been a blessing in this regard." A weak smile flickered across his lips.

"Faith isn't something you lose; it's something you lay aside, and as such, it's something you can pick up again."

"I wish it were that easy."

"Who's to say it's not?"

The weak smile faded from Zedikiah's face. "You look tired. When was the last time you slept?"

"This morning, just before you summoned me."

"No, I mean properly, in a bed."

"Two nights ago."

"Then as your friend, might I suggest you return home and get some rest?"

"Thank you. I will, but the armory is in disarray, and the forge must be swept and cleaned out—"

"No, no. Then as your king, I command it."

Zoram couldn't help but laugh, feeling the toll the past day and a half had had on his body and mind. "As soon as I secure the Sword in the treasury then?"

The king returned his smile. "Agreed."

The two embraced. "I'm afraid Israel may not deserve you," the king said.

"Nonsense. Go and attend to your son and wife and try, at least for a little while, to forget the affairs of state."

"If you feel up to it, I would like you to join us for supper. Mulek has taken quite a liking to you, I can tell, and I want to introduce you to his mother."

"It will be my honor." Zoram bowed and then, with the Sword in hand, made his way through the palace and out into the midmorning sun, the consequences of working his craft fully realized in his physical and emotional exhaustion. But through the numbness and lack of sensation, he could not put aside the many questions he had about the Sword, its patterns, and seemingly odd behavior. Had the events of the morning unfolded the way he now remembered them? Or had part of it been a dream? And if it had happened this way, what did it all mean?

CHAPTER SEVENTEEN

LABAN OPENED A SMALL CHEST and threw Hanoch a small leather scroll.

"What's this?"

"The new key to our success."

Hanoch opened it. "This is your last letter from the princess."

"Is it now? Whose letter is it?"

Hanoch was confused. "Yours."

"Do you see my name anywhere on it?"

Given the nature and content of their correspondence, Laban knew he wouldn't. They had agreed at the outset not to use their names.

"The letter could have been intended for anyone," Laban continued, hoping he wouldn't have to spell it out.

"Like the king?" Hanoch ventured.

Laban smiled. "Like the king."

Laban's new plan was simple, and unlikely as it sounded, Israel's young king would unknowingly play a significant role in Laban's ability to ascend the throne, just as his predecessors had. Once the title of Keeper of the Records had been thrust upon him after the tragic deaths of his father and elder brother, Laban had begun quietly suggesting a new alliance with Egypt, knowing that once this act of betrayal was discovered by Nebuchadnezzar, the king would be killed and Israel utterly decimated. Laban, being of royal lineage as a descendant of Joseph, would quickly intercede, offering the records at the insistence and pleas of the people. It was a brilliant plan. Laban would have proven his loyalty to Nebuchadnezzar and at the same time demonstrated his love Israel, forever establishing himself as Israel's savior, its messiah. But it was not the throne, alone, he desired. The ultimate aim of his plan was to win Amytis's heart—or at least her bed.

But then Zedekiah's older brother, fool that he was, acted on Laban's traitorous advice prematurely, resulting in a swift invasion during which he'd been killed. Outraged but undaunted, Laban pursued his plans with the next king only to have him carted off to Babylon in chains. Which left Zedekiah. But Amytis's most recent letter changed everything. Laban was out of time. This new plan to frame the young king would remedy all this.

Laban tilted his head and drew Hanoch's attention to the wooden box on the table in the corner filled with letters from Nebuchadnezzar's daughter. "Who do we have in the king's palace staff?"

"Someone we can trust?"

"Someone we can buy."

"These are hard times. I am certain it will not be difficult," Hanoch replied.

"Be sure it is someone who will not be missed later."

Hanoch nodded. He understood perfectly.

"We need these planted in his personal chambers, out of sight but easily discoverable."

Hanoch picked up the box of letters. "Consider it done."

"Also, I have sent word to Pashur to call an emergency meeting of the council, in your name, of course."

"Pashur? Why involve the High Priest?"

"If we are to do this right, we will need the support of the priestly class. I need you at this meeting of the Sarim," Laban said.

"Me? Why me?"

"To present your findings and proffer the accusation against the king."

"Why don't you do it?" Hanoch eyed Laban suspiciously. "Your word carries more weight than mine. You will be believed much more quickly than I will be."

"True, but I need to maintain a certain . . . *distance* until the right moment. It must be you. As head of the city's security forces, you must be the one to present the charges. But you must do it with tact and respect. Your allegations will portray him as a traitor to his country and his people, but he is still the king. Do I make myself clear?"

Laban could see Hanoch struggling to grasp the entirety of this new plan. "But with the king under arrest, there will be no one left to negotiate with the Egyptians."

Laban only just hid his frustration with his dimwitted accomplice. "Forget the Egyptians. We don't need them. There will be no alliance.

There will be no threat of armed uprising. With Zedekiah out of the way, Babylon will need to appoint a new king—someone who is a direct descendant of the royal line; someone of Joseph's lineage; someone with influence and power and command over the aristocracy, the High Priest, and the Sarim."

"Someone like you?"

"Someone like me. And with my union with the princess, I will be the one to finally bring peace to this land. My name will be remembered forever."

"But what of the king? What if the Sarim does not convict him of treason quickly? He will deny that the letters are his and demand an in-depth investigation. This might take weeks or even months. He will not be *out of the way*, as you say, for some time."

Laban didn't move or speak right away as a heaviness descended throughout the room. He then produced a small scrap of paper and handed it to Hanoch. "Do you know what this is?"

Hanoch read the printed words. He didn't.

"It is a singular and rare request, and I need it given to the apothecary in the lower city markets. Find someone to deliver it, a nobody, an urchin. Pay him in advance to pick it up and deliver it back to you. You must be absolutely certain you are not seen. This must not be traced back to you, and thereby me, in any way. There must be no mistake on this."

Laban waited silently as Hanoch thought hard on this new plan.

"What you're proposing presents too much risk to guarantee success," Hanoch finally said. "There are too many factors we have no control over."

Laban fought the urge to censure Hanoch for his concerns and, instead, just sat there listening to his lieutenant go on and on about how the new plan would never work. And while Laban didn't really care what Hanoch thought was possible or not, a skilled leader always at least listens to dissenting voices. Who knows? His subordinate might actually make a good point or two—but he doubted it.

He had expected this much from Hanoch. What he was proposing was risky, to say the least, but it *would* work. He had spent the better part of the day, since leaving Zoram in the treasury, running his plans through every scenario he could think of. The plan was fraught with rushed dangers and relied on the support of others, including the Council of Elders, but they were easily swayed and deceived. No, he thought. The new plan was precarious, but it would work.

"But this wasn't the plan," Hanoch continued, not finished airing his concerns. "And I know that with your last letter our timetable has been moved up, but why not just steal them? If anyone suspects or discovers us—"

"They won't."

"But if they do, if it doesn't all play out like you want, we'll be swiftly tried and executed."

"And does death frighten you? Are you so afraid of dying that you would trade the promise of power rivaling my own? You knew this was dangerous from the very beginning. But there's nothing like the threat of death to truly test and reveal the manner of a man. I didn't figure you for a coward."

Hanoch tensed and held his breath for a moment at being called a coward. "You, of all people, know firsthand of my loyalty and my resolve, and while I do not fear death, I much prefer life."

Laban agreed with a smile. "Well said, my friend. Then I guess we should make certain there are no mistakes then, shouldn't we?"

But Hanoch didn't return the confident smile. Instead, he locked on to Laban's stare for several moments. Laban recognized the power play. This was a contest of wills. Laban's plan, as brilliant as it was, did attempt to bring to pass in a day what should take the better part of the year. And while it was a stroke of timing and twisted genius, they both knew it would take Hanoch's full cooperation and commitment to successfully pull it off. This was the one—and only—weakness in the entire operation. Laban didn't have anyone else to help him at this late hour. So it was no surprise to Laban when Hanoch altered his demands.

"I want the land of Judah too. Everything south of Bethlehem."

It was a bold move. "*Too?* You will already be commander of Israel's armies and second to me in power. And now—*what?*—you've suddenly developed a bond with the land? You want to trade your swords and spears for plowshares and till the earth?"

"Land is the only real power. Gold can be lost or stolen, and appointed power only lasts as long as the current regime. Land is how families hold on to their power over the generations. It's where your family's influence stemmed from. I want no less."

"But you don't even like your wife and children. You've said so yourself."

"My reasons are my own," Hanoch said, his voice rising with his frustration. "Whether or not you understand them makes no difference. If I am going to risk it all, then these are my terms."

Laban held Hanoch's stare in true stoic form, unwilling to give away the slightest hints as to his reaction and response. It was best to keep him on edge a little while longer.

"And if I can't?"

"*Can't* or *won't?*"

"It's not mine to give. Nebuchadnezzar is the only one who can grant and transfer title to land that belongs to him."

"That's not true. He occupies the land, but he hasn't yet required landowners to turn over title or vacate their estates. He allows them to live on and work and manage their land as they see fit. This has nothing to do with Nebuchadnezzar."

"It has everything to do with him. The rightful land owners won't take this *reassignment* lightly. They'll protest and send delegation to Babylon."

"But they'll have to go through you. You will have the power— *Babylonian power*—to quiet these dissenting voices."

"And if they send more than their voices to reclaim what has been theirs for generations?"

"I will be the commander of the armies of Israel," he said with menace. "Leave that to me."

Laban couldn't help but allow a small smile. "This is risky. Almost as risky as what I'm planning. And why would I agree to this? Power is easily obtained but difficult to hold on to. If Nebuchadnezzar suspects any fraudulence or treachery, I risk everything I have worked so hard to achieve. You seem to have everything to gain from this agreement while I, alone, bear all of the risk."

Hanoch stood a little taller, more resolved. "You cannot do this thing without me. Without my help you cannot obtain the records in this way and will lose the princess forever."

Laban hadn't thought Hanoch had the courage to say it to his face. He may have underestimated the man he'd chosen to collaborate with. But he supposed it didn't really matter. "And if he refuses to support this?"

"You'll find a way," Hanoch said with a grin. "You're Laban. Nothing is beyond your control. Not even God could hold something from you if you really wanted it."

"True, true," Laban mused. "But Nebuchadnezzar is flesh and bone, and his power is real."

"Swear to me."

"Swear to you?"

"That you'll do it. Title for the lands south of Jerusalem. Swear that the most fertile valleys and hills will be mine once you marry the princess and are finally in power."

"Now, Hanoch—"

"Swear."

Laban's good-natured attitude throughout these 'negotiations' darkened with his hand being forced. And while he didn't like having to agree to terms not of his making, he could see clearly how this deal might actually be to his benefit. A man will fight hard and take risks all in the name of loyalty, but nothing motivates like wealth.

Or, in Hanoch's case, land.

"Done." He raised his right hand. "I swear it. Congratulations. You are about to become wealthy and powerful beyond your wildest imaginations."

Hanoch considered Laban's words for a moment, looking for any signs of deceit before letting the excited thoughts of his newfound fortune creep onto his face. He nodded, and they shook on it.

"Well, now that you number among the land-owning elite," Laban said with an edge of sarcasm, "maybe we can focus again on what we must do to make this little deal, here, a reality."

Laban tried not to let his smug satisfaction show. Men were so predictable. A new inspiration and confidence was taking a hold of Hanoch, one not fueled by loyalty or even power, but a strength driven by pure and simple greed.

"You must hurry. Pashur will have the council assembled in a few hours. You have much to do before then. Do you anticipate a problem with any of this?"

"No," Hanoch said, his tasks clear before him. "No problem at all."

"I suspected you wouldn't," Laban said. "If you will excuse me then; I have a young Keeper to speak with."

"Do you think that wise?"

"Not only wise but necessary. Our young Zoram must be watched carefully these next few days. He will be returning to the treasury."

"How do you know this?"

"He is the Keeper. He is naïve. He'll want to keep his new creation protected. Besides," Laban said with a sense of misplaced sincerity, "I want to see my new Sword."

שומר החרב

Zoram was alarmed when he reached the treasury to find the guards gone and the large, heavy door ajar. He held the Sword tight, gripping the hilt firmly as he experienced a strong and sudden urge to protect the records. Were they all right? Was someone still inside? Where were the posted guards? These and a hundred other questions flooded his mind as he approached the door in a near panic. He wondered if these feelings came with his new title.

Carefully and quietly, he pushed open the door and peered inside. He tried to ease and dismiss his worries when he saw Laban standing over the plates, but his heart wouldn't relinquish its concerns.

Laban must have heard the door move on its hinges or just sensed he was no longer alone in the treasury. He must have also guessed who it was. "They're marvelous, are they not?" he said, not turning around. "Just over a hundred years old, they contain the history of our people and the words of God as He delivered them to the prophets and kings of old, each word carefully and painstakingly etched into these thin sheets of brass. They're all we have left, the only treasure not taken by Israel's many conquerors."

He continued to leaf through the metal pages, speaking to Zoram and to no one in particular at the same time. "Did you know that copies of the law are always made from these, the original source, so as to ensure accuracy in transcription? If we were to lose these our identity, our very heart and soul would be lost as well."

"Laban?"

Laban turned around, a warm, sincere smile briefly creasing his face. "I'm sorry, but these records are very special, very precious to me. I would do anything to protect them."

"You've never borne that weight alone, and like my father before me, it's my duty and responsibility to join with you and share that burden."

Laban looked at him, long and hard. "Indeed." He covered the records with the gold-stitched covering, rested his hand on them, and closed his eyes, almost as if in prayer. "I thought we had agreed you would not begin your work until after your time of mourning."

Zoram was offended at Laban's accusation. He fought the urge to remind the man that there had been no such agreement; there had only been Laban's bizarre and aggressive behavior toward him that morning. Zoram resented, more than anything, the implication that he was somehow controlled by Laban. But he kept his thoughts to himself. "I could see no purpose in waiting. My father is dead, yes, but the way I see it, the needs of a nation far outweigh the need to mourn the loss of one man—even my father. There will be time to mourn later. I had a work to do and obeyed my family's charge."

"My people tell me you locked yourself in the armory shortly after we spoke and did not emerge until just this morning."

"An act that seemed to attract more attention than I could have imagined."

"Yes. Well, was your time in there productive?"

Whether Laban had meant for his words to do so or not, Zoram was now on the defensive and simply stood in the doorway, unresponsive. A moment or two of silence was all Laban could take. "Is that it?" he asked.

A cautious nod.

Laban stepped forward with an outstretched hand. "May I?"

Zoram tried to blame his ill feelings on the fact that he was sleep deprived and physically, emotionally, and now spiritually exhausted. He ignored the request and fought the urge to flee.

"Come, now," Laban said, this time speaking with more force. "Am I to be the last one in all of Israel to see and hold the Sword that bears my name?"

"It . . . it still needs work. The blade catches—"

Laban would be denied no longer. "Give it here!" he said, snatching the Sword from Zoram's hands with snakelike speed. "It was good enough to show the king and your little . . . girlfriend. Now let me see—"

But he couldn't draw the blade from its scabbard either. He struggled again and again, becoming more and more upset with every failed attempt.

"Here," Zoram reached for the Sword. "It seems to catch—"

Laban thrust it back into his hands. "I am beginning to doubt the wisdom of putting all the people's trust and hope in the product of one man. I had *hoped* that the fortune spent on your training would have netted some greater return than this."

Zoram had to bite his tongue to prevent himself from lashing out at Laban. He would not permit himself to be drawn into a fight not of his choosing. The victor in any confrontation, a wise friend had once told him, is the one who *acts* and not the one who is *acted upon*. And what Laban said next would push Zoram's resolve and control to its farthest reaches.

"Your father couldn't make a decent sword either. You must have seen it. The blade broke clean off, sheared at the hilt. I'm not surprised our armies couldn't stand up to the Babylonians with weapons like that. I'm beginning to think that perhaps the Council of Elders and the High Priest should reconsider your family's position. Maybe it's time a new family of Keepers be chosen."

Laban brushed by him on his way out. "Be sure to lock up when you're through in here. I wouldn't want anything to happen to those plates. You haven't lost your key yet, have you?"

Zoram just stood there, tense and rigid from Laban's scathing and contemptuous words. He had never wanted to hurt another human being like he wanted to right now. Keeper or not, Laban's words were uncalled for and unacceptable under any circumstances. And Zoram would take them no longer. But not now. He needed to rest. Perhaps later his head would be clearer, and he would see some other alternative to taking his newly forged Sword and using it to—

He suddenly became aware of his hands. His fingers and knuckles were white from holding the Sword so tightly. He took a deep breath and forced his hands to relax their grip. As he did, the blade slid effortlessly from its sheath. He replaced it without thinking and set it down on the table next to the records. Before he could let go, a strange sensation shot up his arm. He must be getting delusional in his exhaustion, he thought, because the Sword seemed to vibrate and hum as it he set it next to the plates.

CHAPTER EIGHTEEN

Naomi, Zoram's house matron, was waiting anxiously for him when he returned.

"Oh, Zoram! You had us so worried last night. No one knew where you were, and you hadn't left word anywhere." She was trying to sound concerned, but it was coming out as a motherly reprimand.

Zoram was tired and in no mood for a scolding after his encounter with Laban. "I didn't know I had to clear my comings and goings with you—or anyone else for that matter." His harsh words went unanswered and hung in the air like an embarrassment. He shouldn't have snapped at her. He could see that he had genuinely hurt her feelings. "I'm sorry. I didn't mean . . ."

"That was not my intent, Master Zoram."

"I know. Look, I—"

Naomi ignored his attempt to explain. "We truly care about you. You're part of a family now. Our family. *Your* family. Of course you are free to go and do as you please—not even a mother can hope to control her adult son in this way—but there are those of us who may be troubled for your safety. You're a fine grown man, but you didn't grow up here. Jerusalem today is not the same city you knew as a child. There are dangers and threats that lurk in the street and in the hearts of men unlike anything you've experienced."

"But no one has reason to do me harm." He tried to lighten the mood. "People *might* once they get to know me better . . ."

Naomi was not amused. "Zoram, your return is a symbol of hope, and to those who do not possess it, hope is something to fear. Just be careful. We've already lost one Keeper, and I pray that we don't lose another."

He didn't know what to say. He was embarrassed and ashamed of the selfish way in which he had treated her and the other members of his household since returning. And although his homecoming had been anything but the way he had imagined it would be, it was no excuse for his treatment of Naomi.

"I'm sorry. Truly. I'm exhausted. Forgive me, please. I have been on my own for so long I've forgotten that family cares for one another. And if I am honest with myself, you and everyone here are all the family I have left."

Naomi smiled, her eyes tearing up. He then noticed a place setting for two in the dining room. "Was that for me?"

"Anat prepared breakfast for you. For when you finally returned."

Anat! He had almost forgotten. This would explain her shock and disappointment at seeing Rebekah and him together.

"She waited as long as she could and then decided to bring it to you. She's a good girl," Naomi continued, obviously aware of their brief interaction earlier that morning. "She has awaited your return for years."

"I gathered that from the first day we met. She says she knows me from when we were children, but I don't remember her at all."

Naomi sat down and motioned for Zoram to do the same. "I have no idea whether the two of you knew each other before you left or not. I took over the household a year or two before your mother got sick. Anat was already living in the house as if she were your sister."

"I've tried to think of how we might have known each other. What does her father do? Is her family wealthy or influential?"

"No. She doesn't talk about them much. In fact, she so often referred to your father and mother as her own that I often forgot she wasn't a blood relation. But I think her father was or is a baker."

"Here in the city?"

"I think so. Why? Does it matter?"

"Doesn't that strike you as odd? I mean, she has a father and maybe a mother and siblings, but she doesn't visit them or speak of them?"

"There are many reasons parents and children choose not to speak to each other," Naomi said. "Her reasons are her own, and if your father and mother ever knew, they respected her enough never to speak of it. Your mother was especially fond of her. She never had other children and loved having a daughter around the house, even if Anat wasn't hers by birth."

"And she lived here?"

"In one of the lower rooms. She was of particular help to your mother when she . . ." Naomi reconsidered her words. "During her illness. Your father, in many respects, adopted Anat into the family."

Zoram was beginning to see Anat in a new light—a kinder, gentler light. She was forward and bold and her actions bordered on smothering, but after speaking with Naomi, he was able to forgive her strange behavior. What he had once been told was true in his life yet again—a man judges less the more he understands.

"I know she's reacted to your return with an overabundance of enthusiasm. Even if the circumstances surrounding your return had been more . . . inviting, her words and actions may have still been enough to drive any young man away." Naomi reached over and took his hands in hers. "Who and when you choose to love is your decision alone, but may I say that regardless of your feelings toward her, be kind to her. A young girl's heart is not something to be handled with coarse hands or words."

Naomi smiled and patted his hands before standing. She reached for his outer coat and draped it over her arm. "I've drawn a bath and set out clean clothes for you. I know you're tired, but a kind word might ease her troubled feelings."

Zoram closed his eyes and sighed deeply. All he wanted to do was wash off the night's sweat and grime and slip into bed, his very muscles and bones aching for a reprieve. But Naomi was right, and he was sure his mother would have had the same advice and counsel. He needed to put aside his own needs for a few more minutes and do the right thing.

"Where is she?"

"Her room, I think. Thank you. I am certain a few words of appreciation for her efforts to prepare the morning meal would do her heart good."

"Thank you, Naomi," Zoram said in all sincerity. "It's comforting to know that with all I've gone through these past couple of days, I can always find refuge from the storm in your watchful care. My parents were wise to bring you on."

Naomi looked down, almost uncomfortable with the praise. "Now go along, Master Zoram. I'll see that your clothes are cleaned and you're not disturbed further."

Zoram bowed as she turned and left, leaving him to marshal what was left of his physical and emotional strength, force the exhaustion from his body and his mind, and set off to attend to this one last matter.

שומר החרב

"This is treason!"

"Of the highest degree!"

The members of the Sarim were in an uproar. None of them could believe it. They had been notified of the impromptu assemblage only hours earlier by the High Priest but told very little about it. The messengers knew only that it involved an urgent matter of security. Beyond that, they were told to tell no one of the summons, not even other members of the council. It was that sensitive and important. And while many of them had suspected whatever it was involved their Babylonian occupation, none of them supposed it would involve one of their own—especially the king.

But while the rest of the Council of Elders voiced their shock, surprise, and disgust, a solitary level head prevailed against the tumult and eventually found voice loud enough to be heard.

"If it is true." Ishmael was finally heard above the din. He was one of the wealthiest and well-respected members of the council. "Despite the charges, there is no proof that it belongs to the king."

The chaos in the room died down slightly as more and more considered his simple caution. There were breathings of consent and agreement, and all eyes turned to Pashur, the High Priest, who had issued their invitations and who was the voice of the official proceeding. He extended his hands and quieted the room.

"While what Ishmael says is accurate, we cannot ignore the fact that the letter and messenger were intercepted sneaking into the city and making their way to the palace."

"And what evidence do we have of this?"

"Hanoch, our head of security, brought this to my attention the moment it was discovered."

"And is this accuser present?" Ishmael was a businessman, but tonight he was sounding more and more like one trained in the law.

Pashur looked down from the small dais and to his right. "Hanoch? What say you to these concerns? Do you, now, make these statements?"

Hanoch stepped forward. "It is as the High Priest has reported it. What he says is the truth."

But the wealthy oil merchant was not convinced. "And where is this Babylonian messenger? Is he available that we might question him?"

"Alas, in our efforts to discover his purpose, he did not survive our interrogations."

"You killed him?"

Hanoch took a step toward his doubter. The members of the Sarim parted, clearing a large space between he and Ishmael. "We discovered a threat to our city and our nation. We had neither the patience nor the convenience to conduct a full and evidentiary trial. In case you were not aware, sitting in your estate house atop the hill surrounded by every luxury your wealth can afford you, we live in a time of war, and we acted accordingly." Hanoch puffed out his chest. "I will not be questioned or forced to justify our actions to provide you the protection and security you enjoy."

"But he ultimately confessed, isn't that right?" the High Priest asked.

Hanoch kept his attention focused on the voice of dissent and doubt. "Yes. A full confession."

Ishmael didn't respond, holding the soldier's stare with an equal strength of his own.

"But Ishmael," Pashur continued, "the letter refers to other communications, letters sent back and forth for many years. If we can find further proof, there will be no doubt of the king's guilt and conspiracy with Babylon."

"This would explain Zedekiah's appointment and favor with Nebuchadnezzar!" someone yelled out.

"He planned it all along!" accused another.

"We must protect the records!"

To this, Hanoch spoke up. "Security has been discreetly doubled. Members of The Fifty now protect them. They are safe from the king's reach."

"And for that we owe you and your men a debt of national gratitude," the High Priest added.

"And the king knows nothing of this?" Ishmael asked.

"And give him the time and means to hide or destroy any evidence of his guilt?" Pashur said. "Believe me, Ishmael, I have already considered the same concerns you have. I have not come to these conclusions and clandestine actions lightly. I would prefer not to believe the allegations either, but in light of the evidence before us, we would be remiss and traitors ourselves, if we did *not* act."

Ishmael carefully considered the High Priest's words. As much as he hated to, he was forced to admit the logic and precautions were sound. "And what charges are we to level against our king?"

"Conspiracy!" someone yelled, echoed by one and joined in by others. The High Priest raised his hands again to calm the crowd. "Ishmael is right. This decision to present charges is not something to be made based on our anger or fear. Much thought and preparation has been given to this. This is proper and legal. That is why you, my brethren, were called."

"But not all of us are here," someone else pointed out.

"Not all could be reached at this hour. Enough of you are present, however, to authorize a course of action. So let us put this to a vote. Those in favor of taking those necessary measures to protect our nation and our integrity and deliver these charges against Zedekiah, so manifest."

Arms were raised to the square, and affirmative ayes filled the council room.

Hanoch watched all this with a quiet satisfaction. Laban had been correct in his prediction. There was enough fear and arrogance in the hearts of Israel's elite that it would only take a small spark to set off an explosion of irrational thoughts and actions. If any of them stopped and thought about what they were saying and doing, they would choose the more rational course. But that had not been Laban's plan. He needed decisions to be made at the height of their emotions.

But while every other member of the council had already condemned the young king, there was one who continued to resist the charges. Hanoch had expressed concern with Pashur's decision to include the oil merchant in their discreet court, reminding the High Priest that Ishmael was a known associate and close friend of Lehi, but Pashur had insisted.

Hanoch had been reluctant but had consented to Pashur's request. He was now wishing he had gone with his instincts. He could see that other members of the council were beginning to consider alternatives other than the ones he was proposing.

The High Priest noticed it too.

"Now, Ishmael, the vote need not be unanimous, but your support is desired. You must see that until we can determine the young king's innocence or guilt we must act to preserve what order and justice we have left. We know nothing of our king. Until he was appointed, he was unknown to any of us. Though I am loathe to even consider it, we have the letter and the confession of the messenger. The letter makes his intent clear. He must at least be questioned," Pashur stole a quick glance at Hanoch, "and further inquiry completed. If there remain suspicions, then Zedekiah will be afforded a trial and our judges will decide."

"And if he is innocent?"

"Then we will beg his forgiveness. But even the king would have to admit our course of action is the right one given the circumstances."

The rest of the council quieted their voices and hung on what Ishmael would say or do next. Hanoch unconsciously rested his hand on his sword. This was foolish! Pashur was wrong to include Ishmael. There was too much at stake to rest on the opinion of a single man. Especially a man like him. He had his wits about him and was not easily swayed or manipulated. When Hanoch was finally given title to the lands to the south, he thought, his first action would be to assume Ishmael's groves and businesses and put this portentous old man out of business. And then, if Ishmael didn't take his own life out of despair . . . Well, Hanoch thought with a sly smile, he may just have to help separate the man's head from his body.

But for now he waited, holding his breath in anticipation of Ishmael's response.

Ishmael held Pashur's stare for an uncomfortable minute, clearly debating how he should answer. Finally he raised his right hand and consented to the proposed actions. The room erupted in cheers and shouts and applause. It was obvious to anyone not caught up in the commotion that Ishmael was not pleased with his decision, but there truly was not another responsible alternative.

"Then, brethren," Pashur called over the din, "a small delegation will accompany us to the palace. The rest of you are charged with secrecy until the charges are announced. Hanoch, are your men in position?"

"They are stationed throughout the complex. I and a small team will accompany you to keep the peace."

"Since when are soldiers charged with keeping the peace?" Ishmael muttered under his breath. Pashur either ignored the comment or simply didn't hear it, but Hanoch did. Ishmael was a danger to their plans, and he wasn't sure he dared wait until after Laban's plans fully unfolded before silencing the man's tongue permanently.

Following the High Priest's lead, each member of the five-man delegation—a representation of business, government, and the aristocracy—fell into place behind him, and they were all flanked on either side by a combination of palace guards and Laban's Fifty, walking with single purpose toward their unsuspecting king.

שומר החרב

Anat hadn't been able to calm herself down all day.

"How could he?" she hissed under her breath for the thousandth time. After all she had done for him over the years—for the family, for his mother—and this was how he repaid her kindness! Seeing the two of them like that . . . touching each other . . .

Anat growled through gritted teeth. How did he meet her? Was she waiting for him to return too? She hadn't considered that. Just because she wasn't aware of anyone else with eyes on the new Keeper didn't mean they didn't exist. How could she have been so stupid?

And why *her* of all people? Wicked thoughts entered her mind. Maybe it wasn't his fault. Maybe she'd seduced him somehow. Anat burst into a fit of laughter. Not possible. What did the girl have to tempt him with? Her looks? She was nothing to look at. Maybe she'd smooth talked him. More malicious laughter. Everyone at least knew of Rebekah, the eldest daughter of the wealthy merchant Ishmael, and her stuttering tongue. How could she live with herself with a handicap like that?

Anat hoped she might feel better when the laughter dried up. She didn't. Did Zoram know Rebekah from before? Had they been friends then? Anat didn't know and didn't really care. The more important question— the *only* question on her mind—was whether or not Rebekah was trying to steal him away from Anat. It didn't matter. He wasn't Rebekah's yet. She felt the small, thimble-sized glass vial gripped tightly in her sweaty palm. And he never would be. Not if she had anything to do about it.

Just as her anger and her desperate fears began to recycle again for another assault, noises from upstairs caught her attention. He was home! And by the sound of it, he had come alone. She stepped to her door and listened carefully, hoping that her 'broken heart' performance had fooled the old woman. She held her breath as Naomi and Zoram spoke. Straining to hear their conversation, Anat could only understand about every other word, but by the sound of things, her act had paid off.

She heard Zoram ask where her room was, and she sprang into action. Just as she had rehearsed earlier, she quickly went to the small table where two cups were set out next to a pitcher of wine. She fumbled with the vial as she unstopped it and poured the contents into one of the glasses. This would work, she told herself. She hadn't wanted to resort to this, but he had left her no other choice.

She deftly hid the empty vial in the folds of her dress, hurried to the divan in the corner, the one under the window, and quickly conjured up some tears. It wasn't difficult; her feelings were so strong that all she had to do was think of Zoram and that stammering freak living the life that, by right, was hers, and the tears began to flow. It was time to get into character.

All her hard work, all her years of planning came down to what happened next. The pressure was on to be convincing, but Anat felt remarkably calm, as if it was all supposed to play out like this, as if it was all destined to be this way.

Zoram knocked at her doorpost. "Anat?"

She acted startled and stifled her sobs and soft whimpers. She wiped her eyes and sat up, smoothing out her clothes.

"I'm sorry. Thank you for preparing breakfast up there."

Anat's eyes filled again with tears, and she looked away sharply. Her breath came irregularly and in gasps. He started to step into the room but stopped just inside.

"Naomi said it would be good if . . . if I came down and talked to you."

Okay, she thought. *Here goes.* "About her?" she accused.

"About who?"

"That . . . that other woman," she said, successfully producing more tears for effect.

"Rebekah? I don't see how this has to do with her."

"Of course you do! You know good and well this has everything to do with her. And with you. And with me."

Zoram added confusion to his tired look. "I really don't. Maybe we can have this conversation another time. I'm not sure what you're talking about, but I did notice the meal and wanted to tell you thanks. You must have gone to a lot of work. I'm sorry I missed it."

"Sorry?" She turned around, a hopeful smile across her face. "Really?"

"Of course. We were interrupted the other morning—"

"No one knew where you were."

"I know. I already got the reprimand." He cracked a smile at her.

Oh, he was so handsome! She deserved a man like him. "So," she said, sitting up straighter, "what were you doing in there all night? You weren't working on that sword-thing, were you? You do know that the *avelut* forbids work so soon after—"

"Anat?" he interrupted, forcing a smile. "I'd really rather not debate this right now. I was up all night and need to get some rest. Again, thank you for your efforts and your concerns, but if you'll excuse me."

"Please don't go." She sprang to her feet and stepped to the table. "May I pour you a glass?"

"What? No, thank you."

"But you're parched. I can see your lips."

"I think I just need to—"

She slumped her shoulders and lowered her head. She stopped mid-pour. "I knew it."

Zoram turned back around. "Knew what?"

"You don't like me. I'm not even worthy to share a glass of wine with you. Is it because I'm not the daughter of an oil merchant? Is it because my family is poor, and my father is a common baker?"

"What? No."

"It's okay, you know. My social status didn't bother your mother or your father, so I just thought . . ."

"That's not it at all."

"Then why won't you stay?"

Zoram hesitated for a moment but then relented. "One glass?"

Anat perked right up. "One glass. I promise."

She resumed pouring Zoram's glass and then filled one for herself. "Please," she said, motioning to the divan. "Have a seat. You look exhausted."

Zoram was thirsty and drank deeply.

"I'm sorry about what I said earlier." She joined him on the cushions but kept a respectable and nonthreatening distance. "I was just so looking forward to sharing breakfast with you. I even baked the honey bread myself. Being the daughter of a baker does have a few advantages."

"Naomi tells me you've been staying here for a while, that you were of particular help to my mother. I cannot begin to thank you enough."

"She was an angel. Everyone who knew her loved her. And when she got sick . . ." Anat couldn't finish. "Half of the city mourned her passing. Some of us, though, preferred to celebrate her life."

Zoram settled into the comfortable cushions and relaxed. "You know, I only have a few memories of her from when I was younger, before I left."

"Do you remember her sense of humor and quick wit? You probably don't, but she was the funniest person I had ever met. She could observe people doing ordinary and mundane things and make some witty comment that lightened any mood."

Zoram closed his eyes. "I remember her smile. And the way her perfume smelled. And her laugh."

"And then there was her love of children. Some suspected that her generosity and attention toward little ones was a kind of displaced affection to make up for the fact that you were no longer around. And she did miss you greatly, but she loved children for other reasons. Personally, I think she was just blessed with a heart too big to love just one. I wish I were more like her in that way."

Zoram breathed in deeply and sighed. "I'm so tired. I really must get going . . ."

Anat put her glass aside. "Here," she said gently, swiveling to her knees and positioning herself behind him. "Let me help you relax." She placed her hands on his shoulders and began to squeeze and rub. Zoram groaned in pleasure at her massage.

"You're so tense."

"Hmm?"

Anat had learned the shapes and placement of the muscles over the years and could apply the right pressure in the right area to relax a man. She knew just where to rub. Zoram's resolve was beginning to wain.

"Zoram, I wouldn't be honest if I didn't share something with you."

"You're very good," he said, slurring the words together to the point they were almost unintelligible.

"This is hard for me to say. I can't tell you how many times I've practiced this over the years, whenever I was alone, thinking of you, looking forward to the day when you returned. Oh, Zoram, promise me you won't laugh. I don't expect you to answer, but"—here it goes—"I love you. I always have."

Zoram mumbled something, but she couldn't understand what he was trying to say. Had she used too much? She was losing him and fast. The contents of the vial must have been more potent than she had been led to believe. She didn't have much time left.

She got to her feet. "Come on. Let me help you up," she said, reaching down and taking his hands. "You're filthy. Let me clean you up."

Zoram barely had the strength to stand, and it took considerable effort to help him across her small room. With her help he stumbled over to her bed and collapsed into her thick bedding.

"Here, your clothes are filthy. Let me help you with that."

"Nnn . . ." he weakly protested but was unable to stop her from removing his shirt. She then proceeded to dip a small towel in a bowl of warm water she had prepared ahead of time, wiping the residue of his hard work from his muscular chest and arms.

"Mmm . . ." she sounded under her breath. "You are even more beautiful than I had hoped."

Zoram made one more sound, a faint grunt, before succumbing completely to the drug and his own exhaustion. Anat continued cleaning him, softly humming a traditional song of young love penned by King Solomon himself. She caressed his face gently, rinsing the towel several times as she moved it over his body, neck, and hair. She then removed the rest of his outer clothing, washing his legs and feet. He was handsome beyond anyone she had ever seen before. Even Laban on his best day didn't have the shape and definition Zoram's strong, bronzed body had. He was the very specimen of perfection—What was this?

She put the towel away and ran her fingers across his chest and side. She hadn't noticed them at first, but his torso and upper arms were covered in little scars, small cuts. Some were nearly and completely healed and almost invisible, while others—especially one on his side across the bottom of his ribcage—were not. She reached out and carefully, hesitantly, touched it. The wound was larger than the others. It was healed, but by the look and feel of it, she guessed he had received this injury not more than a year earlier. What adventure or act of bravery had marked him so? What manner of man was he?

A man most desired.

She would have him at any cost. She had worked too hard to let him slip through her fingers now, at the eleventh hour. And though she had only truly known him during the few, short days since his return, she was certain she had discovered his one and only flaw. She had suspected it from the beginning, especially the way his father and mother had spoken of him. He was young and naïve enough to still believe in things like honor and integrity. If he wouldn't *choose* to love her, then she would *make him* love her. He would do the honorable thing. She was counting on it.

She quickly crossed her room and closed the door. Then she deftly removed her clothing, slipping into the bed beside him and snuggling up to him, feeling the warmth of his body. She nuzzled her face into his neck and ran her fingers through his hair. She could not be happier. After a minute, she moved her hand to his back, drawing small circles over his ample muscles, listening to his deep, rhythmic breathing.

"I will make you a good wife," she whispered. "One who will meet your every need and desire, one who understands and appreciates what it means to be a Keeper's wife."

She closed her eyes and laid there, thinking of the rest of their lives together, of her position of importance and respect, of bearing his children and forever being part of the Keeper's legacy. It didn't take long until her thoughts gave way to dreams as she joined him in deep sleep.

He would have to love her now . . . He just had to.

CHAPTER NINETEEN

"WHERE IS THE MAN WITH the Sword?" Mulek asked for the third time since being seated for dinner. By this time his father could sense the boy's frustration.

"He is a very busy man—"

"Making swords?"

Zedekiah smiled warmly. "Yes, son. He's busy making swords."

"But can't you *make* him come to dinner? You are the king, aren't you?"

The boy's mother looked to her husband. They had tried to keep this fact from him when he was younger, but the boy was bright and not easily deceived. Despite his youth, he understood quite well the dangers that he and his mother faced with their little charade.

"Your father is not that kind of king."

"Well, what kind of king is he then?"

"He is a king that leads, a king who makes *requests* of people, not demands." Her eyes returned to Zedekiah. "A good king, trying to do what's right."

Mulek noticed the look between his father and mother. "So he can't make him stop working to come to dinner?"

Zedekiah chuckled. "No, but I will be certain to tell him how much you wanted to see him again."

"And the sword," Mulek added.

"And the sword."

But though Zedekiah spoke comforting words to his son, inwardly he was more than a little concerned. Zoram didn't strike him as the type of man to make plans and then not even send word that he was unable to make it. It was true that it had been ten years since they had last seen each other, but still Zedekiah had the pestering feeling that something wasn't right.

Their evening meal was a private one. Zedekiah often dined alone, choosing the quiet solitude of his own thoughts to the bustling and pretentious formalities of entertaining pompous guests and dignitaries. A meal was first and foremost a meal, though he was occasionally obliged to spend his mealtime with affairs of state and religion.

What transpired next happened so fast that all Zedekiah could do was move to the other side of the table and gather his family in a protective embrace. The small dining room was quickly overrun by a dozen or more men, most of which were soldiers or palace guards. These armed men immediately took up offensive positions throughout the room, surrounding the king, each resting their hands on the hilts of their swords.

Terrified, Mulek burst into tears and clung tightly to his mother's neck. She rubbed his back and whispered in his ear that everything was going to be all right, trying to convince herself as much as her son. In the chaos, it took a moment for Zedekiah to look past the immediate threat the soldiers posed and focus his attention on their taskmasters. He recognized several of them as members of the Sarim, but he did not know any of their names. Then he saw two men that he did know: the High Priest and Laban's lieutenant and right-hand man, Hanoch.

"Pashur! What is the meaning of this?" He knew Pashur well enough to know that despite the man's power and position he was weak and easily controlled. Hanoch, on the other hand, had the reputation of being as severe as his captain. If he hoped to maintain at least some level of control over whatever was happening, it would be through the High Priest.

But Pashur spoke quickly and directly. He had clearly rehearsed his words. "King Zedekiah, protector of the people and anointed of God, by vote and order of the Council of Elders, you are charged with conspiracy and treason against the state. In full consideration of the suspicions and charges herein leveled against you, you are hereby arrested and taken into custody."

At these last words, the soldiers nearest the king reached out and took Zedekiah by the shoulders. He tried to shrug off their grips, but it was no use.

He was no longer merely concerned or confused. His fear included more than just his immediate safety. He had taken great steps to shield his young wife and child from the purview of Babylonian and Israeli officials. Word of these accusations, baseless as they were, would surely reach the courts of Nebuchadnezzar in no time. In fact, he was surprised that a member of the Babylonian delegation was not with them. This both relieved and worried him. On the one hand, he would have time to sort through and prepare a defense to these charges before having to answer to the emperor. But—and this sent a nauseating ripple through his stomach—maybe Pashur didn't want Babylon to know.

"This is ridiculous! You have no right!"

"Sit down, my king. No one need get hurt tonight. I assure you this decision was not easy for any of us."

"You will leave us at once and join me in the judgment hall in the morning." The king tried to regain at least a measure of his authority and command. "This is neither the time nor the place for such actions."

Pashur stepped closer. "With all due respect, Your Highness, given their nature, these allegations cannot wait."

"What allegations?" Zedekiah demanded. "I have done nothing wrong. I have broken no law, civil or religious. You have no right to burst into my private chambers and spew forth lies and falsehoods!"

"That has yet to be seen." Pashur motioned for Hanoch to join him. "The charges, please."

Laban's lieutenant opened a letter and began reading. "To Zedekiah, king of Judah and over all of Israel, heir to the most holy throne—"

"Skip it," Zedekiah interrupted. "We all know who I am."

Hanoch narrowed his eyes, and Zedekiah thought for a brief moment that he saw him almost smile at the king's defiance, even at this desperate hour. He continued, "You are charged with acts of conspiracy and treason against Israel, her people, and her God."

Zedekiah was speechless for a moment. He couldn't believe it. "What?"

Hanoch handed a leather-bound letter to Pashur, who held it up for the other council members to see. The High Priest addressed Zedekiah. "This letter was intercepted by Hanoch's men on its way to your hands, my king. It contains the final stages of a plan to betray the very heart of Israel in exchange for Babylonian power and other . . . shall we say . . . *favors.*"

"That's not true. There must be a mistake. I've never seen that letter."

"Of course you haven't. We intercepted it before the conclusion of your plans with the Babylonian princess could be realized and your love consummated."

Zedekiah couldn't help but quickly glance to this wife and young son before further answering the changes. "This is not true. I have absolutely no knowledge of this letter or this princess or this plot you allege I am involved in. Let me see the letter. I demand to see the evidence you supposedly have against me."

Pashur's confident air broke ever so slightly at the king's demand, and he looked to Hanoch for permission. Zedekiah was right. Hanoch was the one overseeing and controlling this operation. Which meant Laban was ultimately behind it.

Receiving the permission he sought, Pashur passed the letter to one of the soldiers, who laid it on the table before the king. It took only a moment for Zedekiah to notice the flaw in their argument.

"Nowhere is my name on this letter. You say a messenger was caught delivering this to me personally? He must be lying. I will instruct our lawyers to question him further and discover for myself who the letter was intended for."

"I am afraid that will be quite impossible."

"Nonsense. Any accused is granted the right to confront his accuser. It is the law. You will not deny me this."

"It's not a matter of *will not* but rather *cannot*. You see, the Babylonian spy carrying your letter died shortly after confessing your name."

This is not happening, Zedekiah thought to himself. If this was not a simple misunderstanding, then it was a carefully planned conspiracy. He would have their heads when this was all finally cleared up. But, he thought with a glimmer of hope, this one fact may actually work to his favor. "Then you have no second witness to implicate me and must, therefore, abandon these charges and release me."

But before Pashur and the others could consider his defense, they were joined by three other men—two additional members of the Sarim and another of Hanoch's men. They were carrying a small chest. By his reaction, it was obvious the High Priest had been expecting them.

"High Priest," one of them said. "It was as we suspected."

A cold shiver passed through the king.

"Where did you find this?" Pashur asked.

"In the king's personal chambers."

"What? You had no right—" Zedekiah began.

"You are the subject of an investigation, my king. It was unfortunate but necessary."

"Where in the king's chambers?" Hanoch asked specifically.

"Sir, in the closet of a small room," the soldier replied. "Beneath a pile of blankets."

"Would you say it was hidden?"

"Yes, sir."

"What say ye, council members?" Pashur inquired further. "Was the chest found as just reported?"

The councilmen were firm in their answer. "It was. We were the first to spy it."

"This is not true!" Zedekiah asserted. "I have never seen that box before! It should be obvious that someone has planted those letters in my room." As crazy as it sounded, it was the only possible explanation.

"Are you accusing these members of the Sarim of scheming to implicate you?" Pashur asked.

"No, of course not."

"What purpose would they have for doing such a thing?"

"No, not the councilmen."

"The soldier then?"

Zedekiah was getting flustered. "No. No one here, but—"

"Then who?" Pashur pushed. "You would have us believe that someone else—"

"The one these letters belong to."

"Someone else wrote these letters—someone who had the means and the motivation to trade what treasure and dignity Israel has left for personal and political power—and then stashed them in your private chambers and hid them out of view?"

"Yes. That's the only explanation." Zedekiah closed his eyes and took a breath, trying to calm the troubled seas of his mind. He fought the instinct to lash out and accuse anyone. He didn't know who to trust anymore, and he doubted if he could have ever trusted any of them. They were all guilty of treachery in one form or another. Even the High Priest. His fear of the men who claimed to hear God had resulted in illegal imprisonments and even officially sanctioned executions without the benefit of trial. But Zedekiah kept his tongue, choosing to remain silent rather than give the High Priest additional opportunity to berate him or imply his guilt.

Pashur called for silence. "We are not your judges," he said softly. "We assume no guilt. That is not our law. There will be a trial. You will be able to have counsel and present your evidence there. But until then, in light of the evidence before us and in the name of the people of Israel, you are hereby placed under arrest and restricted to the palace. You will be under the strict and constant supervision of state security."

Zedekiah didn't know what to say that wouldn't appear desperate, invite further suspicion, or just plain sound crazy. The letters were not his. Whoever they belonged to had gone to a great deal of trouble to shift the blame to him and draw attention away from himself. The more he thought it, the less confident he became about discovering the perpetrator. There were any number of a hundred men hungry enough for power and wealth to sell out Israel and its king. In fact, he suspected that half of his staff, advisors, and even members of the council would all jump at the power that was thrust upon him a year earlier.

And do you know what, he thought, *any one of them can have it!* Anyone who wanted his position deserved to get it. He didn't ask to be king. He never sought after it and the stress that wearing the crown had brought him. All he had ever wanted was a simple life, a long life to spend with his wife and child.

He was suddenly aware of them again and reached out to take his wife's hand. Her gentle but firm squeeze restored his hope and resolve. A small movement from a side entrance caught his attention. It was behind Pashur and Hanoch and largely out of sight by others in the room. It was Ammon. Under house arrest, Zedekiah would be unable to conduct his own investigation, and even when he was finally permitted to speak to his advisors, he didn't think he could trust them. In fact, there were only a handful of men he could trust, and Ammon was one of them. He had to get word to his friend without drawing attention to him.

"With my movements and communications limited as they are," Zedekiah said loud enough to be conspicuous and heard by Ammon, "how am I expected to clear my name and discover those responsible for this subterfuge? I need someone I trust to look into this to help me clear my name and, more importantly, to keep the records safe."

Ammon stopped and then slipped back out of sight. Message delivered. He hoped.

Pashur, unsuspecting of anything, continued acting the part he had rehearsed. "You will be given access to your advisors, and I suspect your lawyers will review the evidence and allegations before they are presented before the judges. For the time being, your communications will be restricted to preserve the evidence and testimony—"

"What is the meaning of this?" a loud voice boomed from the back of the room.

The crowd of soldiers and Sarim parted, revealing Laban. He was dressed in casual house clothes. "Hanoch? Pashur? What is going on here? My king?" he asked, sounding surprised.

Pashur fearfully looked to Hanoch, who responded abruptly. "Sir, evidence was discovered against the king."

"What evidence?"

"Letters—" Pashur started to say before Hanoch cut him off.

"Letters conspiring to steal the records and deliver them to a Babylon princess."

"The records?" Laban's concern appeared genuine. "Why was I not informed of this immediately?"

"We tried to reach you, but no one knew where you were—"

"I don't want your excuses."

"But word did reach you, did it not?"

Laban was clearly upset at the delay in his notification. Maybe he wasn't the one behind this conspiracy, after all, the king thought.

"The safety and protection of the records are my first responsibilities. News of their endangerment should have been delivered to me first—no exceptions. Are we clear on this point?"

Hanoch's jaw clenched, and it took a few moments for him to relax the muscles enough to respond. "Yes, sir."

Laban surveyed the room. "How certain are you of this plot?"

Hanoch showed him the confiscated letter and the chest full of the correspondence.

"No, no, I mean of the king's involvement."

"Sir, well," Hanoch stammered, "this letter was intercepted on its way to the king, and the others were found hidden in his personal chambers."

"Circumstantial, at best," Laban said. "Release him. He's our king, not a criminal."

Hanoch stood taller, planting his feet firmly on the ground. "I'm sorry, Keeper, but as head of security I cannot do that. The law requires that he be held until innocence or guilt can be more clearly established."

Laban stared down Hanoch for a long moment while the councilmen and soldiers nervously watched on. Zedekiah found all this very interesting and not at all like he had suspected it might unfold.

Finally, Laban broke the stare. "Everyone out!" he commanded.

"But, sir, the king cannot be left—"

"Leave your men posted at the door then. I want a word with our king. Alone."

Zedekiah watched with some satisfaction as the room cleared out. Laban didn't hold the official or political power to command Pashur and the other members of the Council of Elders, nor did Zedekiah think Laban had the actual authority over Hanoch in this matter, but what he did possess was attitude and raw charisma. But while the man intrigued him, and despite his uncharacteristic support right now, Zedekiah still couldn't help but think that he was somehow tied to all this. Laban approached and, with permission, joined them at the table.

"Thank you, great Keep—," Mulek's mother started to say but stopped when Zedekiah put a hand on her leg. Being the king and in someone's debt was a dangerous position. Laban may, in fact, be deserving of the king's thanks, but that still remained to be seen.

"They're wrong, you know. I could never betray my people. I would never do such a thing. I may be a lot of things and have many weaknesses, but being a traitor is not one of them."

Laban smiled warmly. "I know."

And in that instant, so did Zedekiah. The letters, the timing of the deaths of Laban's father and brother, his ascension to the position of Keeper—it all became so clear to Zedekiah. How could he have been so blind to the unabashed ambitions of this conceited and unrelenting man? But why? Why would he commit these crimes? His mind raced, trying to match Laban's means and motivations. From what he knew of the Keeper, Laban had everything he could ever want: wealth, power, authority, and an army to command. He had heard rumors since taking the throne of Laban's fetishes and tastes in women, but they never seemed to be in short supply to attend to his every whim. Zedekiah couldn't fathom a reason why Laban could commit so much effort for the love of an exotic princess half a world away when half the women in all of Judea would throw themselves at him for the chance to be his.

Laban never once took his eyes off the king, unsettling Zedekiah under an intense and threatening stare. Laban raised one eyebrow slightly, betraying that he, too, knew of the king's deductions and conclusions. There was no purpose in continuing the charade any further.

"You won't get away with this."

Laban was unaffected by this, his calm grin unchanged. "I'm sure I don't know to what you are referring."

"What I don't understand is why. Why all this? Why not just take them, secretly, in the night? You are the Keeper. You have access to the records, more so than any other man alive, including me. You don't need to do any of this."

Laban held Zedekiah's stare for another moment, impassionate, then reached for the cup from an unused place setting and poured himself a glass of wine. "Expecting someone else for dinner?"

Zedekiah refused to respond, and in the silence Laban took a drink. "Why is it that the king's wine always tastes so much better than what the rest of us can get? It is possible that the grapes themselves know they're destined for a royal palate and give only their sweetest juice?" Laban finished off the glass and placed it back on the table.

"And who are your dinner guests tonight? Who had to witness these serious charges and ugliness? This is not the queen." He cracked a smile. "I've spent time with the queen in the past."

The gravity of this question weighed on Zedekiah to the point of suffocation. He could not imagine anyone worse knowing about Mulek and his mother. He was worried to the point of paralysis, and it felt like ice water coursed through his veins.

"Old friends," he struggled to say. "From the country."

"Of course they are." Laban reached out to tousle Mulek's long, curly hair, but the boy pulled back, clinging tightly to his mother. "And who is this little man? The woman's child, I assume?"

Laban looked at the child and then to Zedekiah and then back to the boy. "And where is the boy's father? Rumors of affairs and scandal would only further damage your standing in light of current circumstances."

"They are friends," he said again as forcefully as he could, "nothing more. I must insist that they be released. They have no connection to any of this."

"Indeed. And while I am largely persuaded of their innocence, the charges are of conspiracy. Until we know who's involved and how far it goes, I'm afraid they will be kept under arrest by your side."

Laban leaned in close to the boy. "And what's your name?"

"Leave him alone!"

"Now, there's no reason to raise your voice, my king."

"You will leave them out of this!"

Laban pulled back and began picking at the food left on the table. "Such powerful and protective feelings you have. Almost . . . *fatherly*. Interesting."

Zedekiah pulled his family closer to him. "We have nothing more to say to you. You are dismissed."

But Laban made no move to leave. Instead, he picked through the bowl of sugared dates, selecting and eating only the most plump. "How far would one go to protect his family?" Laban mused. "Especially a secret one, a family started before one rose to power? And what if there was an heir to the throne . . . ? It is surprising that news of this hasn't reached, shall we say, *royal* ears. I can only imagine the work it would have taken to keep such things secret."

Zedekiah tried to square off against Laban, but stronger men had tried, and none had ever succeeded. Laban was just too strong. To the Sarim, he was a trusted member; to the military, he was a great leader and skilled fighter; the men of the city respected his prowess and position; and the women just loved him. Zedekiah might be wearing the crown, but Laban wielded power the king could only aspire to. It pained Zedekiah almost to the point of death to admit it, but everything he held dear was now at the mercy of Laban.

"What do you want me to do?" He had no other choice. He was defeated.

Laban smoothly produced a small glass vial and placed it on the table in front of him. "The right thing."

Zedekiah eventually picked it up and turned it over, examining it. "And what's this?"

Laban poured himself another glass of wine and downed it in one breath. His grin disappeared and was replaced by a serious and grave look. "The right thing."

CHAPTER TWENTY

"Did you get it?"

Naomi nodded, looking around the estate gardens nervously to make sure they were alone before pulling Zoram's key to the treasury from her coat pocket. She was taking an awful risk taking the key like she had, but there wasn't time to do it any other way. She hoped that Zoram had not noticed her eager hands reaching for his outer coat, feeling to make certain the key to the treasury was still inside. Her accomplice showed some relief, but worry still darkened his features.

"What's wrong, Joshua?"

"You haven't heard? Lehi's gone."

"What do you mean gone? They didn't . . ." She didn't dare finish her question for fear of the answer.

"I don't know. No one does. Word is that his canyon estate is abandoned. The last time anyone saw him was at Jharom's funeral."

"You don't think Laban . . . ?"

Joshua shook his head. "He would have shouted it from the rooftops if he had. No, I think it all just became too great for Lehi to handle."

"No, Lehi would never just leave us. He isn't one to run away in the face of persecution. He's stronger than that. He's stronger than any of us."

"Then why didn't he tell anyone? And where did he go?"

"I'm sure he had his reasons. He wouldn't just pull up stakes and disappear without a good explanation. But the more important question is do you have the plates?"

Joshua pulled back his long coat and showed her the contents of his shoulder bag. There were several thin metal plates inside. "He delivered them before the funeral."

"Are they complete?"

"They seem to be. But Jeremiah still lives, and while he does, I suppose God could still choose to speak through him."

Jeremiah had not been afraid to speak against the actions and intents of Israel's kings. Instead of being heeded, the man of God was imprisoned in a futile attempt to silence his words. But his words were prophetic and could not be so easily silenced. Lehi had been the first to approach Jharom with a plan to include them with the records. The Keeper had agreed to help, and over the past year Jeremiah's words were recorded and engraved on similar plates made of brass and secretly included with the records. The plates Joshua possessed represented the latest, and possibly the last, words of the imprisoned prophet.

"I fear that God may be done speaking. How long will He continue to speak when we refuse to listen?"

"Not all of us turn a deaf ear."

"Yes, but there are so few of us left."

"God said He would spare even Sodom and Gomorrah if Abraham could find ten righteous souls living there. We may be few, but we number more than ten. Perhaps God will spare the city for our sakes."

Naomi didn't answer right away. "I can only hope so."

They were taking an awful risk without Jharom's aegis and protection, but what choice did they have? Naomi and Joshua were counted among the faithful few who had taken it upon themselves to further protect and preserve the word of the Lord. When Laban took upon himself the mantle and title of Keeper of the Records, it wasn't long before it became apparent that his focus was more on what his position could offer him and less on a concern for the records.

"Give me the plates," Naomi said.

"No, it's too dangerous. Give me the key. There are rumors surrounding security at the palace tonight. I'll do it."

Naomi shook her head sharply. "It doesn't feel right."

"What doesn't? Of course it's right. Laban has refused and even prohibited the inclusion of Jeremiah's words. Future generations will need them. They're a warning voice to all those who doubt the Lord and His mercy and patience."

"No, not that." She held up the key. "This. It doesn't feel right going behind his back like this. I can't shake the feeling that we should tell Zoram what we are doing. He has a right to know what work his father started and that we are seeing it through to the end."

"And we will, but only after we are convinced of his intentions. We don't know anything about him yet."

"I know, but I—"

"And until we do we cannot risk the work we have done these past years. In fact, it's a miracle that no one has discovered it yet. This is no longer about simply recording the words of Jeremiah while he sits and suffers in prison. From the servants who compiled his words to the scribes who recorded to Jharom, who fashioned the plates, to Lehi, who engraved them, this has grown from a mere labor of love to an essential part of God's will for His chosen people."

Joshua made sure Naomi was still following him. "If Zoram is anything like his father, then he will be an ally and power for good and the protection of the records. But we don't have the time. With Lehi's disappearance, we cannot wait another day." Joshua gripped the bag hanging from his shoulder. "We must include these tonight."

Naomi knew all of this, of course, and knew in her head that Joshua's reasoning and logic were sound. And while she was forced to admit that there *was* the possibility that Zoram would not understand or support what they were doing, in her heart she had every confidence in the young Keeper. But approaching him and bringing him into their confidence was not her decision alone to make. He was right. She felt the urgency as well. There wasn't time to approach Zoram properly. They had to act tonight.

Naomi held out her hand for the plates. "Hand them over. If suspicions are being raised, then let me go. They will question you before they stop me. I have legitimate reasons for being within the palace walls. You were Jharom's apprentice, not Zoram's. The risk is too great."

As passionate as he was, Joshua was a man of logic and couldn't argue with her on that point. "Then I'm coming with you. If we're discovered, we won't live long enough to see the dawn."

"We'd be fortunate to die so quickly," Naomi replied grimly. They both knew the truth of Laban's temper and sadistic streak. He would take pleasure in their torture and pain and suffering. There was something not right with him.

Naomi quickly considered Joshua's offer. "Agreed," she said, secretly grateful for his insistence and his company. She had attended to the records once or twice with Jharom and knew the basic mechanics of unfastening the metal spines to include the additional plates. Joshua, on the other hand, had much more experience adding Jeremiah's words to the records.

The streets of the city cleared out after dark, allowing the two of them to make their way to the palace compound unnoticed. They knew each and every door and gate into the palace grounds and chose the way in that would likely avoid the staff and guards that patrolled its perimeter and hallways. But once inside they knew something was wrong.

Largely dark after sundown, tonight the palace grounds were lit with many torches and lamps, illuminating even the unused and forgotten passages. Where the shadows would have normally hidden the pair's movements, tonight they had to be careful. They narrowly avoided one set of guards on their way inside, holing up in a small alcove off the main house.

"I don't like this," Joshua whispered.

"Why the heightened security?"

"Maybe they know."

"No. Look, most of the guards are concentrated on the far end of the palace. The treasury is on the other side. There must be something going on in the palace. A reception, perhaps."

"I hope so."

"Keep an eye out, just in case."

A few minutes later, there was no doubt that something was amiss, and what they had to do had gone from difficult and risky to utterly impossible. As they neared the antechamber of the treasury, Naomi was the first to spot them.

"There are four of them."

"And look at their uniforms," Joshua added. "They're not regular palace guards."

Naomi recognized the uniform. "Laban's Fifty."

"He must have known we were coming." Joshua was beginning to panic.

"Impossible. You and I were the only ones who knew we were going to do this tonight." She raised an eyebrow toward Joshua. "Right?"

"Don't look at me. I may have many faults but a loose tongue isn't one of them."

Naomi offered him a quick smile. "I know. Then they don't know. And look at the way they're standing. Relaxed and not at attention. They're not expecting anyone."

"Laban would have their heads if he knew they were anything less than completely vigilant."

"You can rat them out later, assuming they don't kill us first. So what are we going to do?"

Naomi didn't like this. "Maybe we should go back. Wait for the palace security to return to normal. Then maybe we can . . ." But she didn't believe this. And neither did Joshua. They had waited too long as it was. Jharom was dead and Lehi was missing. If she and Joshua didn't add these words of Jeremiah to the records, they might be lost forever.

Joshua studied the guards, gauging the distance then checking the hallway behind them. "What do we know about The Fifty?"

"What? What kind of a question is that?"

"They're the best," he answered. "The elite of Israel's military forces."

"They're killers," Naomi added. "They're animals."

"Precisely." He unshouldered the bag containing the plates and passed it to Naomi.

"What are you doing?"

"Someone's got to draw them away from the door."

"No, Joshua!"

"They're animals, you said so yourself. Big, dumb, hungry animals. And there's nothing like a little wild game to bring out the hunter in them."

"They'll kill you!"

"They'll have to catch me first. I know this part of the palace grounds a whole lot better than those goons. Besides, if they do end up catching me, they'll find that I'm not such easy prey. Jharom was an excellent teacher."

"I won't let you. There must be another way. I'll think of one if you'll just—"

"It's no use. I've decided. I'm not too thrilled about the idea either, but there's no other option right now that I can see."

"We can wait," Naomi pled. "It doesn't have to be tonight. Come, let's rethink this." But he wasn't listening to her anymore.

Joshua readied himself and began breathing faster, shallower, as his courage built. "The way I figure it, in their surprise they'll all follow after me. I'll give them chase as long as I can, but I suspect at least one or two of them will realize they've abandoned their post and return. You'll have a minute—two at the most. Just be sure you're far from the palace grounds by then."

"But—"

Joshua put his hand on hers. "This work is more important than any one of us. The extra security was unexpected, but there's nothing we can do about it besides move forward with what strength we have. If we don't include these plates *tonight*, they might be lost and forgotten forever."

Naomi wanted to fight him on his decision, but the weight of the metal plates confirmed to her heart that this was the right thing, the only thing to do. But these feelings did little to comfort her heart. "If they . . ." She couldn't bring herself to say the words, so she just skipped them. "I mean, what should I tell your wife?"

He flashed a warm smile trying to cover his fear. "I'm sure you'll think of something nice."

Naomi wanted to cry. "I'll meet you back at the house."

"Until we meet again," he said, withdrawing his hands from hers. Then he sprinted down the hall toward the unsuspecting sentries.

Naomi watched, sick and her whole body trembling, as Joshua dashed for the treasury door, knowing full well that it would be locked; but gaining entrance was not his intent. He yelled and pushed through the guards, acting wild and insane and repeating over and over at the top of his lungs that they needed to repent. One of the soldiers grabbed at his shoulder, but he was too quick, too focused on what he was there to do, and slipped free. He returned with a right fist to the soldier's face. At this show of aggression, the others marshaled into action, taking an offensive stance. The one he'd hit drew his sword.

Joshua was no soldier, but he had been a close friend of Jharom and had spent a good deal of time handling swords. Up against regular infantry, he may have stood a chance in a fair fight, but not against members of The Fifty. Even the newest, youngest member possessed skills that far exceeded his own.

"Stop him! Stop him! Get around him!"

Four of them surrounded him and then cornered him against the treasury door.

"You gonna let this fool touch you?" one of the older soldiers taunted. "Nobody gets in a strike like that without paying for it."

Joshua acted swiftly, delivering a kick to this same soldier, who moved to one side to avoid the full force of the attack. The movement gave Joshua a small opening to burst through. He reached for one of the other soldier's swords hanging from his belt, tugging at it but not freeing it. Undeterred, he fled farther down the hall, still shouting at them, egging them on. Naomi watched as all four soldiers pursued him into the darkness and around the corner, out of sight.

Naomi had to act fast. She knew she didn't have much time, but as she stared at the empty hall and deserted anteroom, she realized in horror that she couldn't move. She was completely paralyzed with fear. She tried to will her feet to move, to take that first step, but she couldn't. They just wouldn't respond.

She sent a desperate plea heavenward for the courage to do what was right and closed her eyes in an attempt to clear her mind. With one hand she reached into her pocket and felt Zoram's key, and with the other she touched the words of Jeremiah engraved on the plates of brass. In that instant, connecting the two as she did, a surge of sudden strength passed through her body, and she started running toward the treasury door.

Almost without thinking, she inserted the key and turned it, unlocking the heavy wooden door and hastily pushing her way in. Her sudden rush of confidence waned, though, as darkness met her eyes. She began to panic. Jharom had always seen to it that a lamp was lit and left inside the room, and though she knew how to manipulate the clasps and rings of the records, she didn't think she could do it in the dark.

Gradually her eyes adjusted, and she noticed a dull light emanating from the narrow windows and vents where the wall and ceiling met. This weak light combined with the light slipping in through the door illuminated the room just enough for her to do her work.

Which she did quickly and with purpose.

Removing the royal cover, Naomi had to fight the overwhelming desire to just stare at the plates in awe and reverence as she had done every other time she had been blessed to view them with her own eyes. She shook the feeling, hoping not to offend God, put the new plates on the table, and started working the fasteners.

The plates were heavy, and it took all her strength and focus to tip them over. She used a small lever that had been inconspicuously placed under the far end of the table. She winced the instant before they finally turned over, filling the silent room with a loud thud as the heavy metal came to rest again.

She held her breath and listened.

No sign of alarm.

She worked fast, with a skill and dexterity not her own. She freed the small interlocking bars from one another using both hands to manipulate the intricate metal machinery. She had to repeat this process for each of the three binder rings that held the plates in place.

She then took her new, additional plates, turned them over to match the orientation of the others, and carefully slid each one into place over the bindings. Her hands worked deftly, and in no time the words of Jeremiah found their place with the other inspired words and warnings of the prophets of God.

She locked the new plates in place, wedged the lever under the mass of metal, and pushed down.

Snap! The small wooden lever broke in two under the weight.

Naomi broke out in a cold sweat, and her legs became weak with a flood of dread and fear. She couldn't lift and turn them without the lever. There just wasn't enough strength in her old hands. With Joshua's help, perhaps, but not alone.

Outside the treasury she heard a distant voice and could hear noises getting louder.

She had to get out of there!

She looked at the records. It would be blatantly obvious to anyone who might see the plates that they were upside down. Fortunately, only a small handful of people were even permitted to see them and then only on special occasions. She would have to return as soon as she could to right the plates, but for now all she could do was pray that their orientation would not be noticed. But she had to get out of there unseen or all her work—and Joshua's sacrifice—would be in vain. If she was discovered, it would undo their years of work and endanger many faithful others.

She threw the empty bag over her shoulder and draped the gold-trimmed covering over the plates, stepped quickly to the slightly ajar door, and peered out. She could hear approaching voices from the far tunnels, but it was too dark to see their sources. She slipped out and quietly closed the door, wincing as it locked and echoed softly throughout the small room.

The hallway was still empty. She started walking away as fast as she could, careful that her steps didn't make undue noise. As she neared the safety of the corner, the constriction in her throat eased up as she began to allow herself to think that she may have actually completed her task unnoticed—

She ran into a guard, this time a member of the palace guard, coming around the same corner. His sudden appearance forced a startled yelp from her lips.

"Excuse me," he said. "Forgive me. I didn't—"

"Oh, it was my fault," she stammered. "I wasn't watching. I should have been more careful."

The guard looked at her, and then his eyes moved past her to the deserted hallway behind her. After a moment he returned his attention to her. "And what business do you have here tonight?"

Naomi's fear paralyzed her tongue as she scrambled desperately to come up with a story to explain her presence.

"Do I know you?" the palace guard asked before she could respond. "Yeah, you serve the Keeper of the Sword."

"That's right." She forced a smile and hoped her faltering voice didn't give away her panic. "I am the house matron."

"I was saddened to learn of his accident. I had the privilege to train with him on several occasions over the years. He was a good man."

Naomi could hear the voices of the returning soldiers behind her. She needed to get as far away as possible right now!

"He will be missed. Now, if you'll excuse me." She passed by him, trying her best to assert a confident air and demeanor.

"Ma'am, wait," he said firmly.

She froze. She could neither outrun him nor overpower him, and she was suddenly and painfully struck with Joshua's likely fate. Was he alive? Would she soon join him in the hereafter? Never had her regret for doing this without Zoram's knowledge been so deep as it was at that moment. He could have protected her. Now, instead of a long life into her twilight years, her life would be cut short. But still she knew her life had been one of elevated meaning and purpose. She would meet God with a clear conscience.

"Ma'am," he said again.

She turned around.

The soldier was holding out Joshua's bag. "You dropped this."

Naomi took it and had to fight the urge to laugh from the sudden and deep relief that drained what was left of her energy.

"You'd best be careful if you have other business at the palace tonight."

"Why is that?" She knew she had only a few moments to make her escape, but she thought that knowing the reason for the heightened security might be helpful when she planned her return to the treasury. "What's going on?"

The guard looked apologetic. "They haven't told us much, only that there was an emergency meeting of the Sarim planned for later tonight. Some important matters of state, I suppose."

Naomi nodded and thanked him, hoping not to appear in too much haste as she made her way out of the palace. By itself, a meeting of the Council of Elders was not unusual, and that might explain the lights throughout the palace grounds, but the fact that Laban's Fifty were here meant that he was personally involved in it, and that concerned her.

She paused the moment she was clear of the palace and alone. She sobbed quietly for the loss of her friend and brother in the Lord.

Oh, Joshua!

But she had to keep moving. She would not be safe until she returned home, and even then wondered if she, and the faithful men and women like her and Joshua, would ever be truly safe as long as men like Laban and the High Priest maintained their tyrannical hold on power. Zoram was their hope. Joshua couldn't see it, but he didn't know the young Keeper like she did. He would help them. The Lord wouldn't preserve and return him without having some great purpose in mind for him.

For all of them.

CHAPTER TWENTY-ONE

THE SMALL VEDIC ARMY WAS swift and struck with ruthless ferocity. The monastery had no time to prepare for the attack. Zoram and Wu Yien were sweeping the freshly fallen snow from the courtyard high above the rest of the monastery when they first heard the large brass bell, which usually called the monks to prayer and meditation, ring the alarm. This was followed by the shouts of the invading horde. For a moment the two of them just watched, not fully comprehending, as armed men, several on horseback, stormed the gate before it could be closed. Zoram wondered if it might be some kind of training exercise until he watched as one of their masters, one of their favorite mentors, a man they considered a friend, was cut nearly in two by one of the marauders.

Zoram was stunned at the sight of violence playing out before them. It wasn't until he hit his head on the short stone wall that he realized Wu Yien had pulled him down out of sight.

Seeing his friend cut down in a manner so cruel and barbaric sent Zoram into a rage. But at the moment he started to leap from their hiding spot, Wu Yien reached out and pulled him back again.

"Let me go! They need our help! We can fight!"

"We can also be killed," his friend said plainly.

Zoram struggled with his grip. "I said, let me go!"

"Listen to me! It will take more than our swords to defeat them. They're clearly skilled and organized, and they have the advantage. If we are to hope to save even one life—"

"Then we must act!"

"Yes, but not like this, not without a plan."

Wu Yien stole a peek over the half wall. Zoram's moment of unbridled shock and anger passed, and he could see now that his friend was right, as always, especially in matters of warfare. He relaxed and joined Wu Yien in observing what was going on in the monastery below. The soldiers were completing a search of every hall and residence, dragging everyone out into the central courtyard. Threats of violence and death filled the stone streets and drifted up to the friends' ears. Finally, the invaders had gathered everyone and surrounded them with swords drawn.

"Where are the other apprentices?" Zoram asked, noticing that the intruders had only gathered two of them.

"They've hidden the others," Wu Yien said. "They're protecting their investments."

"Why aren't they fighting?" Zoram couldn't understand their masters' compliance, especially in light of the death of one of their own. "They don't outnumber us, and there isn't an army in the world that could defeat our masters with the sword."

"It's not their way. Theirs is a peaceful and nonviolent religion and heritage. They have taken oaths not to take another's life."

"But shouldn't one fight for his life? Is it wrong to defend your life?"

"Perhaps not," Wu Yien said, "but why should the actions of others control and dictate your own? To die for what you believe is the highest display of faith and devotion."

"But if they die, their knowledge and skill dies with them."

"Not true. They have bestowed it on others over the years."

Zoram shook his head. "Well, they may have taken an oath of nonviolence, but we haven't."

Wu Yien smiled mischievously. "No, I suppose we haven't."

The friends, as close as brothers over the years, shared a look of assurance that whatever they decided, they would do it together. Wu Yien's attention was drawn back to the scene below.

"I don't think they're simply here to kill us though." Those soldiers not guarding the prisoners were busy going through the monastery, house by house, and presumably room by room. "They're looking for something."

"What could they possibly . . ." Zoram's words caught in his throat, and he froze in fear as a man on horseback was ushered in through the gate. He was not dressed like the others. He was covered in heavy skins and coats to protect him from the bitter cold this last storm had brought with it. He was wearing the colors and patterns of the Magadha Empire but not that of a soldier. Zoram immediately recognized him. It was the same delegate who had paid them a rather unpleasant visit in the fall looking for—

"They're looking for me."

"Yes," Wu Yien agreed, "and the gift from your God."

Zoram's very soul rallied within him to protect what God had given him. "They will never possess it."

"Are you willing to die to keep it safe?"

"Yes." He didn't hesitate.

"Are you willing to let *them* die to keep it safe?"

Zoram hadn't considered the extent of the sacrifice that might have to be made.

"And are you willing to kill for it? You see, to die for something—that's easy," Wu Yien said. "But to *live* for something, or worse, to be willing to take another man's life for it . . . Well, that's the difference between victory and defeat."

His friend was right. Suddenly the thought of giving his life to protect the strange metal that had fallen from the sky and that he had risked his life to obtain seemed meaningless. He would accomplish nothing by simply rushing into the fight driven only by his resolve to give his own life in exchange. It was a fool's sacrifice.

But he had never taken a man's life before, and as he sat there, he wasn't sure he could do it. Sure, he thought, he was better trained in using the sword and in close hand-to-hand combat than most anyone in the world. But there was a marked difference between knowing *how* to take a life and committing his blade to *actually* kill another human being.

Zoram was torn. On one hand it was written by the hand of God Himself and given to Moses, their great lawgiver: thou shalt not kill. Yet the records and their history were replete with instances where God had commanded men to kill. Was Saul not commanded to destroy and lay waste to every man, woman, child, and every living thing of the Amalekites? Did not David slay Goliath? Maybe there wasn't just a time to sow and a time to harvest; a time to laugh and a time to cry. Maybe there was also a time to save and a time to kill.

Even if there was a way to escape without killing, Zoram knew he wouldn't be able to live with himself knowing that his friends and brothers had died at the hands of men looking for him. He knew he had to do more than stay and *fight*; he would likely have to stay and *kill* to save everything he loved and cherished.

But while Zoram knew this in his head, he worried he wouldn't have the strength to deliver the fatal blow when the moment came.

Before he could answer his wise friend's question, there was more movement in the courtyard. They had found the last of the apprentices and monks, pushing them brutally into the mass of the others.

Wu Yien did a quick count. "That's the rest of them." But still men searched.

"They'll never find where I've hidden it," Zoram said, mostly to himself. "Not even the High Sadhus knows."

Just then one of their instructors, a younger master by the name of Rajesh, was allowed to pass by the soldiers and approach the delegate on horseback. "Maybe he's negotiating their release," Zoram said. "Explaining that the instructors don't have what they're looking for."

"Then why is High Sadhus not speaking?" Wu Yien watched for a moment longer. "No, I think we have a traitor among us."

"A traitor? Impossible."

Wu Yien motioned to a tower far out on one of the ledges on the lower side of the monastery. "Do you know the purpose of that lookout?"

Zoram did. "From there you can see the roads below and the pathway up the mountain."

"Does it not strike you as odd that we didn't even have time to close the gates before they were upon us?"

"No one was standing watch."

"Or someone *was* watching and did nothing as they stormed our walls."

Zoram was appalled that one of their own could do such a thing. "I don't believe it."

"He is right now, as we speak, betraying everything he was ever taught, everything he professed to believe."

"No, you're wrong," Zoram insisted, refusing to believe that one of their masters would consent to or play a part in this act of horror and violence. "How can you be so sure?"

"I was scheduled to stand watch this morning," Wu Yien said, "but relieved at the last minute. I'll give you one guess who took my place."

But he didn't need to. So it was true. Rajesh had betrayed them all. Anger fed his betrayal, and Zoram had to fight the sudden desire to see to his death personally.

"Hey." Wu Yien nudged him back to the present and motioned to the central square below. "I need you to focus. Look."

One of the soldiers made his way up to the large bell atop their meditation hall and rang it three times. When the loud reverberations subsided, the royal delegate stood in his saddle. "Zoram!" he called out. The little man's voice carried in the crisp morning air. "I am Nagendra, royal vizier and envoy to Lord Ajatasattu, heir to the Haryanka Dynasty, and ruler of all Magadha. I am told that you possess something that does not belong to you, a visitor to our empire."

"He knows my name," Zoram said in disbelief.

"It would appear that our secret did not go entirely unnoticed."

"We wish no harm upon you or this monastery," the delegate continued, "but we are prepared to obtain this fire from the heavens at any cost!"

"Do you think he knows where we are?" Zoram asked.

"No, but he knows we're hiding and likely within the sound of his voice."

"My patience wears thin and the time quickly passes for peaceful negotiations." The little man on horseback paused and waited for a reply. His countenance darkened as no reply was forthcoming. "You and your reclusive friends have now forfeited our mercy and goodwill and will be punished! Make no mistake; we will not leave until what you have stolen is returned to our possession!"

The delegate raised his hand, and a soldier forcefully grabbed one of the monks, dragged him into the open, and forced him to his knees. "I suspect you can hear me, Zoram. If you can also see me, then let both of your senses witness the determination and resolve of the Magadha Empire." At the conclusion of his words he dropped his hand, followed immediately by the drop of the soldier's heavy sword. Zoram turned away sharply and fought to keep from getting sick. This couldn't be happening! He knew both of the men killed this morning. They were good and honorable men and deserved more than a pointless death at the end of a tyrant's sword. Did all of God's gifts come with such a heavy price? He hoped God would receive them for their sacrifice in his behalf.

The outcry from the young apprentices was silenced under threat of further death, and the delegate spoke again. "Another will be chosen and will die every hour you hide yourself and withhold what is rightfully ours. Their deaths will be on your hands."

Zoram slumped against the base of the half wall, scared, confused, and full of doubt. His courage and resolve were taken with the life of his friend and teacher. It was one thing to keep a secret, but it was something entirely different to keep that secret at the expense of their lives.

"I can't let this go on," he said. "I can stop the killing."

"What are you talking about?"

"I'm going to give it to them. It's not worth all this."

"You just got through saying you were willing to die or kill to protect it, and now you just want to give it away?"

"I know, I know," Zoram said, shaking his head and on the verge of tears. "I may be willing to sacrifice my own life and even kill to prevent them from taking it from me, but this is different. You were right. You're always right. I cannot and will not let one more of our brothers lose his life when I have the power to save it."

"And you think that once these men have what they have come for, they'll just leave us and let us bury our dead? Look at them. They sent a vicious army to retrieve it, not a diplomatic herald. Their purpose is clear, and the way I see it, the only reason they aren't all dead already is because you *haven't* given it up. The fact that it remains hidden is the only thing saving them. But mark my words, the moment you turn it over, you will have hastened all our deaths. And I, for one, plan to live a long and prosperous life."

Zoram wiped the tears from his cold cheeks. "What do you expect me to do?"

Wu Yien could not hide his excitement. War and battle strategies and tactics never ceased to thrill him; it was what he excelled at, and he took the next few minutes to carefully and deliberately lay out a course of action to overpower their assailants.

When he was done, Zoram could only shake his head. "There are too many of them. Are you certain this will work?"

Wu Yien was not disheartened and flashed that mischievous smile again. "Certain? No. Confident? Yes. Look, I wouldn't let you rush into the fight earlier because that wasn't the best strategy for engaging a force with superior numbers. If our brothers had resisted and a call to arms had been made, then our skills and numbers would have joined theirs. But there was no army to join. We are forced to take more . . . *indirect* methods to achieve victory."

Zoram was hearing the words, but he still couldn't catch the vision of what Wu Yien was saying. "I counted thirty men. As good as we are, we're no match for an army of that size."

"True, but how would we fare against two or even three of them?"

"There is no question we could defeat them."

"Then all we have to do is break that group of thirty into smaller numbers."

"And just how are we going to do that?"

Wu Yien smiled as if he knew Zoram would ask this very question all along. "If I'm right, we won't have to."

ख़ेपेर ओफ़ ष्वोर्द

Zoram and Wu Yien had one distinct advantage. They knew every corner, every house, and every hiding place in the monastery. After all, they'd grown up here. Just as Wu Yien had predicted, after a short time, the Magadha emissary became impatient and sent the men not directly guarding their prisoners to search the compound again. And as his friend had also anticipated, they broke into smaller groups of two or three.

"They're ill-equipped to take hostages and lay siege to the monastery," Wu Yien had said. "They were expecting a fight, not compliant and willing prisoners. That lapse in judgment, if exploited properly, will be the key to our victory where twenty men would otherwise fail."

Zoram's heart beat as fast as a bird's while they prepared to make their way into the monastery below. He and Wu Yien were defenseless except for the brooms, which they broke down into lengths approximately that of a sword. They were clumsy weapons, but the wood was strong and the tips were sharp. This would have to do until they could procure swords or other weapons.

"The true warrior doesn't wait for fortune to smile upon him but instead makes his own luck." Wu Yien took pride in the makeshift weapons they had forged. "Keep low and follow me."

They made their way down from the upper terrace along a ledge that traced the rock face of the deep mountain canyon. No alarm was raised. They had made it undetected. So far.

They took a defensive position along the outer wall, flanking either side of a narrow alley, listening intently as the sound of a small group of Magadha soldiers approached in search of their prey. Zoram could hear them speaking in a dialect similar to the language he had been taught when he first arrived but different enough to be unintelligible. Though he couldn't understand their words, their tone was unmistakably feral. These were not good men simply following orders. They were animals, angry and bloodthirsty—bred for a single purpose. Zoram thought this would make him feel better about taking their lives, but it didn't.

Wu Yien slowly and silently raised his wooden stick over his head and settled into a strong, grounded stance. He flexed his fingers to better grip the handle. Zoram took a deep breath and did the same. Their plan was to systematically and quietly pick off one small group at a time. It was critical, then, to strike hard and strike fast before the rest of the soldiers learned what was happening. Failure meant not only their own death but the death of all their brothers. Without a blade, however, their attacks had to be brutal and barbaric. Unfortunately, they didn't have any other choice. At least for this first strike.

Zoram wasn't sure he was ready for this. He had excelled in fighting practice and, with the exception of Wu Yien, was better than any of the other apprentices. But this was real. There were no forms to follow, no techniques to exact, and no punches to pull.

The heavy steps got closer. He could hear the rustle of thick coats of skins and the brush of metal and leather. He held his breath for a moment before making himself exhale. Zoram stole a quick glance at Wu Yien. He was focused and unaware of anything but the grisly task at hand.

This is a mistake! Zoram panicked. *There isn't enough time to—*

At the first glimpse of the soldiers, Wu Yien struck, using all his strength to bring the wooden staff down on the closest soldier's head. A split second later, Zoram struck the other, but in that time, the soldier was able to brace for the attack and move to avoid a similarly crushing blow. It glanced off his shoulder.

What followed happened so fast Zoram didn't register it until it was over.

Zoram had hesitated, doubting his resolve, which was the one thing Wu Yien had warned him about. But the reality of actually inflicting harm and even death onto another was too great to overcome with mere thought. His life wasn't in immediate danger, nor was the life of his friend, and while it was one thing to accept that he had to smash a man's skull in, it was quite another to actually swing the club and deliver the blow.

Zoram's strike didn't kill him, but it did stun him enough to wince in pain and add to the confusion over the unexpected fate of his fallen comrade. Zoram instinctively struck again but missed any vital areas, hitting the man's back and shoulders as he recoiled from the assault. He raised his head and opened his mouth to yell out and warn the others when Wu Yien spun his small staff over his head, connecting with the man's exposed throat. The alarm was silenced before it could be sounded. The man dropped to his knees, his hands clawing at his neck as if he could strip the excruciating pain away.

"Finish him!" Wu Yien whispered.

Zoram knew he had to. He had committed to follow the plan, but now, with the soldier unarmed and suffering, his resolve seemed even farther away. "I . . . I can't."

So Wu Yien did, striking at the base of his skull and instantly putting an end to the man's pain. The soldier crumpled to the ground, lifeless, next to the other. Wu Wien immediately took hold of the man's coat. "Help me!"

Zoram was in a daze, and for the third time that morning, he fought to keep from getting sick, taking deep breaths and trying to push the images of death from his mind.

"Zoram!"

He suddenly snapped out of it and found the strength to help move the bodies out of sight. The moment the strenuous job was done, Zoram was surprised to find himself slammed up against the wall, nose to nose with Wu Yien.

"What was that?" He had never seen his friend so angry before. "If we have any hope—any hope at all—of saving lives, I have to know that I can trust that you'll be able to follow through on your end of the plan! I get that this is no longer practice and that you've never killed anyone before. Neither have I! But what you don't seem to fully understand is that today we either *kill them* or they will *kill us* and everyone we have known and loved since we arrived!"

Wu Yien kept a grip on Zoram's shirt. "We cannot simply defeat them and take them prisoner. There will be no negotiation. I would be the first one to tell you to leave a defeated army intact and let them return home with some measure of pride and dignity. In my studies I've found that these once-enemies often later become strong allies. But this is not that type of army, and this is not that kind of war. These are killers, bred and hired for one thing. We have to strike where they are weak and unprepared."

Wu Yien released his grip on his friend. "And that means looking them in the eyes before you send them into the next world. War is not waged between faceless masses of men and soldiers; it is fought—won or lost—one man at a time. Do not forget this."

Zoram tried to hold back the tears of a cathartic release. Wu Yien knew what he was feeling; Wu Yien was feeling it too. His friend was right about everything, and just as he was unwilling to sacrifice the lives of his friends by doing nothing, he knew that if he didn't do what was expected of him, the sentence of death would be the same.

"So are you with me?" Wu Yien asked earnestly. "Will you help me save them?"

Zoram felt the knots in his stomach unwind and a heavy burden lift from his heart as the last of his reservations melted away. "I won't let you down again."

Wu Yien nodded once. "Good. Here," he said, offering Zoram one of the soldiers' swords. "This should make what we must do easier."

Zoram gripped the hilt and hefted the weapon. It was bulky and of primitive design compared to what they forged and used at the monastery, but the blade was sharp enough.

"Come. Once the Magadha emissary starts to suspect something, he'll begin executing them without mercy or restraint."

Zoram settled into the mental and emotional state he needed to be in. "Then we'd best hurry."

Sneaking around the perimeter, the two fugitives spotted another pair entering one of the smaller halls. Careful not to be seen, they slipped in behind the soldiers. The men were taken by surprise, and the fight was over almost before it started.

This time the emotions surrounding what they had to do were not a hindrance to Zoram. He did what he knew in his mind—and now in his *heart*—he had to do to save his friends. And he did it quickly.

When it was over, Zoram stood confidently over the body of the soldier he had engaged. The man was dead, run through by the sword and silenced before he could sound an alarm. Zoram was surprised how little emotion accompanied the kill. He had rushed into the room and, with a hand over the surprised soldier's mouth, pushed him back into the wall, driving the rough blade through him. He was not proud of what he had done. There was no sense of pride. He would always be of the belief that life was precious, but he also knew now, firsthand, that sometimes harsh measures must be taken to protect and preserve *innocent* life. It was a sobering thought, and in that moment he felt any childhood innocence slip away. He would forever be different, changed by the action to save the lives of his friends.

If this was what it meant to be a man, he had the strange thought, he wasn't sure it was worth it. He shook it off. There would be time for reflection and introspection later.

They found two more groups, for a total of five more men, dispatching them like the others. They had eliminated nine men, and at the thought of this, Zoram began to feel nigh invulnerable. Wu Yien wielded the foreigner's sword with precision and exactness, efficiently accomplishing the awful work before them. If their counting had been correct, they had single-handedly reduced their enemies' numbers by almost a third, but they had run out of time.

The brass bell sounded from the central courtyard, breaking the silence that had descended upon the mountain monastery.

"We're too late!" Zoram cried softly.

Wu Yien cursed under his breath in his native tongue. "We need more time!"

Suddenly Zoram's actions felt meaningless. He had taken the lives of three men, and still his friends and masters were going to die. He was horrified and began to question their plan, which had wasted the last hour. What had he done? He should have given up the metal. Maybe the emissary would have let them live. Maybe he really was just after what had fallen from the sky. Maybe—

Zoram had to stop this line of thinking. It was a panicked response. There was no use second-guessing their decision. It had been a good plan, the only one that offered any real hope of success. It had felt right, and he needed to trust in himself and his friend. All was not lost. He would have to trust. He would have to believe. He would need to have faith.

And in that moment, he knew what he had to do.

"Where are you going?" Wu Yien said, grabbing his arm.

"I'm going to give myself up."

"What?"

"I'm going to give them what they want."

"You can't! They'll kill you!"

Zoram reassured him with a smile. "Don't worry. Have a little faith, brother." He laid his sword on the ground. "Be ready on my signal."

"What signal?"

"I'm not sure yet, but you'll know it when you see it."

"And what am I supposed to do?"

"You're Wu Yien, master of strategic warfare. I'm sure you'll think of something when the time comes." Zoram winked and then ran out the door toward the central courtyard.

खेपेर ओफ़ ष्वोर्द

Nagendra, the Magadha high emissary, stood up from his place beside the fire. He tossed aside a half-eaten bowl of rice, pushed through his advisors and men, and climbed the stairs to a raised dais.

"Your time has run out!" he called out. "Your cowardice will now result in the death of another of your sect. Perhaps, though, your allegiance is not toward the old men of this place. If you will not show yourself to prevent the death of one of your masters, maybe you will show yourself to save a fellow apprentice!"

At this command one of the young apprentices was plucked from the crowd. Two of the masters tried to stop them, but their token resistance was met with an abundance of force, and they were bloodied and knocked to the ground.

The young man cried out, begging for mercy and struggling against his captors. He was literally dragged, writhing and screaming, to the front in full view of the crowd.

खेपेर ओफ़ ष्वोर्द

Zoram knew he didn't have much time. He ducked into one of the meeting halls and grabbed what he needed, hurrying back to stop the execution.

The delegate looked around one more time, only half expecting Zoram to show himself. "May his cries and screams haunt your every waking moment!" He then motioned for the soldiers to carry out their duty. Two of them forced the scared young man to his knees and held him down while the other unsheathed his sword. He raised it over his head, took a deep breath, pulled it back, and—

"Stop!" Zoram yelled.

The soldier did, and all eyes turned to see Zoram standing atop one of the raised garden walls. He was holding something up in his hand. "Stop! Please! I will not have his death on my conscience! I have what you want and pray your forgiveness, Most Honorable Delegate! It was my arrogance and foolishness that has caused so much pain this day! I will not be the cause of any more!"

The delegate raised his hands to stop the killing and then motioned for two of his men to retrieve Zoram. Zoram offered no resistance and let the soldiers push him back to the square. He was forced to the ground and made to bow before the little man as the item he had brought with him was handed over.

"I knew you would show yourself," the Magadha emissary mused. "You and your friends here are all talk when it comes to courage. You are all so feared by men that I was cautioned to bring double the men I did." He laughed. "I could have brought women, and even they would have been too much for you."

Zoram chose to remain silent.

"And what is this?" he asked. He was holding a rock, just smaller than the size of a man's head. It was scorched and covered with soot from a fire.

"This is what you seek, my lord."

"A rock? Is this some kind of joke?" The delegate was not amused. He turned sharply and called for the member of the order Zoram had seen him speaking to earlier. "What manner of treachery is this?"

The traitor stammered his answer. "No, no, Your Excellency. I . . . he has been extracting ore and preparing it for a master work."

The delegate considered the rock again. "Is this true?"

Zoram nodded respectfully. "Yes . . . I mean, no. What fell from the sky is made of the most unusual material. When it is heated, it glows."

"Glows?"

"Green. But it does not consume. We have attempted every known technique and process, but the rock will not break. If you will allow me, I will show you."

The Magadha emissary locked eyes with Zoram for a long moment, trying to discern whether what he spoke was the truth or not. Finally he motioned to his men to release Zoram.

Zoram remained on his knees as he spoke to the little man. "If I may use the fire you sit by, my lord, I will demonstrate." He reached out, and the delegate returned the scorched stone to Zoram, who then slowly walked to the fire pit and placed it carefully in the middle. "It will not take long to show you its curious properties."

Zoram knew from his experiences in the villages below that the people of this land were a superstitious lot, and he hoped that this small army of mercenaries was no exception. It didn't take long before he noticed the soldiers starting to separate from one another. Those guarding the captives moved toward one another while the others unconsciously gathered around the delegate to protect him. But despite their inherent fear of what might happen, everyone in the courtyard leaned in to get a better view of the demonstration.

Everyone, that is, except the High Sadhus, who communicated with a raised eyebrow that he knew this was all a ruse but was confused as to why it was being played.

No one said a word as they all watched the stone heat up. After a minute, though, the delegate grew tired of waiting. He opened his mouth, but Zoram spoke first. "Will one of your men help me remove it from the fire?"

The soldiers all pulled back, afraid to be involved. "No," the delegate declared. "Get one of your masters to help you. We'll watch."

"As you wish." Zoram motioned for the High Sadhus to help him. Together they removed the heated rock with pieces of firewood. When they cleared the fire pit, however, Zoram let the stone slip and fall to the ground. A startled cry burst from the soldiers, afraid of what might happen as it hit the stone courtyard. Zoram did his best to contain his smile.

The rock rolled to a stop. The delegate kept his distance but tried to lean in to see it better. "I don't see anything."

"Of course," Zoram said. "Why didn't I think of it earlier? My most sincere apologies. The faint light can only be seen in the dark. The sky and the snow are too bright, but there's other evidence I can produce. The rock will expel sparks of the brightest green when it is heated and struck. It is a truly magnificent sight, so much so that not even the daylight will be able to conceal it. I will require a hammer, one of the large ones in the forge. If you will instruct one of your men . . ."

With a flick of the leader's head, one of his men hurried to the master forge and returned with one of the larger forging hammers. Zoram accepted it. "This will do nicely," he said as he bowed to the delegate then took a firm stance above the heated rock, gripping the hammer in preparation. The Magadha soldiers leaned in closer to get a better view, pushing past some of those they were charged with guarding. All eyes were on Zoram. He took a deep breath and steadied himself. He tilted his head to stretch his neck and shoulders, casually looking around him and especially into the crowds.

Wu Yien was there, having sneaked past the distracted guards. *Good. Here goes.*

Zoram raised the hammer high over his head. But instead of bringing the heavy metal head down on the rock, he swung the hammer in an arch and hit the rock toward the mesmerized delegate.

"Now!"

The apprentices all yelled out, armed with whatever Wu Yien could find and scavenge while the guards had been preoccupied with Zoram's little show. The soldiers were taken by complete surprise, many not knowing they were in mortal danger until it was too late. The young apprentices were all similarly trained and quickly and fiercely attacked their captors, felling them to the cold ground.

Zoram's attention followed the Magadha delegate as he ducked, narrowly avoiding the lethal projectile, and scurried away. He nearly fell several times on the snow-covered stone courtyard on the way to his horse. But the horse was spooked by the chaos and battle that surrounded them, rearing up as the emissary slipped one last time. The man fell directly beneath the mighty steed's powerful front legs. His life was snuffed out in an instant.

A few of the delegate's personal guards made a stand against an ever-growing number of apprentices bent on ending the siege, but it was clear the soldiers would be no match for the young students. Zoram needed to make certain that what they were all protecting was, in fact, safe. He left the courtyard and ran to his quarters.

When he arrived, his heart fell. His quarters were in total disarray. His bed had been overturned and every vase and basket opened or broken. He fell to the ground, the strength suddenly having left his being. The brick in the floor, covering his hiding place, was out, and the hole underneath was empty.

It was gone!

Fighting the rising bile in his stomach, Zoram forced himself to his feet, reaching for the wall for support. He steadied himself and then stumbled back into the central square.

"What's wrong?" Wu Yien asked.

"It's gone. They've taken it."

Wu Yien looked around at the subsiding fight all around them. "One of them must have escaped, but he cannot have gone far. We'll find him, I promise."

Zoram surveyed the scene too and shook his head. "It wasn't one of them. It was one of our own."

"Rajesh!" Wu Yien spat.

Rajesh, the traitor, author of the morning's death and destruction, was missing.

His strength returning, Zoram ran to one of the towers and climbed to the lookout. Rajesh was nowhere to be found. Everyone was still gathered in the central square in the wake of the battle. The thief could be hiding anywhere, Zoram realized.

Then he noticed the delegate's horse or, rather, it's absence. It, too, was gone. His search widened now to include the surrounding mountainside. There, making his way down the mountain path and toward the pass, was Rajesh.

Zoram leapt from the tower and sprinted past the others, driving everything else from his mind as he raced after the horse and rider on foot, determined to make up the distance and recover what was his. The air was biting on his face as he pushed himself to new limits in pursuit. More than once he slipped on the ice and rocks. The horse would not be as sure-footed on the snowy trail as Zoram, and Rajesh was by no means an expert rider. Zoram hoped that a combination of the two would slow the traitor down enough for him to catch up and engage the man who had brought so much death upon their peaceful monastery.

As Zoram neared Rajesh, the horse stopped and reared up slightly, unwilling to traverse a narrow part in the trail. This gave Zoram all the time he needed to catch up with them. He leapt across the final space between them and tackled the traitorous master from his saddle. The force and momentum of the impact knocked them both to the ground and off the edge of the trail. They rolled down the steep incline for a moment or two before coming to rest on a small landing beneath the road. Rajesh was the first to regain his senses, and he began swinging and kicking at Zoram. He connected a few times before Zoram could scramble out of his reach and jump to his feet.

"How could you do this?" Zoram asked. "We are brothers."

Rajesh was quickly on his feet too. He adjusted the leather satchel over his shoulder. "I am *not* your brother! We are not all *one*, as they teach. Religion is a fool's delusion."

They circled one another. They both knew they could never make the sharp climb without the other catching and dragging him back down. They would settle this. Right here. Right now.

"Two of our order died because of you!"

"They died because of this!" He shook the satchel. "They died because you refused to tell them what you had found. Their blood is on *your* hands, not mine."

"It was never theirs to begin with. It was sent by my God for His purposes."

"You are deluded, aren't you? I always figured you and your friend as being more intelligent than that."

Zoram recognized this as a tactic to draw him into a discussion that would distract him enough for Rajesh to gain the advantage. Zoram refused to take the bait. Instead, he brought the conversation back to what was clear and asked the question that was foremost in his mind. "How much did he pay you? What was the price you agreed on to sell out what was most sacred to you? To all of us?"

Rajesh was taken aback by the blunt question. "What do you know of our ways? You are a foreigner. For decades we have been teaching the world our trade and secrets, and where is the reward? Where is the recognition and wealth? You're not so naïve to believe that this service is done out of some sense of duty or honor, are you? We, and the masters before us, do it for the money. Do you think that the fortune your people spent to send you here was used to feed you the daily handful of rice you were afforded or the rags you wear for clothes? The gold is taken and deposited away—gold that should be distributed and given to those of us who toil and sweat trying to teach you and your incompetent friends what has taken my people centuries to perfect."

Rajesh eyed Zoram while he slipped the satchel from his shoulder and tossed it out of reach behind him and settled into a fighting stance. "Is it so wrong to demand more than a life of poverty for dedicating all we have just to send you back with the skills to conquer nations and make your people rich? Is it wrong to want a taste of comfort and luxury before one dies?"

"Not at the expense of innocent lives."

Rajesh shrugged it off. "Who's to say who is innocent and who is guilty?"

"God only," Zoram said, almost without hesitation.

Rajesh scoffed. "There you go again. You're a fool, nothing else."

Zoram settled into a low and steady stance of his own. "You can't take what God had rightfully given me."

"The way I see it, I already have."

Zoram slowed his breathing and quieted his beating heart. "I will have it again, either willingly or through force, though I suspect you will insist on the latter."

"It's too bad we have to end it this way. You were the most promising student the order had ever seen. You truly have skills and talents worthy of what we have to offer. It saddens me to take your life."

Zoram cracked a small smile. "It is not yours to take, but I invite you to come and try."

Rajesh wasted no time on formalities or displays of prowess and skill but lunged for Zoram, his strong hands flexed and outstretched like the claws of a tiger searching for the satisfaction of young flesh. Zoram had only a split second to react and avoid Rajesh's expert skill. While his moral fortitude may be lacking, the instructor's strength and skills were not. Rajesh continued to advance, swinging and reaching, spinning and kicking. Rajesh was relentless as Zoram struggled to block and deflect each deadly strike.

This was not practice, Zoram tried to tell himself. This was real, and he needed to use and apply what had been ingrained into his very being to survive and reclaim what was his. Rajesh, on the other hand, had no reservation or restraint in using his martial skill for what it was designed for.

Rajesh's stance was low, his feet timed perfectly to sweep Zoram's legs as his hands struck with ferocious brutality, but Zoram's years of training and conditioning saved him time and again from almost certain death at the hands of his former master and friend. With every step backward, though, Zoram's confidence waned and fear crept in. Had he expected that same feeling of detachment like he had experienced with the Magadha soldiers? Yes, he had. But this fight was different. This was not a fight against nameless barbarians and brutes. He'd had no past with them, no memories or feelings to contend with. But he knew Rajesh well. He had eaten with him, trained with him, and laughed with him over the years. Despite what the man had done and Zoram's strong and violent feelings toward him earlier, the apprentice now wanted only to disarm and disable him. He didn't want the man's life; he only wanted that satchel.

Zoram didn't know he'd been hit until he tasted dirt and rocks and realized that he was on the ground. Then there was a sharp and debilitating pain in his back and legs. He tried to crawl away but couldn't make his body move. Craning his neck he saw Rajesh standing over him, an arrogant and contemptuous look about him. He had won. Death would be swift and certain.

The feeling in Zoram's legs was returning, but he feared not fast enough. Rajesh had delivered a crushing blow to his lower back. If Zoram hoped to survive the next few moments, he would have to think of something, and fast. While his legs refused to obey him, his arms and hands were only too eager to assist him. In a desperate move, he took the small rocks and pieces of ice littered all around him and started throwing them at Rajesh, but even the ones that connected caused little pain and distraction.

"A child throwing stones," Rajesh said, mocking his feeble efforts. "Again you disappoint me. You do not lack the skills necessary to defeat me; what you lack is the courage to use them." He tapped his finger to his head. "You could not beat me in here. It was already decided. We can teach you the techniques and science of combat, but without the nerve to use them, they are useless to you. It takes strength, unrestrained, to achieve power and greatness. It is my strength that will make me wealthy beyond anything I have ever allowed myself to dream. It is my strength that hones and sharpens my mind and muscles. It is my strength that takes what might once have been yours."

Rajesh violently kicked at Zoram, intending to deliver the final blow, but Zoram was too low and still too agile to be killed that easily. He could feel the life coming into his legs the more he moved them, but he didn't have the strength yet to do what he knew he needed to, so he tried to avoid the attacks for a few more moments.

Rajesh's strikes were now little more than exaggerated stomps trying to crush any part of his foe. Zoram became aware of the master's timing and rhythm and could anticipate when and where the strike would land next. He knew it wouldn't last long, that Rajesh would realize his error. This was his chance! Zoram positioned his legs together in order to offer a target that Rajesh would be a fool to ignore.

The next few moments seemed to happen in slow motion. The attack came for the knees, a paralyzing blow if executed, but at the last moment,

Zoram parted his legs to let the foot pass to the ground. He then closed up his legs again and turned, trapping the master's foot and forcing it to turn, bending the knee forward and throwing him off balance. He crumpled next to Zoram.

This time it was Zoram that struck first. Taking advantage of Rajesh's momentary disorientation and surprise, Zoram wrapped his arms around the other man's head and dragged him completely to the ground. He worried he wasn't strong enough to defeat Rajesh as long as he had full use of both his hands and feet. What he needed was leverage—literally.

Zoram's powerful arms wrapped around Rajesh's head and neck, wrestling him to the snow and rock, trying to contain the fury of his traitorous brother, but it was proving more difficult than Zoram had imagined. The master was desperate and driven mad by greed and fear. Zoram was promptly overcome and lost what little control he'd been able to achieve. Rajesh rolled beyond his reach, and both sprang to their feet, though Zoram was much slower because of the considerable pain he was in.

"Foolish boy!" Rajesh spat.

Zoram didn't have a chance to respond—if he'd wanted to—as a fury of punches and kicks assaulted him from every direction. His feeble attempts to repel them did little good. He finally became numb to the pain, though he remained on his feet, willing himself to make a stand. Then a blow to his solar plexus drove the breath from his lungs, and he was forced to drop to one knee.

The attacks stopped. "I don't have time for this," Rajesh said.

Zoram looked up to see Rajesh reach into the folds of his coat and pull out a small dagger.

"You are a worthy opponent, indeed, Zoram," Rajesh said with some level of sincerity. "May your God welcome you into your afterlife."

Zoram tried to defend or at least move out of the way, but he was too hurt. All he could do was turn slightly. The blade meant for his chest cut into his lower back instead. The sharp pain registered fully, and Zoram screamed out. His vision flashed red and then white, and it was as if the knife had not only cut his flesh but also severed his restraint.

Rajesh circled around and regrouped for another stab, a final blow, when Zoram's hand shot out and struck his wrist, jarring the dagger from his grip. On his feet now, Zoram faced down his former master, mentor, and friend. But he was none of those anymore. Rajesh was now nothing more than an object and the cause of pain and fear.

Rajesh didn't wait to better understand this renewed energy and lashed out again. This time Zoram's lifetime of training took over; he blocked the onslaught of strikes with relative ease and unleashed a round of furious attacks of his own. The pain in his legs and back disappeared as he incorporated his whole being in the vicious offensive. Blocking, pivoting, grabbing, pulling—every strike Rajesh let fly was quickly turned against him.

Finally, Zoram stepped in close with a particularly strong punch and took Rajesh by the arm on either side of his elbow. Shoulder to shoulder, he pivoted to the right, throwing Rajesh off balance. Taking advantage, Zoram continued to spin around, pitching Rajesh headfirst into the side of the cliff. Rajesh immediately went limp. But Zoram wasn't finished with him just yet.

Rajesh was dazed and stunned but still conscious. Barely.

"You killed them!" Zoram doubled up his fist and struck Rajesh's bloodied face. The blow caused Rajesh's body to go completely limp and listless. But still the storms of anger and rage thundered in Zoram's heart. The bloodlust was too strong now. Not entirely in control of his actions, Zoram found a large rock. Rajesh twitched as he fought to regain consciousness.

The traitor had caused so much pain, so much death. He did not deserve to live. Zoram's anger boiled hotter with every thought. *He is not worthy of mercy. He had consented to the deaths of every last one of them, and for what? A handful of gold? Blood money.*

Zoram stood directly over Rajesh and raised the stone high over his head. "You don't deserve to live." He then yelled out to vent a portion of his pain and threw the rock with all of his strength.

But it did not strike Rajesh. Instead, it struck off to the side of his head.

"You might die," he said aloud, aware now that he was crying, "but not today. Not by my hand."

Exhausted beyond his capacity to endure it another moment, physically or emotionally, he dropped to his knees and let out the emotions that had built with the terrible things he had been forced to do that day. He had taken life today, that sacred gift that God only can bestow and that God only should take. Zoram couldn't think straight as he knelt there sobbing in the snow. He had almost killed in cold blood. What kind of man had he become? He had used enough force to subdue his opponent and then taken it further. He had almost committed an act that he did not think he had the strength to carry. The burden would have just been too great.

He looked as Rajesh, struggling still to regain consciousness. "What have I done?"

"You, Zoram of *Je-ru-saa-lum*," a familiar voice called down to him, "have demonstrated mercy and restraint usually reserved for men many times your young age."

Zoram was startled and turned to see the High Sadhus standing amid a half dozen of the other masters. Wu Yien was with them.

"You have performed admirably and worthily of our respect." The line of priests then bowed with utmost honor. Wu Yien flashed a quick smile and winked before joining with the others in their show of esteem.

Zoram was overcome. He was ashamed at how close he had come to losing control and succumbing to his basest desires. He had never felt so much pain and anger toward anyone before; he had never wanted to take the life of anyone so badly. He prayed he would never feel that way again.

But as the High Sadhus had pointed out, he hadn't followed through with those heinous acts. He had stopped short of letting his anger consume him. He had risen above those impulsive and base instincts. Though trained to kill, he was not a killer. He had proven that today. He was not condemned to be a slave to his impulses and faults for the rest of his life. He had shown that he could rise above them, even in his darkest hour.

Wu Yien followed four of the masters down the sharp incline and helped Zoram up while the others lifted Rajesh to his feet. He was only now coming to. He tried to struggle against his new captors, but he lacked the strength to do any more than tug lightly at their hold.

"What will happen to him?" Zoram asked.

"Our ways are simple and our commitments clear," the High Sadhus declared. "We do not ask members of our order to remain against their will. Any of us are free to leave without judgment. But betrayal of our sacred trust cannot and will not be tolerated. The punishment is known to all."

By this time, Rajesh had recovered his senses and listened intently as sentence was passed.

"He will be taken to the fields beyond the village at the foot of the mountain," the High Sadhus said, his voice quivering, "where he will be tied to horses and quartered to the four winds. There he will be left to die alone and broken."

Rajesh screamed in protest, struggling now with more strength at the pronouncement of his fate. He was dragged up to the road, where he was bound and gagged to silence his curses and protests. He was then thrown over the back of the Magadha emissary's horse and led away down the mountain. Punishment would be swift and without appeal.

Zoram finally had the strength to stand on his own, but Wu Yien wouldn't let him go, embracing his friend with all the emotion he possessed. "Do not ever do that again!"

He winced in pain. "Do what?"

"All this."

Zoram smiled. "You didn't really think I was in danger, did you? I'm touched that you worried so."

"Danger?" Wu Yien slapped his shoulder. "What are you talking about? No. I knew you could take him. I meant be the hero. They're going to talk about this day for generations, and I ask you, do you think they'll remember Wu Yien and his brilliant strategies that saved the lives of everyone present that day?" He shook his head good-naturedly. "Or will they retell the heroics of Zoram, who chased down the traitor, outrunning his horse, tackling him from the saddle, and facing off against him in a feat of mortal combat, only to spare his life in a show of mercy and compassion?"

Zoram chuckled but didn't answer. He didn't have to.

Wu Yien left him briefly to retrieve the leather satchel that held the formed block of strange metals. The moment of levity between them passed as he handed Zoram the coveted object. Zoram took it as another wave of regret for the day's deeds swallowed him up. "How did this happen?"

Wu Yien let a span of silence mark his own anguish and turmoil over the decisions they had made to save the lives of others. "We should have seen it coming. We should have been better prepared. It need not have ended this way."

"Looking back now it seems all so obvious, but at the time . . ."

"It is as I've always said," Wu Yien offered as Zoram secured the satchel over his neck and shoulder. "The most cunning captains and generals know that victory in war is achieved by deception and diversion. Next time we will not be taken unawares."

"No," Zoram said. "This is a lesson I will never forget. For me there won't be a next time. This I vow."

Wu Yien offered a sad smile. "Then this experience, as horrible as it was, was not without value. May the lives lost today serve to prevent similar deaths tomorrow."

"Listen to you. You're starting to sound more and more like our masters every day. You really should consider writing some of this stuff down." Zoram laughed. "You never know. Future generations might want to bask in the wisdom of Wu Yien."

Wu Yien joined him in a good laugh. "We'd better get you back to the monastery. That cut looks pretty bad. And besides, I think all this excitement is finally starting to go to your head."

CHAPTER TWENTY-TWO

ZORAM WOKE WITH A START; a feeling of panic. The room was dark, and while he couldn't quite place it, he could sense that something wasn't right. He was disoriented. Had night fallen? What time was it? Where was he? He couldn't remember going to bed. In fact, he couldn't remember much of anything. He blinked a few times, slowly, and noticed that the back of his eyes felt as if they were being tugged at by lead weights. The sensation was nauseating.

He tried to sit up but fell immediately back into bed with a sharp, immobilizing pain. He had felt this way once before, albeit to a much lesser degree. It was years ago when he had first been introduced to rice wine, but he didn't recall having any strong drink—

He pulled back his hand as quickly as if it had touched a snake. Someone was in bed with him!

No! Horror opened the pit of his stomach. Where was he? This wasn't his bed! He recoiled from the stabbing and paralyzing pain in his head and neck but forced his body to sit up. The bedding, the pillows, the room, the windows—they were all wrong. None of it looked familiar.

The cool air on his bare chest caused him even more alarm. He was naked from the waist up and—what was this? Lying next to him was a woman still asleep and breathing deeply. Zoram kicked off the covers and scrambled out of the bed, falling to the floor. The pain and disorientation were too much for him. When he tried to get up, he found his legs were weak and felt as if they were being continuously pierced by a thousand needles. But the worst was the excruciating agony in his head, neck, and shoulders. He almost cried out as he pushed himself across the cold floor and propped himself against the wall. He marshaled what little strength he could and rose to his feet. Every jolt and jar felt like a dull knife blade digging into and splitting the back of his skull as he struggled to regain his balance.

Where was he? This wasn't his room, but his clothes had been thrown and scattered on the floor. How did he get here? He closed his eyes and tried to push the pain away long enough to think back through the jumbled whirlwind of images and recollections: He had completed the Sword. Rebekah. He had seen the king, Matteniah. Then Laban. He returned home. He was tired. Naomi. But that was all he remembered.

The woman stirred, mumbled something still dreaming, and turned over.

It was Anat!

Her eyes fluttered open; she seemed completely at peace as she stretched and drifted into consciousness. He turned away as she rolled over, careful to avoid seeing her nakedness.

"Good morning," Anat said softly and yawned. "Sleep well?"

Zoram was unable to speak; his tongue would not form the words he *might* say even if he knew *what* to say. What was happening?

Morning?

Had he slept through until morning? Why couldn't he remember anything after coming home? And why did his head hurt so much?

"A-Anat?" Oh, it hurt to speak. His voice scraped over his throat and thundered in his ears. "Why . . . ? What's going on? Why am I . . ."

"Oh, my love, you look ill," she said, pulling back the sheets. "Come, lie down, before you fall."

My love?

"Here," she said, sitting up and reaching for a carafe of wine. "You must be parched."

Zoram turned away sharply and nearly fell to his knees with the pain. "Put some clothes on."

Anat sounded offended and dejected. "Am I not pleasing to you, my lord?"

"I don't know what you're talking about. I don't know how I got here or why I spent the night in your bed."

"I could *tell* you why," she said softly, inviting, "but come back to bed, and I'll do my best to help you remember."

"Stop it! I don't know what you're talking about. There is nothing to remember. Nothing happened." But he wasn't so sure.

Anat's look switched to one of concern. "You really don't remember, do you?" She got out of bed and slipped into a robe.

"What am I supposed to have forgotten?" he asked hesitantly.

Anat looked at him for a long moment and then stepped to the window. She moved one of the wooden shutters aside and looked out. "I knew it was a mistake. I shouldn't have encouraged you like that. I mean, I like you. It's like I've known you all my life. Your father and mother would tell stories . . ." She sighed. "And when they received your letters, well, they would speak of you as only proud parents can. How could I be anything but enamored by you and look forward to your return?"

Zoram vaguely recalled hearing this before. Somehow he knew all of this—the letters, her feelings—but where had he heard it? His head still hurt, and trying to remember anything was like trying to look through cheesecloth. But while he couldn't quite remember where he had heard it, he knew it was recent. His memories may be clouded and vague, but his feelings were clear. He—

Naomi! That's who had told him these things. Just a little while ago. No. Yesterday afternoon. She had told him of Anat's feelings and asked him to pay her a visit. Something about young hearts. "I stopped by when I returned from the palace, after my work with the Sword."

Anat nodded. "You were tired. We shared a glass of wine . . ."

Zoram knew by her look how that story ended, and while it made him sick to his stomach, it did explain that manner and place in which he woke up.

"I should have been more persistent in resisting your advances, but to be honest, I had hoped and dreamed of your love and affection for years. I always knew we were destined to be together"—she reached out to take his hand—"forever."

For the second time that morning, Zoram recoiled from her touch. "I . . . I . . ." *don't believe you,* he wanted to say but couldn't. What had he done? His thoughts went back to the stories he had heard as a child. Why did he not flee yesterday, as Joseph had from Potiphar's wife? But there wasn't the chance. There were no signs or warnings. How could he have been so weak willed?

And why could he not remember?

He knew he wasn't thinking clearly. He was smothered with guilt and utter and complete disappointment in himself. How could he have been so easily overcome? How could he have traded something so beautiful for something so base that he still had no memory of? What would his mother or his father have said? But overriding his moral and social guilt was the horror of Rebekah learning of this night. Above all he was concerned about violating her trust and the buds of their emerging love. How could he face her again? He had betrayed her, and for a moment nothing mattered but her.

"Zoram?" Anat asked softly, sitting on the edge of the bed, sensing his internal struggle. "What are we to do?"

Anat's simple question ultimately drove away his hope and concern. *What are we to do?*

"I don't know." And he didn't. But he did know that she was the last one he wanted to discuss it with. He wanted to blame her, but being a man is owning up to your actions—right or wrong. Thoughts of stoning or banishment weighed down uncomfortably on his mind. What was the punishment for such sins?

"We . . . we could . . ." She turned away as if the very words embarrassed her. "We could make it right. It's not too late. I mean, no one knows but us, right?"

He didn't think his dilemma could have become more complex and convoluted. Did he understand her words correctly? Was she now proposing—

"*Marriage?*"

"I know this is all happening so fast, but it really does make sense the more you think about it. In fact, many people assumed that we'd be wed once you returned. Even your mother and your father supported the prospect of our union." Still sitting on the disheveled bed, she waited until he again looked at her. "I know this might be hard for you to see right now, but maybe what happened last night was a sign that this—that *we*—are supposed to happen."

She stood and slowly stepped toward him until she was standing right in front of him. This time, however, she refrained from touching him. "I recognize that I know more about you than you know about me. I've had years to learn of you and hear the stories of your childhood and plan for this day, whereas you have not. You may not love me now, but in time you will grow to share my love. This I promise." She gave him a soft smile and offered her hand for him to take.

The shock of the morning had begun to lose its grip over Zoram's thoughts and emotions. The panic and humiliation that had consumed him since waking up in her bed began to give way, and he was able to start thinking more clearly. And while he didn't know or understand how he could have let his guard down enough to share Anat's bed, he did know one thing for sure. "No," he said. "This was a mistake. We're not the first to make it nor will we be the last. And while I agree with you that we must make it right, simply pretending it didn't happen and announcing our marriage does not fix things. You've been good to my family, and for that I will be forever grateful. What I have done I beg your forgiveness for as I will beg mercy under the law. But I will not compound one mistake by committing another."

Anat's pleasing and demure manner dissolved as Zoram's words registered. She stood motionless for a minute, her eyes wide with hurt as the reality of his true feelings struck her. "Mistake?" she said with a sharp edge to her tone. "Is that what this is? Is that what *we* are?"

He could see she was hurt, but there was something else lurking beneath her anger. "All I'm saying is that to proceed like nothing happened, or that . . ." He couldn't finish. He didn't have the words to express what he was feeling. Besides, he realized, she was clearly not receptive to what he was trying to say. "I think it's best if I just go. Perhaps we can talk again after we've both had time to sort all this out."

Remembering that he was wearing only his undergarment wrapped around his waist, he started gathering up his clothes.

"Don't do this," she said. The way she said it, though, Zoram couldn't tell if it was a plea or a threat. "She could never make you as happy as I can."

"What?"

"She doesn't know what it means to be a Keeper's wife. She couldn't make you proud. Not like I could."

"Who are you talking about—" But then he knew. He remembered, and it was all becoming clear. "You saw us yesterday at the armory." He put his fingers to the sides of his head. "What have you done?"

"You deserve a woman who can make you proud, a wife skilled and schooled in subtlety and discretion, a wife who can blend with and be accepted into society and the ruling class. You *need* me."

And with that last declaration, Zoram rocked back, realizing what he had fallen victim to. The visit, the wine, the pain in his head and neck, his lack of memory. "You drugged me." He could tell from her expression that he was right.

"I didn't mean for it to happen this way, for *us* to happen this way. You must believe me. But when I saw you and her—You can't love her! You deserve more in a wife. You deserve more than a stuttering, mad merchant's daughter could offer you."

Without thought Zoram raised his hand to strike her but stopped short of actually delivering the blow. The threat stopped her string of insults as she recoiled and turned away.

"You are no longer welcome in my house," he said. "You have until nightfall to gather your belongings and leave."

When Anat turned back around, however, she had a sly smile across her lips. "No one will believe you."

"I am the master of this house and the Keeper of the Sword. Of course they will."

She shook her head slowly. "Do you know the consequence prescribed by the law for what we did last night?"

"Nothing happened!"

She reached out and traced her finger down his bare chest. "And if a man find a damsel—that's me—and lie with her, and they be found, she shall be his wife—"

"Silence!" He slapped her hand away.

"And he may not put her away all his days." She stepped boldly toward him until he finally backed away. "You're a vigorous young man who could not resist or deny his natural urges anymore and took advantage of the poor"—she continued to step forward—"innocent"—forcing him farther backward—"girl, who had dedicated her young and tender years to the care of his ill and aged parents."

"Stop this! Get out of my house!"

"I will offer you one more chance before . . ."

"Before what?"

Anat didn't move for a long pause and then drew in a quick breath and let out a loud, high-pitched scream at the top of her lungs. Instinctively Zoram dropped the clothing he was still holding to grab her by one hand, trying to cover her mouth and stifle the scream with the other. After a brief struggle, he had her under control, but not before he realized that she had baited him into doing exactly what she wanted—what she *needed*— him to do.

Her bedroom door burst open. Two of the house staff were followed immediately by Naomi. They had come running at the sound of the alarm.

Zoram looked at the conniving serpent in his hands and saw a brief flash of satisfaction in Anat's eyes before she turned on the tears and slipped to the floor, her robe falling from her shoulder as she shuddered and sobbed.

He didn't have to be experienced in the ways of the world to know that the scene could not have looked worse. She had manipulated not only him but everyone around him. Anat was right: no one was going to believe him now.

"Zoram?" Naomi said, her voice thick with disbelief.

He finished picking up his clothes. "This is not what it appears," he stated simply without apology or explanation, stepping past the stunned and confused onlookers.

As soon as he was out of their sight, he ran, taking the stairs two and three at a time until he reached his own room and closed the door behind him. It was dark. Thick curtains hung at the windows, letting in only thin slivers of the morning sun. He closed his eyes and leaned against the door. The wood felt cool on his back as he forced himself to breathe deep and rhythmically to calm the raging storm that swelled within him. How could he be so foolish? So easily manipulated? He hated himself for being so naïve and trusting, and he vowed never to trust anyone ever again. Matteniah was right, he thought. There was no one left to trust in all of Jerusalem.

Including himself.

He shut his eyes even tighter, as if he could simply will the night and morning away; maybe when he opened them he would find himself alone in his own bed, what had just happened only a fading nightmare. But when he opened his eyes, he wanted to cry. Nothing had changed.

He felt helpless. Anat's little performance was convincing enough to implicate him in a most serious transgression of the law that would likely result in shame and dishonor on his name, his family's name, and the office of Keeper. How could he have let this happen? Was he not stronger than that?

Cool water filled the tub in the other room, drawn and prepared yesterday before his return from the armory, he suspected, but left unused. While his personal hygiene was of little concern to him at that moment, the thought of washing away what he could of this morning appealed to him very much. He wanted to be clean again.

He began to undress then stopped. His undergarment wrapping had been cut. Not all the way through, but here, on the top and only through the first few layers. He was confused at first, but then a feeling of relief washed over him, cleansing his mind and heart more than all of the water in the Jordan. Did Anat think he wouldn't notice? But then she would have had no way of knowing. How could she? He did not wear the same manner of loincloth and undergarment as other men of Jerusalem. His was called a *dhoti* and worn by the men of his monastery. It was nothing special, just a rectangular piece of cloth about fourteen cubits wrapped around the waist and legs. The part that brought sunshine to his soul again was the knot still tied at the waist. He could not have retied the same knot in his drugged state. It was difficult enough to do fully awake. He had not retied his dhoti because he had never removed it. Anat couldn't untie it and had tried to cut through it.

He started to laugh at the sudden release of his guilt and shame. Anat was a convincing liar, to be sure, but her confident control of the circumstances was far from complete. And while he might find it difficult to answer Anat's allegations given her skills and cunning, his faith and confidence in himself was restored. He was pure and had not compromised his virtue after all.

Any fears or concerns about what she might say or what might happen were swept away. She no longer had any hold over him.

He bathed quickly, washing away his aches and pain with the two days of sweat and grime. He was reborn and renewed.

As he dressed, a small stack of clothing in the corner caught his eye. He hadn't noticed it the other day.

He pulled back one of the curtains and let in the first rays of the morning sun. They were clothes, but not his. He picked up the top piece—a linen undergarment covered in dirt and dark stains.

"What . . . ?" he wondered softly, laying that garment aside and taking up the cloak and mantle, gritty and covered in sand. He then noticed the pair of shoes on the ground beneath them, and suddenly he knew what he was holding. He recognized the patterns and style. These were his father's clothes, the ones Jharom had been wearing when he died. The garments took on an almost holy reverence, especially as he touched the dark stains with his fingertips. Blood. His father's blood. Someone must have delivered them to his room thinking Zoram would want to have them. Or perhaps they didn't know what else to do with them.

Standing there in his room, his *father's* room, in his father's estate, bearing his father's title, Zoram felt like he was ten years old again, a little afraid and wholly inadequate for the calling that would one day be his.

The problem was that the once distant "one day" was today, and reflecting on the events of the past three days, he didn't think he was measuring up to his mother and father's expectations.

He recalled the words of Laban during their first meeting. The news about his father's faults and weaknesses had been hard to take, and Zoram still didn't want to believe it. But his father was gone. He had left Zoram to find his way alone.

Why did you leave me like this? he wondered, tears welling up in his eyes as childhood memories mixed with feelings of abandonment. He was lost, and the images of his father's internment and burial now consumed him. He lowered himself to the floor before his strength entirely left him. He hadn't experienced the depth of sadness and loss at the time, but his body, heart, and mind were struck with it now.

His mother's death had been traumatic in its own way, but he had taken some comfort that her death had been an end to her pain and suffering. But his father's death made no sense to him. It didn't seem that a man so racked with guilt, so deep in iniquity, could hide it from those so close to him. To everyone, his father was the very pillar of faith, good words, and good deeds—everyone, that is, except Laban, in whom his father had confided the canker on his soul and the flaw in his character.

Zoram reached over and took the pieces of clothing, feeling especially close to his father. The thin stream of sunlight had crawled across the floor and now rested on the shoes. Zoram then noticed something odd and seemingly out of place. He took a closer look, and in a moment of clarity, Zoram suddenly doubted the story he'd been told about his father's death. He dressed quickly and took the shoe with him. He had some questions that demanded answers, but as much as he wanted to ask them, his confrontation with the one man who could provide those answers would have to wait. There was still much Zoram needed to uncover first.

CHAPTER TWENTY-THREE

"Masterful performance last night."

"Thank you." Laban didn't look up as he continued to brush his favorite stallion. He took great interest in seeing that his prized horses were well treated and cared for. He fed them, bathed them, and brushed them every morning. He felt a special connection to the powerful beasts and often retreated to his stables to find solace from the world.

"In fact," his lieutenant continued, "there were times *I* actually believed what you were saying."

Laban acknowledged the compliment with a grunt. "That's the first rule of an effective lie. You must first lie to yourself. You must actually believe what you're saying, at least for the time being. If you don't believe it yourself, neither will anyone else." He took a break after working his way down the horse's neck and back with his bristled comb. Stepping to a table in the corner, he drank deeply from a large goblet of wine.

After a moment, Hanoch asked, "You don't really think he'll take the poison, do you?"

He shook his head. "No, he doesn't have the courage or the foresight to do it. He's still a boy—a frightened little boy."

"Then why give it to him? Why tip him off?"

From his pocket Laban produced a vial similar to the one he had given to the king the night before. He then tossed it to Hanoch. "So that when he is found poisoned . . ."

"The authorities will conclude that he did it himself. Brilliant."

"I presume you have secured the means to have a drop or two administered with his food?"

"You have but to indicate which meal, and it will be done."

"I've heard that he has refused the breakfast that was taken to him. He may still have resolve enough to refuse the midday meal as well. See to it that our king is prepared an especially appetizing meal for dinner."

"Should I just be concerned with the king's plate?"

A smile crept across Laban's face. "Maybe it would be fitting to make his death a family affair."

"Family?"

"The woman and child. You saw them, I assume. You're not blind."

"But that wasn't the queen," Hanoch said, trying not to sound foolish. "And he's produced no heirs yet."

"Obviously," Laban said with some level of disappointment in his accomplice. "He married the queen less than a year ago. The boy is from a prior marriage—a marriage before he was made king."

"But I was not aware of this."

"No one is. I doubt if even Babylon knows."

It took another moment before the value of this knowledge began to register with Hanoch. "A secret heir."

"He must realize that whether by his own hand or at the command of Nebuchadnezzar, this little secret will eventually and ultimately result in their deaths. It was foolish to think he could keep this from the world."

Hanoch considered the small container. "This is a more merciful end."

"Oh, make no mistake. When the poison makes it to their hearts, our king will plead for a swift end to their lives, especially as he watches his young wife and child suffer." Laban shrugged, unaffected by the visual. "But at least they'll die together."

"As a family," Hanoch added.

"As a family."

Laban returned to his horse, brushing in small, circular strokes to loosen the dead hair, burrs, and other irritants. This particular stallion, bred from a long line of Egyptian stallions, was the pride of his stable, and it was this love that tempered the frustration that prompted summoning Hanoch this morning.

"I am told that there was an *incident* at the treasury last night," Laban said as he worked. "Have you learned any more about this?"

"No. Nothing, I'm afraid."

"Nothing *yet*, you mean."

Hanoch shook his head. "He died in the night. Most of his injuries were internal and the cuts too deep to stop the flow of blood."

Laban momentarily stopped midstroke at the update then continued on. "Forgive me if I am not as easily assuaged. I find it more than a little concerning that on the very night we level charges at the king, a nameless man makes a run on the treasury and then dies before we can learn his motives, if he was acting alone, and what he knew. Are you certain the records were safe?"

"The door was still locked when they returned—"

"Returned? They left their posts?"

Hanoch swallowed hard and unconsciously took a step back. He stammered his explanation, clearly not having meant to reveal this small detail. "I-they . . . when he attacked and then fled—"

"They chased after him?" Laban finished, his voice rising with his anger. "He drew them away? Why was this not in your initial report? Other than the fact that it proves you and your men incompetent!"

"They were all members of The Fifty."

"Not anymore. I'll deal with them later. For now I need to know everything you do. Leave anything out—even the smallest detail—and I will separate that thick head of yours from your even thicker neck. Am I clear?"

Hanoch didn't answer. Instead, he stood a little taller and puffed out his chest as if to invite the fight. But his show of defiance did not last long against Laban's intense stare. As good as he was, he knew he was no match against Laban.

"They quickly realized their mistake and sent two back. When they returned, they found the anteroom empty and the door still locked and secure."

"Are you certain that the plates are secure?"

"There are only two keys to the treasury: yours and the new Keeper's."

"And you are certain Zoram wasn't involved?"

"We had him followed, as you instructed."

"And . . . ?"

"He left the treasury shortly after you did. He then returned home and did not emerge until earlier this morning."

"Is that so? Don't you find that just a little odd?"

"Upon informal inquiry, it appears he paid a visit to Anat and did not leave all night." Hanoch couldn't help but allow himself a slim, satisfying smile. "The woman is ambitious, if nothing else."

"She's an opportunistic snake," Laban said flatly. "A serpent of the most devious and vile kind. Jharom might have been fooled by her caring pretense, but I've already danced with that devil and know of her utter abhorrence for life as the daughter of a common laborer."

"Zoram deserves everything she has in store for him."

"Now, now, are you still sore over your little skirmish the other day?"

"I underestimated him once. You can be certain I won't make that mistake again."

"I know, I know. You can seek him out later, and if you run him through, I will applaud your skill," Laban said. "But not until after we've completed what we've started. Suspicions will be raised when the king and his family are found dead so soon after Jharom's 'suicide.' We cannot afford another prominent death in such quick succession."

Laban gave Hanoch a serious and stern look. "Swear to me. Swear upon your life that you will wait to engage young Zoram."

"I will not seek him out. I swear."

Laban could see the fires of hate in Hanoch's eyes the more they spoke of Zoram. It was more than just simple embarrassment. There was envy and resentment for the young Keeper. "If all goes as planned you can have his head in less than a week. Never trade what you want most for what you want at the moment. You must learn patience."

Laban paused to gauge Hanoch's commitment. Satisfied, he returned to his line of inquiry. "You're certain the records were not compromised?"

"Yes, as I've said."

"And you know this because you have seen them?"

"How could I have? The door was and is still locked." Hanoch was showing his irritation at Laban's redundant questioning. "There was just one man. The halls were empty and otherwise quiet. Every soldier and sentry was questioned. No one out of the ordinary was seen coming or going."

But this explanation failed to satisfy Laban. "Out of the ordinary? So there *were* others?" It wasn't a question. "Did you get names?"

"No—"

"Get them. Deceit and treachery often come from those closest to us. I want to know the names and stations of every single man or woman who was seen there last night."

Hanoch wasn't convinced. "I don't understand. If you're so worried about the records, why don't you just take them and hide them? In your personal chambers, perhaps? No one is aware or suspects a thing. And even if some eventually do, you're the Keeper of the Records. You can justify any efforts to protect them. Why keep them in the treasury if you're so concerned?"

Laban's suspicions were confirmed by the simplistic idiocy of this last question. Hanoch would forever lack what it took to be a leader. He'd been a soldier for too long, accustomed only to taking orders and planning short-term strategies. No amount of explanation or elaboration would broaden his restrictive and myopic view. It would be like trying to pour the Jordan into a small cup. But Laban had to tell him something. "Nothing is done until it's done," he finally said. "And just as our young Keeper must remain unharmed until we have our prize, the records need to be remain where they are." Laban could see that Hanoch didn't completely understand but was glad when he just nodded and left it alone.

Laban continued to work in silence on his horse. This stallion was going to be the steed upon which Israel's new king would ride triumphantly. Appearances, he knew, were everything in the acquisition of power. There was much to do still, including the first of several meetings with the Sarim and the other Elders at Jerusalem to further discuss the fate of their treacherous king. He was about to dismiss Hanoch when they were interrupted. Standing at the gates was the person Laban considered the largest unknown factor in his plans.

"Zoram," Laban said. *Sleep well?* he so desperately wanted to add but held his tongue. He noticed Zoram looked upset and serious and switched his own look to that of concern. "What's wrong?"

"I need to speak to you about my—" Zoram stopped abruptly when he noticed Hanoch standing off to one side in the shadows.

"This is Hanoch, my lieutenant and chief of security forces in the city. He's also my most trusted confidant. In fact, if I am not mistaken, I believe the two of you have already met, briefly, and under admittedly less-than-ideal circumstances. Hanoch," he motioned for him to step forward, "this is Zoram, son of Jharom, and new Keeper of the Sword."

Hanoch offered a curt bow but kept his distance and his mouth shut. *Good boy*, Laban thought.

Zoram returned the nod but paid him no real attention. "I need to speak with you . . . alone."

Laban feigned sincere interest. "What is it? Please, do not mind Hanoch. We have no secrets in matters of security. He knows what I know. Please, go on."

Zoram hesitated for only a moment. The news was threatening to burst from his chest. "I don't think my father killed himself. I think there might have been more to his death."

Laban quickly caught his surprised look and replaced it with a more subtle, blank one, burying his concerns deep within his pounding heart. "What? Why would you say that? What's happened?"

Zoram stole one more glance at Hanoch and then completely ignored him, opening the bag slung over his shoulder. "I've been thinking about what you told me about my father, and while he might have had these weaknesses—though I cannot find any evidence of this—I don't believe that he died by his own hand."

Zoram held out one of his father's shoes. "These are the shoes he was wearing when he died. Look." He turned it over and pointed to the sole. "Do you see this? These are fresh olives. The oil has stained the leather. Here," he touched it, "it's still moist."

Laban moved to take a closer look. "Indeed. That is what it looks like. But he could have picked up those stains on his shoes anywhere."

"I know, but both shoes were covered with fresh olives, not just a stray fruit in the markets during his travels of the day."

Laban thought about this for a moment. "True, but perhaps he took a walk earlier in the day. Men with heavy hearts often seek comfort in long and solitary walks, and we are surrounded by hills of olive trees and groves."

"I know. I've considered this as well, and if the remnant of the fruit on his shoes was the only inconsistency, I might be convinced that he did just that." Zoram reached into his bag and pulled out his father's coat. "Then I noticed this."

The garment was dirty and torn almost to shreds by the sharp rocks at the base of the city wall. Laban was confused. "What am I supposed to be looking at?"

"Here," Zoram said. "Do you see it?"

Laban did, and an uneasy feeling weighed heavily in the pit of his stomach. He looked up and over at Hanoch, whose look of contempt and hatred for the young Keeper was replaced by curiosity tinged with fear. He, too, stepped closer and leaned in to look at what Zoram was pointing out.

"It looks like a rip," Hanoch said.

"On first inspection that's what I thought too. But look at the clean cut, the precise entry point. And then there's this." He removed his father's linen undershirt. "An identical cut here in the same area."

"A sharp rock," Hanoch protested. "He was cut when he hit the ground, nothing more."

But while Hanoch tried, weakly, to deny it, Laban knew that his little piece of evidence posed a serious threat to the flawless execution of his plans. News of this would spread quickly and to ears he preferred to remain deaf to the notions of conspiracy. Too many coincidences begin to look a lot like a plan.

It was time to take control of the situation as only Laban could. "Hanoch," he said. "There's no reason to keep our young friend out of this anymore. I think he deserves to know what happened and the recent events that led to his father's death."

Hanoch, just as Laban had expected, displayed a convincing look of shock and surprise. But before he could voice his concerns and protest, Laban began.

"The night after your father's body was found, Hanoch's men discovered, gave chase, and apprehended a Babylonian spy as he was attempting to sneak into the city." Laban looked around to make sure they were alone and continued in a hushed voice. "He was a messenger carrying secret letters between a Babylonian princess and the king."

Zoram was only mildly affected by the news. "The king must have many lines of communication open between here and Babylon."

"Agreed, but it was the nature of those letters that is the subject of grave concern. In them, he plots to steal the records and trade them for the love and union of this woman."

This last revelation invoked the response Laban was hoping for. Zoram was in shock and disbelief. "That's . . . that's not . . ."

"Possible? I didn't want to believe it either, but the evidence is what it is."

"He must have been lying, a plot to implicate the king in some scandal."

"Who? The messenger? Perhaps. In fact, some members of the Council of Elders believed so too when these allegations were raised. An official investigation was conducted and multiple letters were found hidden in the king's personal chambers. Some of them go back several years, each more convincing and damaging than the one intercepted. He'll receive a fair trial, but it does not look good for our king."

Zoram was speechless, standing there, his father's clothing hanging loosely off his fingers. Finally he found the ability to speak. "When did all this happen? I . . . I was with the king just yesterday morning."

Laban looked to Hanoch. "If I'm not mistaken, the messenger confessed yesterday morning, a meeting of the Sarim was called, and the charges presented last night. It all happened so quickly." He paused to let Zoram wrap his mind around the news. "We now have reason to believe, especially in light of what you have just brought to our attention, that your father may have stumbled upon this plot and, not knowing who to trust, fell victim to the desperate actions of those involved."

"Are you saying . . . ?"

"I now believe he was killed. He may have spotted the spy from atop the wall, where he sat awaiting your return. Your father must have chased him through the hills around the city. When he returned and reported this to the king, Jharom must have been killed and thrown from the wall. The knife cuts in his clothing would indicate a struggle, but whether with the messenger or from men acting under orders from the king, it makes little difference now."

Laban reached out and gently touched Zoram's arm. "I am so sorry." Zoram's eyes glassed over as the shock of these words cut him to the very center. His arms and hands went limp, and the shirt and coat fell to the ground. Laban clapped his hands loudly, and two servants appeared a minute later. "Zoram, you're not well. Here, allow my staff to help you."

Laban gingerly picked up the articles of clothing and began replacing them in the bag. "I would caution you against speaking word of this to anyone. We don't know how far this conspiracy reaches. I will keep your father's clothes as further evidence."

Zoram was almost nonresponsive. Laban spoke quickly to his servants. "See that he receives anything he might need. Return him to his estate and see that a physician is called. Am I clear?"

Zoram muttered his thanks and offered no resistance as he was led out of the stables and through the gates of the estate.

When they had been gone for a full minute and were clearly beyond earshot, Laban's caring demeanor changed dramatically. "Where did he get these?" he yelled, holding up Zoram's satchel. He spun it over his head once and then threw it against the stable wall, startling his horse. "I trusted you to take care of this!"

"How was I supposed to know the clothes would be returned to him?"

"What did you think would happen to them?"

"I . . . I didn't—"

"You didn't *think*, did you? It's missed details like this one that can unravel *everything*!" Laban was shaking with fury and rage.

"Do you think he told anyone else?"

"You had better pray he didn't." A tense moment later, Laban picked up the clothes. "Here!" he said, throwing the bag at Hanoch. "Burn these. Watch them go up in smoke with your own eyes."

"But what do we do about Zoram? He won't just let this go."

"We stall him as long as we can."

"Then what?"

Laban didn't answer right away. The young Keeper's fate was sure. Hanoch was right: Zoram would never give up this search for the "truth" about what happened to his father. He was a smart man. And persistent. It would only be a matter of time before he could conceivably ruin all Laban had worked for and put into place.

"See that he is kept far away from the king," Laban instructed. "The punishment for failing to keep the two of them apart will be immediate and cursory death—yours as well as theirs. I will not permit you to be the weak link in this chain of events!"

He paced in anticipation of the next round of threats he would breathe against Hanoch when they were interrupted by a sharp rap on one of the stable posts. "What is it now?!"

One of his house staff stood, head bowed, at the far end of the stables. His posture and body language conveyed his fear at interrupting his master. He shuffled forward. "There is someone requesting an audience with Your Eminence, great Keeper."

"Send him away! I have no time to entertain." Laban dismissed the servant with a wave of his hand and returned his attention to Hanoch but stopped, sensing that his command had been ignored. The servant had remained, a terrified look plaguing his face.

"I said I was not to be disturbed! Tell whoever it is to go away!"

But the servant just stared, wide-eyed, trying to speak. But while his lips moved, he made no sound.

"Well, man, speak up!" Laban snapped.

"I . . . I . . ." he started. "I b-believe you may wish to s-see him."

Laban's initial rage passed, and he had to admit he was curious who this caller could be and what he'd said to convince the servant to disobey a direct order, especially delivered with such anger and force. "Who is it that you believe I'll want to see?"

The servant suddenly looked to Hanoch and then back to Laban, his fear renewed. He swallowed hard. "His name is Laman."

Laban looked at Hanoch. "Laman? I don't know anyone by that name. Is he a member of the council?"

The servant shook his head hastily. "No, my lord. He claims to be . . ."

"Yes?" He was in no mood to guess.

"The eldest son of . . ."

"Do I have to beat it out of you? Speak up! Who is it?"

The servant finally blurted out the name. "He claims to be the eldest son of Lehi."

Laban might have been upset at the interruption, but he couldn't help raising an eyebrow at the name and lineage. "Does he now?"

"Should I have him arrested?" Hanoch asked.

"Arrested? For what? Being the son of a wanted man? Where's the fun in that? No, let's hear what he has to say. Who knows, maybe he's here to surrender his father." Laban amused himself.

"Not likely."

"You know him?"

"I didn't recognize the name, but if it's who I'm now thinking of, he enlisted to serve in the military a few years back."

"Was he any good?"

"No. He had the size, and he was strong, though not particularly muscular. You know the type. I think all of Lehi's sons are big like that. Anyway, despite his size and potential, he was uncoordinated and clumsy." Hanoch thought harder. "He also had a problem with authority. He didn't take orders well."

"You don't say?" Laban put down the horse brush and cracked a devious grin. "Well, let's not keep our esteemed guest waiting."

שומר החרב

Laban agreed to meet with Laman in the large reception hall built into the estate. The room was large and spacious and better furnished than the palace. Sunlight streamed in through open windows while silks and exotic animal skins adorned the walls. Laban had even directed that a small banquet be set for his guest. Laban had bathed and dressed and now sat upon a raised chair in anticipation of the meeting. Hanoch, as always, stood at Laban's side in full military uniform.

With a clap of Laban's hands, his servant disappeared behind the door and reemerged a minute later with a man a full head taller than his escort and a face covered in dark, coarse hair. He seemed to lurch into the reception hall, his eyes wide and gawking. Laban could see why Hanoch remembered this man—he had a look that was hard to forget. Laman looked around the room, clearly intimidated. His attention finally settled on Laban, seated in the oversized stone chair.

Laman cleared his throat and came to attention. "G-Great Keeper . . ."

Laban didn't wait for the formal greeting and got right to business. "Welcome Laman, son of Lehi, to my home. You bring us great honor by your visit." His tone shifted from pleasant to accusatory in an instant. "Or at least you would if your father was not a fugitive, wanted for questioning in connection with crimes against our law." Laban shifted in his chair. "You are, no doubt, aware of this."

Laman nodded, fear now added to his look of intimidation.

"In light of this fact," Laban continued, "I have to admit I'm more than a little curious as to the reason for your visit. We both are, isn't that right?"

Hanoch, playing the heavy, didn't respond but stood tall and looked menacing.

Laman looked around the room when the servant who had ushered him in had left. They were alone. He cleared his throat again and started to fidget with the sleeves of his coat. "I have come on the errand of my father," he said after taking a deep breath. "He respectfully requests that you release into my control the plates of brass."

Laban could not have been more stunned if his guest had declared himself king and demanded his allegiance. This was the last thing he had expected to hear coming from his guest's thick lips. *Lehi flees in the middle of night, eluding capture, then sends his brute of a son back to ask for the records?* Oh, this was intriguing—unsettling, given the attention the records were receiving of late—but interesting. Laban had so many questions for this dolt but knew he should start with the most important one.

"Does he now? And why should I acquiesce to your father's request?" he said with an air of feigned nobility. "He's a criminal and a wanted man. What possible reason would I have to give him the records?"

Laman hesitated as if gathering courage for his reply. "Because he says the Lord commands it."

Laban didn't speak for a long moment then burst into laughter. Even Hanoch cracked a smug and condescending smile. "God wants me to turn over the plates? God, you say? Well, it's hard to refuse a command such as that, now isn't it?"

He continued to mock and laugh. "Well, by all means then . . ." But he couldn't finish. The situation was outrageous. After enduring his laughter for a time, trying to smile and join in the derisive ridicule at his and his father's expense, Laman spoke again, this time with even less conviction than before.

"He says," Laman started, "it contains the genealogy of his fathers and for that and other reasons, the Lord has instructed him to send us to obtain them."

Laban's laughter died abruptly as Laman's words heightened his every sense and momentarily struck fear into his heart. Genealogy? Was it possible that Lehi knew of his plans? Laban needed the records to confirm his royal lineage. This fact was key to his plans for power. A cold calm descended on Laban and sharpened his heart and mind. He had heard enough. "Is that so? Well, then, if God wants your father to have what is rightfully mine, He will have to send more than a buffoon like you to take them. Hanoch," he said sharply, "arrest this intruder, this thief, this robber who is part of the king's conspiracy to steal and dispose of the records to nefarious ends."

Hanoch stepped forward, his hand gripping the hilt of the sword at this side.

"What? No!" Laman exclaimed in a panic. "Wait!"

"You are a traitor to Israel, like your father, and you will be tried and punished according to the law."

Lehi's eldest son backed up as Hanoch approached. "No! I'm not . . ." He didn't finish, turning and throwing open the door, running out of the room in a frantic escape. Hanoch started to pursue him but was called back.

"No," Laban said. "Let your men give chase."

"But he's getting away."

"Let him go. I only wanted to make an impression."

"But if we lose him, we lose Lehi's location."

"We'll have him soon enough. But did you hear what he said? He said his father sent 'us.' There's more than one of them. I need you to secure the plates. Bring them here."

"Why? What's wrong?"

"He wants them for genealogy."

"So?"

"Lehi is a descendant of Joseph too." Laban was frustrated when Hanoch failed to see the significance of this fact. "With the sudden death of the king, Lehi would also have claim to the throne. We cannot let that happen. My claim and ascension must be without objection or question."

Laban got up and paced the room, pausing to fill a cup of wine. "I don't like this. It's too much of a coincidence. And if there is one thing I do *not* believe in, it's coincidences."

"But how could Lehi have found out? That's impossible, isn't it?"

"Maybe he knew all along."

"Then why send his son simply requesting them?" Hanoch wondered. "Why not steal them?"

"Or blackmail us with what he knows? Or wait until the eleventh hour to make his move? I know, I know. None of this makes any sense."

After a moment of reflection, Hanoch ventured, "You don't think it's possible that . . ." But he didn't finish his thought.

"That what? That God actually told him to retrieve them? Don't be ridiculous. God is dead. And you know what? We killed Him. Oh, no, not literally, of course, but we live in an age where we no longer need to look to a god on high to direct us or lead us from on high. These are foolish stories and traditions, nothing more. The sooner we start relying on what's real, on our own strength, and not some mythical deity, the sooner we'll be free and come into our own power among nations."

Hanoch stood there, not certain if he believed as fully as Laban did, but certain enough not to disagree. "And the records?"

"I want them safe here with me."

"Shall I bring them in secret?"

"No. The records are in danger. In fact, make it known without making it obvious. I am concerned for their well-being."

Laban finished off his cup of wine.

"Besides, who better to protect them than the great Keeper of the Records?"

CHAPTER TWENTY-FOUR

REBEKAH FLOATED THROUGH HER MORNING routes, delivering oil to her lower city customers, offering smiles and genuine wishes for a wonderful and glorious day. She had hoped to meet up with Zoram the day before, after he had left her in the armory, but he had retired to his estate and not emerged all that day and night. He must have been exhausted after fashioning a sword like the one he had shown her. It was amazing and still gave her chills whenever she thought of it. The workmanship was unlike anything she had thought possible, and then there was the way in which he had folded the dark and light metals to form those words. There was no other explanation: it was a miracle.

So was he.

She had never let herself feel this way about a man before. The very thought of him sent her heart racing. She couldn't wait to finish her work so she could call on him again. But was that proper? It wasn't the place of the woman to pursue the man. It was . . . unnatural, wasn't it? But then why did it feel so right? Why must *she* wait for *him*? Did a woman feel any less love than a man? The whole tradition felt archaic and outdated, if you asked her.

Rebekah loved her early morning assignment and route through the markets. In the quiet of the morning, she was able to think clearly and see things that others might miss. She loved the more . . . humble parts of the city. There seemed to be a certain air among those with wealth and power. Though she would never voice her opinion, it seemed as if so many of those who sought after riches and influence only held on to them by control and fear. If their value and sense of worth were so dependent on material possessions, what happened when those things were stripped away from them? She had seen that firsthand with many of her father's associates and business partners. They were left with nothing. *No*, she thought, *they were left with* less *than nothing*. And while those people had tried to cope with having nothing—and now *being* nothing—those who worked by the sweat of their brow and put in an honest day's work for a honest day's wage continued to push through life with some measure of happiness and dignity.

She saw the former attitude in her sisters. While their father maintained his priorities, putting faith and family above business and riches, she feared her sisters did not. They had never known want for anything. Life came easy to them, and while Rebekah believed they were good people, they were accustomed to wealth and a life of ease. She believed they would all marry for wealth instead of looking into the heart and soul of the men they would wed. For them, financial comforts and security meant more than love. That was why she had refused the list of suitors over the years.

That and the simple fact that none of them ever made her feel the way Zoram did.

She nearly missed the street of the old lamp maker in her wandering thoughts. Her morning stops nearly complete, she was walking with a spring in her step, so when she rounded a corner, she nearly ran headlong into someone. She giggled and apologized to the woman.

"Stay away from him," the stranger said, an edge and threat of violence to her words. "He's mine now."

Rebekah didn't know what she was talking about but smiled anyway. She nodded her apology and stepped around the stranger, but the woman moved to block her.

"Whatever your angle, whatever it is you hope to achieve by wooing him away from me, it won't work."

This time Rebekah lowered her yoke of oil and studied the woman bent on interrupting the morning routine. She was young, about Rebekah's own age; pretty, but there was something unmistakably *un*attractive about her. It took Rebekah another moment, standing toe to toe with the woman, to recognize her.

"You're A-Anat."

"No. Not 'A-Anat.' Just Anat. Do you see? That's what I'm trying to figure out. How is it that you can even carry on a conversation with him without him tiring of y-y-your st-st-stutter? I mean, really."

The insults washed over her easily and without pricks or pain. But she was still confused. "Who are you t-talking about?"

Anat had a look of disgusted frustration. "The young Keeper, Zoram. Who else?"

Rebekah's peace and good feelings slipped away at Zoram's name. She was filled with a mix of overprotective and jealous feelings. What had Anat said? That he was *hers*?

"I'm surprised he didn't tell you about us. But he does have a big heart. He probably just didn't want to hurt your feelings." Anat's words were sickly sweet. "Zoram's not like other men. He's one of those rare individuals that actually cares about others."

"Wh-what are you t-t—"

"Talking about?" Anat finished. "Why, that he has chosen me to be his wife. He's declared his love for me and only me."

"He told you th-this?"

"Not in so many words . . ."

"Th-then it's not true."

"Oh, it's true, all right. You can be sure of that. Do you know where he was last night? *All* night?"

Rebekah started to feel sick. It wasn't true. Was it?

"And while he may not have said so in words, his actions spoke loud enough for me." Anat cocked her eyebrow and smiled.

"I d-don't believe you."

"I didn't expect you to. No matter, though."

"You're l-lying."

Anat continued to smile, as if remembering a secret pleasure. "You should ask him about his scar." She traced a small line from her lower back down her hip, "Right through here." She took a deep and dramatic breath. "He is magnificent."

Rebekah was unprepared for the flash flood of anger and fury that coursed through her. Part of it was directed at Zoram. How could he? Though they had met only a few days earlier and had spent only a scant few hours together, she felt betrayed by what she was hearing. That anger quickly turned inward. She cursed herself for opening up to him and having allowed her heart to soften. She felt deceived and used, and she loathed the very thought of him.

But the greater part of her anger was focused white-hot on Anat. She knew a little about this woman and her aspirations of power and status and suspected—no, she *knew*—that Zoram did not know the true type and character of this woman standing before her. Oh, how Rebekah wished she could have warned him. And while Rebekah continued to cling to her disbelief, she suspected that Anat was capable of all manner of treachery to obtain what she wanted. As innocent as Zoram was, he must have fallen prey to her wiles.

"G-g-g-g—" She tried to tell Anat to get away from her, but her mind was racing too fast to allow the time her mouth needed.

"Don't hurt yourself, dear. I know you must be upset, but did you really think a man like him, with so much responsibility and status, could really love you? Listen to you. You're an embarrassment to your family, and you would only be one to him too. It would only be a matter of time before he hid you away, or at least instructed you to remain silent in public. Being dumb is easier to explain away than a wife who can't form a word, not to mention an entire thought, without stuttering and stumbling over every sound."

Anat gave her a false smile. "You should really be thanking me. Your life isn't meant to be shared with him or men like him. Stick to your own kind. I'm sure you'll be much happier there."

Her own kind? Rebekah's feelings flared up again, in one terrifying instant releasing in the form of a slap. She connected squarely with Anat's cheek and with such speed and force that it left her hand stinging and hot. Anat, not suspecting the physical assault, was stunned, her own hand coming to her cheek. Rebekah knew that violence was seldom, if ever, justified and was punishable by the law, but she couldn't help it. She also couldn't help but notice how *good* it felt.

"You have no right to speak to me that way," Rebekah said without the slightest stammer or pause. "What you have done is inexcusable, and God will judge you accordingly. Zoram may not have been born into a life of manual labor, but he has a good and honest heart and will never be one of *your* kind."

Anat's face quickly went from humiliation at being struck to anger at being insulted. She inhaled sharply and held her breath, her eyes alight with the fires of retaliation. But then, just as quickly, all traces of her resentment dissipated and disappeared. "You really love him," she said with a smirk. "And you really think he loves you back. Oh, that's precious." She started to laugh. "And here I thought you were just pursuing him for his status and wealth. But you really care for him. Then I guess the pain you will feel when he is either wed to me or banished for what he did to me will be all the more deep and heartbreaking."

" B-banished?"

"I told him to stop . . ."

"You're lying!"

"He'd had too much to drink . . ."

"Enough!"

". . . and I will see him run out of the city for his offense, if they don't stone him first."

Rebekah didn't know what to say. It was all too much.

"I have a meeting with the city's head of security later today. I'm sure he won't take to this allegation with much sympathy or mercy."

Rebekah didn't have the strength to contend with her anymore. Anat had cut her to the very center, but not with the condemnation of her speech impediment. What really hurt was the fact that she had allowed herself to love him, to believe, even for a day or two, that she might have found love at last. She had opened up and let down her defenses and trusted someone who—

Who had done what, exactly? In fact, a new thought emerged and drove away her growing pity.

"He f-found out about you," she said with new confidence. "D-didn't he?"

Anat was taken aback. "I don't know . . ." She started to protest.

Rebekah took a step forward. "He knows what you d-did. Th-that's why you came here, isn't it?" It was all becoming clear as her perspective shifted. "You can't have him so you've come to turn m-me against him."

Anat stepped backward to maintain her distance.

"You are a p-pathetic and evil woman. You w-won't get away with th-this."

Anat found her strength again and stopped, standing nose to nose with Rebekah. "And who's going to speak on his behalf? You? He'll be dead and buried before you can get two words out."

"I'll st-stop you."

"You can try, but you won't. In fact, go to him, make haste and declare your love. Tell him anything you want. It won't matter. If he doesn't consent to marry me, he'll be dead or driven out by sundown. Either way, you'll have nothing to cling to but a few scant memories, and the pain will linger for years." Anat smiled devilishly, turned, and walked away.

Rebekah's heart was beating like a frightened bird's. She knew enough about Anat to know the woman was not bluffing or merely trying to scare her. Anat meant to see Zoram banished or worse, and Rebekah had to warn him without delay.

שומר החרב

Zoram had been escorted out of Laban's house in a stupor. He had suspected more concerning his father's death, but he didn't know quite how to take the news Laban had offered him. Once the sun hit his face, he shrugged off the servants' hold on his arms. No, he didn't need any help, he told them. He just needed some time alone.

His thoughts enveloped him as he wandered the streets of the city. Was it possible? Could Matteniah be involved in his father's death? Matteniah and he were friends from their childhood. They had played together, learned the law together. With Daniel and the others, they had dreamed of a better, brighter future for Israel. Could what Laban said be true? He didn't want to believe this any more than the initial report of his father's death, but what of the evidence? What of the letters? What of Matteniah's lack of compassion and abundance of distrust and guilt?

And then there was the Sword. The king couldn't draw it. At the time, Zoram couldn't explain it, but when the king's son drew the blade easily and smoothly . . .

But neither could Laban.

Zoram was perplexed. As fantastic and ridiculous as it sounded, it had been as if the Sword had chosen who could handle it. It would be a miracle if it were true, but he had no other explanation. The purpose of the Sword was to protect the word of God, to protect the faith of a nation. It was a divine calling. Why was it so hard to believe that the Sword was more than mere forged metal? Didn't he already profess to believe this? If he believed in God, why was it so hard to believe in His power? Who was he to limit the workings and will of the Almighty?

But just because the king could not pull the blade from the scabbard didn't mean he'd had a hand in Jharom's death.

Zoram shook it off. He refused to feed his fear and suspicion. He deserved to know the truth, and there was only one place to look for it.

An uncomfortable and unnatural silence filled the halls of the palace. The king's arrest had spread throughout the city faster than a late summer wildfire. Zoram had passed groups of men and women protesting and calling for the king's head, while others spoke in whispered circles, and everywhere, armed men stood guard. But these were not palace guards or even members of the military. Strategically stationed at most corners and intersections were members of Laban's elite guard, The Fifty. Though if the two at Jharom's funeral were representative of their skill and training, Zoram would have no problem besting the lot of them.

But a direct, full-on assault was not what he had in mind. In fact, he wanted his meeting with the king to be as inconspicuous and private as possible. Keeping out of sight as he skirted the palace grounds, he learned that the king was under house arrest. When he approached one of The Fifty to inquire whether he could pass, he was told that not even he, the Keeper of the Sword, was permitted to see the prisoner. Zoram's first thought was to force his way through the posted sentry, but that, he knew, would only aggravate the situation. He needed answers, not more problems.

As he turned away, wondering how he was going to reach the king, he remembered the tunnels. Not only were there underground tunnels connecting the treasury and the armory, there were also smaller passages, secret ones, which he had played in as a child. Some, he recalled, were so small that only a child could fit through them. Royalty was a paranoid class, and Israel's kings were no exception, building and carving out secret tunnels and hidden passageways between rooms and even in and out of the palace itself. When he was younger, Zoram and his childhood friends could only imagine exciting uses for them. But as he thought about it now, he wondered if there weren't more amorous reasons for moving about unseen.

But none of that really mattered now. Zoram had to calm his mind, pushing the allegations against the king—against his friend—from his thoughts to allow him to remember. In a few minutes, he was squeezing through a narrow and hidden passage long since forgotten, that connected a small, unassuming peripheral garden to a chamber in the west wing of the palace. He struggled to orient himself after all these years, but he was relatively sure it was near the king's personal chambers.

Sneaking through the deserted rooms and halls, he found a familiar section of wall and quietly pushed on a hidden portal, a stone door cut to resemble the surrounding hall. Slipping in unseen, he was in a back room in the king's personal chambers. There he found the king; the boy, Mulek; and the woman he presumed to be Mulek's mother huddled on one of the large divans, sitting in silence, just holding one another. Mulek, lying on his mother's lap as she ran her fingers through his hair, was the first to spot him.

"Father!"

Matteniah was startled and jerked his head around. "Zoram?"

"Shh, keep your voice down."

"Where did you—? How did you—?"

"The secret passages. When we were kids."

Matteniah's look of confusion gave way to recognition as he remembered. "Of course."

"Is he here to rescue us?" Mulek asked hopefully.

The king held Zoram's hard stare for a moment. "I'm not sure."

"Can I speak with you? Alone?" Zoram's tone left no question that he was not here for a social visit. Instead of dismissing the mother and child, the king gathered them close.

"We will not be separated. Speak what you will to all of us."

Zoram considered the questions he would ask. They were not for a child's ears, but if his old friend wanted it this way, then so be it. As he opened his mouth, however, the words got stuck in his throat. How did you ask someone if he killed your father? What if he did? He had refused to believe it on the way here, rationalizing that it just wasn't possible. But now, at the very moment of inquiry, he wasn't so sure. He had planned to start out with fact-gathering questions and then work into more direct and accusing ones, but now he couldn't think clearly and rationally. He just wanted to know. He needed to know.

In an instant, he was flooded with a surge of emotions from sadness to grief, from anger to despair, and all he could ask was, "Did you?"

Matteniah sensed Zoram's internal struggle and was confused at the question. "Did I what?" He was sincere.

"My father," Zoram said, his voice cracking. "Did you . . . ?"

The king got to his feet and stepped forward, reaching out. "I don't know—"

Zoram slapped his hand away. "Kill him. Is it true? Did you kill him?"

The king froze, dumbfounded and shocked at the accusation. "Why would you think this?"

"You don't deny it?"

"No, I mean yes. Yes, I deny it. No, I didn't have anything to do with his death. In fact, news of it only reached my ears hours before his funeral. I wasn't even in the city. I was . . ." He stopped and looked to the woman. "I was away but returned straightaway. Your father was a great man and more of a role model to me than my own family. Who would say such things and spread such horrible lies?"

Zoram felt a weight slip from his heavy heart. And while he largely believed the words, he still had questions to ask and gaps to fill in. "Laban and others suspect this. They say that when my father discovered this plot, this conspiracy with the Babylonian princess, you had him killed and thrown from the top of the wall."

"These are lies!" the woman exclaimed. "Matteniah would never—"

"Be still, woman!" the king ordered.

"But what of the messenger? The letters? He said they were found in your chambers."

The king shook his head. "I can't explain it, but you must believe me. They are not mine. I had never seen them before last night."

"Tell him," the woman said. "Tell him about when the letters were said to be written."

Matteniah held up his hand to quiet her. "Forgive my wife. She's a very passionate woman and protective of her husband. But what Jerusha says speaks to the truth. Some of the letters, we were told, were written when I lived in the country, even before my uncle took the throne. Someone must have planted them in my room; that's all I can think."

Zoram was surprised how quickly he believed his old friend. The king was innocent, Zoram was certain of it. "Is there anyone you suspect?"

The king sighed. "It would be easier to ask if there's anyone I *don't* suspect. There's no one I can trust. My advisors are corrupt and self-serving, my generals have their own agendas, and always this pressure from Babylon." He returned to his family and put his arms around them. "There are few I do trust. You are one of them, Zoram."

Zoram bowed slightly at the waist. "I am the Keeper of the Sword, bound to serve the One True God and His people. You are my king."

"Thank you, my friend."

There was a space of silence as their trust was forged anew. Finally the king spoke. "There is a plot and conspiracy, of that I am certain."

"You suspect someone?"

"I do." Matteniah hesitated. "Laban."

"Of course," Zoram said. "Because he suspects you."

"No, no, that's not it. After the charges were leveled against me, he had the room cleared. He spoke to me, to *us*, alone. None of this seemed to be a surprise to him. Oh, he expressed his concern, but it was all too . . . rehearsed."

Zoram wasn't convinced. "Laban may have many faults, to be sure, but he's the Keeper of the Records. It's his sworn and solemn duty to *protect* the records."

"I know, I know. This all sounds too incredible to believe, but there's a great deal he isn't saying."

"Nor does he have to. If he truly suspects you, he will, undoubtedly, keep things from you. Suspicions and feelings are one thing, but—"

The king held up a small vial.

"What's that?" Zoram asked.

"Poison, I suspect. He slipped me this as we spoke and urged me to do the 'right thing.' He also made it clear that he knew about Jerusha and Mulek."

Zoram held out his hand and took the vial. Opening it, he took a cautious whiff. "I don't smell anything, but many poisons have no odor. But assuming it is, maybe he wanted to save you, your family, and the crown you wear the shame and controversy allegations like this will cause."

"Laban knows nothing of mercy. He is a cunning serpent. He is a shrewd manipulator."

"He's also my counterpart and master."

"Your master?"

"As Keeper of the Records, I and the Sword are servants to the records and their Keeper."

"I mean you no disrespect. You are a good man, honest and true. I do not mean to speak ill of anyone not deserving, but I will caution you not to turn your back to him."

Zoram accepted the advice. "No one saw him give this to you or heard what he said about your family?"

"The Elders had all left the room by then, but I believe there was one who might have witnessed it."

"Then you must send for him."

"I can't. He's the only one I trust to help me. He's looking into these allegations and conducting an investigation of his own."

Zoram knew instantly who Matteniah was referring to. "Ammon?"

The king nodded. "Besides you, he is the only one who knows everything. We have known each other for years. He's the only other soul I can trust right now."

"And where was he when Laban spoke to you?"

The king motioned to a doorway on the far end of the other room. "I spotted him out of the corner of my eye but got a message to him before he made himself known. I haven't spoken with him, but he heard enough to know where to start looking. But he is only one man, and if he's caught digging for information in the wrong place . . . Well, I'd hate to think what might happen to him. I couldn't bear to have his death on my conscience."

The more Zoram thought about what the king was telling him, the more he could feel a cold stone forming in the pit of his stomach. "If Laban *is* involved, then the records are in grave danger. I must see that they are kept safe." He turned to leave.

"Wait," the king called out. "Take Jerusha and Mulek with you."

"There isn't time."

"Please."

"You can take them yourself."

"No, no I can't."

"Sure you can. You remember, the passageway is in the back of—"

"I know where it is, but I cannot leave. If I am found missing, my guilt will be confirmed in the eyes of the Elders. I must stay and fight this if I am ever going to be free of these allegations. But I cannot risk my family. Will you please help them get beyond the palace walls? They can make travel arrangements in the city, but I do not dare send them unaccompanied. Please, Zoram, will you do this for me? I am asking you as a friend."

Though Zoram knew his duty and calling were to do everything in his power to watch over and protect the records, he also knew he could not refuse the righteous request of a friend in need. And besides, he noted for the second time in as many days, there was something special about this boy that almost compelled Zoram to help him.

Zoram reached out his hand to the boy's mother. "Come with me."

שומר החרב

Leading Jerusha and Mulek out of the palace, past the guards, and deep into the streets of the city took much less time than he had feared. The mother and child were quick on their feet and followed instruction without deviation, question, or complaint. It seemed to Zoram that their travels were almost too easy, as if they were being watched over. There was one time when, if one of the soldiers in Laban's Fifty had simply turned one way instead of another, the trio would have been spotted, but for the grace of God, he didn't, and they were able to escape unnoticed.

Zoram watched with amazement that quickly became respect as the boy's mother found a small caravan and convinced the master to include them on a trek north through the mountains. She was a strong woman, and Zoram could see Matteniah's attraction to her and his concern for her safety. He was fortunate to have found a woman like her. In another time she would have made a magnificent queen.

The arrangements made and money exchanged, Zoram excused himself and started to leave when a pair of small hands pulled on his coat.

"Thank you," Mulek said, giving his legs a hug. "The Lord is with you; I can feel it."

Unaccustomed to being hugged by a child, Zoram dropped to one knee and gave an awkward squeeze back. "Be good. Do as your mother says, and never give her reason to doubt your love." Zoram was surprised at these last words, wondering where they had come from. This was not what he meant to say, and he suspected they were meant more for his own benefit than the boy's. He was suddenly at peace, knowing that he had never—and would never—give his departed mother and father cause to question his faith and resolve.

"Will I ever see you again?" the boy asked, his eyes tearing up. "Or that great sword you made?"

A rising surge of emotion constricted Zoram's throat and threatened to make him cry. He caught himself and tried to smile instead. "Perhaps, the Lord willing."

Mulek looked as serious and somber as a wise man well taken in years. "I think we will." Then he gave Zoram one last hug and took his mother's hand, disappearing into the crowds of people that filled the streets.

Zoram stood there, mesmerized by the boy's almost prophetic prediction. Would they meet again? He couldn't explain the feeling he had, but he sensed that he had done the right thing in seeing them safely out of the city.

The records!

With a greater sense of urgency than before, he turned and sprinted back toward the palace grounds.

CHAPTER TWENTY-FIVE

Zoram couldn't risk making his suspicions known to anyone. There was no way to know who was involved in this conspiracy or how far it had spread. He kept to the back roads and alleyways on his way back up the hill to the palace grounds. He didn't really have a plan—there wasn't time to formulate one. He could almost hear Wu Yien arguing with him, a world away, that without a plan the battle's outcome was determined even before the first encounter. But he needed to reach the records before they were taken.

A loud commotion of voices yelling farther up the hill near the palace startled Zoram. Ducking down a side street and crouching behind a stack of discarded lumber and broken crates, he watched as a big man came barreling down the street as if his life was in danger. Three armed men chased after him, though their speed and determination could not match the fleeing man's. One of the pursuers yelled for him to stop. "Thief!" he called, and then they rounded a corner and were gone again. It took Zoram a moment or two to recognize the clothing they were wearing. They were servants of Laban. Had the man they were chasing tried to steal the records?

His sense of urgency rose to unprecedented levels. He needed to get to the treasury, and fast.

The palace grounds were crawling with even more soldiers than before. This apparent attempt to steal the records had precipitated the call for reinforcements. If he was going to get inside the walls—

"Hey! You!"

Zoram stopped and turned around. A guard approached. "This area is restricted to official—" He suddenly recognized who he had stopped. "Forgive me, Keeper."

Zoram had no other option than to play along and see how far his title and position could get him. "What is going on here, soldier?"

The man hesitated for only a second before answering him. "There has been a threat made on the records. Laban has issued the call to all loyal men to help protect them. You have, no doubt, heard about the king? "

"The king?"

"He is a traitor to his country and his people."

"Yes, but I'm not yet convinced," Zoram said, trying his best to sound authoritative. "I am glad, though, to see so many men out ensuring the safety of the records."

"But it may not be enough. There have already been at least two attempts to steal them since yesterday."

"Two?"

"I heard that last night a religious fanatic stormed the treasury, and then, just now, another broke into Laban's house and demanded the plates. It's hard to believe."

Zoram agreed. It *was* hard to believe. It was almost impossible. Neither attempt sounded legitimate. What was going on? "That is why I must see to their safety and add my own strength to their protection."

"I'm afraid I can't let you do that."

"I am the Keeper of the Sword. It's my right."

"Our orders are clear and absolute. No one is permitted access to the records. Not even you, great Keeper."

"This is outrageous!"

"You'll have to take it up with Laban. I'm sure he'll make an exception."

Zoram had learned what he needed to know. It was time to act. Zoram casually took in his surroundings and made sure they were alone and unobserved. "And where might I find Laban at this moment?"

The guard turned away and pointed back the way he had come. Zoram deftly wrapped his right arm around the man's neck and squeezed, locking his hands to make certain the grip was sure. Zoram then slowly pulled down and back. It was a simple move but one of the most effective nonlethal ones he had mastered. The pressure on the man's neck cut off his airway, but that was only to prevent him from screaming out and alerting the others. The real key to this technique was the angle of the head as it was pushed forward while the body was pulled backward. This temporarily cut off the blood to the brain and caused the victim to pass out. When he awoke, he would only suffer a splitting headache and perhaps a sore throat for the balance of the day.

Once the man lost consciousness, Zoram dragged him out of sight and inside one of the abandoned shops that ran parallel to the palace wall.

He knew he would have to act quickly. Once the man awoke, the whole city would be alerted. Zoram knew of only one possible way to bypass the scores of men who would be guarding the treasury, and that was by way of the tunnels that connected it to the armory.

He encountered no sentries at the armory. Why should there be? It wasn't part of the conspiracy. He paused as he passed the heavy door that he had barricaded himself behind as he worked his craft. The miraculous undertaking only a day or two before already seemed distant. Would he eventually forget the sweat and toil it took to forge that extraordinary blade? It was a magical feeling, creating a work of art from a thick block of unsightly metal. To the casual observer, it did not seem possible, but Zoram had been trained and conditioned to see not what *was* but what *could be.* In the hands of one skilled in the uses of fire and extreme heat, the crude, unsightly block of metal couldn't help but become the most precious steel. *Much like each of us,* he thought, pressing his palm against the cool wood of the door. *Are we so different in the hands of God?*

He felt for the key. He was almost surprised to find it still in his coat pocket. He hadn't given it a second thought since leaving the treasury the day before. His father's key. His family's key. Now his key. If what Laban said was the truth, then there were only two keys like this in existence, which only troubled him more. Could the king be right? Could Laban be involved in the conspiracy, after all?

He left the armory, a strange longing tugging at his heart, like he was never to pass this way again. He ventured into the far recesses of the anteroom, the dark passageway still hidden from view. He paused at the mouth of the tunnel and listened. He held his breath, straining to sense any presence or sign of a sentry. In the silence, he could only hear the thumping of his own heart in his ears. Not wanting to risk a light, he felt his way through the narrow and twisting corridor. As he neared the exit, Zoram picked up the faint light and sounds coming from the treasury anteroom. Stealing a quick glance, he was confused to see that the room was empty— the sounds were coming from inside the treasury. The door was ajar.

Had he arrived at the exact moment to catch the conspirator and thief in the act? He didn't stop to consider the fact that he was unarmed and made a dash for the door. He startled the man at the table, busy wrapping the heavy plates with leather straps to carry them out. He had hoped it wouldn't be Laban but had prepared himself for it if that was who turned around. It wasn't, and for a long moment, Zoram was confused. It was Laban's lieutenant.

"Zoram," the man said, the name spoken with vile contempt. It was as if they were lifelong enemies. They had scarcely just met. Why would he—

Then Zoram remembered why the man had looked familiar earlier at the stables. They *had* met before, at his father's funeral. He had only partially listened when Laban had introduced them. He'd had a lot on his mind, but he knew now. This had been the third soldier he had defeated that night, the one Laban intervened to save. And while Zoram hadn't given it another thought since, it was clear that the soldier had not forgotten their little skirmish.

What was his name? He strained to recall. "Hanoch!" he ordered. "Step away from the records. You have no right to them."

"I have no right?" Hanoch asked with calm confidence. Zoram noted that he didn't sound like a thief caught in the act. His tone sowed seeds of doubt in Zoram's mind. This didn't make sense. "And I suspect you're going to try to stop me."

Zoram's eyes flicked to the Sword he had only just fashioned hanging on the wall above the plates. Hanoch noticed the quick eye movement, followed it, and took the Sword before Zoram could reach for it. Zoram stopped as Hanoch tried to free the blade. But he couldn't. Zoram lunged for it, but Hanoch tossed it far into a cluttered corner and out of reach.

Hanoch's hand went to the hilt of his own sword. He drew it before Zoram could stop him. Zoram leapt back, narrowly avoiding the sharpened blade as Hanoch sliced upward in one fluid and ferocious motion. Falling against the wall, Zoram reached out for something, anything, to fend off the soldier's blade. His fingers wrapped around a wooden stick, a staff of some kind, and he brought it up over his head just as Hanoch's sword drove downward. He heard the wood crack and splinter under the force, but it held enough to block the attack and give Zoram time to move past Hanoch and assume a defensive ready stance.

"You should have stayed away," Hanoch said.

"I cannot let you take them."

"I don't think you're in a position to do anything about it."

"I will stop you. The records belong to God and His people. You cannot take them."

"We can, and we will."

"We? You're not acting alone?"

"You ask too many questions. Like your father."

Zoram was not prepared for a reference to his father, but looking into the eyes of the animal in front of him, he suddenly knew the truth. "It was you."

Hanoch grinned. "He was so trusting. He didn't see it coming until it was too late. It was pathetic. Personally I expected more from him, being the Keeper and all. But he was weak. Weak and useless."

Zoram refused to listen to another word. He took the splintered staff and broke it fully over his knee. Armed with both hands, he began an all-out assault on his father's killer. But where lesser-trained men would have panicked at the attack, Hanoch skillfully deflected everything Zoram threw at him. And then, in a surprise move, Hanoch delivered a powerful kick with his heavy boot to Zoram's stomach, driving the air from the Keeper's lungs as he fell backward.

"You're good," Hanoch said, "but I'm better. How you got the better of me at your father's funeral, I'll never know—and I'll never forget. Those were my men you humiliated me in front of!" He was becoming more upset the more he thought about that night. "We had him! And you let him escape! If Laban hadn't stopped me, I would have killed you then. You could have joined your father in a coward's death."

Zoram scrambled to his feet, leaning against the wall. He forced his abdomen to relax as the first breath of air entered his lungs, bringing with it the cool assurance and prospects of standing up to the next round of attacks. He struggled to keep his emotions in check. He couldn't afford to let them control his actions. Hanoch was too skilled a fighter.

"Why?" Zoram was able to say without betraying his weakened state. He needed just a little more time. He needed to keep the other man talking to stall the next attack.

"Why? Why else? Power. Riches. You really have no idea what we plan to do with these plates, do you?"

Zoram shook his head. "It doesn't matter." He paused to take another shallow breath. "All I know . . ." *Breathe.* "Is that I have to stop you." He could feel his strength returning.

"And how will you do that? Who would you go to for help? The king? The Elders and the brethren of the Sarim? You're all alone. You are but one man—a *boy*, really—while we are many."

Hanoch stepped closer, weary of Zoram's lack of retaliatory action but still confident of his superior skills. "You know, he made me swear not to kill you, not until this whole thing went down. He said it would be too suspicious, it would raise too many questions. But here we are. And do you know what? I don't care what he said." He flexed his fingers around the hilt of his sword. "I'm really going to enjoy this."

Hanoch sprang into action with an overhead strike, but Zoram was ready for it. He used one half of the staff to deflect the blade while the other half struck at Hanoch's wrist. Then, in one flowing motion, he moved next to his attacker, out of harm's way, shoulder to shoulder, his left arm pressed up against Hanoch's right. Still moving, he applied the simple but effective technique he had practiced a thousand times over the years, pushing Hanoch's arm up and out of the way while his palm came up and connected squarely with his opponent's chin.

Hanoch cried out but, with a strength fueled by rage, spun to his left, bringing his arm down, effectively trapping Zoram's arm and throwing him off balance and into the wall. Zoram recovered quickly but not quick enough as Hanoch drove his shoulder into his chest. Already weakened by his loss of breath, Zoram fell to the ground, his strength having completely left him. Hanoch was better than most.

"He said you would put up more of a fight," Hanoch taunted, rubbing the pain from his jaw. "'Be careful', he said. But I knew you were no match for me. You just got lucky, that's all. You're just a boy. You don't deserve the title or the inheritance."

It hadn't happened very often—the last time being just over a year earlier and halfway around the world—but at that moment Zoram was afraid. Not just for his life, but for what Hanoch was implying. Had the faith of all of Israel failed them? Maybe he was right. Maybe Israel didn't deserve the records or the Sword anymore. But that was not his decision to make. It wasn't for him—or anyone else, for that matter—to pass judgment on that scale. The one thing he knew for certain was that he would not shirk his duty to protect both of them. With his dying breath, if necessary.

Dying breath. He would have chuckled at the irony of his choice of words because that's what it looked like he was quite literally about to do. The Sword was hopelessly out of reach, and if he didn't find a weapon of some kind, he couldn't withstand his next round of attacks.

Taking his eyes off his opponent for the briefest of instances to steal a glance at the walls on either side of him, Zoram spotted what looked like a rusted rod of iron, neglected and half hidden behind stacks of decaying scrolls and other remnants of their nation's past. He couldn't imagine what it had been used for or why it had found place in the treasury, but he could use it. Snatching it with the speed of a striking cobra, he brought it over his head just in time to meet Hanoch's mortal blow. Sparks showered over Zoram's head as the two metals collided.

Still unable to breathe freely, Zoram kicked at Hanoch's shins and knees to force him back enough to give Zoram the room he needed to get to his feet. He forced small, sharp breaths in through his nose to slowly inflate his lungs. He could tell the worst of it was past as he spun the iron rod in his hands to get a feel for its weight, speed, and balance. It was only a little longer than a traditional sword—about the length of a man's arm—but it weighed nearly double. He would have to wield it with both hands.

Zoram was still forcing air into his lungs when Hanoch regained his footing and began his assault anew. But this time Zoram was sufficiently armed and ready. Hanoch's blows were swift and powerful but were met with equal force by Zoram's makeshift weapon. He was content to simply defend against Hanoch for now. First, it allowed him to observe Hanoch's patterns of attack, looking for flaws to exploit; and second, it might tire his attacker out. But after only a few moments, it became clear that neither was going to happen.

Hanoch was better trained than Zoram had expected. Perhaps it was his own pride, but he hadn't expected anyone in Jerusalem to be so well trained. Hanoch must have possessed some inherent talent in hand-to-hand combat. He was light on his feet, and his every move was smooth and effortless. Zoram had learned how to "read" an opponent over the years—the way he shifted his balance or moved his shoulders and hips or how the eyes could give away the next move. These, and myriad other signs, could be used to tip the scales. But Hanoch had none—at least that Zoram could observe—and it took every bit of training and conditioning he had received over the past ten years to meet the attacks and get in one or two of his own.

Zoram decided there was only one thing he could do, one strategy left to try. If Hanoch was as good as he appeared to be, maybe that fact could be used against him. As dangerous as it was, Zoram feigned a feeble attack, turning his foot in just such a way as to weaken his stance, and hoped that Hanoch's keen eye and instinct would exploit it.

Like a hawk, Hanoch noticed the exposed weakness and struck fast, knowing Zoram would now have to shift his weight to adequately defend a blow to his left side. But knowing where and how the attack was going to come gave Zoram the edge he needed. Continuing his foot rotation, he pivoted on his back foot, spinning off to the side and away and avoiding the blade's edge. Extending his arm as he spun, Zoram whipped the iron rod to gain even more momentum and struck Hanoch's lower back and rib cage. Hanoch screamed out in pain, but even the level of his voice couldn't completely mask the sound of his ribs cracking and being crushed under the force of the substantial strike.

Hanoch was thrown by the force of the iron rod as he stumbled and fell to his knees at the treasury door. He started coughing, spitting up blood with every violently expelled breath. Zoram had seen this before. Hanoch's lung was punctured. In every case the result was the same. He would die a swift but painful death. There was no hope for him. And while Zoram knew he should feel at least some sympathy, he also knew that he had to learn all he could about the conspiracy before Hanoch succumbed.

Zoram tried to catch his breath and approached the dying traitor. It was possible Hanoch was at the heart of the plot to steal the records for the promises of wealth and the love of the princess, but Zoram didn't think so. The king had said that the entire Sarim had been persuaded to support these charges. Hanoch was a soldier—and a good one, at that—but Zoram thought he lacked the political and religious influence to command such a conspiracy. And besides, he'd admitted to working with someone else, someone who had discouraged Hanoch from trying to kill Zoram until their schemes were realized.

Hanoch hadn't moved. He hadn't even tried. He remained on his knees, one hand resting on his sword and propping him up while the other gripped his side. He still coughed, producing a pink foam and froth with each hack. He didn't have much time left. Zoram needed to pry what information he could from the dying man's lips—and fast. Zoram dropped to one knee, but Hanoch lashed out with his sword, slicing Zoram across the right calf, cutting deep into his muscle.

Zoram sprang backward and fell to the ground using both hands in a futile attempt to stop the pain and bleeding. Just then he heard his name.

"Zoram!"

But it wasn't Hanoch. It was a woman.

It was Rebekah!

Zoram turned and saw her, horrified, looking in on him from just outside the treasury door. She started to run to him.

"No!" He tried to warn her, but it was too late. Hanoch had somehow found the strength to stand and was waiting for her. Positioned off to one side of the door, he grabbed her the moment she set foot inside the treasury. Though Hanoch was weak and injured, she was caught unawares, and immediately he had his sword pressed up against her throat. She let out a short, sharp scream. A thin line of blood emerged at the blade's edge. This was no idle threat. He meant to kill her.

"Let her go!"

Hanoch held her tight and pressed even harder on her throat. Rebekah squeezed her eyes shut. Her captor smiled, his mouth frothing with every labored breath. "Well, well, well," he said, spitting out mouthfuls of blood and spit. "Looks like the day"—*cough*—"wasn't a total loss"—*cough*—"after all."

Zoram was frantic. He knew where this was headed. He had to save her before it was too late, but he couldn't put weight on his leg at all. He was crippled and helpless to do anything but try to persuade Hanoch to let her go.

"She poses no threat to you! She knows nothing of this. Let her go! You can't take an innocent life."

Hanoch started to laugh, but it immediately turned into a fit of coughing and convulsions, spewing blood on everyone and down his face. "Innocence? What do I care about one innocent life? We will take a thousand innocent lives before you or anyone else can stop us. You're too late. The records will be far beyond your grasp by sun up."

Hanoch tried to suppress another wave of painful coughs and hacks. When they subsided there was a sharp hatred in his eyes. "I will not die like this! At your hand!" He pressed his blade even harder against Rebekah's skin. "You care for her? Do you *love* her?" A bloodstained and malicious smile twisted his face. "I'm going to enjoy this!"

Zoram looked around for something—*anything*—to stop him, but there was nothing. There were no weapons, nothing he could use—

Then he saw it. At the base of the wall. A smooth, polished stone. He looked up. Above it was the sling young David had used to fell Goliath. Could this be one of the smooth river stones from the story? Hanoch was hiding behind her. It would take a miracle to hit him and then another for Rebekah to get away, but Zoram didn't have any other options. He grabbed the stone, and with a prayer in his heart he let it fly.

Hanoch flinched and ducked out of the way. The rock went wide, striking the wall behind him. It wasn't even close.

What was he thinking? Did he really believe he was on equal ground with David, the beloved of God? He abandoned every hope of saving Rebekah—or would have, if not for what happened next.

In avoiding Zoram's stone and paltry attempt to strike him, Hanoch relaxed his hold on Rebekah and the sword at her throat. She must have sensed this as well and at that instant jabbed her elbow into Hanoch's side. What otherwise would have been a feeble attempt to get away was, instead, a crushing and paralyzing blow to his broken ribs. He recoiled, and Rebekah was able to force her way from his clutches and run to Zoram's side.

Hanoch's strength left his legs, and he collapsed in a heap. It was only after his body stiffened and then relaxed that Zoram saw that he had fallen on his own sword. Hanoch's surprise turned to contempt and then faded into the nothingness of death.

Rebekah, still confused and in shock, had the presence of mind to turn her attention to Zoram's leg. It was a deep cut and bleeding profusely. Almost instinctively she ripped off part of the hem of her dress and tied it around the wound.

Zoram tried to get up.

She pushed him back down. "You need a d-doctor."

"There's no time."

"You've lost a lot of b-blood."

"I'll be all right. Help me up."

Reluctantly, she put his arm over her shoulder and helped him to his feet. The sight of Hanoch's lifeless body, impaled and doubled over on the floor, forced Rebekah to look away. She looked like she might be sick.

"Is he . . . ?"

"He was trying to steal the records," Zoram said, taking the focus off the body and turning her back to the table. The leather straps securing the large block of brass plates still needed to be tied. "I need your help—"

A shrill shriek pierced the silence of the room, sending fear flooding through his heart like ice water. They turned to see the source of the bloodcurdling scream, but Zoram recognized it immediately. He had heard it earlier that day. If he lived to be a hundred, he feared he would never forget that sound.

It was Anat. She was fixated on Hanoch's body and the pool of blood that had pooled around him. She screamed again and looked up. "You killed him!"

"He was trying to—"

"You killed him!" she repeated with an edge of hysteria creeping into her words.

Zoram reached out. "Anat—"

"Help!" she yelled, stepping back into the anteroom. "Help! He's been murdered! Help!" She turned and ran off.

Rebekah began pulling on him. "Come on!"

"Not without the records."

"Leave them!"

"I can't!"

"They'll kill you if th-they find you."

He resisted for another moment or two, but he knew she was right. Hanoch was the head of security in the city and second in command over the armies of Israel. No one would believe Zoram's story about him stealing the plates. Zoram would be summarily executed if they found him like this. They both would. Rebekah was right. They needed to get far away from the treasury as quickly as possible. He would have to find another way to protect the records—a task he couldn't do if he was dead.

So with one arm around Rebekah's shoulder, he took her hand with his other and followed her out as the sounds of approaching soldiers filled the distant halls.

CHAPTER TWENTY-SIX

LABAN HAD JUST RETURNED FROM the first of many meetings he had scheduled with the Council of Elders, and if he dared pay himself the compliment, he had those simple and short-sighted old men right where he wanted them. It was almost too easy. His ascension and play for power were all but assured.

Or so he thought. The news that awaited him once he stepped inside threatened to undo it all. Laban exercised every bit of self-control he possessed not to take out his anger and frustration on the soldier standing before him.

"What do you mean he's dead? When did this happen?"

The soldier hesitated with his answer. "It was decided not to interrupt your meeting with the Elders."

Laban wanted to lash out at the young soldier, but he restrained himself. He *had* left word not to interrupt him, but that did not excuse their neglect. "And the treasury? The records?"

"Both safe."

"You're sure of this?"

"I've seen the records with my own eyes."

At least the soldier had the forethought to make certain of this. "So tell me. What do we know?"

"Hanoch is—"

"Dead. I know this much already. By whose hand?"

The soldier stammered and stumbled over the name. "Zoram."

"Zoram?" Laban said with a potent combination of anger and surprise. "Are you sure?"

"He overpowered one of the palace perimeter guards after demanding access to the treasury."

Laban had no reason to doubt the report, but he still needed to feign disbelief. "Circumstantial at best. Zoram is the Keeper of the Sword and a respected member of this city. You saw him kill Hanoch?"

The soldier shook his head and glanced to an adjoining room.

"Then how—" Laban followed the man's gaze. A short distance away, in the next room, Anat sat on a stone bench, a blanket draped over her shoulders.

"There was an eyewitness," the soldier said.

Anat looked over at Laban with a dazed expression. But Laban discerned something else too. He turned back to the soldier. "If you'll excuse us for a moment."

The soldier snapped to attention then left.

Laban took a deep, calming breath and smiled at Anat as he joined her. Pulling another bench from along the wall, he sat across from her. "You *saw* Zoram kill Hanoch?" His voice was smooth and comforting. Anat nodded. He could see her shaking, no doubt in shock. "And Zoram was alone?"

She shook her head. "Rebekah was with him."

"Rebekah?"

"Ishmael's daughter. The oil merchant."

Laban kept his smile on, but inside he was writhing. He would have to take care of the old man too. And his family. He didn't have time for pleasantries anymore. "Tell me," he said softly but with a hint of accusation and malice. "How did you get past the guard?"

Anat seemed to snap out of her stupor. "I . . . I followed Rebekah to the palace." Her words slowed with caution. "But she didn't go to the treasury. There was a tunnel. Hidden. Connecting the armory to the treasury."

Laban could scarcely believe it. "A secret tunnel?"

"I think Hanoch was there to steal the records."

"You mean Zoram."

Anat shook her head again. "But why would Zoram want to steal the plates? And Hanoch wasn't alone. He said 'we' and 'us.'" Anat stared past Laban, her confused thoughts starting to connect. "But how could he have gotten into the treasury . . . ?" Anat started to sit up taller and move away as a new realization began to dawn on her, but Laban grabbed her wrist, holding her down.

"How, indeed?" Laban asked. "Tell me, how do you think Hanoch got in?"

Anat didn't want to answer. Laban tightened his grip.

"A key," Anat forced out.

"That's right. And whose key?"

"Zoram's?" The pain and fear were too much, and Anat started to cry.

"But how would Hanoch have gotten access to our young Keeper's key?"

"I-I don't know—"

Laban squeezed Anat's wrist and twisted. She cried out in pain.

"Whose key?" he repeated.

"Ow! You're hurting me!"

"I'll do more than that!" he said through clenched teeth. "Tell me! Whose key?"

"Yours!"

Once she said the word, Laban let her go, but Anat had sense enough not to run. She just sat there, rubbing her wrist. Laban stood and began to pace in silence. His methods were crude but effective. He needed to know what she would say if pressured. She would have to be dealt with too.

Without warning, Laban rushed Anat and slapped his hands on either side of her, leaning in so their noses nearly touched. He spoke just above a threatening whisper. "The only reason you live at this moment is because explaining your death would prove difficult!" He leaned in closer, forcing Anat to lean back. "Should I tell you what I think you saw tonight?"

Anat nodded, paralyzed with fear.

"Zoram was there to steal the records with this Rebekah—"

"But—"

Laban brought a finger to her lips to quiet her. "Zoram was the thief, and Hanoch—loyal, brave Hanoch—surprised them in the act and tried to stop them." Laban pulled back and pasted on a fake smile. "In fact, you're fortunate to be alive. Wouldn't you say?"

When Laban was certain that Anat understood fully the threat against her life, he tended to the blanket that had slipped from her shoulder. He then called for the soldier waiting in the other room and clapped loudly for his house staff.

"Sir?"

Laban went to the table and poured Anat a small cup of wine. "Our young friend, here, has been through a great deal today." Anat skittishly accepted the drink. "My staff will see to it that she is taken care of tonight. You're to see that she's not disturbed. Do I make myself clear?"

The soldier snapped to attention. "Sir, yes, sir!"

Laban shot Anat one final hard look before leaving for the treasury.

שומר החרב

With every hastened step, Laban mulled over the new complication to his plan. Zoram had risen from mere annoyance to an outright threat. His presence at the treasury meant he didn't trust Laban's capacity to protect the records. Or worse. Perhaps he suspected Laban's involvement. While the young Keeper didn't have the reputation or influence to make a case against him to the Council of Elders, his father had been well respected in such circles. If Zoram worked it just right, he might be able to use his father's name in his favor. Laban couldn't let that happen. He had to let the people know what kind of man their new Keeper was. But first he had to attend to the matter at hand.

Without acknowledgment, he marched past his men standing guard throughout the palace on the way to the treasury. He paused at the anteroom to peer down the dark entrance to a tunnel previously unknown to him. "Incredible," he whispered to himself. He wondered how many more mysteries Jerusalem might hold for him.

Laban saw a large heap in the corner, covered with a coarse blanket. A dark, wide stain stretched between it and the treasury door. "Is that him?"

One of the soldiers spoke up. "We felt it was best to remove him from the treasury as to not further desecrate a place as sacred as this."

"Yes, of course." Laban squatted down and pulled the blanket back. Hanoch was dead all right, and the cause of death wouldn't be a surprise to anyone. The men had even failed to remove his sword. It was a pity. He wanted to be angry at Zoram, but he found that he couldn't force it. It was what it was. In fact, he thought, trying to hide the smile that threatened to emerge across his face, he should be thanking Zoram for killing Hanoch. This was a cleaner, more believable end to the fool's life. Laban would've had to kill him sooner or later to protect their secret. Why was it, he wondered, wishing he had strong drink right now, that fools were so easily convinced they could actually achieve the dreams of more deserving, more cunning men like himself? Men like Hanoch lived a fool's deception and sooner or later were brought to the harsh reality that they were destined to a life of mediocrity.

Yes, it was a pity.

Laban rifled through Hanoch's coat pockets, feeling for what he needed. Keeping his hand from view, Laban slipped the key into his pocket.

Laban then stood and strode with purpose and power to the treasury. He didn't have to use the key, though, as they had left the door open. He looked inside. There were the records, askew on the table and partially unwrapped, the leather carrying straps as Hanoch must have left them before Zoram showed up. Taking a minute to make sure all was as it should be, Laban covered the records and closed and locked the door. Outside, he called for his men to gather around him. Once they had formed a semicircle around him, he made the announcement that would remove Zoram as a threat.

"The Keeper of the Sword is now wanted for the murder of your brother, Hanoch. He is a traitor and coconspirator with the king. Send word throughout the city. Anyone found helping or harboring him will share in his punishment as he *or she* will be presumed an accomplice." He let his order settle in their ears before he continued.

"Hanoch was one of us. He was a patriot and a hero to Israel, and while I cannot order it, nothing would please me more than if his killer were found dead rather than alive. Do not take any chances with him. He is a skilled and dangerous man. I trust you will do the right thing when he is found." The members of The Fifty looked at one another, each clear on their objective and command. "Now, go, and bring me word when it is done."

He left a sufficient number of sentries to guard the door, though he didn't think Zoram would be returning anytime soon, especially if he was hurt as badly as was reported. The rest were released to join the citywide manhunt. Zoram couldn't hide forever. Laban might even offer a reward, place a bounty on Zoram's head—that would ensure prompt apprehension if more traditional methods proved unsuccessful.

שומר החרב

Laban returned to his estate and ordered that a bath be drawn for him. He felt dirty. He wanted to be clean. While he did not fear any religious consequences, he found the thought of having to touch Hanoch—alive or dead—repulsive.

Clean and dressed in new clothes, he ordered that more wine be brought. There was still so much to complete before his second meeting with the Council of Elders. This one, scheduled for later tonight, was critical to the success of his plans. Tonight, with records in hand, he would announce the king's confirmed treachery and offer his willingness to ascend to the throne. With the support of the ruling class, he would make his offer to Nebuchadnezzar, offering the one thing no other invading emperor had been able to attain: a peaceful and complete surrender of Israel. Nebuchadnezzar would have his treasure, and Laban would have the princess.

Laban had initially been concerned with Hanoch's death, not for the loss of the man's life but with his failure to arrange the king's poisoning. But where he had once been reliant on this act of murder, he didn't think it really mattered much now. The Sarim was so afraid and irate over it he doubted Zedekiah would last to morning. There was nothing like fear and anger—but mostly fear—to bring about acts of violence.

But, oh, how he would miss rescuing Israel from another ill-advised alliance with Egypt, employing his brilliant diplomacy and trading the nation's last treasure to save them all. He had so wanted to be their savior, their deliverer, their promised messiah.

But he would settle for being their king.

Laban drained another cup of wine and smiled to himself. He had expected to tell the council later tonight of the king's unfortunate death, but instead he would tell them of Zoram's involvement and connection to the conspiracy. The Elders would be so incensed they would cry for Zoram's immediate death, which, if they didn't have the backbone to carry out, he would arrange himself. Either way, his plan to ascend the throne would go forward as planned.

Laban raised his glass to an empty room and silently offered a toast to his cunning and masterful intelligence. With Zoram wanted for murder and the records safe behind the locked treasury door, there was little to do but put the finishing touches on the words he would speak to incite the Sarim to swift action.

Laban ordered the evening meal brought to him in his personal quarters with another decanter of wine. Tonight was a true celebration. Tonight he was going to get all he deserved. He dismissed all but the essential house staff and had just begun to partake of his supper when a young woman, one of the kitchen help, knocked warily on the doorframe.

"Laban, sir?" she said in a nervous, mousy voice. If not for her attractive face and shape, he would have shouted at her to leave him alone, but as it was, he was rather hoping she had plans to stay.

"What is it?" he said. He was firm but not enough to frighten her away. He may require her . . . *attention* later.

"There are men here to see you."

Laban shook off the effects of the wine best he could. "Did I not leave instructions not to be disturbed?"

"Yes, Laban, sir, but they insisted you would want to see them."

"Who are they?"

"I . . . I don't know."

"And you just welcomed them in? You have allowed strangers into my house?" Good looks or not, he was losing his patience with her. "They could be thieves, for all you know, and you've simply thrown open the door and ushered them inside."

"They're not thieves."

"And you know this because . . . ?" The young woman had made a mistake in letting them in, but she was either very brave or very stupid to correct the master of the house—and not just any master, but Laban, the Keeper of Records.

"Why would thieves bring gold and silver *into* a house?"

Laban was outright baffled at what he thought he heard her say. Had he heard her correctly? Was the wine already clouding his senses? "They *brought* gold?"

"Coffers of it," she said. "They told me you would see them and then showed me some of what they had brought with them."

Laban felt the stirrings of fear and alarm deep within him. "Did they say what they wanted?"

"I didn't ask. I didn't think the master's business was mine to know."

"Never mind. That's not important. And you didn't recognize them?" She shook her head.

"They were not dressed as priests or merchants or other businessmen?"

"No, but I'm not sure what a businessman would look like."

Laban started to get up, but he was light-headed and a little dizzy. He reached out to steady himself before he fell and made a fool of himself. The feeling passed as quickly as it had arrived, and he stood, straightening and smoothing his clothes. "Where did you seat them?"

"In the reception hall, my lord."

"Very good. Offer them food and drink, and tell them I will be there presently." Laban tried to shake off his growingly intoxicated state and retired to his closet to find more appropriate attire to receive guests such as these. As he dressed, however, he became more suspicious of who the men might be and why they had come bearing gifts, or at least a show of their wealth. Then a horrifying thought crossed his mind. Had Hanoch let slip the nature of their plans? Had these men, whoever they were, come to offer a preemptive bid for favor and influence from their new, soon-to-be king? But then the thought and panic passed, and he dismissed this line of thinking. It did no good to worry about matters that were unknown. He was nothing if not pragmatic, and it was foolish to waste energy on baseless fears. He finished dressing and made his way to the lower level reception hall.

The moment he saw who was waiting for him, recognition gave way to suspicion, which promptly turned into anger. "It's you!"

Laman, the eldest son of the fugitive voice in the wilderness, stood next to three other men. Though judging by their looks, at least two of them were little more than boys. He was about to call for his guards when the size of the coffers at their feet interrupted his building tirade.

"Great Laban," the eldest son said with even less conviction and confidence than he'd had before, "forgive our insistence at this late hour. My brothers and I know it is not the custom to request an audience after the evening meal, but this issue is of some importance."

Laban eyed them all very carefully. "I have to admit I didn't expect to see you again." In fact, he would have strong words with the men dispatched to chase Laman out the first time. Not only had he escaped their pursuit, but he was able to make his way back into to Laban's house again. They would all answer to him personally. "Are these the 'others' you were referring to?"

The four men all exchanged glances. Laman nodded. "Our father has charged us concerning the records."

"And my answer remains the same. You cannot have them."

Laman started to reply when one of his brothers stepped forward and threw open one of the coffers. Light from the recent sunset filtered in through the open windows. Joined by the artificial lamplight, it danced on the pieces of gold piled high in the small chest. Though he was one of the wealthiest men in the city, Laban thought one could never have too much gold.

"We do not expect you to simply give them to us," this younger brother declared. "So we offer you this ransom in exchange for the plates."

Laban took a moment to consider the younger brother of Laman. Were it not for his youthful and boyish face, Laban might have taken him for a full-grown man. He was tall—about as tall as the others—and broad shouldered. Laban's first thought was that this boy would make a fine soldier, but that was where his admiration ceased. The boy had a determined fire in his eyes that Laban knew would not be easy to extinguish.

"And you would bribe the Keeper to obtain them? I told your brother and you can tell your father—you cannot have them!"

But while his brothers cowered at Laban's forceful words, this one remained unaffected, standing tall and confident still. "It is God, not our father, who commands us to obtain the plates."

"That's right," Laban mocked. "Your father had a *dream*."

The boy held Laban's stare. "Do not mock the Lord, our God."

Laban's smug smile leveled away as his jaw clenched, and his whole frame began to shake with rage. There was something about this boy that repulsed and unnerved him. "You cannot have them!" he shouted. "Not now! Not ever! Guards!"

Laman tried, unsuccessfully, to intervene and curb Laban's anger. "Forgive my foolish brother. He is mad, like our father." He thrust his hand into the deep well of gold and pulled out a handful. "Surely this is enough to pay for a new set of records."

But Laban was well past the point of bargaining. "I will see you all stoned for your crimes and your bodies quartered and cast aside to feed the wolves and birds."

"But we have committed no crime!" Laman yelled in terror.

Though he was alone and outnumbered, Laban knew he was in no danger from them. His skills were such that, even unarmed, he was confident that he could easily defeat Lehi's sons. Except maybe this youngest one. Laban kept his eye trained on the young man's reactions and stepped toward the cowering lot.

"As criminals you forever forfeit your estate, wealth, and position in Israel. And I hereby charge that as thieves and conspirators, according to martial law, you are sentenced to arrest and summary execution."

The clanging of armor and weapons sounded outside Laban's window and down the halls. Laman turned and fled when he heard the approaching soldiers. Two others followed behind him like frightened rabbits. The youngest brother, however, remained steadfast and immovable, refusing to flee, his stare fixed on Laban.

Laban tried to maintain his air of confidence and superiority, but something about this boy stripped him of his power and presence. He felt a cold sensation that started deep within his chest and spread throughout his body.

"This is your last chance," the boy finally said, as if the roles were somehow reversed and it was Laban who was in danger of swift judgment and execution. "I will not return to the tent of my father without them. God has required this of us. Who are you to stand in His way?"

Who was he? He was Laban, the Keeper of the Records and soon to be king of Israel. "I am the man who will see you beheaded for your audacity and impudence! Who are *you* to think you can come into my house and demand the records? I will take great pleasure in watching you die."

Laban took another step closer. "And as for your father, I will not rest until he and those cowards you call brothers are hunted down and slaughtered. But before Lehi meets the end of my blade, I shall deliver to him your heads so that the last *vision* he has is the certainty of the deaths of his sons."

Laban had expected those last words to break the young man's spirit, but they had no such effect.

"If I am to die, then it will be in the service of the Lord, our God," he said calmly and without the slightest fear in his words, "for He commands, and I must obey."

The soldiers were near now, just outside the door. One of the brothers returned through the back entrance, panicked and frantic. "Nephi!" He rushed to him and took his younger brother by the arm. "Come away! Now!"

As soon as this brother opened his mouth, Laban could tell there was something not quite right with him. Maybe it was the way in which he ran his words together quickly, like a young child might, but it was clear he was not as old mentally as he was physically. *Fitting*, Laban thought. Lehi sends two clod sons, a half-wit, and an impertinent boy to fetch the records. Maybe he had given Lehi too much credit. But no matter. He would have their heads for this.

But instead of yielding to the frantic persuasions of his brother, Laban noted, this youngest boy, this Nephi, resisted the arm tugs, keeping his stare fixed on Laban's eyes, as if to reinforce his commitment to obtaining the records.

"Come!" the brother pleaded. "He means to kill us. Forget about them. Come! Now!"

Nephi held his gaze for another long moment then ceded to the forceful enticing of his brother, and they disappeared out the back hall.

Laban was furious, but if pressed he was uncertain he could explain why he was feeling the way he was. He had felt exposed standing toe to toe with the boy, like Nephi had seen right through him. And all this talk of God. If God wanted the records He was free to come get them; but until then they were staying right where they were.

For now.

The reception hall was suddenly filled with estate guards. The soldier charged with watching Anat stood ready to lead them.

"They went out the back," Laban said, pointing. "Four of them. I want them hunted down and killed on sight. Except for the youngest one. See that the others are killed, but bring me this youngest boy. I would have a few words with this one."

The guards all snapped to attention, their orders clear. As they turned to follow after Lehi's sons, Laban called for one soldier to remain behind. "What is your name, soldier?"

"Micah, sir."

"Where is . . . my *guest*?"

"When I heard the commotion, I secured her in the room."

Laban approved. Returning to his pressing problem, he continued. "Micah, none of this would have happened had Hanoch succeeded in apprehending this eldest brother the first time he visited my home. You will find them, at all costs. In fact, I am holding you personally responsible for their capture and demise. One might say that this task is so important that you should endeavor to find them as if your very life depended upon it. Am I clear?"

All color drained from the young man's face as he nodded, under-standing perfectly what fate awaited him should he fail. He saluted and followed after the others with a new and grave determination. They would not escape this time.

But Laban couldn't shake this nervous, unsettling feeling that threatened to bring him to his knees. And the more he thought of the timing of all this attention to the records, the more this feeling made him light-headed and sick. What was once a simple plan was now complex and convoluted, all which brought more attention to him than he cared for.

Then a fear struck him with such force and intensity that he felt as if he might be engulfed and drowned by it. What if others had been sent to steal the records while his attention was distracted with Lehi's sons?

What if this was a carefully orchestrated plan to steal them from under his watchful eye? He needed to see them for himself. Now!

To calm his nerves, Laban drank directly from the carafe of wine set for his intended guests then ran in a frenzy from his house to the treasury, pushing past the guards stationed outside. A few of them tried to ask him about the rumors of another attempt to steal the plates, but he wouldn't be distracted. Nothing mattered now but seeing them safe with this own eyes; to hold them with his own hands. He needed to know that what he had killed for—and would kill again for—was safe.

Laban fumbled for his key. His thoughts were cloudy and unfocused, and his actions matched.

"Sir?" one soldier dared ask. "Is everything all right?"

Laban gave him a sharp shove and found the key. He had to try a couple of times to insert it and unlock the door. Without hesitation, he made for the table. There they were. He ripped off the royal purple veil and beheld them with his own eyes. Nothing appeared amiss.

He stripped the leather straps away and gazed at the plates in the glow of the lamplight. Opening them to a random place in the first book of Moses, he ran his fingertips over the chiseled metal. They were an odd treasure to be sure. The whole of it could be melted down and be next to worthless in the markets. Brass was nothing compared to the value of gold. But he knew the true value was not in the brass but what was inscribed on it. It seemed foolish to him that these myths and stories of gods and angels could command such a place in the hearts of the people. No one was fool enough to believe them anymore, were they?

But, he reasoned, there would always be men, insane and drunk on the fervor religion, to stir and manipulate the masses all in the name of this god or that. Men like Jeremiah, who was locked away in the darkest prison Jerusalem had; or Lehi, who had fled in the night instead of owning up to his beliefs. But still their cries were heard by the dwindling few.

What was the difference, Laban wondered, between the God of his ancestors and the hundreds or thousands of gods in other lands? What of the gods of Babylon? Were they any less "real" or true? He supposed the High Priest would take offense at this notion. God was an intoxicant, a drug to ease away the pain and realities of life. He was the balm to sooth the harsh realities of poverty and failure. Who was God to the rich man? But to the peasant and the downtrodden, He was everything. The truth was, Laban thought as he felt the engravings on the metal plates, God wasn't to be found in these writings. He was to be found elsewhere. Laban's god was gold; he was power. And those too stupid or lazy to work hard for wealth would rather invent a god with promises of treasures in heaven, of a paradise *after* this life.

Well, not Laban. He much preferred his treasures real, tangible, in *this* life.

Laban continued to leaf through the thin plates, words and phrases jumping out at him—fire from heaven, chariots, visions, angels, stone tablets—nonsense, the whole lot of it. And if it wasn't for their intrinsic and sentimental value, Laban would cause the forge to be lit and stoked and the records melted and recast into something useful.

But, he thought with a measure of satisfaction, they were useful. They were the means to a very desirable end. The princess wanted the plates; he wanted the princess. And in a few weeks' time, they would each have what they so wanted.

A tremor of excitement coursed through his body. There was not a woman like her in all Jerusalem, not in all the world. And soon, very soon, she would be his.

As long as he kept the records locked up a little while longer.

Laban closed the metal book and replaced the gold-trimmed cover, satisfied that they were, in fact, secure in the treasury. As he turned to leave, though, he noticed the blood stains smeared on the floor. Hanoch's blood. He had been an undeserving and unsuspecting stooge, who, while having played his role well, still deserved his untimely death. It was ironic that in the end it was his thirst for Zoram's blood that ultimately caused his own to be spilled.

Laban looked over the room, noting the destruction his fight with Zoram had caused. With the exception of the table and records, the place looked as if a bull had been locked inside, kicking and struggling to get out. And then, near the back of the room, something caught his eye. It was Zoram's new Sword. It was cast off with the other "treasures" in the room. But as beautiful as the hilt and sheath were, it came as no surprise that it had been cast aside. He pushed his way to the back to get it. He tried to pull the blade free.

It was still stuck.

"Worthless," he said under his breath. He was about to toss it away again, but he stopped. No, he would keep it. It could always be repaired. And besides, he thought, it was *his* sword, after all. The Sword of Laban, forged to protect the records. He liked the sound of that. Its place was at his side, hanging from his belt. It would be a nice adornment to his dress uniform when he stood before the Council of Elders in a few hours.

He called the guards together as he emerged from the treasury. "Listen up, for I will only say this once. Tonight these records are to be kept under the strictest watch." He inserted his key and locked the heavy door behind him. "No one is permitted entrance or access to the treasury. No rank is high enough, no position exalted enough to override my orders right now. Do not be deceived—I will not send anyone in my place. If I need the records, I will come and get them myself. If anyone claims to be on my errand, run him through first and ask questions later. Am I clear?"

Laban felt a sharp jolt from the sword in his hand, like the shock of touching metal on a hot day. If he believed in such things, he might have thought the thing cursed. It was the effect of the wine, he reasoned, nothing more.

"You will guard this door with your life and defend it with your last breath," he said. "Because if you do not, rest assured that your punishment will extend not only to you but to your wives and children as well."

Laban returned their salute and then placed his hand on the thick door, locked and secure from any incursion. "Let's see God take them from me now," he threatened under his breath.

CHAPTER TWENTY-SEVEN

AMMON WAS CERTAIN HE WOULD never see the king or his loved ones again. It amounted to suicide, after all, to sneak into Laban's house on a reconnaissance mission to search for incriminating evidence against the foul-tempered Keeper of the Records.

Out of the sight of the others, he had listened to the charges leveled against the king the night before. They were outrageous. If any of the council members had given the matter any rational thought, they could have seen that the evidence was being manipulated. It was impossible for the young king to do what they accused him of. Personally, Ammon knew the allegations were false. He had been the king's only real confidant since his appointment to the throne. The king would admit to many faults, partly because of his age and upbringing, but a traitor he was not.

While he'd wanted to burst into the room and defend his friend, the king's subtle instruction had been clear and unmistakable. He was to remain on the "outside" of this drama and offer aid in the defense. It had been a wise decision because the entire palace was sealed up, from staff to palace guards—anyone connected to the king or his household was placed under arrest. The entire palace was a prison. Only those directly connected to the Sarim or Laban's Fifty were allowed on or off the grounds. Ammon suspected he might be the king's only ally beyond the palace walls.

He wasted no time in his discreet investigation, spending the rest of that night and much of the next morning inquiring of young lawyers he knew and believed he could trust about the charges and the letters that had been found. Of course, without more information no one could give him any hope of how to defend against these accusations. They all agreed that the future looked bleak for the king. Then, when Ammon tried to find out the names of the guards who had apprehended the Babylonian spy, no one could produce one. There was no recognition, no awards, no official or unofficial credit given for the capture. There was nothing, no trail to follow. Beyond the official claim, there was nothing to suggest it had ever happened.

And then there was the more recent news of Hanoch's death at the young Keeper's hand and the presumption that Zoram was part of the same conspiracy. A warrant was issued for his immediate capture, but Ammon knew it was really a thinly veiled death sentence. There was almost fanatical loyalty among soldiers. Killing one of their own would not go unpunished under their own brand of vigilante justice.

He had wanted to speak to members of Zoram's house, but here, too, members of Laban's Fifty guarded the estate and grounds closely. They were, no doubt, hoping he would return home. Despite the reports, Ammon had trouble believing Zoram's guilt. True, he had only met the new Keeper once and spoken no more than a dozen words with him. Still, there was something about Zoram that radiated faith and devotion and service to Israel. If he had killed Hanoch in the treasury, it must have been to protect the records not to steal them.

This realization led Ammon toward thoughts of Laban's involvement in this conspiracy, as outrageous as that might seem. But it was well-known that Hanoch was Laban's dog; the servant did nothing but what the master knew of and sanctioned. He didn't want to believe it possible that the Keeper of the Records could have a hand in these accusations, but Ammon had not been able to discover one piece of evidence elsewhere to clear the king's name. With a rising lump in his throat and an unsettled feeling spreading through his chest, Ammon made his way to Laban's estate in the upper city.

With the manhunt underway, Ammon found approaching Laban's house relatively easy. When four men requested an audience with the Keeper, Ammon was able to slip inside unseen through a servants' entrance. At one point, Laban had passed within an arm's length of him on the way to meet the guests, but Ammon had remained undetected.

Not wanting to waste a precious moment, he hurried to Laban's personal quarters and began searching through everything he could. He rummaged through drawers, chests, and stacks of books and papers that lined shelves along the walls. He found official papers and correspondence but nothing to aid him and the king. His heart began to sink. It would take several men the better part of a week to go through the amount of records Laban had on site. It was maddening. But what did he think would happen? Did he really think that Laban, if he was involved, would just leave incriminating evidence out for anyone to see? He knew Laban had scheduled meetings with the Elders later that night to give further testimony and more fully seal the king's fate. Would such proof just be out and easily accessible? It was foolish to think so.

Then another thought struck him. There was one place he hadn't looked.

Ammon quickly inspected Laban's bedroom. Though the lamplight only dimly illuminated the room, he could see no scrolls, no letters lying around anywhere. Then a box caught his eye. It sat atop the edge of the large stone bathing tub in an adjacent room.

A sudden commotion elsewhere in the house startled him, and it felt as if his blood turned to ice water. Laban had raised his voice, yelling and calling for his guards.

He had to act fast. Taking the small wooden box into the other room, he examined its contents in the better light. There were four or five letters, written on papyrus and affixed to a leather backing. They were similar in look and construction to the ones found in the king's bedchamber. The top one was open, and he started reading. Ammon had convinced himself that Laban *might* have a hand in all this, but he was wholly unprepared for what he now read. The letter was from King Nebuchadnezzar's daughter, a princess in Babylon, written to Laban expressing her love and anticipation of the promise of receiving what she called the "last" of Israel's treasures.

Ammon was in shock. What had he uncovered? He put the letter back and glanced through the others, quickly skimming each until specific words from one of them commanded his full attention. In it, the princess praised Laban's genius and commitment to their union by seeing to the death of his father and elder brother to secure his place as Keeper of the Records. And while she did not understand why he could not simply take the plates and deliver them to Babylon to speed the consummation of their love, she trusted that his plans were for the best.

Ammon's strength had nearly left him. Laban would trade their heritage, their tradition, their faith, for the love of a woman? This was treasonous and criminal in the most serious sense. If what he read was true, Laban had been plotting the theft of the records for years. And now he had the evidence to prove it. He had to get these letters to the council and to the king as quickly as possible. All of Israel needed to know that Laban—

"Find something interesting?"

Startled, Ammon dropped the ornate box and spun around. It was Laban. How long had he been standing there, watching him?

"She is exquisite," Laban said calmly, as if in confidence with a friend. "Though you have only her handwriting to see. The once-fragrant perfume of the chrysanthemum and other flowers have long since faded, but trust me when I tell you there has never been a woman so beautiful, so alluring as Amytis."

"You cannot do this." Ammon's hand dropped to the hilt of his sword. He then noticed that Laban held Zoram's Sword loosely in his hand.

Laban took a step toward him. Ammon stepped back, partially out of fear. Laban didn't look concerned in the least. In fact, his attention was focused on the box and letters now scattered on the floor.

"I couldn't give these up," he said as he lay the Sword down and carefully gathered the parchment. "Though we agreed not to use our names in our correspondence, these were several that were so intense, so passionate, that she could not help but use my name, even if it was only on parchment."

With one letter still in his hand, Ammon gripped the sword on his belt, trying to muster the courage to draw on the most skilled swordsman and fighter, the most feared man in all of Israel.

"I know you, don't I?" Laban replaced the letters in their box. "You're one of the king's personal guards."

"I know you framed him." Ammon had to force the words from his lips. "The letters that were found in the king's chambers were yours." He held up the parchment in his hand. "This is the proof he will need to clear his name."

"Perhaps." Laban grinned, standing and setting the Sword and box of letters on a small table. "But seeing that you and I are the only ones who know of these letters, I fail to see how this is a concern of mine."

Ammon knew a confrontation was inevitable. He drew his sword, expecting Laban to reach for and draw Zoram's Sword, but no counterstrike came. Amnon pointed his blade at Laban's chest. "You are charged with treason and conspiracy. In the name of Israel, her king, and her God, I command you to stand down and surrender yourself to my authority!"

Laban's grin melted away, leaving a cold, empty stare. "You have no idea how tired I am of being commanded by Israel's God to do this or that. Save it. I've heard it all before." Laban continued to step forward, closing the distance between them to just over an arm's length between him and the end of Ammon's sword.

"Stop!" Ammon commanded. "I will use force!"

"No," Laban said calmly, moving closer until the blade's tip touched his chest. "You won't."

Ammon saw him move a split second before he registered the searing-hot sensation cutting through him. He was confused. One moment he was staring down the length of his blade at the Keeper of Records; the next instant his wrist hurt, and he was nose to nose with Laban, the smell of wine heavy on the Keeper's breath.

Ammon blinked several times trying to clear his vision. His eyes were watering, and it was getting increasingly difficult to focus on Laban's face.

"The princess will be mine if I have to kill every last one of you who would stand in my way."

Ammon blinked the water out of his eyes and looked down to the source of this unique feeling spreading throughout his body. Laban was pressing the hilt of Ammon's sword against his stomach. But where was the blade? Ammon stumbled backward. He watched, fixated in horror, as the blade pulled free of his stomach. It was covered in blood. His blood.

It was funny, Ammon thought with an odd humor. He had expected more of a fight, but he'd never stood a chance. He guessed, as the room around him began to darken, that the rumors of his speed and skill were, if anything, underestimated.

His last thoughts moved to his family, his king, and his faith.

"Oh, one more thing," Laban hissed. "Tell God, if you see Him, that the plates are *mine*."

שומר החרב

Laban let the body slump to the floor, cursing as he noticed a small patch of blood smeared on his silk dress shirt. He gave the body a sharp kick to vent his irritation before reaching down and taking the letter from the dead man's hand. He smoothed out the parchment and replaced it with the others. Fortunately there wasn't any blood on it.

He stood in the silence that filled his quarters as a thousand thoughts flooded his mind. He hated to admit it, but he was sufficiently unnerved to the point of questioning—if only for the briefest of moments—whether or not to proceed with his plan. Perhaps he should just run away. With Lehi's treasure now his own, Laban was wealthy beyond most men's unchecked imaginations. Maybe he should join up with a caravan and leave the plates and the princess to whatever fate awaited them. He had survived thus far without them. He didn't need either one.

But then the moment passed. And while it was true he didn't *need* either one, he wanted them with the very deepest, most base desires that lurked in a man's heart. He would do anything to satisfy those desires. His plan was still sound, and with Hanoch and this king's guard now silenced, there was no one left to stop him; no one knew anything of his deceit.

But, no, that wasn't entirely true. Zoram still lived. He had suspected enough to seek out the records, and there was no way to know how much Hanoch may have shared with him. He had, no doubt, believed he would emerge the victor over the young Keeper. No, Zoram was the last obstacle in the path of his success. His voice could eventually arouse suspicion and doubt among the Sarim. There could be no room for error this time. He would see to it, personally, that Zoram was discredited to the point of being forever dishonored.

Or dead.

He preferred dead.

There was only one more loose end to tie up. Laban almost chuckled. Or untie.

Laban nearly lost his balance twice as he made his way down the hall to where Anat was being kept. He was drunk. As he fumbled at the locked door, he wished Hanoch was still with him. Laban had grown accustomed to Hanoch making his problems disappear. Like Anat. But tonight Laban would have to do his own dirty work. A thrill shot through his body. He was going to enjoy this.

Laban swung the door open, expecting to see Anat bound and "secured." In the moment it took him to register that she was nowhere to be seen, a deafening crash followed by a sharp pain registered. Instinctively, Laban fell to his knees, but his years of training and conditioning took over. Protecting his head from another blow, Laban spun around and drove his palm upward, connecting with Anat's chin. Anat dropped the brass wine decanter and stumbled backward, tripping and falling to the floor. Even as drunk as he was, she was still no match for Captain Laban.

She was, however, tenacious. Spinning around, she crouched on all fours, waiting for Laban's next strike. He had underestimated her. She knew he planned to kill her. She had heart, though, thinking she stood a chance against him. He would have been impressed if not for the nauseating pain radiating from the back of his head, blurring his vision.

Anat leapt at him, a small serving knife in her hand. The attack was so simple, so straightforward, that he barely had to react, grabbing her wrist and slapping her hard enough to daze her. She went limp, but he continued to hold her wrist, squeezing tighter and tighter, grinding her tendons against her bones. She screamed out, paralyzed in pain and fear.

Laban raised his hand to strike her but stopped short of contact. Instead, he brushed her disheveled hair from her face. He laughed, devoid of mirth. Demeaning. "You couldn't seduce Zoram, could you? You wanted so desperately to elevate your status, to forever distance yourself from the ugly poverty you were born into." He continued to brush her hair with his fingers. "But you will always be poor. You will always be ugly."

Anat recoiled at his touch.

"No amount of fine clothing or jewelry or flowered perfumes can hide it." Laban knew he was hurting her more than any physical pain would. "Your repulsive nature is not, however, the fault of your parents. *They* are decent people. You have *made* yourself ugly. No decent man will have you. Ever."

Laban reached for the discarded serving knife. "But I'm not unkind. You want release from your circumstances, from your curse? I will provide it." Laban gripped the small knife tightly but stopped as he heard the familiar rustle of leather and metal of a soldier's uniform.

"Captain."

Laban turned around to face his interrupter, but he did not let go of Anat's wrist. The soldier, not one of The Fifty, looked both confused and concerned at the sight before him.

"What?!"

The soldier snapped to attention, but he could not tear his eyes away from Anat. "Sir, I-I'm here—"

"I can *see* that." Laban had no patience for the disruption.

"Yes, sir. I am here to escort you to the council meeting of the Sarim."

Laban took a deep breath and stood up, roughly pulling Anat to her feet.

"We were . . ." Laban fought to keep his words from slurring, "having a little disagreement."

The soldier didn't look convinced, but he had enough sense not to voice his concerns.

Laban looked at Anat once more then threw her at the soldier. "Take her away," Laban said.

The soldier held the crying woman. "Sir, my orders are to take you—"

"You have new orders now!" Laban screamed. "Get her out of my sight! Get her out of my house!" He reached down, picked up the spilled decanter, and started drinking what remained. The warm wine calmed his nerves. "Take her home to the lower city. Take her back to her own kind." Anat looked at him, her spirit broken, unable to stand up to him. "She knows the way." Laban smiled, satisfied in his contempt. "She never really left."

The soldier stood there for a moment, unsure about his conflicting orders. "Shall I return for you?"

Laban gave him an exaggerated wave of his whole arm. "I know the way. I will not be treated like a child."

"But, sir," the soldier started but stopped, knowing he risked more than his rank if he angered Laban further.

"Now! I said leave me! I will not have my orders questioned. Inform the Elders that I have new . . ." He lost his train of thought. "That I have new evidence against the king and that I will be along once I've had time to dress."

The soldier remained, a look of doubt strewn across his face. "But, sir, you can hardly stand . . ."

In an explosion of temper, Laban threw the empty brass decanter of wine at the soldier. He missed, the heavy vessel chipping the stone wall next to him.

"I don't need your help!" he yelled in a drunken rage. "I don't need you! I don't need any of you! Now, get out of my sight! Do as I command! I am Laban! There is none greater in all of Israel!"

As the soldier put his arm around Anat and led her out of the room, Laban cast his eyes heavenward and lowered his voice to a growl. "There is none greater in all of heaven or hell!"

CHAPTER TWENTY-EIGHT

ZORAM HAD BEEN CUT PRETTY bad. Hanoch's skill was every bit as sharp as his sword, and as he had lashed out, he sliced through a good portion of the muscle in Zoram's lower leg. Without Rebekah's help he would have remained maimed and unable to flee; he would have been caught and most likely killed. He owed her his very life.

"I n-need to get you home," she said as they had fled the scene.

"No, that's the first place they'll look."

"Th-then I'll take you to m-my father's home."

Zoram shook his head, wincing at the excruciating pain that accompanied his every step. "She saw you too. Anat will tell them you were part of all this. It's not safe there, either."

The trouble was, he realized with a sober thought, he didn't know where to go or what to do next.

Rebekah seemed to sense his despondent thoughts and secured her grip on him as he leaned on her for support. "I know a p-place."

It was as if a weight suddenly lifted from Zoram's heart. His own death did not worry him, but he could not bear the thought of being responsible for Rebekah's.

But that was not entirely true. His own death *did* concern him—not for the loss of his life but for the thought of being separated from Rebekah. He had never been so scared in all his life than when Hanoch's blade was pressed to her neck. His own life seemed inconsequential to the overriding need to see her safe. And while he wished he could send her away from the danger, she was now tangled in all this almost as much as he was. She would be safer with him than on her own.

Rebekah led them through the dark streets of the business district, partway down the hill and situated between the upper and lower cities.

There were few people on the streets at this hour, so the pair was able to move largely unseen. They traveled unrecognized, likely presumed to be young lovers leaning on one another.

Eventually she stopped at an empty storefront and pushed her way inside. The owner, she explained as she hefted Zoram to the upper room, was a customer along her oil route. He was out of town for another few weeks on business. "He always s-said if he could d-do anyth-thing for m-me he would. I'll be sure to th-thank him wh-when h-he returns." She smiled as she helped Zoram down onto a small couch by the open window.

"Let's t-take a look." She checked his hastily-made bandage. It was soaked and was doing little to staunch the flow of blood. Even in the dim moonlight, she could see it didn't look good. "You need a d-doctor," she said, tearing off another strip of her dress to replace the blood-soaked one. She tied it tightly, making Zoram cringe and cry out.

"No," he said through clenched teeth. "We can't let anyone know where we are. They'll either be seen or word will get out, and then . . ." He couldn't finish.

"B-But we need to stop the b-blood."

She was right, he knew, but they couldn't risk letting anyone know where they were. Without any witnesses to challenge Anat, he suspected— no, he *knew*—that an order to arrest or even kill them on sight had been issued. There may even be a bounty on their heads, which, he knew from experience, could make even good men go bad. Money was a powerful motivator.

Rebekah left him and began searching, almost blindly, through the room until she found what she was looking for. In the dim light, he could make out a small oil lamp in her hands. "St-stay here," she said, and then with a smile to her voice added, "D-don't crawl off anywhere."

"Where are you going?"

"We need towels and water and m-more bandages."

"No, don't. You might be seen."

"I won't." She looked on him with such compassion and—love?—that his worry and concern for her far surpassed his own injury, however grave it might be. But there was something else too. It was determination, that stubborn, I-don't-need-your-help, don't-tell-me-what-to-do look he had first encountered in the hills outside Jerusalem just a week earlier. He had seen it again when he offered to help her a few days later in the city, and he was seeing it again now. If she was set to leave and return with medical supplies, there was nothing he or anyone else could do to stop her. The only thing he could do was see to it that her time away was minimal and limited to one trip.

"All right," he said, "but you and I both know I need more than simply clean water and more bandages. The blade cut too deeply. Can you sew?" he asked.

"S-sew? Like clothing?"

Zoram nodded.

"Yes, of course," she said, confused at the strange question.

"Can you find a needle at this hour without drawing any attention to yourself? Without returning to your father's home?"

She thought for a moment then nodded. "Th-there's a seamstress a few streets over. She is a g-good woman."

"You trust her? Completely?"

She nodded. Confused.

"Will she insist you explain your visit at this late hour?"

She shook her head. Still confused.

"What about hemp, or . . ." he was trying to think of something else, something better, ". . . or flax. Yes, flax would do just fine. Can you also get a stalk or two?"

Rebekah nodded again. "I can, b-but why?"

"You're going to sew me up."

Even in the dim light, he could see her face turn pale as fear and doubt filled her thoughts and heart. "I d-don't think I can."

"Don't worry," he assured her. "I'll walk you through it. Where I have been these many years, it is a common practice. It's the only option available to us now. Are you sure you can bring back what we need?"

Rebekah could not form the words and nodded instead.

"Then hurry. I'll keep pressure on it while you're gone, but what we need to do must be done while the cut is still fresh. Do you understand?"

She nodded again.

"Then go." He tried to ease her fears with a smile. "And I promise I won't go anywhere without you. Ever."

She took a deep breath and returned his smile, his feeble declaration of love clear. She suddenly bent over him and kissed him on the forehead. "I'll be right b-back," and then she was gone.

He waited for a full minute before the last sounds of her retreating back into the night faded. He was having a hard time comprehending the depth

and breadth of his newly ignited and intense feelings for Rebekah. Where
before he had suspected what he was experiencing was budding love, with
her kiss—as brief and pure as it was—he was now certain of it. This was
what the poets wrote of, what he had only heard or read about—the kind
of love he remembered his own mother and father sharing. This love was
calming and exhilarating at the same time, and for a while nothing else
mattered. He longed to be reunited with her and then never part with
her again. She was beautiful and smart and funny. But what was most
enticing about her was that her faith had not become tarnished as a result
of her struggles. If others couldn't see past her lips and their own ears,
they did not deserve such a noble woman. He could not envision a more
perfect companion and helpmeet—or mother to his children. And though
he dared not dwell on it for long, he could see himself spending the rest of
his life meeting her every need and trying to make her happy.

When she did return, he was unable to take his eyes off her, her beauty
amplified in the warm lamplight.

"Stop th-that," she said gently.

"Stop what?"

"Looking at m-me like th-that."

"Sorry," he said, embarrassed. "I . . . I couldn't help it."

Rebekah had brought a pitcher of water and some towels. She unpacked
a small shoulder bag and laid the contents out on the floor between them.
Her frightened look returned. "Are you sure about th-this?"

Zoram picked up the needle. It was thin and had a slight curve to
it. He replaced it and picked up the stalk of flax. It was fresh, young,
and—"Perfect."

The euphoria he had experienced thinking about Rebekah had
departed at the sight of the simple materials before him. He still had a
sacred duty to perform, but first he had to repair what that traitor, Hanoch,
had done to him.

"Wh-what d-do you need me to d-do?" She was anxious and nervous.

He started stripping the stalk, peeling away the outer fibers to reach
the strong wet ones inside. "I'll guide you at every step. And don't worry,"
he added with a smile. "You'll do just fine."

As they worked cleaning his wound and preparing the thin fibers of
the flax stalk, Zoram explained that the people he had lived with followed
a medical practice of stitching flesh as one might stitch a ripped or torn
garment. The procedure was first used by a great sage and physician

named Sushruta, who had lived over two hundred years earlier in that area of the world. His instruction and unorthodox methods had saved many thousands of lives over the centuries. Zoram had seen his masters use similar needles with hemp or even cotton fibers to close wounds.

"B-but you've never actually . . ."

"Sewed someone up? No." He knew this wasn't what she wanted to hear. "But I was never good with a needle anyway." He tried to laugh and break the tension they were both feeling, but it did little to ease their troubled moods.

Zoram struggled to keep his hands steady as he threaded the needle with a long flaxen strand and tied it tight. He handed it to Rebekah.

"Don't think of it as skin," he instructed. "Think of it as you would a shirt or a dress. You'll have to make sure the needle penetrates deep into the skin. If it doesn't, the skin will rip when pressure is put on it."

Talking about it didn't help ease her fears. "I d-don't th-think I can."

"You have to. I'm scared too, but we have no other choice. Your skills will take over, you watch, and I've heard that the needle doesn't hurt much when it's that deep into the skin." He knew it was a lie, but he couldn't have her worrying about hurting him. "I wouldn't ask you to do this if I didn't know, beyond all doubt, that you're capable of it. If I could do this myself, I would, but I need you . . . I—I mean," he stammered, "I need your help."

Rebekah's serious and apprehensive look melted, and a smile crept onto her face seeing him embarrassed and uncomfortable around her. She took a deep breath. "Let's d-do this."

Zoram cleaned his leg one more time with a clear, damp towel as Rebekah practiced holding the needle several different ways in her fingers, trying to anticipate the best way to approach her unusual mending task. He positioned his leg on the edge of a small table. He knew his leg would bleed less if it was elevated.

"Are you ready?"

He nodded and began focusing on his breathing. In and out, slow and rhythmic, inhaling peace and calm while exhaling fear and doubt and pain. His mind was carried away to the day, as a young apprentice, he had joined his masters in their strange meditation practices. They had never required it of their students, respecting the many and varied faiths, but the offer to participate was standing and open. What he had learned had enhanced his own faith. There were secrets of the mind and the inner power that all men possessed but few understood and harnessed. He had practiced slowing his own heartbeat, letting his thoughts drift on the ebb and flow of nothingness, shutting out the world around him. He had advanced with them enough to learn the techniques of withstanding extreme cold, heat, and even pain. It was these last stages of the meditative journey he now sought.

But those had been practice only and in a controlled environment. He tried to focus and push these few, persistent doubts from his mind as he lay there, anticipating the first stab of Rebekah's needle.

The sharp, sudden, piercing pain took him by surprise. It seemed as if the small needle hurt worse than the blade that had sliced open his leg. And while he was able to bite his tongue, he was unable to stop himself from flinching in pain.

Rebekah, though, instead of pausing or stopping, continued through both flaps of skin and pulled the flaxen fibers through, effectively beginning the stitch. Even if he could, he didn't dare turn around to face her. She was softly crying, knowing she was hurting him, yet she pushed on. This strength of character and determination to do whatever needed to be done gave him new resolve. He refocused his wandering mind and focused again on a place far away from the pain, a place where only peace and quiet control over his every sense prevailed.

Rebekah proceeded to sew up his leg, her movements becoming more confident and sure with every stitch. Zoram had lost all sense of time and was surprised to hear her talking to him, telling him that she had a few smaller areas to stitch up for good measure, but that other than that she was done.

Fully conscious now and curious to see all that she had completed, he strained to watch her finish up her surgical efforts. But every time he craned his neck to see, his leg would move and turn.

"Hold still!"

"Aren't you done yet?"

"If I was d-done, you'd be the first to know. Now, d-don't m-move."

But he was anxious to return to his responsibility and task at hand.

"I said hold still!" she said again, this time with more force. "I'm almost d-done."

Zoram was disoriented, wondering how much time it had actually taken for Rebekah to sew him up. It must have taken longer than he felt, and he was suddenly pricked by an impulse to return to the treasury and seek out the records. Every passing moment endangered them further.

"That's good enough," he said, pushing himself up off the floor. She tried to push him back down but was not prepared for his sudden movements. He stopped and sat back down, though, as a wave of dizziness passed through him.

"No! St-stop! I'm not—"

He knew he had hurt her feelings and reined in his urgency to leave. He took her hand. "Thank you. I have never seen such a meticulous and perfected work. The High Sadhus, himself, would be impressed."

"Who?"

"An old friend. You have great talent as a healer."

"B-but you need to rest."

"I know, but I can't. There simply isn't time." He reached out and took one of the remaining clean towels, pressing it to his leg. Then he took one of the strips of cloth and tied it tightly around his leg. "There."

Zoram used his arms to push and pull himself up to his feet. Rebekah stood as well and took a step back. She just watched, not sure what to say. The first thing he noticed was the peculiar sensation of the skin pulled tight where she had sewed him up. He tested the sutures by putting a little weight on his leg. He took a few careful steps around the room.

"Don't," she pleaded, reaching out to steady him, but she pulled back seeing that he didn't need her help. She looked down and away from him, and Zoram got the feeling that there was more to her plea than just a concern for his leg.

"What?"

She didn't turn or answer right away, and in the silence he knew something was wrong. He was about to ask her again when she spoke.

"Is it true?"

He started to open his mouth to ask if what was true when he suddenly knew what she was talking about. But as much as he wanted to, he couldn't find the words to explain what had happened.

"She told me th-that . . . th-that you and her . . ."

Remnants of shame and guilt and an intense longing to protect her from these lies filled his frame, and he could feel his emotions gather and catch in his throat. How could he explain what Anat had done without sounding like he was simply shifting the blame to her and away from himself? And while he was largely the victim in her web of lies, he had to admit that had he followed his instincts and left before she offered him that drink, none of that would have happened.

"I d-don't b-blame you if—"

"I'm sorry you had to hear this," he started, his voice cracking and filled with emotion. "We did nothing wrong, but I should have been more guarded with her advances." He swallowed his embarrassment. "May I tell you what happened?"

She looked up at him and listened without interruption as he recounted what he could remember and piece together from that night and morning—from his conversation with his house matron to his intention to offer an apology and Anat's invitation to stay for one drink. He paused as he gathered strength to tell her of the horror of that next morning and how he had learned of her treachery and lies.

Rebekah didn't answer right away, but he could tell that she had listened carefully to every word. He wanted her to answer or say something. Did she believe him? Would she forgive him?

Then she tried to smile. "I came to w-warn you about her." She took his hand and stood. "I could see th-the lies in her e-eyes and h-hear it in her v-voice."

"Then you—"

"You never have to sp-speak of it again."

There was so much he wanted to say to her, but all that came out was, "Thank you."

They shared a long look, then Zoram reached down, felt the stitched wound on his leg, and took a few steps around the room. Their heartfelt talk didn't change what he still needed to do.

"Wh-what are you d-doing?" she said. "You'll tear the flax."

Zoram took a few more steps, walking with more confidence and purpose with every passing moment. "I don't think so, but I'll be careful."

"You n-need more t-time to heal."

"I know I do, but I can't afford it. Hanoch wasn't working alone. Every minute I stay here, away from the records, the greater danger they're in. I cannot allow that."

"Wh-what d-do you intend to do?"

"Return to the treasury," he said after thinking about it. "I still have my key. If the plates are there, I'll take them and hide them away until we can uncover this conspiracy."

"B-but isn't that Laban's d-duty?"

Zoram considered this briefly. "I'm not sure where he stands. As crazy as it sounds, I'm starting to think he might actually be involved in all this somehow. I don't know who I can trust to help me with this."

He suddenly looked down and then back up at her, smiling. "Well, actually, there is one person I trust completely. Thank you, Rebekah." He had expected her concerned look to soften at this, but it didn't.

"I d-don't want you to go," she said, panic sharpening her words. "You can't do th-this by yourself. Let m-me tell my father. He's a m-member of the S-Sarim. He'll know how to help."

"There isn't time. Besides, there's no telling who else might be involved. I trust that your father would help, but others in similar positions of power, those he might call on, might not be. We know it reaches Jerusalem's chief of security. Involving your father will only put him in danger too. No. Until I can get to the bottom of this, we must be careful where we place our trust."

Rebekah just stood there for a moment, unmoving. Then she wiped her hands on the towel draped over her shoulder. "Th-then I'm coming with you."

"No," he started to say, but he didn't think it would do any good. There was something in her eyes and in her tone that communicated more than a mere concern for his safety. Much more. She cared for him too, he was certain of it, and she couldn't bear the thought of him risking his life. And as much as he dreaded the thought of being separated from her, he refused to risk her life for something that was his duty.

"No," he said again, gently. "This is something I must do. It is my calling. It is my purpose and what I and my family have been set apart to accomplish. I have involved you too much as it is. I could not bear to live knowing I had been responsible for endangering your life any more than I already have."

She was crying. "But I—"

He took both of her hands in his. "The men behind this plot to steal the records will not hesitate to kill anyone who might get in their way. They killed my father because he stumbled on their plot, and Hanoch nearly killed you back there. I cannot risk your life . . . not again."

Rebekah tried to pull her hands free, but Zoram kept a hold of them. "I know you want to help, but—" He stopped, realizing this course of persuasion was simply not going to work. She was not the kind of woman to sit idly by as he risked his life. She needed to help. She needed purpose. "You may be right. We can't fight this alone. Your father may be able to help. Go to him. Keep out of sight. You know the streets better than most. Tell him what we know and who we suspect, but stay with him under his care and protection. If the Elders and brethren of the Sarim are part of his conspiracy, as Hanoch claimed, then we will likely need your father's power and influence to right this wrong."

She finally pulled away. "You th-think I can't help you. You th-think th-that because I'm a woman—"

"No, that's not it at all. I've said this before and I mean it. You're stronger than most of the men I have ever known."

"Th-then why?"

"Because I love you."

The words escaped his lips before he could stop them. Despite having thought it many times over the past couple of days, to hear himself say it out loud was a surreal experience. He did love her. He was more certain of it now, at this moment, than he had ever been before.

Neither spoke, and the words just seemed to hang there in the lamp-lit room. Zoram became more and more uncomfortable in the silence. He suspected she felt the same way about him, but why didn't she say it? She was kind and compassionate, but was that love? He didn't know. She had kissed him, but it was on the forehead, something a sister or a good friend might do. Had it been a mistake?

He was beginning to wish he could take the words back when Rebekah smiled. She took his head in her hands and pulled him to her for a kiss. Sensations unlike any other he had ever experienced before flooded and coursed through his body. He felt light and invincible and more complete than he had ever felt before. He did love her; he would always love her, and now that he knew she loved him too, he wished he could never let her go.

They held each other in a gentle but passionate embrace for what felt like forever, neither wanting to be the first to end it. Her hair smelled of wildflowers, and Zoram let himself get lost in the sweet fragrances. Everything he had ever imagined love would be like was manifest in this one moment and in this one extraordinary woman who held him tightly.

Eventually, ever so slowly, their embrace released. Rebekah wiped her tears on her sleeve and then took his hands in hers. "Is it wrong for m-me to wish you wouldn't go? Th-that you would stay with m-me instead?"

Zoram shook his head. "No, and as much as I want nothing more than to stay with you, leave this city, and commit the rest of my life to you, I cannot forget the duty I have to Israel and to God. It is a choice I do not make lightly, but it is one I must make nonetheless."

Rebekah seemed to relax. "I could never love a m-man who d-didn't take his oath to G-God with fidelity. Be careful though. If Laban *is* involved . . ."

"Don't worry. I can take care of myself."

"Laban has never b-been d-defeated. He cannot be beaten. M-many have tried. All have d-died." A tear spilled down her cheek, then she whispered, "I d-don't want you to d-die."

Zoram squeezed her hands gently. "I can't live knowing I didn't do everything in my power to protect the records." He could see that his words offered her no comfort. "So," he said with conviction and faith, "we will rely on the Lord's help and hand. He is still Lord of all, is He not?"

She smiled, comforted. "Yes," she said. "He is."

"I must know you are safe with your father. Agreed?"

She nodded. "Agreed."

"Can you make it home unseen?"

"I know these streets better th-than anyone."

Zoram felt a stirring of strength flood his whole being. This was what he was called to do.

"Wh-what will you d-do when you get to the t-treasury?"

He shrugged and smiled. "Whatever I can, and I'll trust that God will provide a way to keep the records safe. There's not much more that I can do."

He turned to leave, but she took a hold of his shoulder. She turned him around and kissed him again. "Come back to me."

He wanted to put his hand over his heart and utter the promise that he would, but he couldn't. As he looked at her, the desperate sincerity in her eyes, he couldn't lie, even for love's sake. She deserved more than a hollow and empty promise. Despite his brave words and front for Rebekah's sake, she was right. As good as Hanoch was, Laban was known to be his superior. It would take more than skill alone to defeat him. And while she would have never used the words, Zoram was likely to die tonight. But he would trust in the Lord.

He opened his mouth to confess his love for her again but stopped. What more could he say? Instead, he tried to offer up a confident smile.

She appeared to understand the magnitude of this, quite possibly their last farewell. She let one final cry escape her lips, but she bit back the rest of her tears and tried to remain strong for him as he turned and was gone.

CHAPTER TWENTY-NINE

ZORAM PROCEEDED WITH EXTREME CAUTION as he wound his way back toward the palace grounds. Every sound, every voice, as few as they were at this late hour, sent his heart racing. He had to make it back to the treasury, though he didn't really expect to find the records there. But he needed someplace to start his search. If they had been taken, perhaps there might be a clue as to who took them.

The streets were dark and the shadows wide under the quarter moon, giving him ample places to conceal himself. Except for the soldiers—most likely looking for him and Rebekah—Zoram was alone and the streets still. As he approached the upper city though, he had to watch his every step a little more closely. The palace and surrounding grounds were lit by what seemed to be every lamp and torch in the whole city. The yellow glow from inside the perimeter walls illuminated not only the streets and houses below but the surrounding hills as well. The light, however, wasn't the worst of his troubles.

That was the legion of armed men posted at every corner and gate.

With every step Zoram cautiously took toward the palace, his confidence in obtaining and protecting the records waned. Climbing atop the roof of a deserted house, he could see that the royal compound and surrounding streets were crawling with men, armed and no doubt under explicit orders to not only protect the grounds from other "conspirators" but to also apprehend—or kill—him on sight. Making a wide circle, Zoram made his way around to the secret entrance he had used to sneak the king's wife and son out, only to see a fire lit and two men guarding it. They must have discovered it when they learned of the woman and child's absence.

Circling back, he made his way toward the Keeper's armory. This way, too, was heavily guarded and impassable without first taking out the four soldiers guarding it. And while, even unarmed and favoring one leg, Zoram was sure he could prevail against them, the alarm they would raise would bring numbers that no man could defeat singlehandedly.

No. He had to find another way inside.

A cursory study of the perimeter found a single man guarding a section of the wall without a door or gate. While there was no apparent entrance, he did notice a stack of crates and grain sacks across the narrow street. It was chancy, but if he could silence the lone guard without alerting anyone, he might just be able to go over the wall. What awaited him on the other side, however, he had no way of knowing, but he figured he'd deal with that dilemma when the time came. He didn't have the luxury of speculative worry right now.

Looking around, he found some discarded gunny sacks and blankets, and for a moment he considered dressing up as a beggar to approach the soldier.

No, he decided, opting for the more direct approach. He moved through the shadowed streets as quietly as he could as he approached. At the last moment, he stepped into the light and walked right up to the guard, startling him.

"Soldier!" Zoram said as authoritatively as possible. The combination of his command and sudden appearance momentarily confused the guard. Out of habit and years of military conditioning, he snapped to attention before he realized Zoram wasn't wearing a uniform. Though his confusion lasted only a brief second, it was time enough for Zoram to charge him, throwing him into the wall. The soldier's hand went for his sword, but he wasn't fast enough. Zoram hit him square on the chin, whipping his head back and into the stone wall. He was unconscious before the pain had time to register, and he dropped to the ground.

Zoram quickly dragged the body into the shadows across the street, took the man's sword, and straightway began building his crude stairway over the wall. Peering over to the other side, he relaxed a bit to see this section of the grounds relatively dark and deserted. Not thinking, he slipped over the wall, remembering too late about his leg. He tried to favor the uninjured one in the short fall as he landed, but the impact was absorbed by both. A sharp and painful cry escaped his lips before he could stop it. He instinctively curled into a ball, cradling his leg and gripping the bandage. Once the shock of the pain wore off, he realized with a sickening feeling that his hands were wet with blood. He had torn one or more of Rebekah's stitches. He only hoped her work would hold a little while longer, at least until he could return to her.

He managed to get to his feet and tested out his injured leg, putting pressure on it to test the stitches. He was relieved that he could still feel the tension from the flaxen fibers. He could walk, albeit with a pronounced limp. He knew he would have to move more carefully if he expected to complete his divine mission.

Getting his bearings in the dark, he started in the safest direction to the treasury, avoiding the lit streets, pathways, and gardens. Shortly, however, he was forced to stop. He couldn't get any closer without being noticed by at least a half dozen men. Zoram knew he was skilled but he wasn't *that* good, especially given his injury.

He fell back to a dark corner and closed his eyes, leaning his head back.

Think. Think.

It was only a matter of time until the sentry he had rendered unconscious either came to or was discovered and the break in their security shouted from the rooftops. He had to get in, rescue the plates, and get out before his presence was known and all hopes to save the records dashed. He needed a plan. *Ponder and deliberate before making even the first move,* Wu Yien had reminded him time and again over the years. His friend would be disappointed if he could see the mess Zoram had created. Unable to go back but prevented from going forward, he knew it was foolish to go on without a plan, but if he didn't go now, there might not be any records to save later.

He sent a silent prayer heavenward, wiped the blood from his hands on his cloak, gripped his sword, and stepped to the corner. Before he could start his assault though, he stepped on a small, sharp rock with his bad leg. The pain jolted through his entire body. He was about to kick it away in anger when he suddenly stopped. All warfare was based on deception, his friend had once told him. *When he is close by and ready to strike,* Wu Yien had explained, *the wise general will make it appear that he is far away.*

Zoram was no general, but the meaning was not lost on him.

He bent down and picked up the rock. His plan, if that's what it could be called, was painfully simple, and while he didn't fully expect it to work, it was the best—and only—one he had. Easing up to the corner again, he cast the stone across to the far end of the guarded courtyard. It hit the wall and bounced on the ground just loud enough to draw their attention.

While only three of them were sent to investigate the noise, all of their backs were now to him.

He had to move now!

Sprinting the best he could while landing softly with every footfall, he limped across the lit corner of the courtyard. Fortunately, it was only ten or fifteen paces. The guards began to call out to one another, inquiring about the source of the sound. Any one of them could turn around at this moment and spot him, thus ending his ill-planned attempt to secure the records. A familiar pain in his leg returned, but he forced himself to keep moving. He held his breath for fear of inadvertently crying out, willing one leg to follow the other, not looking back nor to the right or left to check on the distracted soldiers. He would know, all too soon, if even one of them turned around before Zoram could blend with the darkness.

"Hey!" someone shouted just as he crossed through the archway and into an inner hall. He tripped in his sudden panic but managed to roll out of the fall and back to his feet, favoring his good leg and spinning around to face his opponents.

But there was no one there.

"Why aren't you at your post?" the owner of the commanding voice demanded.

"Sir, we heard something over there," one of the sentries answered.

"And did you find anything?"

They hadn't.

"Two watches can take a toll," the newcomer said, "but we must stand our ground, or Laban will have our heads . . ."

Zoram didn't hang around to listen to the reprimand once he realized his ill-conceived plan had actually worked. He slinked through the labyrinth of rooms and passageways that made up the royal grounds, not giving much thought to which way he should go. He had a general sense of direction and did what he could to follow it, ducking into dark rooms to avoid the sentries who patrolled the hallways.

There were voices up ahead around the corner. He recognized the way now and knew that the treasury was almost within his reach. Zoram paused, out of sight. There were at least four soldiers, and judging from their casual tones, they were all friends, likely from the ranks of Laban's infamous Fifty. The topic of their conversations didn't interest him much until one of them said a name that made him stop and take heed.

"He was working with Naomi," the sentry had said.

"Who?"

"Naomi, the house matron for the Keeper of the Sword."

"You think she was working with Jharom?"

"That whole house is corrupt."

Had Zoram heard them correctly? Was Naomi involved in trying to steal the records?

"At least she's in custody."

"I heard she didn't even try to resist, babbling on about God's will and how we're all blind."

One of them scoffed. "Lunatics, the lot of them."

"Even this new Keeper . . . what's his name?"

"Zoram."

"Yeah, they say he killed Hanoch, snuck up on him from behind and ran him through."

"I hope he tries to steal them again. If I ever see him . . ."

Zoram was so intent on what he was hearing that he didn't notice the sounds of someone approaching him from behind until it was too late. He spun around, alarmed, startled to be facing—

"Laban," he said, surprised.

They stood facing each other in the dimly lit hallway, neither saying a word. Laban was dressed in his full ceremonial uniform, complete with arm, leg, and breast plates. He was even wearing his polished helmet. But the uniform was not what seized Zoram's attention. His eyes darted quickly to the sword on Laban's belt. It was his Sword, the Sword. He had hoped to retrieve it when he reached the inside of the treasury, but Laban had already claimed it.

Which meant he had likely moved the records as well.

Zoram waited for him to call out to his Fifty, ending the ill-fated attempt to save what his family had been charged by a prophet of God to protect. But Laban didn't move, nor did he raise the alarm. Unsure what kind of game the commander was playing, Zoram bowed and decided he could do worse than play along. "Laban," he said again.

"Do you have the key to the treasury?" Laban asked after another moment of uncomfortable and peculiar silence.

Did he have his key? "Yes."

"Then come with me." Laban started around the corner and down the hallway toward the treasury.

Zoram was confused. He didn't know whether to follow or not. Was he leading Zoram into a trap for sport, to surround him as a hunter would his prey? Laban hadn't seemed to recognize him or perceive him as a threat.

Maybe Zoram had been wrong about Laban. He was arrogant and wealthy and accustomed to speaking down to those around him, but Zoram had no clear evidence that Laban was directly involved in any conspiracy. Was it possible that Hanoch had been acting alone or at least with *other* men?

With his every sense heightened and on alert, Zoram followed. He didn't know what to think of this strange behavior, and then he caught the unmistakable smell of strong drink wafting from Laban's clothes as he led the way. Laban was drunk. That would explain his disorientation at their meeting and his question about the key. Well, Zoram thought, this just might work to his advantage.

As they approached the treasury anteroom, the soldiers snapped to attention at the sight of their captain but just as quickly took a defensive stance when they noticed Zoram following in step behind him.

"Stop!" Laban commanded. "He's with me. Put your swords away. Now!"

Laban must be drunk. There was no other explanation for his strange behavior and choice of words to his men.

"Do as I say! I am Laban, and I command you to put them away."

"But, sir—" one of them started to protest.

"You are dismissed."

"Sir?" another asked.

"You heard me. Go . . . check on . . ." Laban couldn't finish his command, and frustrated at his lack of words, he swept his arm out in front of him. "I said leave us!" He faced his men, standing his ground, but only barely.

"But you ordered that . . ." the ranking soldier started but trailed off, confused.

Zoram flexed his fingers around the hilt of the sword he held loosely at his side.

"What? What did I order?" Laban's words were beginning to sound unsure.

"That Zoram," another answered, pointing, "be arrested on sight."

Laban turned around and stole a quick glance at Zoram. "He's with me now. The situation has . . . changed."

"Changed, sir?" The ranking soldier was beginning to gain courage. Perhaps he too smelled the alcohol that emanated from his master. Zoram slowed his heartbeat and calmed his nerves with slow, deep breaths in anticipation of the challenge and fight that was unavoidable. Laban, however, remained firm in his stand and stared down his skeptic.

"Sir?" the soldier asked again.

Laban's hand went to the new Sword. "I will not be spoken to in this manner nor will my commands be questioned! You are dismissed! Now go. Zoram and I have much to do. Am I clear?"

His words and voice might have been weak before, but the soldiers now recognized the rising anger and power in their captain. They came to attention. "Sir! Yes, sir!"

"And you will see that our presence is not made known until such time as I will it. Do you understand?"

"No," the courageous soldier replied. "I don't understand, but I'll obey." He bowed, not taking his eyes off either of them, then gathered the others and left.

Once they were alone, Laban said, "Open it."

Zoram fished the key from his pocket and unlocked the door to the treasury. Taking a lit torch from the wall, Zoram led Laban inside. Zoram was relieved beyond words and comprehension to see the records sitting on the center table right where he had been forced to leave them. Laban stepped toward them and removed the gold-trimmed covering. The plates, made of polished brass, shimmered in the lamplight. Laban's gaze was fixated on them.

"Laban," Zoram dared to ask. "What's going on? I know about the letters and the allegations made against the king, and you must know I do not find them credible. I also know you're meeting later with the Sarim. The Elders hold much power, and I would urge you to be cautious in your dealings with them. I fear some of them may be involved in this plot to steal the records."

Zoram wanted to get him talking. In his inebriated state, Laban might let slip everything he knew about the conspiracy.

"The plates aren't safe here," Laban suddenly said. "You will help me take them."

"Where, Laban? Where are we taking them?"

"To my brethren," he said in a voice not quite his own. "They're waiting for me."

"You want me to help to take them to the council? Are they assembled in the meeting hall?"

He shook his head. "They're waiting for me outside the city walls."

This concerned Zoram. If Laban had made arrangements to meet the conspirators beyond the city walls, they could have riders waiting and ready to spirit the records away to Babylon. His first thought was to end this charade now. He had the records, the guards were gone, and Laban was in no condition to offer any real resistance. He could take them now and have a reasonable chance of escape. But there remained the larger problem of identifying and exposing the dissenters. Zoram might win the battle and save the plates now, but without knowing who to trust, he would eventually and surely lose the war. He needed evidence. He needed to know who was involved. He needed to see this through to the end. It was the only way to ensure victory over this insidious plot.

Laban was looking around the room as if disoriented. Then Zoram realized he was looking for something. Knowing Laban's plan, Zoram located what he was looking for—the two wooden poles and wide, leather sling. He laid them out on the table next to the records. "If you plan to leave before your men return, we must hurry. I'll need your help to load and secure them."

"Of course," Laban said, taking the other side of the ringed stack of metal plates and helping place them in the center of the sling. Zoram had never felt the full weight of the records before. They were solid and much heavier than they appeared. In a moment of reflection, he wondered if their weight was in part due to the importance of what was engraved on them. This was the history of God's people and His dealings with them, and Zoram suspected their value was represented in their heavy mass. It also struck him that he could not have taken them by himself. Moving them was a two-man job.

With the records balanced and tied on the leather, Zoram picked up one end of the wooden poles and placed one on each shoulder. He waited for Laban to do the same. "After you."

Laban paused just outside the treasury door as if debating which direction he should go.

"If I might suggest our course," Zoram said. "There's a secret passage to the armory this way." He motioned to their right. "We're likely to encounter fewer of your men if we go this way."

Laban nodded. "Agreed." He took one of the torches from the wall, and together they proceeded through the dark tunnel.

They were stopped by no less than six guards on their way out of the city. Each time, Zoram lowered his head to hide his identity while Laban dismissed their questions without explanation or apology. Zoram followed

Laban's lead down into the dark shadows of the merchant sections of the city, but where was he taking them? None of this was making any sense. But of one thing Zoram was certain: Laban was very much involved in the conspiracy. His silence during their clandestine travels and his odd behavior, intoxicated or otherwise, confirmed his guilt. Though why Laban hadn't tried to have him killed yet escaped him. Surely the man could have enlisted any one of his hundred servants to help him carry the records, so why Zoram? Zoram was puzzled, but still he followed, listening and looking for the first signs of Laban's coconspirators.

"I've not been in this part of the city before," Zoram offered by way of casual conversation. "Where are the Elders you speak of meeting?"

Laban kept walking, stepping up the pace, but didn't answer. Zoram noticed that, while his footing was a little unsure at times, Laban was moving quite well for how drunk he must have been. In fact, Zoram was having a difficult time keeping up with him. The occasional sharp pain in his leg reminded him that he needed to be careful not to further reopen his wound and undo everything Rebekah had done for him.

Rebekah. The mere thought of her gave him courage, and he prayed with all sincerity that God would keep her safe until he could return to her.

Laban suddenly stopped. They had traveled to a section of the lower city that was deserted and in a state of extreme ruin. Even in the dim moonlight, Zoram could see that the stretch of wall that was not reduced to rubble was scarred and scorched by a long-ago fire. Piles of rocks and refuse littered what once were streets. He could only imagine what a horror those days and weeks of the Babylonian invasion must have been. This corner of the city must not have been worth the effort and resources to rebuild.

Zoram was surprised when Laban put down his end of the carrier and started pulling large wooden beams and stones from a section of the war-torn wall, revealing a hole in the outer wall just big enough for a man to pass through.

"Come," he said, picking up the poles again and leading them through the narrow breach.

On the other side, they had to pass through a thick, gnarled cypress that seemed to be strategically positioned to disguise the passage in and out of the city. How long had it been there, and who else knew about it?

The hills and surrounding countryside were as dark as the lower city and covered in long shadows. Zoram had expected to find members the council or whoever Laban was meeting with just beyond the wall, but all was quiet. They were alone. Laban must have made arrangements to meet the others in the hills. The possibility of an ambush concerned Zoram. He would have to keep his eyes and ears open to the first and slightest hint of danger. He briefly considered disabling Laban and taking the records somewhere safe, but he knew he needed to see this through to the end. He needed to know what Laban knew.

"I know the reports are otherwise," Zoram started, "but when I went to secure the records earlier today, I found Hanoch there, preparing to take them. He must have stolen your key to gain entrance."

He waited for Laban to take the bait and either admit or deny involvement or at least knowledge of his lieutenant's actions, but Zoram was met again with silence. He needed to take a more direct approach.

"He said he wasn't working alone. He kept saying *us* and *we*. I believe he had help from others, from men with more skill and cunning and power than he possessed."

Still nothing.

"I spoke to the king today," Zoram said. Surely this would elicit a response. It didn't. "He claims you gave him a vial of poison, that you encouraged him to kill himself. Why would you do this?"

Nothing. Was he now deaf too?

"Do you know what I think? I think Hanoch was doing your bidding when he was in the treasury, that you are the one behind this conspiracy. And for what? The love of a woman—"

Zoram stopped. Out of the corner of his eye, he spotted movement about a hundred paces up the mountainside. A small group of men had hidden themselves in an outcropping of rocks. But instead of approaching them, the men were scrambling to run away from them. They must have been a band of robbers, who, seeing Laban in full uniform, knew it better than risk being caught and forfeiting their lives.

Laban noticed them too, but instead of ignoring them, he shed the sling and reached out to them. "No!" he called. "Laman! Lemuel! Sam! It's me!"

The voice did not belong to Laban. Zoram was disoriented and confused. Why would Laban—

Laban then removed his helmet and called out again.

It wasn't Laban!

The men in the hills stopped fleeing and instead began running toward them.

Zoram instinctively took a couple of steps back, letting the poles of the carrier fall from his shoulders as well. "Who . . . where is Laban? Where did you get his uniform—?" Then he spotted dark stains on the shoulders and around the collar under the breastplate. Blood. The helmet must have covered it up before. This man had killed Laban and taken his uniform.

The man turned and reached out to him. "Please, stay where you are. We don't want to hurt you."

Zoram took another step back to maintain his distance, but the pretender must have thought he was moving to flee because he sprang into action and leapt at Zoram, tackling him to the ground before he could raise his sword. Zoram was strong, but this pretender possessed so great a strength that he could do little but struggle in vain.

"You killed Laban!" Zoram accused. "You have stolen the records. The sentence is death for both!"

Zoram continued to struggle, but his attacker now straddled him in a way that pinned his arms and rendered them useless. But Zoram was not entirely defenseless. Using his good leg, he brought his knee up sharply into the man's lower back. The man cried out in pain and leaned forward enough to relieve some of the pressure keeping Zoram's arms down. A quick twist of his shoulder and his right arm was freed. He reached for the breastplate and pulled his attacker forward, down, further off balance.

At least that was the plan when another set of hands grabbed his free arm and pinned it over his head.

"Stop, I say!" His attacker reached for the Sword at his belt and freed the blade about a hand's span from the scabbard.

The sharp and clear ring of the steel struck Zoram with more force than the two men holding him down. The blade had been drawn! He relaxed his struggle as the ringing still resonated in the still night air.

"Please," his attacker began, imploring. "I promise you, as the Lord liveth, and even as I live, I and my brothers mean you no harm and will spare your life if you will listen to us."

Just then the other two joined them, panting and out of breath.

"Just kill him, Nephi, and let's be off," one of them said. "We have what we came for."

Nephi? Where had he heard that name before?

"No," Nephi said. "He has done nothing to deserve such a fate. Especially from us."

"Well, we can't just let him go."

"Yeah," the other latecomer added. "We can't just let him go."

"Shut up, Lemuel," one snapped at the other and then said to Nephi, "He's seen our faces, and thanks to you he also knows our names."

"Yeah, just kill him so we can get out of here."

The big one shot the other one a disapproving glance.

Nephi thought about the dilemma, and while he did, Zoram took the time to size him up. He was large and muscular, but he was also young. He still had a child's shape to his face. The others, with their thick beards, looked the part of older brothers. So these were the brethren he was talking about? Not the brethren and Elders of the council. He had meant his *actual* brothers.

"No," Nephi said again. "We'll take him with us."

"As what? Our captive?"

"Yeah, as what? Our prisoner?"

"I told you to shut up!" the eldest brother said sharply. "And what's going to stop him from breaking free at the first instance we turn our backs? Then everyone will know which way we went.'"

"I'm not killing him, Laman."

"Then give me the sword," Laman said. "I'll do it."

Laman pushed Nephi off Zoram and reached for the Sword. The instant he touched it, though, he pulled his hand back and cursed. "What the—"

Nephi quickly got to his feet and placed his hand again on the Sword's hilt. "You will not touch me again! And we are not going to harm this man. Help him to his feet."

The other brother, the silent one, helped Zoram to his feet but kept a strong grip on his wrist. It didn't matter though. Given what he had just witnessed, he had no intention of fleeing. Since its creation, the Sword had possessed strange, almost miraculous qualities. He had seen men and women of faith—and even a child—draw the Sword from its sheath, while others could not budge it. Laban could never draw it, but this man, this *boy*, could. He freed it as easily as Zoram or Rebekah had. It was as if the Sword had *chosen* him. And if the Sword had chosen him, then who was Zoram to fight it?

"What is your name?" Nephi asked.

"Zoram."

Nephi offered a short bow. "I am Nephi. These are my brothers Laman, Lemuel, and the one who still refuses to let you go is Sam."

Sam let go and looked to his brother apologetically.

Laman? Lemuel? Sam? He had met them all before. These were Lehi's sons!

"I know your father," Zoram offered. "He and my father were friends."

"See?" Laman interjected, still rubbing the pain from his hand and fingers. "He knows too much. Don't tell him anything else. If you're not going to kill him, then bag him and gag him and let's get going."

Nephi ignored his brother. "My father keeps company with many good and honest men. What's your father's name? Perhaps I have met him too."

"His name was Jharom," Zoram said. "He's dead now."

Laman looked upset and even a little afraid. He staggered backward a few steps. "The Keeper of the Sword? Your father is . . . you're the new Keeper?" His voice betrayed his fear. "F-forgive me, Keeper. I didn't . . . we didn't know . . ."

"I knew your father," Nephi said. "And your mother. I accompanied my father a couple of times when he ministered to her during her illness. She often spoke of you. She was very proud of you. They both were."

Zoram couldn't stop the tears that suddenly welled up in his eyes and spilled down his cheeks, nor did he want to. Sam stepped to his brother's side.

"I swear to you, Zoram, son of Jharom and Keeper of the Sword, if you go with us, you will partake of the same freedom to live and worship according to the law, without fear of persecution or oppression."

Zoram didn't know what to think of all this. He still had so many questions. "What happened to Laban? How did you come to wear his uniform and Sword?"

Nephi didn't answer right away. The stillness of the night was amplified as even his brothers waited to hear the answers. He tried to remain strong and confident, but his eyes filled with tears, and his jaw began to quiver as he spoke. "The Lord commanded us to return and obtain the plates. We asked for them; we even brought our family's fortune and inheritance, thinking that we might be able to buy them from him, but he refused."

He was crying now. "He tried to kill us, but I wouldn't give up. The Lord commanded us to do this. I believed that if the Lord had commanded us to obtain this thing, then He would provide a way to accomplish the task. I returned to the city not knowing how I was going to get them, only that I would. That's . . . that's when I found him, drunk and passed out."

Nephi was shaking as if in pain as he recounted what had happened. Sam led him to a rock to sit on. After a moment Nephi continued. "I pleaded with the Lord not to do this thing, but I could not argue with Him. He . . . He said that it was better that one man perish than an entire nation perish in unbelief."

These last words resonated loudly in Zoram's mind and heart. Laban's plan, if he had succeeded, would have had catastrophic and lasting consequences on all of Israel for generations, perhaps forever.

"The Lord commanded that I take his life . . ." Nephi looked at his hands then stared at the ground at his feet. "Shall we not be diligent in keeping the commandments of the Lord?" he said softly.

So this boy had killed the great Laban, Keeper of the Records, commander of the armies of Israel, and captain of The Fifty? Surely it must have been the Lord who had accomplished this thing.

Nephi looked up. "Come with us. The Lord has prepared for us a promised land, a place unlike any our hearts or minds can imagine. Join us. Come down into the wilderness to my father, and I promise you will have a place with us."

Zoram didn't know what to say or how to answer. Laban was dead and with him the threat he posed to Israel. There was no more need to flee the city. But, Zoram realized in that moment, Laban was not the cause of Israel's decay; he was a product of it. If, indeed, the Lord had commanded this family to leave and take the records with them, then his place and destiny were clear. And if the Sword he had fashioned did, in fact, have miraculous properties to somehow guide its own destiny, he was compelled to go with them. He was the Keeper of the Sword, consecrated to serve the Keeper of the Records and preserve the plates at all costs, with his very life if need be.

And it appeared God had chosen a new Keeper of the Records.

In the distant city, an alarm had been raised. A loud drum was sounding, and a chorus of voices carried on the night air. The body of Laban had likely been discovered, and where Zoram was the last one seen with him—though it hadn't been Laban at all—he knew he would be hunted all the days of his life. He knew he could never return.

Ever.

But what of Rebekah? His heart longed to return to her. A small part of him wanted to send these sons of Lehi back to their father with what they had come for and live out the rest of his life with her. But as soon as the thought had fully formed in his mind, he knew it could never be so. Her words echoed throughout his entire being; she could never love a man who took the commands of God lightly. She would never be his if he returned without the records. But he knew somehow that it was the Lord, not Nephi and his brothers, who was leading him away.

He was torn in deep and emotional ways he had never before experienced. If he left with them, he would never see her again. Rumors and speculation would brand him a traitor to his people and his God. Whether he left or stayed, his life with Rebekah didn't seem possible. His choice was clear. Painful, but clear. He would have to trust the heart and life of his love to the Lord and prayed that Rebekah would forgive him for the difficult decision that lay before him.

"Nephi?" Laman said, nervous. "We have to go. Now."

"Zoram," Nephi said, standing and extending his hand to him. "I will not force you to come with us. I believe you to be a faithful and good man—like your father—and that our secret will forever be safe with you. But I ask you again. Come with us. Please."

Zoram knew what he had to do. In fact, he suspected that he had always known. It was what he had been raised and trained to do. It was his purpose, his dharma. He was the Keeper of the Sword. His place was with the records. Their safety and preservation was his solemn duty. Nephi was right—shall we not be diligent in keeping the commandments of the Lord?

He reached out and took Nephi by the forearm. "I will go with you, and if you will have me, I will serve you and the God of our fathers with my every breath. Great is our God."

Nephi smiled. "Great is our God."

Zoram felt a bond form between them unlike anything he had ever felt before. It was stronger than his friendship with Wu Yien and even his feelings for Rebekah. He and Nephi were now brothers in the Lord, united in faith and purpose. He was the Keeper of the Sword, an instrument in the hands of the Lord to bring to pass His will among the children of men. Zoram was complete, whole. The pathway of his destiny, his dharma, was clear. He was sure of his relationship with God and knew not only of his of skills and talents but now also had a clear understanding of how he was to use them to serve others. His place was with Lehi and his family, serving the One True God, the living God, and to protect the word of God and the people who would follow it.

He was unprepared, however, for the direction and distance his dharma was taking him. His heart ached at the thought of never seeing Rebekah again. Not just for the loss of her love and friendship, but that he would not be there to protect her. He had inadvertently put her and her family in danger, and while Laban and Hanoch were both dead, he had no way to know how far this conspiracy had spread.

Zoram looked back at Jerusalem and could only offer a fervent prayer for Rebekah's safety under her father's protection. He then turned and helped Nephi lift the records. The men fell in line and followed Nephi's brothers through the darkness and over the low, rolling hills of the Judean countryside, confident in his decision and, once again, putting his trust in the Lord that He would watch over his friends and the woman he loved.

CHAPTER THIRTY

ZORAM SPENT THE MORNING ALONE with his thoughts. He knew this day had been coming for months, but the anxiety and emotional drain still surprised him. The mountain monastery, secluded and hidden away from the world around it, was the only home he'd known for almost ten years, nearly half his life. He couldn't imagine life without the sparse halls and the bare stone paths and courtyards connecting them all together.

Unable to sleep the night before, he had packed his few meager possessions in a single leather satchel, bundled up against the cold, and set out before first light to experience one more mountain sunrise before his time as an apprentice came to an end. As he hiked over the snow and ice and up the mountainside, Zoram couldn't help but remember the night he had arrived. He couldn't sleep then, either, and, he thought with some insight, for much the same reasons—fear and anticipation. His life as an apprentice had been so simple. Not *easy*—he had never learned so much, been tested so completely—but simple in that his every waking hour could be spent working and improving his art. Life at home would be different, more complicated. *Home*—the word suddenly took on new meaning. He would be expected to marry and raise a family, while preparing and forging the symbol of his people's faith and commitment to God. But through his fears and anxiety stood the figure of his father. Surely he would help Zoram adjust to his new life and the host of expectations that would be placed on him.

He only wished his mother could see his return and know that her sacrifice and faith were not in vain. But, he thought with a peaceful feeling warming his heart, maybe she already knew.

Zoram sat on an outcropping of rocks that jutted out over the wide, deep valley below. He watched in silence as the darkness faded and gave way to the light of the sun. Slowly at first, and then seemingly all at once, the stars blinked out of existence as the blanket of night fell to the vibrant colors of the approaching day. The grays of first light were replaced with soft blues and then painted in broad strokes of orange and shades of red. The magnificent and awe-inspiring colors reminded him of the fires he had spent so much time working with over the years. The display was a fitting tribute to his purpose in being here—a final farewell to the land that had raised him and taught him so much. He knew he would never look at a sunrise or sunset in quite the same way.

The morning bell had been rung nearly an hour earlier, and he could hear the noises of preparations and departures carried on the wind. A few of the apprentices had already left for their respective homes, traveling the precarious roads down the mountain between spring storms. His group was scheduled to leave today, and a small part of him wished for another storm to delay his journey home. But he knew it was time to leave. It felt right.

Across the valley, he took one last look at the side of the mountain that had and would continue to change his life. So much had happened since that fateful night a few short months earlier. There was no trace of the fire or the impact; there never had been. If he wasn't a man of faith, the coincidence of the events of that night would have been too staggering to even consider. But Zoram knew now—more than ever—that there were no coincidences in the Lord. If one could hold on to even a fragment of faith through the dark night, the light of a new dawn would illuminate His benevolent future and plan. *Our lives are truly in His hands*, Zoram thought. *He guides us through the dark valleys and leads us atop high mountains*. Zoram wondered where his life would take him.

He took in one more deep breath, feeling the crisp morning mountain air purify his body and mind in anticipation of the difficult day's journey before him.

"I'll miss you," he whispered, and while he knew it was only his imagination, he thought he heard the mountains whisper back on the winds.

Sure in his footing, he made his way down the rocky hill to the monastery. As he neared the outer wall, he spied Wu Yien taking in the majesty of the Himavant that surrounded them. Zoram had spent the better part of the week helping the priests prepare the rooms and halls for the next generation of apprentices. Most were scheduled to arrive later, in the summer, but one new apprentice had already arrived—a young boy from Wu Yien's homeland. Zoram had only glimpsed the boy when he'd arrived. Like Zoram's friend before him, the boy was accompanied by a small entourage of attendants and kept separate and isolated from everyone else.

It was the boy who first noticed him. Wu Yien put his arm around the child as an older brother might and motioned for Zoram to join them.

"Zoram," he said with an air of formality, "I'd like you to meet Sun Tzu, young prince from the Ch'i providence of the Zhou Dynasty. Sun Tzu, I present to you Zoram, Keeper of the Sword, and a man closer and dearer to me than a brother."

Zoram was stunned at his friend's sincere and heartfelt words. Though they never doubted their feelings, neither had ever voiced them like the before.

The boy bowed. "It is an honor to meet you."

"You already speak the language?" Zoram was impressed.

"Tutors from this land were sent to join him on his journey," Wu Yien explained.

"I have heard much of you and your brotherhood," the boy added.

Zoram smiled and playfully slapped Wu Yien's shoulder. "Don't believe half of what he tells you, and remember—the half that *is* true was somehow his fault." He laughed and had expected the boy to join him in his jest but was met instead with a serious stare.

"It was a . . . I was . . . Never mind."

Wu Yien, though, appreciated the humor. "Forgive my young student. He has known nothing outside the world of study and instruction."

"*Student?* But aren't you—"

"Leaving?" He shook his head. "My plans have been changed. I am to remain behind and help mentor Sun Tzu. Arrangements have been made for him to stay for only a year or two, then we are to return home."

Zoram waited for his friend to break into laughter at the joke, but he never did. Zoram had conflicting thoughts about this news. Part of him, he had to admit, was jealous. Change always brought with it nervous energy. This place was home, and the prospect of staying here, with their routines, consistency, and focus, appealed to him very much. But on the other hand, they both knew and felt it was time to move on with life. This was their dharma and a critical part of their journeys. Wu Yien's had just taken a new direction.

"You?" Zoram said with a wry grin. "A mentor?"

"I know. I'm not old enough to be a teacher. Oh, speaking of which . . ." He dug deep into his heavy coat and pulled out a small package wrapped in a thin blanket. "Here."

"What is it?"

"Go on, open it."

Inside were dozens of flat, thin bamboo slats tied together at the edges with string and rolled up tightly. Zoram loosed a piece of purple ribbon and unrolled part of it.

"I took your advice," Wu Yien said.

"My advice?"

"That day, when we were attacked. You don't remember? You told me I should write down some of my thoughts on warfare and military strategy."

Zoram ran his fingers across and down the smooth, narrow planks.

"I thought recording what I knew would be difficult. But after a while I found that I couldn't stop."

"This is amazing." Zoram moved farther into the scroll. "'There are only two methods of attack—direct and indirect—yet used in combination with each other the strategies are endless.' I remember when you first shared this with me. It was true in sword training when we were younger, and it's true still."

Zoram continued to read silently, mouthing more of the words to himself in quiet reflection. "This is an incredible undertaking. I . . . I'm honored with your gift." Wu Yien bowed. "But I cannot accept this."

Wu Yien was confused and a little hurt.

"This treasure is of enormous, immeasurable worth and value. What you have composed belongs with you and your people." Zoram carefully rolled the scroll back up and offered the bamboo scroll to the boy. "This does not belong in my hands. Your thoughts and words belong in the hands of your student. This is your talent and part of your dharma, not mine."

The boy held the bestowed gift gingerly in his hands, unsure what his mentor would do or say next. Wu Yien remained silent.

"But don't worry," Zoram offered. "It'll take more than the miles to erase the years of lessons and instruction from my mind . . . and my heart."

Wu Yien searched Zoram's eyes and found only sincerity and love. He nodded then cracked one of his sly smiles. "You'll never be free of me."

Zoram's heart felt as if it might burst. What he had said was true in every sense. In fact, Zoram couldn't imagine life without him. Since that first night, they had never really left one another's side. Wu Yien had been a constant in his life, and he felt as if a large part of who he was and who he had become was being ripped from him and left behind. His friend was right—he would never be free of his brother, despite the reality of living out the rest of their lives a world apart. There was so much he felt and wanted to say, but the only word that came out was, "Never."

There was a comfortable and warm stretch of silence between them. The boy, the new apprentice, Sun Tzu, looked between Zoram and his new mentor, unsure what he should say or do next.

Finally, Wu Yien spoke. "Aren't you supposed to be gone already?" he joked.

"I leave within the hour. Can I expect you?"

"I wouldn't give you the satisfaction of a farewell without me."

Zoram inhaled his hidden relief. He then tousled the boy's hair. "You're fortunate to have Wu Yien as a mentor. Listen to what he has to teach. There is none other who possesses more strategies and tactics of warfare. In fact, one could say he's turned warfare into an art form, to be studied and mastered, like any other."

The boy gripped the rolled up bamboo tighter and returned Zoram's smile; then he was off.

The few apprentices who had already departed the monastery did so with little ceremony. The High Sadhus saw each young man off and offered parting words of encouragement and counsel as he began the next leg of his life's journey. Their exchanges had been largely private and personal. As Zoram saddled his horse and prepared to leave, however, every priest and sadhus gathered in the central courtyard and surrounded him. Even the remaining apprentices joined in to see him off. Zoram was uncomfortable with the attention and felt a lump in his throat as the reality of his departure washed over him.

The High Sadhus stepped forward. "We have been honored over the years to learn of the world's cultures and customs. Many of them prescribe that it is fitting to bestow a gift upon a departing friend. We have no such tradition, and even if we did, we are poor and have nothing worthy of our affection and gratitude."

He swept his hand across the crowd. "We have only our knowledge, our passion, our very *essence* to offer those whom we invite to our home in the mountains. Most leave us having learned what we intended them to, but you have done much more. In so many ways, it is *we* who have learned from *you*."

There were murmurs of consent among those present. "All we have left to offer you is our respect." The High Sadhus bowed deeply, reverently, and was then joined by the multitude surrounding him.

Zoram felt the strength fleeing his legs, and he gripped the reins of his horse tightly for support. He had prepared himself for a private farewell, attended by the High Sadhus and Wu Yien. All this, he thought, was too much to take in. And they were wrong. He had done so little compared to what they had done for him over the years. Unable to find words enough to express what he was feeling, he could only return the bow, his eyes filling with tears.

Wu Yien stepped forward. "They might not have a tradition of presenting gifts, but I do." He reached into his coat and pulled out a small sheathed dagger. "Do not refuse me this gift."

Zoram took it gingerly. It was the small blade that had served as the forerunner for the steel they had fashioned from the metal that had fallen from the sky. It was a beautiful work of martial art.

"To remember me by." Wu Yien's eyes were filling with tears too.

"How could I ever forget? But thank you. Never has there been a truer friend."

Wu Yien wiped at his eyes, embarrassed. "Or a more mushy farewell. Truer friend? What about 'worthy opponent' or 'brilliant teacher' or 'masterful craftsman'?"

Zoram grinned. "Those too."

There was an uncomfortable and emotionally tense moment between them. Why was it so hard for men, young or old, to express their deepest feelings for one another? Zoram reached out and wrapped his arms around his brother, hugging him and lifting him clear off the ground. "Thank you."

"There is a prophecy," the High Sadhus continued when the two had stepped out of their embrace, "that one day an apprentice would be instructed and awaken dormant skills and talents, the likes of which had never before been seen. He will be an instrument in the hands of the gods to the protection of a nation."

The High Sadhus paused to sanctify the words he had just shared. "While there have been many skilled in the making of steel, and there will likely be many more, even after we are long gone from this world, I, for one, believe this prophecy has been fulfilled in you, Zoram of *Je-ru-saa-lum*."

Nothing else was said. What else could be? Zoram knew not what lay in store for him once he returned to his war-torn and conquered homeland, but he was confident he could do all things with God's help. As he crossed the threshold of the massive monastery gates, the heavy satchel secure over his shoulder, he stole a glance behind him and sent a prayer heavenward for the strength and faith to endure the challenges that awaited him. He had arrived in this place a child—innocent, frightened, and naïve—but was leaving as a man forged, tempered, and steeled by the trials and experiences God had seen fit and proper to subject him to.

But who was he to say that the Lord's work with him was complete? Had these years only been a preparatory period? Didn't his true work and purpose still lie ahead of him?

As the last view of his mountain home finally passed from sight, a strange yet comforting thought entered his mind and quieted his heavy and conflicted heart. As the certainty of this day had approached, he could not shake the distressed feeling that he was leaving his home behind. But at this moment, looking out over the endless folds of snowcapped mountains and shrouded valleys beneath a deep blue horizon, he knew that wasn't true. He wasn't leaving anything behind; in fact, he was taking so much—everything—with him. This was not the end; it was a beautiful beginning. The simplistic genius of the Lord's hand in his life was unmistakable, and he only hoped he possessed the courage to do all that God would require of him. Zoram may have left his father's side and his mother's arms to simply learn a skill, an empty vessel to be filled, but he has been shaped and forged and was returning home to become the next link in a long and unbroken chain of Keepers of the Sword.

EPILOGUE

"Rebekah?" Zoram whispered. "Rebekah? Wake up."

She opened her eyes slowly, calmly, and stared right at him. She smiled warmly, as if still in a dream. Then, realizing that it wasn't a dream, startled awake.

"Zoram! I . . .you . . ." she sputtered, throwing her arms around his neck.

Zoram held her tightly, a weight lifted from his heart, the longing to see her again and be reunited finally fulfilled. After a long embrace, she abruptly let out a hurt cry and hit him, first in the arm and then in the chest as she released him.

"Th-they said you were d-dead." He couldn't tell if she was happy or upset to see him. "I th-thought . . ." Another sob caught in her throat. She again reached for him and hugged him tightly. He wanted to explain, or at least lighten the mood with a bit of humor, but somehow he knew not to say anything. Instead, he let her shock and emotions run their course as she switched from tears to laughter to incoherent mumbling. Zoram wasn't disconcerted with her erratic and confused behavior. He had expected as much. He had left her to think he was dead . . . or worse. Would she forgive him for putting her through this trauma?

A few moments later, her sobs and outbursts subsided, and she released him, turning her head and wiping her tears with her blanket. Regaining her composure, she looked up, eyes still wet, and offered a smile. "I never stopped p-praying you would return."

She reached for a small oil lamp, but he stopped her before she could light it. "Your estate is being watched," Zoram said softly.

She looked at him suspiciously.

"Two men," he offered by way of explanation, "at the base of the hill."

The danger he faced suddenly registered in her sleepy and somewhat disoriented mind. "You m-must be careful. Th-they say you k-killed Laban. Th-that you . . . He was found with his head . . ." She didn't finish. "And th-that you stole the records. Do you have th-them? Are th-they safe?"

Zoram nodded and smiled, calm and confident.

She suddenly tensed up and pulled the blankets up over her nightdress, aware that they were not alone. Zoram sensed her concern and looked over his shoulder. Nephi stepped from the shadows.

"N-Nephi?"

He bowed, slightly embarrassed being in her room after dark. "It's good to see you again."

She looked to Zoram, confused.

"I need you to gather your things," Zoram said.

She sat up straighter in bed. "Wh-what's going on here?"

"I'll explain on the way."

"Th-the way?"

"The Lord has sent us back for you," he explained.

"You want m-me to go with you?" Concern and skepticism returned and were strewn across her face.

"You and your entire family. Laman is right now speaking with your father. He brings word from Lehi."

"B-but I . . . I can't . . ."

Zoram could see it all in her eyes, even in the dim light drifting in from the open window: the fear, the confusion, the unknown, the suddenness of it all. He knew precisely what she was experiencing. Nephi's invitation to him only a few nights earlier had been no less abrupt and overwhelming. But through it all, there was a calm and a peace that settled in his heart, even now, as he asked Rebekah to do likewise.

"I know how this sounds, but if you ever trusted me, trust me now."

"But what of all th-this?" She swept her arm across her room.

"The Lord has prepared for us a promised land. Lehi has seen it. Do you believe he is a man of God?"

She nodded.

"Then you must come with us."

Her fear and doubt diffused and were replaced by an eager look of understanding. She smiled. "Is th-this really happening?"

Zoram took her hands in his. "The Lord forgets not His own." He looked briefly to Nephi and smiled. "Shall we not be diligent in doing all the Lord commands?" Then back to Rebekah. "And though what He asks is often difficult, He requires of us only obedience . . . and patience."

Rebekah couldn't hold back her feelings of relief, love, and gratitude, and began to cry tears of joy. "I love you."

Zoram pulled her in for a gentle kiss. "I will never leave you again." With her hand in his, he put them both to his heart. "I promise."

For information and resources about stuttering, please visit the
National Stuttering Association (NSA) at www.westutter.com

ABOUT THE AUTHOR

GUY M. GALLI *LOVES* THE accounts recorded in ancient scripture. His vivid and boundless imagination takes the black-and-white words and paints marvelous portraits of the men and women who, like all of us, struggle with challenges and rise to meet and overcome them. Their stories become an inspiration and a testimony builder that we are all living out our own personal scripture stories. You can visit Guy at www.guygalli.com